"JEALOUS?" SHE SAID. "WHAT AN ABSURD
THING TO SAY . . ." But it was difficult not to
find it a little heartwarming. How long was it since
she had enjoyed this kind of masculine admiration?

Oh, Hart, she said to herself. Dear Hart, where
are you now?

# WIDE
# IS THE
# WATER

FAWCETT CREST BOOKS
by Jane Aiken Hodge

# WIDE
## IS THE
# WATER

Jane Aiken Hodge

FAWCETT CREST – NEW YORK

A Fawcett Crest Book
Published by Ballantine Books
Copyright © 1981 by Jane Aiken Hodge

Library of Congress Catalog Card Number: 81-3230

ISBN 0-449-24563-2

This edition published by arrangement with Coward, McCann & Geoghegan, New York

Manufactured in the United States of America

First Ballantine Books Edition: September 1982

Oh, wide is the water, I cannot get o'er,
The water lies wide twixt my true love and me
I stand alone on a stranger shore
And never more my true love shall see.

The water is wide, and I cannot get o'er
I long to fly, but I fear to fall,
I wait my love on a stranger shore,
I await my love, for love conquers all.

Anon.

# I

It was cold. Too cold to think; too cold to feel. Outside, a savage wind threw snow against the windowpanes, found cracks in the wood-built inn, blew the flames of a newly lit fire angrily back down the chimney.

"The sledge should be ready any minute now." Hart Purchis reached inside his greatcoat to pull out his watch. "You're sure you won't stay and have some breakfast?"

"After you've gone? No." Like her husband, Mercy was wearing a heavy coat and shivering inside it. She held out her hands to the fire and would not let them shake. "The Pastons will give me something when I get there." He was still holding his watch, and she sensed his impatience to be gone. So much to say. Impossible to say any of it. Not here; not now; not like this. "Hart. Don't wait. There's no need. The landlord will take good care of me, I'm sure. I know you're desperate to get back to the *Georgia,* to get her out with the tide, before she gets frozen in like the other ships. That has to come first, hasn't it? You didn't get safe away from Savannah to be frozen in, helpless, here at Boston. You have a job to do; the British to beat. Please, Hart, let's say good-bye; get it over with."

He took her cold hands in his and chafed them gently. "I'm sorry, Mercy. Sorry for everything. It's not the way we hoped, is it? Any of it. But you'll be happy with the Pastons. They're my good friends. They'll take care of you.

1

And I'll write whenever I can. Come spring, when the harbour thaws, we'll be here to see you, the *Georgia* and I, bringing our prizes with us. The men will miss you."

"Will they?" She raised exhausted eyes to his. "I wonder." Even for an acclaimed heroine of the Revolution, the stormy voyage north from Savannah, sole woman on a small privateer crammed with men, had not been easy.

"Of course they will." His voice came out a little too strong. "Their mascot. The Rebel Pamphleteer."

"And a great nuisance." She thought of the tiny, cramped cabin, every sound audible, it felt, throughout the ship. A mockery of a honeymoon. A disaster. Hart looked at his watch again. "Hart, do *go*. I couldn't bear it if you missed the tide on my account. Where the *Georgia* is anchored, she'd be a sitting target for a British man-o-war. She's not even far enough in to be protected by the harbour batteries."

"I know. But any further and we really would have been frozen in like the others. God, what a winter. I hope you'll be warm enough, Mercy. Comfortable. I wish I knew more about this Cousin Golding Mrs. Paston is staying with. But a Boston merchant rich enough to live out at Farnham should keep a good house. And you'll be able to pay your way, at least for a while. Until I come sailing in with that prize. I wish I could have given you more."

"Don't *worry*, Hart. I'll manage. I always have. I'll find work. Teaching, perhaps. Something. Everyone says the New Englanders have been getting rich while we in the South bore the brunt of the war."

"Better not say that to the Goldings." The sharp answer was characteristic of their new, strained relationship.

"I won't." She had bitten back a protest against his repeated assumption that the *Georgia* would be successful in her next privateering cruise. Not normally superstitious, she had felt a shiver run through her at his first mention of prizes; the second one was almost too much. But she had learned self-control during those cramped months on the *Georgia*, and besides, they were going to part in a minute. Till spring? Till the end of the endless war? No way of telling. And no time to quarrel. She reached up to put both hands on his shoulders. "I love you, Hart. Remember that. Always. And forgive me for everything that's been wrong. It's been a hard time."

"My fault," he said. "All my fault." And then :"Oh, my God!"

"Hart, what is it?"

"Your marriage lines," he said. "The paper Captain Bougainville gave you. It's still in my Bible, on board."

"Our marriage lines." She could not help the sharp correction but winced as she saw it hurt him. "Never mind, my darling." It was a while since she had used the endearment. "I doubt if the city fathers of Farnham would set much store by a wedding performed on a French ship by a French sea captain. But you say Mrs. Paston will believe me, and that's what matters."

"I wish I'd heard from her. I wish so many things. If only we could have got ashore, found a minister, the way I meant, been married again. Properly."

Was that what had been wrong? "It was proper enough for me," she said, "that wedding. But if that's the way you feel, maybe it's just as well there's no chance that I'm carrying a little, dubious Purchis."

Now she had really got him on the raw. "Forgive me. I didn't mean . . . I can't bear it. Mercy—"

But she had turned away from him as the landlord of the inn opened the door to announce that the sledge was ready for her. "Best get going right away, ma'am, before the horses freeze in their traces. And the tide's almost on the turn, Cap'n Purchis."

They looked at each other. "Mercy!"

"Hart. I love you."

"You know I do." He had his arm round her, guiding her out to where the sledge stood dark on the snow, her tiny portmanteau already stowed, steam rising from the horses' nostrils in the grey light of a reluctant dawn.

Their cold lips met. He helped the landlord pile furs around her, repeated the Farnham address to the driver, bent to kiss her one last time. "God bless you, my dear wife, and keep you."

"And you." She was interrupted by the swift forward movement of the sledge as the driver gave the office to his horses. "Good-bye."

"Good-bye!" Already his answer came from behind, against the drive of the wind. God be with you. She found herself crying and praying at the same time.

The driver was saying something in the clipped accent

she found difficult to understand. "I beg your pardon?" she said, and then, belatedly understanding: "Two hours to Farnham, you say? Can the horses stand it?"

"The cold? Yes, ma'am. Don't you fret about them, but see you keep your hood tight round that pretty head of yours. I don't want to get to Farnham and find your ears friz off. Ain't been to these parts before, I reckon?"

"Never. I didn't believe it could be so cold."

"Coldest winter for years." He was proud of it. "Ships fruz tight in the harbour. Sensible fellow, your friend Cap'n Purchis. He's doing the right thing with his *Georgia,* that's for sure."

"My husband," she said.

"Wind's rising." Perhaps he had not heard her. "Bit of luck we shouldn't get too much snow."

She shook her head, hardly able to hear him against the creak of the sledge and the howling of the wind, and settled back among her rugs, grateful for the unaccustomed solitude. On the little *Georgia,* during the storm-tossed voyage north, she had often been lonely, but never really alone. Meeting the fringes of a hurricane as they sailed away from the fiasco of the French and American attack on British-held Savannah, they had been blown far off course, and the voyage to Boston that Hart had hoped to make in a few weeks had taken two exhausting months. They had spent a glum Christmas at sea, and now, counting on her cold fingers, Mercy realised that it was New Year's Day, 1780. A whole new decade. I should have wished Hart a Happy New Year, she thought, and then: What's happy about it?

If only they had taken a prize, the crew might not have been so resentful about what they considered the unnecessary trip to Boston. Hailed as a mascot at first, when Hart brought her on board, the heroine who had fooled the British for so long in occupied Savannah, Mercy had begun, in the last few weeks, as they battled up the storm-swept coast, to feel herself regarded more and more as an incubus. She had begged Hart to send her ashore to Philadelphia, but he could be obstinate, too. The French squadron had sailed away south after the fiasco at Savannah, and the British ships based on captured New York kept sharp watch on the mouth of the Delaware. To put in there was to risk capture, prison for him and his crew and, for her, very likely the spy's death from which he had saved her in Savannah.

Right, wrong? Wrong, right? No way of telling, but the argument had still further strained a relationship exacerbated by the appalling lack of privacy on the *Georgia*. And of course, Hart had meant to spend some time in Boston, for the refit his ship badly needed, to see her settled with his friends the Pastons, and, as she had learned only today, to marry her again. She put up a mittened hand to brush away a tear before it froze. It had been a happy ceremony, that swift wedding on board Captain Bougainville's ship the *Guerrier*, with everyone making the most of an occasion for rejoicing after the bitter disappointment of defeat at Savannah. The *Guerrier*'s chaplain had been killed evacuating the wounded from Hart's burned plantation house at Winchelsea. And anyway, he had been a Roman Catholic. Well, so, she supposed, had Bougainville, but that was different. He had officiated, not as minister, but as ship's captain, supreme at sea.

Had Hart had doubts all the time? Was that why he had made such a point of sailing in company with the *Guerrier* so that the ceremony took place, not in the Savannah River, presumably American territory, but at sea, well off Tybee Light in international waters? But for that fatal delay, they might have been clear of southern waters before the hurricane struck Jamaica and its fringes lashed the coast right up to North Carolina. Fighting for all their lives, Hart had had no time or strength for his new wife, and she had understood, or thought she had. There would be time for happiness, for their honeymoon, when they got to Boston.

But in that freak winter Boston Harbour was frozen solid. Warned in time, Hart had anchored briefly and dangerously off Cohuit, south of the town, to put her ashore. She pulled the furs more closely around her. Maybe it was as well that there was no chance she could be carrying his child. She had put a good face on it when he had broken it to her that he could give her only Georgia paper money, and not much of that. But everything she had read and heard about the rich merchants of Boston, who had thriven on wartime trade, made her wonder what they would think of Georgia paper. Well, she would find out soon enough.

"Not long now." The driver turned to encourage her. "You look kind of peaked."

"I'm tired," she admitted, amused at the understatement.

"Breakfast in Farnham. We hit the main road here; it'll be quicker." He shouted to his horses, and the sledge moved forward more swiftly on the firm, ice-covered snow of a well-used road. Even under snow, this country looked lived in, Mercy thought, man-dominated, very different from the wilds and swamps she had got used to in the six years she had lived in Georgia. More like the England she had left. And how strange to find a sudden, homesick knot of tears in her throat at that thought. She was an American now, the wife of an American, and moreover, she had been fighting the English, with all her wits and all her strength ever since they had taken Savannah. Only a year, but it seemed a lifetime.

The driver slowed his horses at sight of the first human figure they had seen, an old man, almost buried in a huge, shabby coat.

"Paston?" He shook his head. "Never heard of 'em."

"Ask for Golding." Mercy leaned forward to remind the driver of Mrs. Patson's cousin's name.

"Oh, him." Something odd in the old man's tone. "Look out for the church. You'd see it now if it wa'nt for this danged snow. Turn right when you get to it. A mile down the road, and it's on your left. And good luck to you." He put his head down and trudged away.

The snow was coming harder now, and the church was merely a darker blur on their left as the driver swung the sledge into its new direction. "Not long now," he said again. "Road's good. A mile's nothing. You all right?" he asked anxiously.

"Oh, yes." But the last mile seemed endless. They had turned into the wind, and snow was seeping into the folds of her hood, settling in her eyelashes, caking on her mittens so that she could not use her hands to brush it away. It was an extraordinary relief when they turned once more, out of the direct blast of the wind, and she was able to look about her again.

On either side of the road big houses stood well back in the huge lots. Farnham was a prosperous village evidently.

Mrs. Paston's cousin, John Golding, must be a wealthy man. It was full morning now, and columns of smoke rising from the chimneys of the first houses they passed spoke of warm kitchens and breakfast being cooked. Hard to decide whether she was more tired, more hungry, or more cold, but at the thought of breakfast she concluded that hunger was the worst.

"Are they expecting you?" asked the driver.

"I don't know. My husband wrote, but there was no way we could hope for an answer."

"Bad times," he said. "Send by sea, the British take the ship. Send by land, they're out from New York and stop the coach. I just hope your friends have heard. Thing is, I can't see smoke. I hope they're home. I don't want to scare you, miss—ma'am," he corrected himself. "But there's plenty people cut and run inland after the British raid on Connecticut and the Penobscot affair last year. They reckoned the British might take the same kind of revenge round here for Penobscot that they did on those Connecticut towns for attacking their ships in Long Island Sound. Well, here we are." As he turned his horses off the road, the sledge crunched into deeper snow. "No one's been here awhile," he said. "But that's no wonder, this weather. We New Englanders reckon to be able to hold out on our own for weeks in the winter if we must. Ah. Someone *is* home." He pointed with his whip to a thin trickle of smoke rising from the chimney at the end of the house. "Now you'll be all right." Had he been wondering what in the world he would do with her if no one was there? "You stay dry in the sledge while I rouse them." He stopped the sledge as close as he could get it to the house and plunged through deep snow to the front door.

It swung open as he approached, and a slight girl in black greeted him eagerly. "Thank God you've come at last." And then, looking beyond him to Mercy in the sledge: "But it's not Dr. Frobisher. Who in the world?" She swayed and caught at the doorframe.

"Easy there." He reached out a hand to steady her.

"Don't touch me!" The scream brought Mercy out of the sledge, plunging through the snow, grateful for the sea-boots Hart had made her wear.

"What's the matter?" she asked the frantic girl, who was

shrinking against the doorjamb as if terrified that the driver
was going to assault her.

"Make him go away." Her eyes were huge with terror in
the thin white face. "You come in. Make him go away. I'll
tell *you*."

Mercy and the driver exchanged a quick glance. "I'll
wait in the sledge," he said. And then, elliptically: "Indians,
maybe? But not here . . . not in New England."

"No, but something. I'll try to find out as quick as I
can. If they need a doctor, maybe you could go?"

"Sure will. We all have to help each other these days.
You just find out what's up." He returned to the sledge,
and the girl let out a great shuddering sigh of relief and
reached out a hand to pull Mercy into the house.

"Who are you?" she asked, and then paused at the sound
of a faint voice from the back of the house. "Coming,
Mother. This way." She pulled Mercy after her down a
cold bare hall and in at the open door of what should have
been the parlour. "Mother fell," she said as Mercy took in
the hastily improvised bedroom and the frail old figure
propped by pillows on a cot bed. Mrs. Paston? But Hart
had described her as a formidable woman in the prime of
life.

"I've done the best I could," the girl went on. "Couldn't
get her up the stairs, so Jed and I fixed the bed for her
down here. But she's hurt bad, I'm afraid. Jed's gone for
the doctor; on his snowshoes, across the fields. Quicker
that way. I wish they'd come. How do you feel, Mother?"
She bent to take the old lady's hand. "You're so cold. We're
out of wood." She turned to explain to Mercy. "Jed went
off at first light. I didn't like to leave Mother. But the fire's
going out. I've done my best." She was crying like a child
but must surely be in her early twenties.

"I'll ask my driver to fetch the wood for you." A quick,
anxious glance from the dying fire to the grey-faced, silent
figure on the cot bed. "She looks bad. Have you sal volatile
in the house, or spirits? Anything to warm her?"

The girl shook her head. "Cousin Golding locked it all
up before he left. Temptation out of Jed's way, he called it,
but I reckon it was just Cousin Golding's meanness." She
was sitting by the bed now, chafing the hands of the invalid, who seemed to have drifted off into something between sleep and unconsciousness.

Something very odd about the girl, but no time to think about that now. Mercy hurried to the front door, found the driver waiting anxiously outside, and rapidly explained the situation.

"Sure I'll fetch you some wood." He reached into a pocket. "And here's something might do the old lady good. British navy rum. If that don't warm her, there's no hope for her. So the Goldings did cut and run?" he asked.

"I think so. There's just the two women and a boy. Wicked to leave them alone like that."

"Yes." He spit reflectively into the snow. "Reckon I'd best stable the horse for the moment."

"Oh, thank you, Mr.—" So far he had just been the driver; now he was suddenly a friend.

"Barnes. Bill Barnes. I'll fetch that wood in right away and get a fire going in the kitchen. You'd best warn the girl I'll be in and out."

"Yes. Thank you, Bill." She turned back into the house, her eyes filling with grateful tears at his instant, practical helpfulness.

The door facing the invalid's room led into a big cold kitchen. Resisting the sudden temptation to forage for food, Mercy dropped her coat on a bench, took down a mug from the big dresser, and poured a generous tot of rum. Back in the bedroom, she handed it to the girl. "Get her to drink this; it will do her good. Mr. Barnes will be in with wood for the fire directly."

"In here?" The girl seemed to shrink into herself.

"Of course." Mercy was still holding out the mug. "You don't want your mother to freeze to death, do you? It is Mrs. Paston?" The girl nodded. "And you're . . . ?"

"Ruth." Once again she broke into those disconcerting, childish tears.

"I'm Mrs. Purchis, Hart's wife." How strange to be saying it for the first time here in this desolate New England sickroom.

"Cousin Hart!" Instead of taking the mug, the girl, Ruth, began to cry harder than ever, and Mercy moved impatiently round to the other side of the bed.

She put a firm arm around the frail shoulders and lifted gently. "Mrs. Paston, try to drink this." Holding the mug to the grey lips, she was relieved when the old lady opened clear blue eyes and looked her over thoughtfully.

Her lips moved. "Rum?"

"It's all I've got."

"Spirits!" exclaimed Ruth, but her mother had taken a good pull at the mug. A little of the strong-smelling spirit dribbled down her chin, and Mercy put down the mug to wipe it away with a corner of the cold sheet.

"More." Mrs. Paston's voice was a little stronger. "I've got to talk to you. You said—you're Hart's wife?"

"Yes." Mercy was surprised and delighted that she had taken this in.

As Mrs. Paston drank a little more, Bill Barnes came quietly into the room with an armful of cut wood and began to make up the fire.

"Hush." Mrs. Paston stretched out a shaking hand and put it on Ruth's. "Hush, child. He's helping us. Hush your crying, child. He'll do you no harm." She drank some more and this time managed without spilling any. "That's better." The blue eyes studied Mercy thoughtfully. "Mercy?" she asked. "Mercy Phillips?"

"Yes." Mercy was beyond surprise.

"I thought he'd marry you. He talked about you. Told me more than he knew, I think." Something almost like a smile flickered across the white face. "I'm glad. You're strong, aren't you, Mercy? I could tell, from the way Hart talked." And then, her eyes clouding: "But where is Hart?"

"Back at sea by now, I hope. He's captain of a privateer: the *Georgia*."

"Oh." Disappointment showed in every line of her face. "But you're strong," she said again, and when Mercy nodded, "Good. Ruth, dear, go see if the man has got the kitchen fire alight."

"But . . ." Ruth stopped crying and looked at her mother with a kind of wild horror.

"He won't hurt you, no more than Jed does. We've a guest, Ruth. Put the kettle on, make a pot of tea. There's bread in the crock, still, and a little butter. We all need our breakfast. Give the man his in the kitchen."

"Mr. Barnes," said Mercy. "He's kind. He won't hurt you, Cousin Ruth."

"Cousin," said Ruth. "That's nice." And left them with one long, anxious backward glance.

"Good," said Mrs. Paston. "You'll be able to manage her. Give me some more of that rum. We've got to talk,

you and I, and there's not much time. You're an answer
to prayer, Mercy Purchis." Once again she drank eagerly,
and a faint flush began to show on her thin cheeks. "That's
good," she said, "but that's enough. I'm badly hurt, Mercy.
I fell stupidly. I was so tired and cold, and Ruth screaming
like that. She does sometimes. But you'll look after her, I
know. An answer to prayer. Hart's wife."

Mercy sat down in the chair beside the bed and took a
pull at the rum herself. "You'll have to explain," she said.
"I don't understand anything, Mrs. Paston. Hart said . . .
Hart told me . . ."

"That I was a thriving woman with a parcel of children."
The ghost of a sardonic smile flickered across the exhausted face. "Well, so I was. . . . So I was. But that was
five years ago. Five long years. First Mark, killed that black
day at Lexington. And the house burned. Dead . . . gone
. . . And then, no money. He kept us all, did Mark. It does
teach you who are your friends."

"You should have written. Told us . . ."

"But I did. I'll come to that." A slow tear rolled down
her cheek. "It's all over now, done with, decided. No use
looking back, and don't you waste my time and strength,
Mercy Purchis, with questions I may not have time to
answer. I did what I did. For the best."

"I'm sure you did." Mercy proffered the mug.

"No. I need a clear head for what I have to tell, to ask
. . . You have to understand about Ruth." A monitory
hand stopped Mercy from speaking. "Her sister married.
Naomi. Her twin. The strong one. He was a good man."
She paused, looking beyond Mercy at something horrible.

"Was?"

"He said we'd all go to the West. For a new life. He
loved Naomi, loved us all. We were his family, he said. He
had none of his own. And Cousin Golding was glad to see
us go. He even helped with the expense of the trip. We
joined a party . . . a small party. If it had been bigger . . .
But he was always impatient, Naomi's George. He wanted
the world, and Naomi for its queen. Lord"—suddenly her
voice changed, warmed—"that was a happy journey. The
two of them so in love. Glowing. The other children happier than they'd been since Mark died. Ruth getting over
the shock of Naomi marrying. They were close, those
twins."

"Yes." She had noticed, once again, that significant past tense. "And then?"

"Indians. Just when we'd camped for the night. Ruth and I had gone down to the stream to wash. She was always shy, my Ruth. We heard it happen: the war cries; the sudden attack; the screams. Then Naomi came, running, screaming, with three braves behind her. We saw it all, Ruth and I. She bit my finger clean through as I kept her quiet. She'd have gone to Naomi's help if I'd let her. And died the same. We lay there, hidden, huddled together, all that night. In the morning a few other survivors came out of the woods. We buried them. All my family. All my children. All but Ruth. The other survivors decided to come back east. They'd had enough. There seemed nothing for it but to come too. Ruth was all right with them. It was when she saw her first strange man that she took on: screaming; hysterics; panic. And nightmares after, and waking screaming again. That's why I was hurrying to her in the dark last night. I'd been trying to teach her to sleep alone," she explained. "I knew I hadn't long. Those hungry years had done for me, even before we went west. I thought I'd see the children settled before I died. Well, I saw them settled. All but Ruth. I've been worried sick what to do for her." She reached out to take Mercy's hand. "I've been a wicked woman. Blaming God for abandoning me in my trouble. I should have known better. He sent you. Hart's wife. He and my Mark were like brothers."

"I know. I'll look after Ruth. You don't need to worry about her anymore." Inwardly she prayed that she could make it good. "But, Mrs. Paston, 'hungry years'? You said you'd written to us."

"Indeed I did. Back in '76, when I faced it that there was no way I could make a living for us all. Prices rising all the time . . . Cousin Golding took the lot where our house had stood in Lexington against our keep. Said the taxes were so high it hardly paid him. My other cousins had gone west. . . . I was at my wits' end. . . ." She was tiring, her sentences running down into little silences, and Mercy held the mug to her lips once more. "Thanks. I don't want to die drunk, but you need to know where you stand. With Ruth. If you'll really look out for her." The tired blue eyes begged for reassurance.

"I promise, Mrs. Paston."

"Thank you. Where was I? Oh, about Cousin Abigail Purchis. I wrote her, back in '76. It was next year before I heard, and then it was a short note from her cousin Francis Mayfield, saying she had asked him to write. Things were terrible in Savannah, he said. Abigail a burden on her aunt Purchis already. Could not bring herself to write me . . . He was sorry for me, he said. . . . That was all. I never wrote again. How could I?"

"You should have written Hart."

"Francis said . . . he'd talked to him. Hart was sorry, too."

"The liar." Long hatred of Francis Mayfield boiled in Mercy's throat. "The scoundrel. I swear to you, Abigail never saw that letter." Francis Mayfield had deceived her, betrayed her, tried to kill her, but nothing he had done to her seemed, now, so bad as this. "He's dead. Francis Mayfield is dead." A horrible death, richly deserved. "He told none of us," she said, "about your letter. I swear Abigail never saw it."

"I see that now. I think I understood it the moment you walked into the room and said you were Mercy Purchis. Dear Hart, I'm so glad . . . He was like a son to me. I hated to think he'd let me down like that. When you see him, ask him to forgive me for believing it."

"I will." But a cold hand clutched at Mercy's heart. When would she and Hart meet again? She pulled the bedclothes round Mrs. Paston's frail shoulders. "Try to sleep now, Mrs. Paston. You look exhausted. I'll see how Ruth is getting on with that tea."

"Yes." The blue eyes closed, then opened again. "When she gets excited . . . if she gets excited . . . I hush her, like a child. It mostly works. Dear Mercy"—the words were coming more slowly now—"I thank God for you."

Bill Barnes was alone in the kitchen, tending a blazing fire over which a kettle was just beginning to sing. "The girl cut and run upstairs when I came in," he explained. "I thought best let her be."

"Yes. It *was* Indians." Hastening to tell him this, Mercy admitted to herself how afraid she had been that it might have been an English raiding party that had done the damage. "The family were on their way to the West. She saw her sister killed. She and her mother were the only ones of the family who escaped. Her mother's dying, I'm afraid."

"I thought she looked right poorly." The kettle boiled. "I found the tea," he said. "There's not much. Nor of anything else. Looks like they've been living on bread and tea mostly. I'd like to get my hands on that Mr. Golding who left them here alone."

"I wish the doctor would come." Mercy warmed the big pot and made the tea, grateful that the nearly empty caddy was not locked. "I'll take a cup to the old lady," she said.

"No," said Bill Barnes, surprising her. "Drink some yourself first. I reckon you've problems enough on your hands without passing out from cold and hunger. When did you last eat?"

She put a vague hand to her brow. "Last night, I think." Chowder and stale biscuit, and the crew grumbling about the fresh supplies they had hoped for from Boston.

"Right." He pulled out a chair from the table, cut a thick slice of bread, buttered it, and handed it to her. "I'll join you in a cup of tea if I may." He took the heavy pot from her and poured for them both.

"Have some bread and butter."

"No, thanks. That's all there is. The girl must be hungry, too."

"Her name's Ruth. Ruth Paston." Mercy took a bite of stale bread and rancid butter, realised that she was starving, and made herself chew and swallow it slowly, washed down with the reviving tea. He was right, this kind Bill Barnes. She seemed to be responsible for this unhappy household and must preserve her own strength.

"Paston?" said Bill Barnes. "Not kin of Mark Paston's, by any chance? Him that was killed at Lexington?"

"His mother and sister."

"And left to starve in the cold! I wish I had Mr. Golding's neck here to wring." His hands twisted an invisible neck.

"You knew Mark Paston?"

"Not to say knew. But we all knew of him, miss—ma'am. A martyr of the Revolution. A hero. And his family left to starve. It serves us right we ain't winning this danged war. We don't deserve to. Not letting things like that happen."

# II

When the doctor came at last, he shook his head over Mrs. Paston. "Nothing I can do. Keep her warm. Keep her happy. It won't be long." He and Mercy were alone in the cold front room.

"How long?"

"My dear young lady, how can I tell? Two days? A week? A month? Light diet; nourishing broth; a drop of wine if she feels like it." Something about her had been puzzling him. "You're the daughter, I take it?"

"No. She's upstairs. You don't know her? I'm surprised. I would have thought Mrs. Paston would have called you to her. She's—mentally disturbed since she saw her twin sister killed by Indians."

"Oh, yes, now you come to mention it, I do seem to have heard something. From my friend Mr. Golding. One reason why he very sensibly took his family away inland. But perhaps a matter more for the pastor than the doctor? And I am afraid I must mention, Miss . . . um?"

"Mrs. Purchis."

"Mrs. Purchis. Must mention that my charges have to be quite high. You know how it is. This deplorable war. The cost of living rising every day. Why, what it costs me just to keep my wife dressed to suit our station in life . . . Appalling. Quite appalling. Madness, the whole business, and the sooner those lunatics down in Philadelphia recognise it, the better for us all. In the meantime, I am afraid that my charge for a house visit . . ." He hesitated, aware at last of some unexpected quality in her silence.

"Will have to be paid in Georgia paper, if at all," she told him. "I take it your friend Mr. Golding did not think to tell you that he left his cousin and her daughter penniless to face the winter, with only a boy to look after them? Where is Jed, by the way?"

"The boy? Why, making the best of his way back on his snowshoes, I suppose. You surely did not think I would take him up in my sledge, Miss—Mrs. Purchis?"

"If I did, I can see I was far wide of the mark." She took out her purse. "So, in Georgia paper, how much, Dr. Frobisher? For your great help and extraordinary kindness?"

"Oh, it was nothing," he began, and then, her savage irony slowly penetrating: "Mrs. Purchis, if that *is* your name, I do not at all appreciate your tone. I will wish you a very good day and send in my account in due course. It must be paid, I should warn you, in Massachusetts paper or in specie."

"Good day, Doctor." She opened the front door and ushered him out to where a man in what looked like livery was waiting by a luxurious sledge.

Returning to the kitchen, shivering with anger, she found Bill Barnes awaiting her with a look of delighted respect. "I listened," he told her. "I've not enjoyed myself so much for years. I hope you don't mind, ma'am. It's men like him and his friend Golding make you despair of our ever winning this war. Just imagine making that poor boy come back through the storm on his snowshoes when he has room for six in that grand sledge of his. Don't you ever pay him, ma'am. You offered, fair and square, and he refused it. Let it go at that."

Mercy made a wry face. "I think I shall have to. I must go and look at Mrs. Paston."

"Don't you fret about her. The girl's with her. Calmer, I'd say. Not much you can do, by the sound of it, but wish her an easy passing. And you and I need to talk business."

"Business?" She was glad to subside onto the chair he pulled out for her, near to the now glowing fire. In her immediate anger with Dr. Frobisher she had forgotten how much she had counted on him for advice and help. Now it hit her that she should have temporised with him, flattered him, blandished help out of him. Where in the world had her wits been? "I'm a fool," she said wearily. "I shouldn't have let it go like that."

"Not much else you coulda done, I reckon. If you think anything you said would have made him help you, you're crazy. I know his kind. We've plenty of them here in New England. The war's a terrible mistake, they keep saying, but they profit by it every way they can. It makes a man mad. Now, Mrs. Purchis, ma'am, can I ask you to sit it out here and look to things while I go into Boston and tell some friends of mine what's happened to Mark Paston's mother? I'll be back with help as quick as I can, but it's bound to take a bit of time. When the boy gets back, you could ask him if any of the neighbours might help, but I don't set much hope on them. Not in a fancy rich district like this. It's where people live close together, the way they do in Boston, that they look out for each other. I'll be back, I promise." He must have sensed her sudden qualm.

"I believe you. And I do thank you, Mr. Barnes."

"Oh, call me Bill, the way you did before. I liked that. Friendly, it was. Are you really from Georgia? You was talking kind of British when you gave the doctor that setdown."

"Was I? What a strange thing. Yes, Bill, I was British once. But I'm American now. Since I married Captain Purchis." She used the title intentionally, and it had its effect.

"Who's fighting for us all," said Bill Barnes, "while men like Frobisher and Golding look out for themselves. Don't you worry, ma'am; what with Mark Paston's name and Cap'n Purchis's, you'll have help before night, or my name's not Bill Barnes. So—I'd best be going. Get some rest if you can, and keep your heart up." He pulled on his shaggy greatcoat and went out the back way into the yard, where she heard him talking encouragements to his horse as he harnessed it up. How long to Boston and back? She should have asked him. But it made no difference. She ought to go and see how old Mrs. Paston was. She did not think, for the moment, that she could get up from her chair. She leant her elbows on the kitchen table and let her head droop onto her arms.

"Miss! Miss! Excuse me, miss?" The anxious voice roused

her from deep sleep, and she looked blearily across the table at the tall, gangling boy, who was gazing at her in amazement. The fire had burned low, she saw, and the room was cold again.

"You must be Jed." She got stiffly to her feet. Terrible to have neglected old Mrs. Paston for so long. "I'm kin to Mrs. Paston," she explained.

"Well, praise be!" He put a basket carefully down on the table. "She could do with some kin right now. I was plumb worried taking so long to come back, but it was hard work, carrying this. Mrs. Frobisher fetched me into the kitchen, the minute the doctor was gone, and packed it up for me. Gave me a good dinner, too. Wouldn't let me come till I'd had it." He was unpacking the basket of provisions, and Mercy moved over to help him.

"Bless the woman. Arrowroot and broth. Would you make up the fire for me, Jed, and I'll heat some for Mrs. Paston? I must go see how she is."

She had slept a long time. The light was beginning to fade, and she could just make out the two still figures in the improvised bedroom. Ruth had fallen asleep on the floor, her head awkwardly propped against her mother's cot.

"Shh . . ." said Mrs. Paston softly. "Don't wake her. There's time enough for her to be unhappy. You are going to look after her, aren't you, Mercy?" Her face had changed, sunk in, the jaw dropped a little, and Mercy thought talking hurt her.

"Yes. But now I'm going to bring you some broth."

"No. I'd rather you stayed. I don't seem to want food, and I do need to talk to you. I've been lying here, thinking what's best for you to do. I think you should go back south, Mercy. To Hart's family. They're Ruth's family too, after all. I don't rightly understand why Hart brought you north in the first place."

"He had to. It's not safe for me in Savannah, not now the British hold it. I was working against them. They found out." Behind the brief statement lay memory of Francis Mayfield's implacable search for her on Hutchinson Island, Hart's last-minute rescue, and Francis's horrible death. "Hart saved my life," she said.

"Dear Hart. I loved him like a son. Like my Mark." Two slow tears rolled down her cheeks. "Hart was lonely here at the North," she said. "Would have been if it hadn't been for us. We New Englanders are a close, closed lot. I'd go back south if I were you, Mercy. If not to Savannah, then why not Charleston? Doesn't Mrs. Mayfield have a house there?"

"There's a rumour the British are going to attack Charleston." She had learned this as a spy in Savannah. "Hart will look for me here. He promised to come in the spring." Once again a superstitious shiver went through her as she remembered that bold promise about prizes.

"Of course. Stupid of me. But I'm afraid you'll find it hard here. They don't like Ruth much. She scares them. I've sometimes been afraid. . . . Absurd, of course. Nobody would. We're civilised these days. Or think so. But these are strange times. They bring out the brute in men. My cousin Golding said he was taking the children away because . . . because he was afraid. Possessed, he called her. My little Ruth. I wish you'd take her south, Mercy."

"I wish I could," said Mercy. "But things aren't so bad as you think, Mrs. Paston. The man who drove me here has gone to fetch his friends. He says they'll be angry at what's happened to Mark Paston's family. He promised to be back tonight."

"I hope he comes," said Mrs. Paston. And then: "Hush, child." Ruth had sat bolt upright with a strangled scream. "It was only a dream, only a bad dream. I'm here. Mercy's here. No one will hurt you. Mercy won't let them. Mercy's going to look after you."

"I'm going to make us all some broth," said Mercy as Ruth's screams dwindled into a quiet, desperate sobbing. "Mrs. Frobisher sent a great basket of provisions, God bless her."

"I hope her husband doesn't find out," said Mrs. Paston.

She made a gallant effort to eat the broth Mercy fed her, but it was no use. "Don't waste it on me," she said at last. "Give me a little more of that blessed rum, and at least I'll die cheerful."

"You're not going to die, Mother." Food had brought colour to Ruth's cheeks. "You're going to live forever and ever and ever."

"I'm glad I'm not," said Mrs. Paston, and Mercy guessed at the pain she was concealing. "And if I should die, Ruth, my darling, you are going to do everything that Cousin

Mercy tells you, just as if she were me. Do you promise me that?"

"You're not going to die," said Ruth mulishly.

"But just suppose I did, I want you to promise me. About Cousin Mercy. About minding what she says. Hushing when she tells you to, just the way you do for me. Promise me, Ruth." With a great effort she pulled herself up against her pillows and took Ruth's hand in hers. "Now yours, Mercy."

Holding it out, Mercy recognised the formidable woman whom Hart had loved and respected.

"Promise to be sisters." She spoke with increasing effort. Moving had hurt her. "You, Ruth, promise you'll mind Mercy the way you did me. And you, Mercy, promise you'll look out for Ruth as if she were your sister."

"I promise." Mercy smiled at Ruth.

Ruth's cold hand writhed in hers. "I don't want . . ." she began, but her mother interrupted her.

"Ruth." Mrs. Paston's voice was stern. "Don't make me ask you twice."

Ruth looked full at Mercy, who realised with a little shock of surprise that, happy, she could be beautiful. There was a short silence; then Ruth leant forward and kissed Mercy on the cheek. "I promise," she said. "I'll try, Mother."

"Thank you, my darling. And now I think I'll sleep a little. I hope that man comes back," she said as Mercy helped settle her on her pillows.

"He'll come." Mercy left Ruth to watch beside her mother and took the dishes out to the kitchen, where she found Jed lighting candles.

"Wax," he said. "That's a good woman, Mrs. Frobisher. I sure hope her husband don't notice."

"So do I. But, Jed, I don't understand. How could Mr. Golding leave his cousin with nothing, like this?"

"Oh, do him justice, he didn't." Jed looked at her sombrely. "He left servants on board wages, a couple, and me, of course, and stuff for the winter. Only they didn't reckon much to Miss Ruth, the couple, that is, Mr. and Mrs. Jacks. Well, Mr. Golding made no secret she scared him, and the kids used to holler when she hollered, and Mrs. Golding wouldn't be in the room with her, so what with one thing and another you can see how the Jackses felt. This was back in the fall. The Goldings left when the roads were still dry from the summer. Long evenings; quiet nights; everything went fine for a while. Until Miss Ruth had her first screaming fit. I *like* Miss Ruth." He coloured as he said it. "She can't help it she was scared silly by the Indians. I told the Jackses, told them and told them that night. We were all kind of wore out by the time Miss Ruth settled. I sleep out back in the shed," he explained. "Time I woke, those Jackses had gone and taken pretty near all the food and stuff with them. And the waggon. And the better of the horses Mr. Golding left behind. I tell you, when it first started to snow, I was right down glad. I could get about again, see. On the sledge. Stock up with a few provisions, but I didn't reckon on the way prices had gone up. Nor on a winter like this."

"None of us did. You were good to stand by the Pastons, Jed."

"Oh, that was nothing. I'm kind of . . ." Once again he blushed. "Kind of fond of them. Besides, I've nowhere else to go. My father was killed at Bunker Hill, and Ma . . . Ma, she took up with an English soldier. I couldn't stay, not with that going on, so I cut and run for it, and Mr. Golding took me in as yard boy. I was just a littl'un then. No wages. I worked for my keep, and lucky to get it, he said."

"And now?"

He shrugged. "Just the same. You don't know Mr. Golding. He cheated Mrs. Paston something wicked over that plot of hers at Lexington. Everyone knew that. She did, too, I'm sure, but what could she do? And him making a favour of having her. It made you sick to hear him. She's dying, ain't she? She has the look Pa had after he was wounded. What's going to happen then, ma'am? What's going to happen to Miss Ruth?"

"I've promised to look after her." Had she been mad to do so? But what else could she have done?

"Oh, I'm *glad*." His reaction was heartwarming. "That's the best news yet. I've been right down worried for Miss Ruth, and that's no lie. A winter like this, no one's got anything to do but sit home and talk. And it's not been nice talk, not about Miss Ruth. I heard something in the doctor's kitchen I didn't like above half. Something about witches and Salem. You'll take her away, won't you, ma'am, and let me come too? No wages, of course. Just the same as ever."

"Thank you, Jed. But as to going away, I don't know what to do for the best. My husband will look for me here."

"You could leave a message," he said. "He's a privateer captain, ain't he?" Awed respect in his tone. "They can get anywhere. He'll find you. I don't like to think what might happen to Miss Ruth if she stayed here through the winter. People act funny since this war. When they get into crowds. I saw a tarring and feathering once. Miss, it was horrible. The man died after."

"I've seen one, too." Mercy shuddered, remembering the times she had encountered the mob in Savannah. "But surely, it could never happen here; not in New England? It all seems so peaceful, so civilised. . . ."

"I wouldn't want to bet Miss Ruth's life on that." Jed jumped to his feet. "There's someone coming now!"

"Bill Barnes, I hope. The man who brought me." But she had caught his anxiety, and they hurried together to gaze out the front window.

She saw Bill Barnes, alone and looking anxious, too. "Thank God it's snowing again." He stamped his feet as he entered the kitchen and dusted down his greatcoat before he took it off.

"Thank God?" Mercy asked, puzzled.

"Yes. I wouldn't have believed it. The things they're saying in town. About Mark Paston's sister."

"Oh, no!" Mercy exchanged a quick glance with Jed.

"And that's not all." Barnes tramped through into the kitchen and held out cold hands to the fire. "There's talk about you, too, ma'am. Being a Jonah. I hate to tell you. But rumour flies fast across the ice. Men from one of the ships frozen in got to speak to the crew of the Georgia while you and Cap'n Purchis were onshore. Heard a bunch of lies and nonsense and passed it on, back to Boston. The place was fair buzzing with talk when I got there. Witches and warlocks and Jonahs and God knows what, all mixed up together. Parcel of rubbish." He was both angry and very worried indeed. "How's the old lady?" he asked.

"Dying."

"We couldn't move her?"

"Not possibly. You don't really think something might happen?" She paused, facing this new threat with a mixture of horror and fury.

"I'm darned glad it's snowing," he said again. "Bit of luck, it should keep those madmen at home. Talk of riding the pair of you out of town on a rail," he said grimly. "And the *Georgia* sailed with the tide, so no chance of help from that quarter."

"Oh, I'm glad," said Mercy. And then. "But the crew. If they were talking like that . . ."

"It don't sound good for Cap'n Purchis, ma'am, and that's the truth. I just hope he gets a fine prize quick and easy. It might make all the difference. You know how it is." Was he apologising for the *Georgia*'s crew? "A woman on board ship's always trouble. I'm sorry, ma'am."

"Oh, it's true enough," she said wearily. "But what else could we do?"

"No use crying over spilt milk. The question is, what's to do now? First of all"—he turned to Jed—"come and help me bring in what I brought. I've some friends still. I'm not empty-handed. And maybe you'd like to have a look at the old lady, ma'am. Just in case . . ."

He hoped Mrs. Paston was dead. Horrible. If she was, would he load them all into that capacious sledge of his and take them away from this lonely, dangerous house? Mercy thought that was what he wanted to do and went obediently into the little room, where Ruth sat immobile by the bed and her mother's breathing had become louder, more difficult. Her hand, lying on the patchwork quilt, was cold as ice, but she opened tired eyes and smiled up at Mercy. "The man came back?" Her voice was a painful whisper.

"Yes. He's brought supplies. They're unloading them now. Everything's going to be all right, Mrs. Paston." If only she believed it.

"Good. God bless you, Mercy. And give my love to Hart."

"I will." If I ever see him again, she thought, and, returning to the kitchen, found Bill Barnes standing a rifle behind the door.

"Oh!" He looked at her sheepishly, caught in the act.

"Bill! You don't really think!" Still, she could not believe it.

"I think anything could happen, ma'am, if it should stop snowing, which it often does at dark. It's a full moon, remember, and with the roads all ice it's no kind of journey out from Boston. And picking up more madmen on the way, from what the boy says. Full moon does funny things to people, besides showing them the way."

"When does it rise?" Looking out, Mercy saw that it was full dark now. Jed was lighting more candles, apparently brought by Bill Barnes, and there were bundles of food on the kitchen table.

"I hear the doctor's wife turned up trumps." Bill Barnes changed the subject.

"Yes, but I can't get Mrs. Paston to take anything." She saw that he was shaking snow from a bedding roll. "Oh, Bill, you're staying!"

"I'll say I'm staying."

"But your wife. Won't she be worried?"

"Daisy's been dead two years," he told her. "Died of grief, I always reckoned, after our boy was killed at Saratoga. We have to win this war, ma'am, just to make it all worthwhile."

"Yes." She thought of her own dead. Her father, killed by the mob, six years ago, at Savannah, and all the friends and acquaintances who had perished during the harsh years of war. "I'm sorry, Bill. And I'm more grateful than I can say that you are staying. Where will you sleep?"

"Jed and I have fixed it all. One of us will sleep in here and keep the fire up, the other watch in the front room, just in case."

"You really think something may happen?"

"I wish it would start snowing again."

"Yes." Mercy took a sacking apron down from behind the kitchen door and tied it round her waist. "Well, we'd better have some supper before the moon rises."

She took Ruth's supper to her but did not try to rouse Mrs. Paston, who had fallen into a deep, snoring sleep.

Finishing her own salt pork and hoecake, Mercy turned to Barnes. "D'you think if they come, they might fire the house?"

"Ma'am, they might do anything."

She picked up a candlestick. "Jed, come and help me carry bedding down for Ruth and me. We'll sleep with

Mrs. Paston, so we're all close together. And you must let me share the watch with you," she told Barnes.

"No, ma'am. You've had enough for one day. You get your rest while you can."

"Promise you'll wake me if they come?"

"Don't worry," he said grimly. "You'll wake all right.".

Her last thought, before exhaustion had its way with her, was of Hart. Hart sailing away with a disaffected crew. Hart, who had never really believed them married . . .

Barnes's voice roused her, speaking urgently to Jed. "Wake up, boy, they're coming."

Moonlight streamed in at the uncurtained window. Ruth and her mother were fast asleep. Mercy, who had slept in her clothes, got quietly to her feet, picked up her boots, and moved softly into the front room. Both Barnes and Jed were there, peering out the window. "Surprise is what we need," Barnes was saying. "I'll fire one shot over their heads, and then you'll cover me, Jed, while I go out and speak to them. If I can't stop them, shoot to kill. It'll give me time to get back and reload."

Mercy had stopped a mob herself in her time and thought he knew his business. "Is there a third rifle?" she asked. "I'm not a bad shot."

"No, but if one of us is hurt, you can take over," said Barnes, unsurprised. "Ammunition's here, see. Get the feel of things. I don't want a light, want to surprise them when they come into view. Soon now."

"How do you know?" She had heard nothing.

"Little things. The birds have been carrying on between here and town. You get to know if you live much in the woods. Ah."

Now she could hear it too: the murmur of voices, somewhere beyond the bushes that fringed the Golding lot; the rattle of harnesses; a horse's neigh.

"They're not trying to keep quiet," said Barnes. "They don't expect to be opposed. They just think they're dealing with three women and a boy. Bit of luck, they won't even have weapons ready. Just planning to walk in and take over."

Mercy shuddered. "Have we any chance?"

"One in ten," he said coolly. "We're ready. They're not. But we won't lay any bets on it, ma'am."

"No." Mercy clenched her teeth to stop them from chattering. This waiting was worse than anything. "I think I'd rather say my prayers."

"Then go right ahead. It sure can't do any harm."

"Will they be able to see you when you go out to them?" She had been worrying about this. "The moon's behind the house."

"I know. But any minute now it will be over. Just you pray they don't come before."

"But then you'll be a standing target!"

"Can't have it both ways. If they see me, if they know me, we've a chance. I've been about a long time."

"You're a good man, Bill Barnes. I do thank you."

"I couldn't do anything else, could I? Ah," he said, "here they come, and here's the blessed moon." He opened the front door and moved swiftly across the porch and down the steps, the rifle held lightly in his right hand. Jed and Mercy followed him quietly and took up their positions to the right and left of the steps, Jed with his rifle ready, Mercy quietly putting some bullets into her pocket, just in case.

As Barnes moved forward into full moonlight, the first dark figures emerged from the bushes. They must have left their sledges up on the road, Mercy thought, and wondered why. But of course, a horse could easily break a leg in an unexpected snowdrift, once it was off the hard-packed road. It meant that they were coming in ones and twos, as they had left their sledges. Now they had seen Barnes, standing immobile in the moonlight, waiting for them. They stopped, silent, hesitating, and Mercy was relieved that he would not need to fire that dangerous shot in the air.

"Good evening, neighbours," he said. "Bill Barnes of Cohuit here. What can I do for you?"

They paused for a moment, surprised, muttering among themselves. Then one figure moved forward. "You can get out of our way, Bill Barnes, and let us deal with this parcel of witches. We've no quarrel with you."

"Witches?" Barnes's tone was an admirable blend of scorn and surprise. "What century do you think you're living in, John Tanner? Yes, of course I know you." This in reply to a strangled exclamation from the figure confronting him. "If you want to do your dirty business in secret, you need a new voice. I stand here as a witness that you are leader in anything that should happen tonight." As he spoke, more and more figures had crowded into view behind John Tanner. He raised his voice. "Friends, what do you think you are doing? There's no one here but a dying woman, two girls and a boy. Haven't we enemies enough without this kind of madness?"

"A witch and a Jonah," came a voice from somewhere in the crowd.

"Some people call your Jonah a heroine," said Barnes, surprising Mercy. "Don't you know how she fooled the British down in Savannah?"

"Savannah!" came the answer. "What do we care for them southerners? Give us the witch and the Jonah, Bill Barnes, and you and the boy can get out of here."

"I'm staying right here with Mrs. Purchis and Mrs. Paston," said Barnes as the crowd moved a little nearer. "One step more, and I fire."

There was a long moment of indecision. John Tanner had been obviously disconcerted at being named, and seemed to have abandoned his position as leader. Mercy was actually beginning to hope that the worst was over when there was a little stir, a kind of whirlpool among the crowd, and then a missile, savagely hurled, hit Barnes on the side of his head, and he collapsed, silently, into the snow.

"Brutes!" Mercy was down the steps in an instant, bending over Barnes, picking up the rifle, standing to face them as they came a slow step forward through the inhibiting snow. "I am Mercy Purchis." Her voice rang out clear across the snow, and she blessed Mr. Garrick for his teaching, all those years ago in London. "Wife of a privateer captain. Cousin of Mrs. Paston, whose son was killed at Lexington. I ask you the same thing Mr. Barnes did: What are you doing here? And what madness is this to attack your friend Bill Barnes?" Did she dare bend to see how badly he was hurt, whether he was suffocating in the snow? No, she knew she must not. She stood there, quiet, facing them, waiting, aware of Jed behind her on the porch, rifle at the ready, breathing hard.

"We've come to see you out of town. You and the witch inside there." The man Barnes had called John Tanner had resumed the lead now that Barnes was out of it, unable to bear witness against him. He took a step forward towards Mercy, and the silent crowd moved behind him. Straining her eyes, she could see weapons in their hands, but no glint of metal in the moonlight. So—sticks, not guns? Very likely, to attack three women and a boy.

"One step more and we fire." As Mercy swung the rifle up, she tried desperately to decide whether to fire over or into the crowd. They were so close. . . . Either way might mean disaster. And besides, to risk killing a man. Horrible. But so was what they meant to do. "There's a sick girl in there," she said as they still hesitated. "And her mother, Mark Paston's mother, dying. As for me, I've done my share of fighting for the Revolution. Don't think I won't fire to kill if you make me." She had made up her mind and meant this as advice to Jed, too. If they still came on, there would be no time for firing over their heads. "Friends, go home," she said. "Forget this madness ever happened." With a quick breath of relief she felt Barnes stirring at her feet. "We'll look after Bill Barnes."

A mistake? Perhaps. It might have reminded John Tanner of the extent to which he had already compromised himself. He gave a scornful laugh. "Parcel of women and a boy." He flourished the stick he carried. "Shoot at us; you'll miss, and we'll be . . ."—an expressive pause—"harder on you. Otherwise, we'll just see you on your way, nice and easy, and no hard feelings."

"On a rail?" Mercy had seen that some of the men at the back of the crowd were heavily loaded, no doubt with the pieces of fence on which she and Ruth were to be ridden out of town. She held the rifle very steady. She would aim for Tanner's shoulder and hoped Jed had had the wits to pick a different target.

"Lucky not to be burned! Come on, boys. Let's get the witch and the Jonah! Tarring and feathering's too good for them!"

As he stepped forward, their two shots rang out almost in unison, and he paused, staggered, and then collapsed slowly into the snow. And behind him another man, who had been a little ahead of the rest, fell too. Reaching into her pocket for a bullet, Mercy blessed Jed for his quick, wise decision.

For a moment the crowd was hushed, uncertain, shocked by the fall of its leaders. She took advantage of it. "Friends," she said, "you see now that we mean business. Go home, I tell you, take your wounded with you." Pray God the two men were not dead. She heard the click as Jed reloaded. "My friend is ready to fire again," she told the now wavering crowd. "One more of you will suffer if you come on." As she talked, she had been working swiftly to reload, by touch alone, as Hart had taught her, long ago, in Savannah. "Two," she said as the bullet fell into place and she raised the rifle. "And this time, I warn you, we shoot to kill." And as she said it, she saw with sharp relief that John Tanner was beginning to flounder about in the snow. "Mr. Tanner needs help." She made her voice carry above the murmuring of the crowd. "Take him, my deluded friends, and go in peace."

The reminder that she knew Tanner's name did it. She watched breathlessly as the crowd changed, became purposeful once more, gathered round the two dark figures on the snow, loaded them onto the pieces of fence that had been brought for a more sinister purpose, and began to shuffle away into the bushes. Only, as they went, one dark figure stepped forward, shook a fist, shouted, "We'll be back."

As he in turn vanished into the bushes, Mercy bent anxiously over Bill Barnes, lifted his head, and began desperately brushing snow from his nostrils. He was breathing, and she thanked God for it.

"How is he, ma'am?" Jed was beside her, bending, listening as anxiously as she did.

"Alive, thank God. Help me get him indoors, Jed. That was good shooting of yours."

"And yours." He lifted Barnes's shoulders, Mercy took his feet, and they managed to struggle up the steps and into the house. Pausing there, wondering where to put him, Mercy felt him stiffen, come alive under her hands.

"He's coming round." Jed had felt it too, and between them they managed to steady Barnes on his feet and hold him there, swaying.

"Knocked me out," he said. "The dirty bastards. John Tanner . . ." and then a string of oaths that surprised even Mercy, hardened by life on the *Georgia*. "What happened?" he asked at last. "Ma'am, did they hurt you?"

"No, but I'm afraid Jed and I wounded two of them. Come into the kitchen, Bill, and let me look at what they did to you. Light the candles, Jed," she said as they eased Barnes into a chair near the fire. "And put some water on to heat. Ah." She had pulled the knitted cap off Barnes's head and felt the wound, a great swelling on the side of his face, just on the hairline: "You've the luck of an angel, Bill," she said. "Two inches only, and it would have been the temple, and you'd be dead."

"I'm glad I'm not. But what happened?"

She told him quickly, wringing out a cloth in cold water as she talked, and pressing it against the swelling.

"You shot one each," he said at last, impressed.

"I'm afraid so. The two leaders. Tanner and someone else. That was quick thinking of yours, Jed. What did you aim for?"

"The shoulder."

"So did I. I do hope they both survive."

"Yes," said Barnes grimly. "I wish I knew who it was said they'd be back. Oh, my good lord, what now?" Ruth's terrible scream had momentarily silenced them all.

"I hoped they'd slept through it." Mercy hurried, candle in hand, into the other room and saw Ruth lying across the cot. "Mother! Mother!" She raised distracted eyes to Mercy. "She won't answer."

"She's dead," said Mercy after a quick look. "She's at peace, Ruth. Nothing will hurt her anymore. She's with the cherubim and seraphim, casting down their golden crowns. . . ." How did it go on? She could not remember. "And I'm here to take care of you, Ruth." She took the girl's cold hand. "We're sisters, remember. Your mother made us sisters."

"Sister Mercy?" Ruth stopped crying and looked up at her.

"Yes." Mercy reached a hand and pulled her to her feet. "And now you must come and sit by the fire and have something hot to drink."

"Well, that settles it," said Bill Barnes half an hour later.

"We leave here in the morning, and I can't say I'm not relieved. You'll have to go back south now, ma'am," he said to Mercy. "You do see that, don't you?"

"Yes. But I don't know how I'm going to manage, and that's the truth. Two of us . . . all that way."

"Three," said Jed.

# III ❧—

The two captains faced each other on the blood-stained deck of the British frigate. "No, no, keep your sword," said the Englishman. "You made a gallant fight of it. But what madness made you take us on? You could have given us the slip, easy enough, when we first sighted you."

"Yes." Hart Purchis had to agree. It had been madness indeed. But how could he explain that his disaffected crew had not summoned him on deck when the strange sail was first sighted; that when he had finally been told, it would have looked like sheer cowardice to have run for it?

"Heroic madness," said the English captain. "Your men fought like tigers."

"Yes," said Hart again. It was the only good thing about this disastrous day. If his selfish decision to stand and fight rather than risk the taint of cowardice had meant the destruction of the *Georgia* and the deaths of half her crew, it seemed to have given back their pride to the survivors after the long disappointment of their unsuccessful winter's cruise.

Shocked silent, thought the English captain, and no wonder. "Come down to my cabin, and let me give you a glass of wine," he said. "Your wounded will be seen to along with mine, I promise you, Captain—" He paused.

"Purchis," said Hart.

"But that's my name! Where are you from, Captain Purchas?"

"Savannah." Hart noticed that the English captain had mispronounced his name, but he still seemed incapable of answering with more than a single word.

"Hence the *Georgia,* gallant little ship. But before that? In England?"

"Sussex." Belowdecks now, Hart looked round the English captain's luxurious cabin, which seemed to have been hardly touched by the little *Georgia*'s gunfire. Already pig-tailed British sailors were busy restoring it to order.

"Leave it for now," said the English captain. "And send me my man with wine." He threw his cocked hat on a chair and took off his heavy uniform jacket, making Hart more acutely aware than ever of his own shabby, almost civilian appearance.

"My letters of marque." He handed over the papers as another sailor bustled in with a tray and glasses.

"That's good." The Englishman looked them over quickly. "I'd hate to have to hang a cousin as a pirate. Dated from Charleston, I see, not Savannah."

"Yes. I commissioned the *Georgia* there after the fall of Savannah."

"Quite so. A glass of claret, Captain Purchas?"

"Purchis," said Hart. "Yes, thank you."

"With an *i?*" He poured the wine. "Then you're from the other branch of the family. They used to have a big house at Winchelsea. That's in Sussex. I remember now, something my father told me. One of them went to the colonies with General Oglethorpe. Your father?"

"Yes. But I never knew him. He was killed in the French and Indian War." Hart was relaxing a little now, sipping his wine, in a kind of limbo between the desperate hours of battle and the unknown, unpromising future. Somewhere above them, on deck, a man screamed, then was silent.

"They're still getting the wounded belowdecks," said Captain Purchas. "I've a good surgeon. He'll do his best for them. Both yours and mine."

"And then?" Hart took another sip of wine and made himself begin to look forward.

"It's a devil of a war, this, and none of my seeking," the Englishman answered obliquely. "My party, the Whigs, have been against it from the start. Criminal folly. Fighting our own kin over some stupid taxes that should never have been levied. As if we hadn't enough natural enemies. Well, look at us now, with the French and Spanish joined against us, and the Dutch looking uncommon unfriendly. But that's not to say I'm not fighting you Americans with everything I've got. That's my job, and I'm doing it."

"You don't have to tell me that," said Hart. "I saw. But the men. My men. What will you do with them?"

"I shall do my best to persuade them to change their coats and enlist with me. I've not seen England for years. I'm shorthanded, of course. I could use some good men like yours. I hope I can persuade them. Otherwise, it will mean a long spell of prison for them. I'm on my way home, you see. With despatches." He had purposely delayed the announcement until his prisoner had drunk half his wine and begun to look a little more relaxed.

"To England?" Hart kept his voice steady with an effort. Idiotic to have assumed that Captain Purchas was operating from New York, where an exchange would be comparatively easy to arrange, at least for himself. As for the men, if they had not put up such a good fight, he would almost have wondered whether at least some of them had not hoped for capture and a chance to change sides. What other explanation could there be for that failure to rouse him at first sight of the enemy?

"Yes. With all possible speed. I'd not have chased you if you'd run for it. Good news for me, bad for you and your men, I'm afraid, but I hope I can manage better for you, Cousin. My family may be Whigs, in opposition, but we've friends in high places just the same. No need for you to languish in gaol, I think. But time enough to think of that when we are there. In the meantime, is there any one you would like to write to in case we should speak a ship bound for New York before we leave American waters?"

"Thank you. Yes. My mother. My wife."

"You're never married!" He had been thinking this new-found cousin of his young to be a captain, despite the hint of white in his untidy fair hair.

"Last autumn." It was March now, nearly three months since that swift, sad parting from Mercy and no possible chance of hearing from her. But she would be safe with the Pastons. Of course she would. If he had left her at

Philadelphia, as she had asked, everything would have been different; none of this would have happened. No use thinking of that now. But he must remember it when he felt himself tempted to blame her for his crew's disaffection. "My wife's staying with relatives of ours near Boston," he said. "I'd very much like to get word to her and to my mother in Savannah."

"Write to them both, of course." Captain Purchas poured more wine. "But I'm afraid your wife is more likely to learn the news from the public prints. Your mother in Savannah is another matter since we hold the town. I know Sir James Wright, the British Governor of Georgia, slightly. If we do speak a ship, I'll enclose your letter to your mother under cover to him." *

"He's an old friend of ours," said Hart.

"There you are. I told you it was a ridiculous war. I devoutly hope we'll get home to find that negotiations for peace are under way. In the meantime, Cousin Purchis, you must consider yourself my guest while you are on board the *Sparrow*. Have I your word that you'll not try to escape or meddle with the men?"

Hart paused for a moment, looking round the luxurious cabin, remembering the sheer size of the *Sparrow*. Thought of escape was idiotic, and as for his crew . . . "Yes," he said.

"Sensible." Purchas breathed a sigh of relief and shouted an order to the marine on duty outside the cabin door. "You'll be glad to get to your cabin. Paper and pen will be brought you directly. If we sight a ship at all, it's most likely to be in the next day or so."

"Thank you. You'll let me have a copy of the list of survivors?"

"Of course. And you'll want to visit your sick. But later, if you please, when the surgeon has had time to go the rounds." He held out his hand. "I hope you will be as happy as is possible on board the *Sparrow*, Cousin."

"Thank you." He could not quite bring himself to call this friendly stranger cousin.

The first lieutenant of the *Sparrow* had presumably been turned out to make room for Hart in this tiny cabin that was more like a cupboard, with a cot, a writing desk, and a chest for the clothes he did not have. It was mercy enough that they had managed to get the wounded off the

*Georgia* before she sank, taking the dead with her. Snatching the ship's papers from his cabin, he had felt the *Georgia* settling in the water. No time to think about his own effects when there were still wounded to be got aboard the *Sparrow*'s boats. It was only now, as a grinning British sailor brought him paper, pen, and a small inkstand, that he remembered the certificate of marriage Captain Bougainville had written for him and Mercy on board the *Guerrier*. He had kept it in his Bible, and it had gone down with the *Georgia*.

An unlucky marriage from the start? He would not believe it. But the loss of their marriage lines did not make writing to Mercy any easier, and he decided to write the letter to his mother first. After all, it was much more likely to reach its destination, and then, surely, his mother would get word to Mercy. After all, so far as he knew, his mother, his aunt Mayfield, and his cousin Abigail were still living very comfortably in the Savannah house on Mercy's earnings. It was entirely thanks to her that they had survived the rigours of the British occupation as well as they had. She had turned the Purchis house in Oglethorpe Square into a kind of club and gaming house for British officers and made a resounding success of it. He smiled wryly to himself, remembering his own savage jealousy when he had come home, secretly, a spy, and seen Mercy flirting with the British officers. And then the astonishing discovery that she, too, had been a spy, egging on her admirers to indiscretions which she had used to good effect in the pamphlets she published in her other, secret identity as the Rebel Pamphleteer.

Lucky for him—he lifted the pen and put it down again —very lucky, that the British had kept the truth about Mercy as quiet as they could after he himself had accidentally led them to discover her. It had not at all suited their book to have been so roundly fooled by a mere girl. In the one letter he had had from his mother, in answer to his announcement of his marriage to Mercy, Mrs. Purchis had said nothing about the Rebel Pamphleteer, unless a glancing remark about how kind the British had been was intended as a reference to the illicit printing press they had discovered concealed in the cellar at Oglethorpe Square. The British had apparently not penalised the household for

this. She, her sister Mayfield, and Abigail Purchis were still
running the club, she had told him: "We do very well."

She had not mentioned Mercy's emeralds, either, which
he knew she and her sister had pawned to meet their expenses, and her comments on his marriage had seemed curiously lukewarm, considering what a tower of strength and
comfort Mercy had been to them all. Well, of course, Aunt
Mayfield would inevitably be mourning her son Francis,
and whatever version of his death had been current in
Savannah, it was certainly not the true one. It would have
suited neither British nor Americans to have it be known
just what a double or even triple game Francis had been
playing, with the Purchis inheritance as the stake.

He picked up the pen again and dipped it in the ink.
Francis had lost. Francis was dead, and Winchelsea, the
plantation house he had coveted, was burnt. "We'll be
back, Hart, you and I," Mercy had said, that last day,
standing under the ruined Judas tree by her father's grave.
Would they ever? He sighed and began to write, slowly:

*My dear Mother:*
   *This is to tell you that the Georgia is sunk, half her
men dead, the rest and I prisoners on board HMS
Sparrow. By a most amazing chance, her captain
proves to be an English cousin of ours—he spells it
Purchas.*

(Captain Purchas would read this letter. It was his duty,
though he had been too polite to say so.)

   *You see how fortunate, all things considered, I have
been.*

(The words came more easily now.)

   *And I hope you will not mind too much that we are
bound for England. You know I have always wished
to go there, and my cousin Purchas hopes to be able
to save me from imprisonment. So you must not fret
about me, dear madam, but take care of yourself, and,
if you will, write to Mercy and tell her that I am un-
hurt and as always her loving husband. I am writing
to her too, to Farnham, but my cousin Purchas is less
sure of the letter's reaching her. I hope that you have*

*had good news of her from the Pastons and that all
goes well with you all.*

He was interrupted by a knock on the door, and a midshipman who looked all of twelve years old announced that Cap'n Purchas wished to see him urgently.

What now? A ship already or some new disaster?

"There's trouble among your crew." Captain Purchas had been gazing out the stern windows at a blazing sunset that reminded Hart horribly of the morning's battle. "I thought you'd want to know."

"Trouble?" Was there no end to it?

"Yes. My bosun had to intervene to save a boy's life. A black boy."

"Bill!" Hart exclaimed. "Hardly a boy. I thought him dead. I swear he was missing when we abandoned ship. But that's good news. He's an old friend," he explained. "His family have worked for us forever." And then: "But who attacked him?"

"Some of your crew. They said he'd robbed your cabin. He had your Bible when one of our boats picked him out of the water. He asks to see you. Urgently. I rather think there's more to it. I'm afraid I must ask to be present."

"Yes. Naturally." His Bible. Bill. Bill, who had insisted on looking after his things, who must have known the precious document the Bible contained. When he himself had forgotten it, Bill had risked his life to save it for him and had nearly been killed for his pains.

Brought into the captain's cabin under guard, Bill was still in wet clothes and bleeding freely from a wound on the head and another on his right arm. He was grey with exhaustion, his teeth chattering with cold, and he was clutching Hart's Bible in his left hand. "Thank God you're safe, sir," he said as Captain Purchas dismissed the guard. He held out the Bible. "I knew you'd want this. I just wish I could have brought your things too."

"You risked your life for it. Thank you, Bill." Hart took the Bible and undid the stiff clasp. Bougainville's precious paper was still there, but the water had got at it. It was an illegible smear, only the heading "On Board the *Guerrier*" still legible.

"Something important?" Captain Purchas had recognised the moment of tense disappointment.

"Our marriage lines," Hart told him. "What made the others think it was theft, Bill? Surely they know you better than that?"

Bill looked anxiously from one captain to the other, and Hart began to understand that misleading description of him as a "boy." He had always been slightly built, but he now looked almost frail, a very far cry from the brave ally who had helped save Mercy's life when Francis had nearly captured her. What in the world was the matter with him? "What is it, man?" he asked impatiently. "Speak up. Why did they turn on you?"

"You should know, Captain," said Bill bitterly. "If they called Mrs. Purchis a Jonah, what do you think they call me, the only black on the ship?"

"A Jonah? Mercy? Impossible!"

"I wish it had been. You should have left her at Philadelphia, like she asked, Captain. They didn't like that long haul north and no prizes. A lot of talk there was, bad talk."

"You should have told me."

"On that little ship, with ears everywhere? It would have sealed our death warrants. I hoped things would get better after Mrs. Purchis was safe onshore. If only we'd taken a prize then . . ."

"I know." Hart was acutely aware of the English captain, silent, listening. . . .

"They turned against *me* then." It was a relief to Bill to tell it all at last. "A black. Sharing their quarters. Treated the same as them. They didn't like it. Made a great deal of my looking after you like I did, sir. Said it was the right job for a slave. Said a lot of things I don't reckon to tell you."

"It's a curious thing," said the English captain quietly, "but I thought that Declaration of Independence of yours said something about equality."

"Tell that to one of us blacks," said Bill. "If your men hadn't intervened, Captain, and I'm grateful, I'd be a dead equal. So I'm going to tell you both something I think you need to know." He turned back to face Hart. "It was no accident you weren't told first thing when we sighted the *Sparrow*, Mr. Hart. Half the crew wanted to be taken, to change their coats, and the other half were as wild a set of death or glory boys as you could wish for. So . . . between them . . ."

"Now I understand," interposed the Englishman. "That's

why you chose to fight against such overwhelming odds, Cousin."

"Too late to do anything else," said Hart grimly. "I wish you joy of your prisoners, Cousin Purchas."

"Oh, we'll sort them out all right." The Englishman turned back to Bill. "Don't look so troubled, man. I'm not going to ask you which are which. I don't need to. They'll be taught soon enough what life is like on a king's ship. The question is, what are we going to do about you?"

"Let me serve Captain Purchis, sir. I'd like to do that. He's—family to me."

"An excellent idea." He shouted an order, and a little, wizened, grey-haired sailor came bounding into the cabin as if he owned it.

"You wanted me, Capting?"

"Yes, Smithers. This young man will be looking after Captain Purchis. Meet my man Smithers, Mr.—" He turned questioningly to Bill.

"Just Bill," he said. "We don't have no other names."

"You do on my ship." He looked at Hart. "We can't have another Purchis, however you spell it."

"No." Hart recognised the reference to slaves who were named after the ship's captain who had brought them from Africa. "But how about Winchelsea? That's the name of our plantation," he explained to his cousin. "Would you mind being Bill Winchelsea?" he asked.

"I'd be right down proud, sir." Bill saw that Smithers was holding out a brown, clean hand, looked surprised, but took and shook it warmly. "How do you do, Mr. Smithers."

"Pleased to meet you, Mr. Winchelsea," said Smithers. "Now come along of me, and I'll show you where we doss down."

"And let him help you look out some of my clothes for Captain Purchis," said the Englishman. "And for himself. We've enough sick already without a couple of deaths of cold on our hands."

"Aye, aye, sir." Turning suddenly nautical, Smithers sketched a crisp salute and departed, taking Bill with him.

"Well?" said the Englishman.

"I'm ashamed," said Hart. "As you say, we talk of equality, and look at us! And calling my wife a Jonah, too!" This had hit him hard. "A heroine like her." But he must not go into that. "Thank God there's no chance that wicked slander got to shore with her. I'd not have liked her to start life in New England with a nickname like that tied to her. As for my crew, Captain Purchas, they're all yours, and welcome to them. Just don't trust them, the way I did."

"Oh, we'll teach them new ways of thinking on the *Sparrow*," said Purchas cheerfully. "Tell me, Cousin, what's your first name? We can't go on Purchas-Purchising each other all the way to England. I'm Richard, mainly known as Dick. And you?"

"Hart."

"Unusual. Just with an *a*, I take it?"

"Yes."

"That certainly settles the question of our relationship. That and the name of your plantation. The member of our family who misspelled his name and moved to the other end of Sussex took a friend from Harting with him. A George Hart and his family. I suppose an intermarriage was bound to happen." He held out his hand. "Welcome again to the *Sparrow*, cousin."

"You're from Sussex too?" Hart returned the firm pressure.

"Yes. My home's in West Sussex. Denton Hall, not far from Petworth. You shall make us a long visit there when we reach England; meet my father, who sits for the Whigs —the opposition interest in Parliament—my older brother George, and my tearaway of a sister Julia. And remember, if you can, that you're a married man."

"I shall remember." But was he? "I look forward to meeting your family, Cousin Richard. It was a lucky day for me when I fell into your hands."

"Maybe luckier than you know," said Purchas. "I wonder what your life would have been worth if you had sailed much longer with that disaffected crew of yours and no prizes."

"So do I," said Hart.

If writing to his mother had been difficult, writing to Mercy was almost impossible. It would have been hard enough anyway, after the fiasco of their marriage, but to have to do so with the knowledge that his newfound cousin must read every word he said . . . He was still struggling with the stilted phrases when they sighted a British sloop, inward bound to New York, and he was forced to a hurried, loving, almost incoherent conclusion. And then, while

Smithers, who had come for the letters, concealed his impatience, he added a postscript:

> *God knows who will read this besides you and me, my dearest Mercy. And God keep you. Your loving husband.*

"Thank you, sir." Smithers took the open letters. "The captain said to tell you he'll see they're sealed all right and tight and safe away."

"Thank you, Smithers. And please give Captain Purchas my best thanks."

"He's a right one," said Smithers. "For a man out of luck, sir, I reckon you coulda done a whole lot worse."

"I know it." His view was confirmed when Dick Purchas took him on a tour of the *Sparrow* next day and he recognised it at once for a happy ship, in painful contrast with his own *Georgia*. Where had he gone wrong? How had he lost the confidence of the crew who had once been devoted to him? It has to be something to do with Mercy and their unlucky marriage. A Jonah, they had called her. Well, no use trying to pretend that she had been lucky for him.

It was disconcerting, too, to see Georgians who had already turned their coats very neat and smart in the blue cloth trousers and flannel frocks that had been issued to them from the *Sparrow*'s slop chest, learning their duties as members of the enemy's crew. Some of them saluted him, awkwardly, unhappily; others looked away, pretending not to see him. "They're settling down well enough," Captain Purchas told him, later, over a glass of wine. "But bless me, Cousin, what kind of discipline do you keep in your navy? They seem to think they have a right to discuss every order. I'm afraid, much though I dislike it, we'll have to take the cat to one or two of them pretty soon, as an example to the rest. I can't have the infection of their free-and-easy ways spreading to my crew. I'd heard about your militia going home from the scene of battle when their time was up, but I had no idea such independent habits spread to your ships too. You'll never beat us without some discipline, Cousin Hart."

Impossible not to be grateful for the impartial tone in which this was said, but difficult also to answer. "When it works," said Hart. "It works to a marvel. You must have heard of the exploits of our John Paul Jones."

"An amazing man," agreed Dick Purchas. "But a wild one, Cousin. More a pirate than a privateer, if you ask me. His kind may win laurels, but they don't win wars. It's the day-to-day grind of duty done and orders obeyed that does that."

"You may be right," said Hart thoughtfully. "You may well be right, Cousin. And if so, God help my countrymen."

"Oh, well." Dick Purchas laughed and poured more wine to break the sudden tension. "God may or may not help you Americans, but your allies the French and the Spanish most certainly are. I have every hope, entirely between ourselves, that we shall get to England to find Parliament talking seriously of peace. The last letters I had spoke of a possible intervention by the Empress of Russia. And my father was in high hopes that Lord North's government would fall at last and be replaced by Fox and the friends of peace. Who knows? Maybe you will be the lucky man who takes the good news back to your country."

"A privateer captain, and an unlucky one at that? I'm grateful for your comfort, Cousin, but I'm not quite a fool yet. If you can really contrive to keep me out of prison, I'll be most grateful, but that's the height of my hopes."

"Then let us hope you will be pleasantly surprised."

# IV

Six members of the *Georgia*'s crew died of their wounds, and three were flogged for disobedience, but otherwise the voyage to England was swift and uneventful, with friendly westerlies behind the *Sparrow* most of the way. Twice a week Hart and his newfound cousin visited the members of the *Georgia*'s crew who had refused to serve the British in their dark confinement on the orlop deck. And every time they did so, Hart would find one or two more missing and knew that they had joined their friends in freedom above-decks. And more and more he was aware of the ugly looks of the men who still held out and who must have felt, with justice, that his lot was shamefully light compared with theirs.

He always returned from these visits in a black mood, which Dick Purchas learned to respect. Shut in his tiny cabin, he would go over and over the whole disaster of the last winter, trying to decide whose fault it all was. His own? Mercy's? The men's? After all, if they had only told him about the *Sparrow* sooner, he would have been able to show her a clean pair of heels, without dishonour and without pursuit, as his cousin Dick had told him.

All past, all over with, all irretrievably done. Blame was for the past. He must think of the future, his own and that of the few of his men who still remained immured below-decks. He had never seriously hoped for rescue, and as day followed uneventful day, he was glad of it. Better not to hope than to hope and court disappointment. And besides, as he got to know the officers of the *Sparrow*, he found it increasingly difficult to think of them as the "enemy." Most of them were Whigs like their captain and would clearly much rather fight Frenchmen or Spaniards than Americans. They spoke with comforting respect of the rebels' successes in the five years of war and then apologised for calling them rebels.

Impossible not to like them, and equally difficult not to enjoy this enforced idleness. There had been no time like this since that day almost five years ago, at Lexington, when Mark Paston had died in his arms. His only other spell of inactivity had been after he was taken prisoner at Monmouth Courthouse, when he nearly died on a prisoner of war hulk in New York Harbour. Mercy had arranged his rescue from there. Mercy had nursed him back to health and had saved him once again when Savannah was taken by the British. He owed her his life. Horrible to feel that in some curious way this seemed an obstacle between them. That and the sea, the ever-widening cold grey waste of sea that lay between them now.

> *Oh, wide is the water, I cannot get o'er,*
> *The water lies wide twixt my true love and me. . . .*

His mother had sung him the ballad when he was young. How did it go on? He could not remember.

"Sir?" Bill had brought his shaving water and was laying out a clean shirt, part of the wardrobe to which all of the *Sparrow*'s officers had contributed.

"Yes?" Hart watched with surprise as Bill opened the cabin door, looked cautiously to right and left, then shut it again.

"I've a message for you. From the men."

"The men?"

"Some of them. Grant that was mate on the *Georgia* and his friends. Grant was flogged the other day, as you know."

"He was lucky to get off so lightly." It was true, but just the same it had been horrible to have to watch the blood-drenched back writhe under the lash. And, he remembered now, he had felt something sinister in Grant's clenched silence and that of the other Americans.

"He don't see it that way," said Bill. "He's had his belly-ful of British discipline, he says. Told me to tell you"—he lowered his voice—"that he and his friends are ready to rise and take over the ship if you'll just lend them a hand. They've found friends in the British crew who say they're sick, too, of low pay and the lash. One of them's assistant to Doc Burnard. He prigged this the other day." He handed Hart a small bottle. "Laudanum. Your part's to put it into the officers' wine the first chance you get. We'll have to think of some way you can let me know you've done it." He looked round the cabin. "Your Bible. Leave it open on the desk. I always come in after dinner to see all's right here. I'll pass the word to the others. And we'll be sailing home in no time. What is it, sir?" He felt Hart's lack of response.

"Bill, I can't. I gave my word. So did the others. Swore allegiance to King George."

"This is war," said Bill. "Sir, think! Think of the Georgians who are still prisoners belowdecks. What's going to happen to them when we get to England? *If* we get to England. Mill Prison, sir. We all know about that. You better than most after that time you spent on the prison hulks at New York. A living death. What's a man's word compared to that? And just think of the other side of it. Sailing the *Sparrow* into Charleston Harbour! The welcome we'd get. And the difference it would make. A spanking frigate like her. We'd be heroes."

"We'd be villains. Bill, I'm sorry. I can't do it." And yet how appallingly tempting it was. "What would happen to the officers?" He realised as he asked it that it betrayed him as wavering.

"Oh, they'd be right enough. Held for ransom, most like, or"—he corrected himself, seeing Hart's expression—"ex-change, rather."

"I wonder." Hart was remembering that writhing, bloody back under the lash. If Grant got the chance, he would never stop short of the fullest possible revenge. "No," he said, "I'm sure you believe Grant, but I don't. He'd kill them all. Captain Purchas is my cousin. He's been—they've all been good to me. To us all," he added with less conviction. "Think how Dr. Burnard cared for your wounds. All your wounds."

"So we could help sail their ship," said Bill. "Sir, it's such a chance." He was pleading now. "For me, most of all. They need me, see; they're treating me like one of them again." He looked suddenly grey. "If you don't agree, sir, and I have to tell them so, my life's not worth a straw. And there's something else. Something Grant told me to tell you if you should be uncertain like." He paused for another quick, cautious look outside the cabin door. "It's about Miss Mercy, sir. Mrs. Purchis, I should say. Grant said to tell you that when you and she were ashore that day at Cohuit, some men came out to the *Georgia* across the ice from Boston Harbour. You never knew that, did you?"

"No?" For a moment he did not see where this was leading.

"No. Well, they heard all about our voyage. About Mrs. Purchis being a Jonah and the bad luck we'd had from her. Oh, a parcel of nonsense, of course." He quailed at Hart's look of naked fury. "But them New Englanders seemed to believe every word of it. I don't rightly know what kind of welcome Mrs. Purchis will have had there, sir. Ask him right, once we've taken over the ship, Grant might even take her up to Boston, and you could see for yourself. He's a Maine man himself; it would suit him well enough."

Without intending it, he had made up Hart's mind for him. "You mean," he said, "Grant would be captain."

"It's his idea," said Bill.

"Then my answer has to be no."

"Good-bye, Mr. Purchis," said Bill.

Later that afternoon there was a cry of "Man overboard," and Hart knew at once that it had to be Bill. But had he gone over alive, in despair, or dead, first victim of his angry accomplices? Certainly, though the ship's boat was lowered, while the *Sparrow* swept in a wide circle back on her own course, there was no bobbing head to reward the search, and by nightfall they were on their way again.

"I'm sorry." Dick Purchas had sent Smithers to summon Hart for a glass of wine. "I know he was almost part of your family. You'll miss him badly."

"Yes." Hart had been battling it out with himself all day, and this friendly, almost family sympathy decided him. "But there's worse than that," he said. "I've been fighting with myself about telling you, but I must. Bill spoke to me this morning." It was hard to get it out. "He told me there was a plot among the Americans to take the ship. They wanted my help. When I refused, he said, 'Good-bye.' I wish I knew whether he killed himself or they killed him."

"I don't suppose we ever shall." Dick Purchas raised his glass in a silent toast. "I'm glad you told me, Cousin. I thought they must have approached you."

"You mean, you knew?"

"Naturally I knew. I run a happy ship. Reckon to. Oh, I expect some of the men Grant and his friends approached really intended to join them—there are always some malcontents on any ship—but he was fair and far from the mark in some he spoke to. Our British sailors like to grumble and curse, but come the crunch, they're solid gold. I won't tell you how the word reached me, any more than you were going to tell me Grant's name, but I can tell you this: If you heard only today, it got to me a long time before it did to you."

"Good God!" Hart stared with backward horror at the danger he had run. "But what are you going to do?"

"Nothing. Oh, I've got the ringleaders closely watched. That's why I'm afraid your man may have killed himself. None of the leaders could have done it. I've a man on each of them. Reporting daily. When we get to England, I'll see they are sent to different ships. We need sailors, not gaolbirds. They'll settle down, I hope. The only one I'm not sure of is the man Grant. I'm glad you spoke to me. Now I can ask your advice about him."

"It's hard to tell." Hart spoke slowly. "He's a damned good sailor but has never liked taking orders. I made him mate on the *Georgia* for both those reasons."

"And did it work?"

"That's what I'm not quite sure of." He was looking back to the day the *Georgia* was sunk. "Grant was in command when we sighted you that day," he said. "It was his responsibility to summon me. He left it so late that I had to fight you. I wonder what he really wanted. I do remember one thing, though. Bill stuck to me close as pitch almost to the end of the fighting that day. I wonder if he was afraid for me. Afraid of Grant . . . Oh, poor Bill . . . If I had told you sooner, you could have protected him perhaps."

"I doubt it," said Captain Purchas. "Certainly not from

himself. As to Grant, I'll see he's watched night and day. One false step, and I'll throw the book at him. But for all our sakes, the last thing I want is word to get out of what he was trying to do."

"I'm more than grateful," said Hart. "I cut a pretty sorry figure whichever way you look at it."

"Nonsense," said Dick Purchas. "You were on the spot, and no mistake. Now we'll drink another glass of wine and say no more about it, if you please. I hope to make Plymouth in three or four days if the wind holds, and then this will be all over, best forgotten. But I must say I'm damned glad I don't have to take you in in irons, Cousin Hart. I was—anxious."

"Thank you." Alone in his cabin, Hart sat for a while, very still, contemplating the disaster he had escaped. And Bill, poor Bill, who had not . . .

The more he thought of it, the more he respected his newfound cousin for the way he had handled the whole business, and the more grateful he felt to him. If the conspiracy had been exposed, his own part or lack of one would inevitably have come to light, and there were no two ways about it—it would have meant ruin for him. He seized the first opportunity to mention that dangerous bottle of laudanum to Dick Purchas, who laughed and said, "You don't think it really was laudanum, do you? Doc Burnard has more sense than to leave that where thieving hands can reach it. No, it was when that was taken that we knew Grant really meant business. He's behaving very well, have you noticed?"

"What does he know?"

Dick Purchas shrugged. "I'm not sure. That he's watched, that's certain. I gave orders that it must be obvious after your poor Bill's death. I didn't want anything else to happen."

"And it hasn't. I envy you your power. I wish we could order things like that in our navy."

"I expect you will one day. We've been sailors a long while, remember, long enough to learn that there's no time for divided command at sea. A split-second decision can so easily make the difference between life and death. No time for your committees here. Do you know, I am beginning to hope that even the man Grant is beginning to recognise that. He's certainly minding his step."

"He must be a very frightened man."

"If he's not, he's a fool. And I never thought him that. If he goes on behaving as he is now, I'm half-inclined to keep him on the *Sparrow* and just split up his friends. He has the makings of a damn good petty officer."

"Cousin, you amaze me."

Dick laughed. "Well, it would solve a moral problem for me. I hardly like to send him to another ship without some word of warning to the captain, and yet how can I give that without telling the whole story, which, as you know, is the last thing I want to do?"

"And for which I'm more grateful to you than I can say," said Hart.

He thought about this conversation a good deal in the next few days, when the *Sparrow* encountered contrary winds almost for the first time and wallowed unhappily to the west of the Bay of Biscay. And the more he thought, the more anxious he felt. Grant, he was sure, was not a man to change easily. He had a wife and children in Maine and had always seemed devoted to them. Impossible to believe that he had given up all hope of getting home. "It's too good to be true," he told his cousin, "the way Grant's behaving. I hope your watch on him is close."

"It certainly is."

But not close enough. The ship ran into fog the next day, somewhere to the west of Ushant, and all attention was centred on the man taking soundings. They had seen no land so far, and though the master's reckoning showed the ship as well clear of dangerous, rocky shore, Captain Purchas was taking no chances. "I don't intend to pile my *Sparrow* up on the rocks, as a gift to our French enemies," he told Hart, who had groped his way up on deck through the strangely silent, fog-muffled ship.

Enemies? Friends? Hart had a sudden vivid memory of Captain Bougainville's French officers crowding round Mercy on the *Guerrier,* Mercy in her low-cut dress of bronze satin that drew all eyes. Mercy laughing, flirting . . . Mercy who had laughed and flirted also with the British officers who controlled Savannah. He had watched her, dangerously, through the window of the house in Oglethorpe Square, teasing, tantalising them. . . . How far had she gone? Would he ever know? The question, gnawing at his vitals, had combined with the cramped, awkward life on the *Georgia* to make him shamefully impotent during that strange honeymoon of theirs. Looking back, he could understand that, but understood it with rage and despair. If he had only been able to take her, he might have known. . . .

"By the mark, ten," chanted the man in the chains. So far they were out of danger. Did he want to be out of danger? A Jonah, the *Georgia*'s crew had called Mercy. And they had passed the word to the New Englanders who had visited the ship when he and Mercy were ashore. He had been so sure she would be safe with the Pastons. And of course she would be. Mercy had a gift for being safe.

What was he thinking now? Hating himself, he could no longer bear the muted, crowded deck and turned to grope his way down to the privacy of his cabin. The fog had penetrated below decks, cutting vision, blanketing sound. Reaching his cabin door, he was surprised to find it ajar with, surely, a faint glimmer of light showing inside. And the hint of movement?

He pushed the door, silently, gently, and, as it yielded to his cautious touch, saw Grant, faintly illuminated by the lantern he had hung from a nail, very busy with something on the writing desk. Papers . . . a pile of something that might be wood shavings . . . Grant reached for the lantern, and Hart sprang at him.

They fought silently, horribly, with bare hands, with teeth, with deep, sweating, grunting hatred. Grant had Hart by the hair, was banging his head against the desk, and for a moment Hart relaxed, letting him do his worst, thinking hard. They both were unarmed. A weapon? It might make the whole difference. Without one, he was lost. Grant knew about his weak right arm, legacy of Monmouth Courthouse, and was taking the fullest advantage of it. But the enforced rest on the *Sparrow* had done it good. And now, lying quiet, apparently helpless, he remembered something. On the writing desk, somewhere under the pile of paper and shavings, lay the penknife Dick Purchas had lent him to sharpen his pen the other day. He had forgotten to return it and now thanked God. Still playing helpless, he rolled a little nearer to the desk. Now his right hand could reach up, if he could only distract his triumphant adversary.

Grant helped him by letting go of his hair and reaching for his throat. This was to be the end. He had worked off

the long rage of his captivity in that savage banging from
which Hart's head still spun. Now he was ready to finish
and get back to lighting the fire that would destroy the
*Sparrow* and, if he was lucky, give him his freedom.

As his hands went from hair to throat, Hart's right one
reached up, groping on the low desk. A small knife, but
sharp. Was his right hand strong enough? It must be. He
had the knife now, and as the calloused, savage hands
tightened round his throat, he drove it with all his re-
covered force, upward, sideways, under Grant's left ribs.

A grunt of angry surprise; the hands went on tightening;
Hart's head swam; Grant's body was heavy on his, stopping
life, stopping breath . . . dark, dark . . . And suddenly, just
this side of unconsciousness, he remembered Mercy, Mercy
offering her breast to his knife. "I can't kill you," he said,
"so I suppose I must trust you." Mercy . . . The darkness
closed on him.

"Hart! Cousin Hart!" Dick Purchas's voice. Hart travelled a long, reluctant way through heavy darkness to find
himself lying on his own cot. His head ached; his throat
hurt. "Grant?" His voice came out as a croak.

"Dead, I'm glad to say," said Purchas. "And glad I lent
you that penknife, Cousin. If I hadn't, I think we'd all be
dead, or in French hands. I should have listened to your
doubts about Grant."

"What happened to the men watching him?"

"Dead, I'm afraid. The fog gave Grant his chance. I
should have doubled the watch on him. But I had other
things to think of. At least we've cleared Ushant now, but
it's thanks to you, Cousin, that we did, and so I shall tell
my masters at the Admiralty."

"Oh, God!" Hart struggled to pull himself up against the
hard pillow. "What have I done?"

# V ❦—

It started to snow again just as Mercy, Barnes, and Jed finished packing the sledge with everything it would safely hold for the long journey south to Philadelphia. "That's good," Barnes said as the first large flakes came floating softly down. "That's the dandy. Bit of luck this will see us safe to the post road south of Cambridge. Though I'm not that worried about the daytime. It's darkness brings out the devil in men."

"Just so long as the snow don't lie too thick." Jed looked up anxiously at the heavy sky.

"Roads are good," Barnes said reassuringly. "Right down to Philadelphia, by what I hear. Orders of Congress when the durned British got a hold on the seaways. And inns every six miles. So they say! Believe that, you'll believe anything. But tonight we'll lie up snug with a cousin of mine, back from the road a piece. Safer like that, so close to Boston. Pity we couldn't get started sooner."

"I'm sorry," said Mercy.

When Ruth discovered that they must leave her mother's body unburied, for Barnes to look after until the spring thaw made burial possible, she had gone first into screaming hysterics and then at last into a numb, biddable silence that Mercy found almost as alarming. It had delayed their start badly, and Mercy had managed an anxious whispered question to Barnes. His answer had been reassuring. Their attackers of the night before had most likely all come from Boston. "They're famous," he told her, "Boston mobs. Infamous. I don't reckon on trouble cutting across to the main road south of Cambridge."

But they all breathed secret sighs of relief when they reached the main road at last. "Reckon it'll get dark kind of soon tonight." Jed, who was driving the sledge, voiced an anxiety that Mercy and Barnes had silently shared.

"Yup," said Barnes. "I wouldn't mind if it was to stop snowing now. I'm not dead sure how often Cousin Joe clears his track. But I know it like the back of my hand." He turned with hurried but not entirely convincing reassurance to Mercy. "*And* the turnoff. And by golly, there it is! Turn 'em easy, Jed boy, right by that clump of firs. The road's posted all the way."

"How high are the posts?" asked Jed.

"High enough, I hope." Barnes leaned forward, peering anxiously ahead through the dwindling light that was reducing the landscape to a dangerous grey sameness. "I reckon I'd best get down and lead the horses. Looks like the snow's pretty deep."

"It certainly is." Like him, Mercy had noticed that when the track dipped into a hollow, the posts marking it were almost hidden by drifting snow. And the light was failing moment by moment.

"Not long now." Barnes looked exhausted, and she was angry with herself for giving way when he had insisted on tying his horse behind the sledge and joining them on this dangerous first stage of their journey. On the other hand, would they ever have managed without him and this useful cousin of his? Would they manage now? The sledge was moving at a snail's pace, as Barnes groped his way through heavily drifted snow. To distract her mind from the instant, immediate anxiety, she made herself face another. She had only, with luck, and thanks to Barnes and his friends, enough money to get her little party to Philadelphia. So— what then? Her best hope was that one of Georgia's representatives at the Continental Congress would be prepared to help them, but she knew it for a forlorn one. In Georgia's present chaotic state, it would be a miracle if representatives had even been elected, still less made the long, hazardous journey through the war-torn Carolinas to Philadelphia.

But perhaps nothing had come of the rumoured British attack on Charleston. If Charleston was still free, and the Mayfield house standing, she had only to get them there, and they would have a home where she could surely find work to support them all. If she dared. Remembering the British capture and the French siege of Savannah, she shivered with more than cold. Ruth was in no state to be exposed to such an experience. Was she mad to have taken on the added burden of Ruth? Well, mad or sane, there was nothing else she could have done.

It was a relief when a cheerful shout from Barnes brought her back from these gloomy thoughts to the cold present and the happy sight of lights ahead. Joe Meigs and his plump, silent wife welcomed Barnes with enthusiasm and his friends with hospitable kindness and a blessed dearth of questions. That they were friends of Barnes's was good enough for Meigs, but, like Mercy, he was anxious about Barnes's haggard appearance, which Barnes attributed to an accident the day before.

"Not like you to have accidents," was his cousin's reply, and Mercy wondered what he really thought and was grateful for his pointed abstinence from further questions.

"Snow's stopped," were the cheering first words with which cousin Joe's wife greeted Mercy next morning. "My Joe reckons the worst's over, and you might be lucky for a while. He's good at weather telling, is Joe. How's your poor sister then? She surely did take your ma's death hard." Mercy and Barnes had decided that the little party should pass for brother and sisters.

"She slept well, thank you." Mercy and Ruth had shared a tiny slip of a room that opened off the kitchen, and Ruth had indeed slept almost too heavily and had waked wild-eyed and silent as ever. Well, for the moment the silence had its advantages.

After a huge breakfast of ham and home-baked bread Barnes and Jed reloaded the sledge while Mercy tried to pay Cousin Joe's wife.

"No, no." She waved away the money Mercy offered. "Friends of Bill Barnes is friends of ours. You keep your money; you'll need it all before you get to Philadelphia, by what I hear. Some of the innkeepers along that road are proper sharks, I'm told. I wish your brother was older, ma'am, and that's for sure."

"Oh, we'll manage," said Mercy with a confidence she did not altogether feel.

It was a very bad moment when they reached the main road and said good-bye to Barnes, who looked a little better this morning but agreed that he must get home. "I do *thank* you." Mercy pressed his hand with her mittened one. "For everything. You will watch out for my husband in the spring, won't you? Explain what happened. He'll pay you what you and your friends have so kindly lent me." She prayed inwardly that Hart would have been lucky at last.

"Course I'll look out for him," said Barnes. "As to paying back, well, we'll see about that. When he comes. If he comes. It's been a pleasure to help you, ma'am. I do pray you get safe to Philadelphia."

"Thank you, Bill. For everything." She was silent for a moment, fighting a lump of tears. "It's too cold to stand." She made her tone brisk. "Good-bye. God bless you."

Now that they were on the main road, the going was good, the snow already packed down by other travellers on this well-used post road between Boston and Philadelphia. The clouds were high and much lighter. "We should make good time today," said Jed.

"Not too far for the horses." They were one of Mercy's many anxieties. She had left a note for Mr. Golding explaining the emergency that had compelled her to borrow his sledge and horses and promising to send them back from Philadelphia, but had to recognise that she was very much on the windy side of the law over the whole affair. How soon would his friends in Farnham let him know what she had done? But that was an anxiety for the future. For the moment: "Are we crazy, Jed?" she asked. "Will we get there, do you think?"

"Sure we'll get there," Jed said stoutly. "Now we're clear away from Boston, there'll be help when we need it. See" —he pointed with his whip—"smoke there—and there. Houses . . . people. You don't see them, cos of the weather. But get in trouble, they'll come. We hang together, we New Englanders. Mind you"—he had been thinking about the journey, too—"I reckon anytime we find company, for a day, or more, we take it. But we'll get there, don't you fret. We'll get there, in God's good time."

He was proved reassuringly right when the sledge bogged down in a snowdrift later that afternoon, and Mercy and

Ruth both got out to try and help shift it. As if by magic, a man and a boy appeared from a nearby wood and helped them free the sledge. When Mercy thanked them, the man urged them to spend the night at his house. "My wife won't forgive me in a hurry if I let female company by. She reckons she's sick of us men."

In a curious way, that set the pattern for the journey. There were constant crises, but help always did arrive in the end, and if there were not, in fact, inns every six miles along the road, there were enough so that they could always find somewhere to sleep, usually on the advice of their previous landlord. The innkeepers were often retired militia officers full of war stories, and their charges were usually reasonable enough, running at somewhere round eight dollars a night for the whole party. Mercy had shared the money Hart and Barnes had given her with Jed, and they both of them had it stowed in different places, some in Jed's pocket, some in the sole of his shoe, some in hers, some in the hem of her skirt, carefully stitched there before they left Farnham. She always took care, before they started out for the day, to have the price for the next night's lodging ready in a carefully arranged mixture of hard and paper currency, blessing Barnes daily for the amount of hard coinage that he had managed to give her.

Her experience of running the British club and gaming house in Savannah was a godsend to her now, and many a landlord who had begun by planning to fleece the young party ended up with a grudging respect for her hardheaded bargaining. She knew exactly what discount she should get for the proportion of hard money she doled out each day and began to think that with luck and good management she would be able to eke out their resources to last them at least as far as Philadelphia.

The continuing icy weather was a blessing. Travellers from the South, questioned the night they spent in a crowded Providence inn, assured her that there was no need even to consider the long northern detour that might have been necessary if the Hudson had not been frozen at Fishkill. If it thawed there, she had been told, it might take as much as a week before it was possible to cross the ice-filled river by boat, and a week in Fishkill's expensive inns, where space was at a premium because it was the main supply depot of General Washington's army, would have gone far to ruin her.

As it was, they contrived to pass through Fishkill early in the morning and turned south towards West Point, where they crossed on the ice, under the frowning fortresses —Putnam and Wallis and West Point itself—that had been so miraculously built in the last two years. Safely across, they stopped at a little inn on the west bank for beefsteaks and tea and some good advice from a friendly landlord.

"You must on no account think of going the shortest way to Philadelphia, by Brunswick and Elizabethtown," he told Mercy. "General Washington don't let his soldiers go that way, and what makes sense for them most certainly does for you. It's not just British parties out from New York," he explained, "though they're bad enough, but the Cowboys and Skinners is worse. And not much to choose between them, ask me, though the Cowboys do call themselves Tories and the Skinners Patriots. Bandits is what they are, miss, the whole lot of them, and you want to keep clear of them, pretty young things like you and your sister."

"Thank you." Mercy found the compliment both surprising and heartwarming. She had noticed only the day before that though she still did not speak, Ruth was beginning to look much better as a result of the days spent in cold, invigorating fresh air and the exercise they all got when they walked uphill to spare the horses or pushed the sledge out of a soft patch of snow. They were hungry as hawks by night and slept like logs, despite the cramped quarters where they sometimes had to sleep all together, fully clothed, and Mercy was grateful that they were passing as brother and sisters. She called them all Paston, because she thought it would be easier for Ruth, and was glad of it when the friendly landlord went on to warn her of the danger of British raiding parties out from New York.

"They can cross on the ice, easy as kissing your hand," he told her. "Harbour's fruz clear over to Staten Island. Pity General Washington ain't got more than the rags of an army, or we'd take New York back easy as winking while the British generals wine and dine their fancy ladies. If only he could surprise them in New York the way he did in Trenton in '76, there might be some life in it. Specially now most of their fleet has sailed south."

"South?" It was what she had feared.

"You hadn't heard? Word is their General Clinton got clear of Sandy Hook just before the harbour froze in December. Ten warships and I don't know how many transports. For Charleston, they say. I reckon that figures. The British have found us northerners too tough for them and fancy the South will make easier pickings after the way Savannah fell."

"That was a bad day," said Mercy. "But surely Charleston will never fall so easily. Isn't General Lincoln there, one of the heroes of Saratoga?"

"Well," said the landlord dubiously. "Yes he is. A Massachusetts man, miss, and maybe not all that much of a hero. Anyway if I were you, with that young brother and sister of yours to look out for, I think I'd make plenty of enquiries in Philadelphia before I took the road for Charleston."

"First we have to get to Philadelphia," said Mercy.

"Oh, keep to the post road, and a bit of luck, you'll get there all right. The mails get through, mostly, and the roads are busy enough this time of year, with the snow hard and the sledging easy. The damn British do take the mails from time to time and publish extracts from people's letters in *Rivington's Gazette,* as I'm sure you know, but I doubt if they'd trouble with a young party like yours even if you should be unlucky enough to meet them."

"I do hope we don't," said Mercy with feeling. It was partly with this hazard in mind that she had called them all Paston, but suppose by sheer bad luck they should encounter one of the British officers she had duped in Savannah? It did not bear thinking of.

The next few days were anxious ones as they had to avoid Paramus and take a wild, rough road by way of Haverstraw to Morristown, where the American army had built its winter huts and they were hailed with friendly cheers by bands of scarecrow soldiers. Mercy had been warned that Mr. Arnold's inn at Morristown was expensive and always full as it could hold with officers, so they had made an early start, hoping to press on to Somerset Courthouse, where there was said to be a reasonable inn. It was a relief to get out of the area occupied by General Washington's army, for she had been anxiously aware of tension building in Ruth as they received the cheerful catcalls and

sometimes ribald salutes of the tatterdemalion winter
army. They passed through Middlebrook, where Washington had stopped General Howe in 1777, and descended
from the heights by way of a valley whose frozen stream
leapt down in a series of glittering icefalls. The sun
gleamed greyly through cloud for a moment, and Mercy
heard Ruth draw a sharp breath. "Pretty," she said.

"Beautiful," agreed Mercy, delighted at the change in
Ruth's mood. And then: "What are you doing, Jed?" He
was fumbling with something he seemed to have concealed under the seat of the sledge.

"Mr. Barnes gave it me." He looked at once awkward
and proud as he produced a heavy old-fashioned pistol.
"He said he'd feel safer if we had it for the debatable
ground, and from what I heard last night, I reckon we
should be grateful to him."

"What did you hear, Jed?"

"Oh . . . talk." The inn had been a small one, and
Mercy and Ruth, the only women travellers, had slept with
the landlord's three buxom daughters, while the men
dossed down in the big, warm kitchen which served also
as dining and living quarters.

"What kind of talk?"

"Cowboys," he said grimly. "Or Skinners. No one
seemed sure which, and it don't seem it makes much
difference. They raided a farm over there a piece." He
waved a hand vaguely in the direction of New York.
"Took all the cattle," he said. "And all the food they
had."

"Did they"—she paused—"hurt anyone?"

"I dunno." He looked quickly at Ruth.

"We'd best keep going then." She twitched the reins,
and the sledge moved smoothly forward. Jed was right, she
knew. It made little difference whether the marauding
bands that ravaged the farms round New York were Tory
Cowboys or Patriot Skinners. All they really wanted was
loot. She shivered a little. "If we should meet them, don't
fire unless you have to. We'll give them the money I've
got out for today, and pray God they believe it's all we
have. But I'm glad you've got the pistol."

"So'm I," said Jed.

The morning passed quietly enough, but as the country
grew less mountainous and the road better, Mercy was

increasingly aware of the menacing nearness of New York. They were in a district, she knew, where a landowner like Mr. Vanhorn, whose handsome country house they had passed, might entertain the British general Cornwallis for breakfast and the American Lincoln for dinner. As to whose side he was on, that was his secret.

They passed through Monmouth Courthouse, where Hart had been wounded in 1778, and saw the relics of the huts where Washington's troops had spent the following winter. The light was beginning to fade, and Mercy to look anxiously ahead for signs of the village that surrounded Somerset Courthouse, when she saw a dark band of woods ahead and heard a shot and the sound of shouting.

"Trouble." Jed pulled the horses to a halt. "What's to do?"

She looked about her, her first instinct to hide. But frozen piles of deeply drifted snow would make it an impossibly dangerous business to get the sledge off the road, and even if they did, there was no cover except for the wood ahead of them. "I think we'd better go on, get into the wood, hope to hide there," she said. "It looks quite big. There might even be a side track we could take."

"I surely hope so."

As the sledge moved forward again, a horseman emerged from the wood, riding hard, sparks of ice flying up from his horse's hooves. He was holding his reins left-handed, Mercy saw, and swaying dangerously in the saddle. Whether friend or enemy, he was badly hurt. And now, behind him, she could hear shouting from the wood. How many voices? Not many, she thought.

He had seen them. "Help!" he cried, and then, near enough to see that two of them were girls: "No, save yourselves! I'll hold them as long as I can. I killed their leader, I think. Quick! Back the way you came. It's your only hope." Level with them now, he pulled his horse to a sliding halt and made a fumbling effort to reload the pistol he held in his left hand. "Save yourself, madame. There's no hope for me."

Now she recognised his slight accent. He was French, one of America's new allies.

"The British?" she asked.

"No. Some *canaille*. They ambushed me in the wood.
I killed their leader, hoped for a moment the others would
run for it. They're on foot," he explained.

"Then we can all escape them!" exclaimed Mercy.

"No. I can ride no further."

It was too obviously true. Blood was showing now, a
dark stain on the right side of his coat.

"Give me your pistol." Mercy had made up her mind.
"You can't use it. I can. And will. Jed, turn the sledge
across the road. We'll fire on them from behind it, try
to keep them from seeing how few we are. Better that
than trying to run for it. Besides, we can't leave him.
Sir"—she turned to the Frenchman—"let me help you
dismount. Then they need not see that you are wounded.
It will make us seem more of a threat. Quick! They'll be
out of the wood any minute now." The sounds of shouting
were much nearer. "How many?" she asked as she steadied
his difficult descent from the horse.

"Five. Four now. And I may have wounded another."

"Then we have a chance. The light's going. When they
appear, you must speak to them. Tell them to stand, or we
fire. Make it sound as if we were friends of yours, soldiers,
a threat. That's right, Jed." He had been manoeuvring the
sledge so it lay at an angle across the road, the horses to
one side in a passing place. "Fire when I give the word,"
she told him, swiftly examining the Frenchman's pistol.
"Does it fire true?" she asked.

"Yes, if you can handle it."

"Oh, never fear for that." She was trying to decide
whether to leave Ruth in the sledge. It was a good deal
darker now, and she thought that they would present a
fairly formidable-looking group silhouetted against the
snow. "Keep down, Ruth," she urged. "And keep quiet."
Fatal if she should scream. "Jed, you take the one to your
left, I'll fire to the right. Here they come!" A little group
of dark figures had emerged from the wood and hesitated
at the sight of their party. "Now, monsieur. Frighten them
if you can," she urged.

"Halt, there," he shouted as they began to come forward, rather hesitantly, Mercy thought. "I have met my
friends. We are armed and ready for you. Come any
further, and we fire."

They paused, an indistinct huddle against the dark of

the wood, and Mercy turned to Jed. "We'll have to hold
our fire until they are clear of the trees," she told him.
"We'd never hit them now. When they are outlined against
that bank of snow, that's our time."

"If they don't fire first," said Jed.

"I doubt they can see us any better."

"I hope they don't hit the horses."

"They don't want to," she said. "That's why they're not
firing already." The men had started moving forward now,
spreading out to present a wider field of fire. Four of them,
as the Frenchman had said. "We'll have to reload fast."
Despite the cold, her hands were damp with sweat on the
pistol. The outlaws were coming forward steadily now,
silently, drawn by the irresistible target of sledge and
horses. If either she or Jed missed a first shot, they would
be lucky to get a second. "Now!" she said, and the two
shots rang out, dull-sounding against the snow. For a horrible moment she thought they had both missed, then saw
the man to the right of the group begin to crumple down-
wards while the one on the left was cursing and holding
his right arm with his left one. No time to be looking
at them. She was reloading with cold hands that would
shake.

"After them, my friends," shouted the Frenchman.
"Don't let the villains escape!"

That did it. The three who had remained standing turned
and fled, leaving their comrade where he lay. The Frenchman turned shakily to look at Mercy for the first time.
"Thank you, mademoiselle," he said. "You saved my life."

"Then I'd better make a job of it by bandaging that
wound of yours," she told him. "Jed, help me get his coat
off. Ruth, there's a petticoat at the top of the valise. Get
it out for me, would you?"

"Yes, Sister." To Mercy's immense relief, Ruth re-
sponded to the tone of command and began obediently
tearing the petticoat into strips as Jed and Mercy eased
the Frenchman out of his coat. The wound in his forearm,
though bleeding freely and obviously incapacitating, was
less serious than Mercy had feared. "But we must get you
to some shelter," she said as she bound it up. "Do you
know these parts, monsieur?"

"Call me Charles," he said, pronouncing it in English.
"Or *Charles?*"

"Quick of you, mademoiselle, but English is better. You Americans do not seem to take kindly to strangers. I believe those ruffians back there might have let me alone if it had not been for my accent. No," he replied to her question. "I am quite a stranger here. I had intended to spend the night at the inn at Somerset Courthouse. The other side of the wood, I take it."

"So had we." Mercy looked unhappily at the dark bulk of the wood, which seemed increasingly sinister as the light faded. "And it's a long stretch back to the last inn." She had been thinking about this. "It would be quite dark before we got there."

"It will be dark in the wood," said Jed.

"And the longer we stay here talking, the darker it will get." She made her voice as positive as she could.

# VI ❧

"Listen!" said Jed. "Someone's coming."

Mercy had been helping the Frenchman into the sledge but straightened up at the sound of voices, a horse's neigh, the creak of a sledge, clear in the twilight hush. "Thank God," she said. "Someone else on their way to the inn. We'll wait for them, go through the wood together."

"Excellent," said the Frenchman. "Have you a lantern, mademoiselle? I think we will need it."

"Madame," she said. "Mrs. Purchis. Yes. Would you light the lantern, Jed? My brother and sister," she told the stranger. "Ruth and Jed Paston." What had made her give him her real name?

"And I am Charles Brisson, your most indebted servant." He pronounced his name English style to rhyme with prison. "I am here on business for my government," he explained. "But the less said about that, madame, the better. I shall hope that these people have less acute ears than yours, and pass myself off as an American merchant on his way to Philadelphia." She noticed that since the moment of crisis had passed, he was speaking with much less of an accent.

"I am sure you will succeed," she told him. "Of course, we will say nothing. I doubt my brother and sister have noticed."

"You are all goodness." A sparkling glance from large

dark eyes made her feel like a woman again. "Ah, here
they come."

The new group of travellers approached cautiously
through the gathering dusk, and Mercy raised her voice
to call to them. "We've been attacked," she said, "by
bandits. We beat them off but are hoping for your company through the wood."

"You were lucky," came a friendly voice from the
shadows. "We had wondered if you were bandits yourselves, but I don't believe there are women brigands yet.
We'll be glad to join you. Safety in numbers. Ah!" Jed
had got the lantern lighted, and the stranger could see them
in its light. "So few of you, and you fought them off?"

"As you say, we were lucky. I'm Mrs. Purchis. My
brother and sister, Pastons. Mr. Brisson, who is wounded."

"Then we must lose no time. My name's Palmer. George
Palmer. My brother, Henry; our servant. We are bound
for Philadelphia. And you?"

"Are going there too." While they talked, Jed had turned
their sledge round to face once more towards the wood.
Let us go," she said. "Time to talk when we are safe at
the inn."

"Let me lead," said George Palmer. "I know the road."

"That's good. Jed, let them by, we'll follow."

"How many outlaws?" asked Palmer as the servant
edged his sledge past.

"Only two now, I think. We wounded two, but I saw
them struggle away. I doubt they'll attack again." She had
been relieved to see that she had not actually killed her
man.

"Then let's go. Keep close behind. Sam—" he spoke to
the servant—"light our lantern so our friends can follow
it."

Even with company, it was unpleasantly dark in the
wood, and Mercy doubted if they would have found their
way without the providential appearance of the Palmers.
When they reached the inn at last, Charles Brisson was
half-conscious from loss of blood, and Mercy was glad
to find a capable landlady very ready to help change his
makeshift bandage and get him into bed, while her husband looked after the other travellers.

"The wound's nothing much," said the landlady when

she and Mercy left him at last. "He should do well enough."

"'I hope so." Mercy shared her slight surprise that a mere flesh wound had weakened the Frenchman so much, but then she had no idea how far he had travelled. He was younger, too, than his voice had made him seem, slightly built, with large dark eyes set deep in a pale face that just missed handsomeness. If he was a civilian envoy of the French government, this might, she supposed, have been his first encounter with violence and therefore much more shocking than it would have been to an American, after five bloody years of war.

She found the rest of the party gathered in the kitchen, the men drinking rough cyder while the landlord's daughter cooked their supper. The cyder was on the house, the landlord's tribute to their encounter with the brigands, and he insisted that she drink some too, since she and Jed were the heroes of the hour. "I reckon it was the Bartram brothers attacked you." The landlord handed her a brimming pewter tankard. "Been plaguing these parts two years or more. If you've rid us of two of them varmints, you've done us a favour, ma'am, and no mistake. I drink to you."

"A formidable young lady," said George Palmer. "I certainly hope to have the pleasure of your company for the rest of the way to Philadelphia, Mrs. Purchis, if it's agreeable to you."

"It is indeed." She had been hoping for such a suggestion. "But we are travelling with our own horses. Will we not go too slow for you?"

"We are doing so too," he told her. "Slower stages, but I prefer it." He rose to move over to the big scrubbed table where the landlord's daughter was laying out steaming platefuls of salt beef and beans.

As always, conversation over supper was general, and careful, but the Palmers, too, had heard the rumour of an attack on Charleston. Eating with appetite herself, Mercy noticed anxiously that Ruth was picking at her food, pale and even more withdrawn than usual. After a while she excused herself and took Ruth up to the little garret room they were to share with the landlord's daughter. It was not late, and after she had settled Ruth for the night, still without a word spoken, she went back to join the rest of the company for the rare treat of the landlady's own pre-

served blackberries. "We picked a bushel last fall," she
explained in answer to Mercy's compliment. *"And* I laid
hands on some sugar. We have to make the most of what's
going these days."

"We certainly do." Mercy had noticed the landlord give
his wife a quick, angry glance in the course of her last
speech and wondered just where the sugar had come
from. Like salt, it was scarce enough these days to make
a very handy bribe. Could it perhaps have come out from
New York in return for services rendered? And just what,
she wondered, had the so friendly landlord's relationship
been with the Bartram brothers, who, he said, had plagued
the district. And were they Cowboys or Skinners? He had
not said. She would be glad to get away from here, she
thought, rising to say good night.

"An early start in the morning, ma'am?" George Palmer
rose too.

"As early as you please."

"But will your friend be well enough?" asked his brother.

It was a natural mistake, and she was about to explain
about Brisson when she heard Ruth scream, and turned
with a quick apology to run up the steep attic stairs.

This bout of hysteria was worse even than the one on the
day they had left Farnham, and Mercy noticed that now it
was the name of Ruth's sister, Naomi, not her mother's that
came over and over again between the horrible half-human
screams. Today's adventure must have brought back memories of the Indian attack. In the end she administered a
short, hard slap and a dose of laudanum supplied by the
landlady in the interests, she said, of a little quiet in the
house for the other guests. "You'll be moving on tomorrow," were her last firm words as she bade Mercy good
night, and Mercy could hardly blame her. Ruth was certainly a formidable responsibility, and it was difficult not
to wish she had never met her or made that rash promise
to her mother. But after all, Ruth was Abigail's cousin, the
family's affair. She only hoped they would see it that way.

To her relief, Ruth waked quiet and docile as ever, and
when they went down to the kitchen, they found Charles
Brisson also up and dressed, his arm in a sling contrived
by the landlady out of an old sheet. His colour was back,
and his dark eyes sparkled as he rose to greet her. "My
guardian angel." For a moment she actually thought he

was going to kiss her hand, but he contented himself with
a look of warm gratitude. "Did you get some sleep?" he
asked as he pulled out a chair for her. "I'm afraid your
sister is not well."

"No." She was grateful for the understatement.

"I hope you will let me travel with you and help you
to look after her." He was speaking quietly, under cover
of a babble of general talk from the rest of the company.
"Indeed, I would be most grateful if you would allow me
a place in your sledge today. My shoulder is much better,
but I am not sure whether I could manage the reins. Perhaps your brother would be so good as to ride my horse?"

It would mean that she had to drive all day, but she did
not see how she could refuse him, and besides, she would
be glad of his company. Last night's scene with Ruth had
been exhausting, and the burden of today's journey, still
through the debatable ground, had been weighing rather
heavily on her. She was very fond of Jed by now, but the
fact remained that he was only a boy and she had to take
all their decisions. She smiled at the Frenchman. "I'll be
happy to have you," she said. "And I'm sure Jed will be
glad to ride your horse."

Jed was delighted. "If you can manage the sledge?" He
had not yet contrived to use Mercy's first name as she had
urged he do.

"I shall help Mrs. Purchis," said Charles Brisson. "I
may not be able to ride, but I can certainly manage those
horses of yours with one hand."

"Poor things," said Mercy. "I do hope they get us safe
to Philadelphia." She was beginning to be afraid that that
was about as far as the horses would ever get and wondered how she was going to pay Mr. Golding for them.
But that was a problem for another day. At the moment
they were facing another dangerous day's journey. The
Palmers were armed too, she was glad to know, and had
undertaken to take the lead, since they had come this
way before. They showed no surprise when Brisson got
into her sledge and probably still thought they were all
travelling together. It hardly mattered. . . .

Brisson proved admirable company, and Mercy realised
for the first time just how lonely she had been since she
parted from Hart. Ruth hardly ever spoke. Jed was a dear
boy, but he had no conversation and was so obviously shy

of her that she was afraid Brisson was bound to see through the pretence that they were brother and sisters.

She drove for the first part of the journey, and Brisson sat beside her and told her about the little town south of Paris where he had been born and grown up in a small château. "We are of the nobility, we Brissons," he told her, "though of course, you Americans make nothing of that."

It was on the tip of her tongue to tell him that she was, in fact, English by birth, but she restrained herself. He had been very careful, she had noticed, to tell her nothing of importance about himself. He had described his voyage from Nantes to Providence in vigorous and entertaining detail, but had given no hint of why he had made it or what his errand was to Philadelphia. Nor, indeed, had he explained why he had sailed to Providence at all, but then she knew that with both the British navy and British privateers at work, one had to take any passage one could and pray for a safe arrival.

He had just volunteered to drive for a while, and she was slowing the sledge to let him take over, when they heard shouting from ahead and saw that the Palmers had been stopped by a small band of militia. "Americans, thank God," said Mercy, recognising the shabby attempt at uniforms. She pulled the horses to a halt and watched the sergeant in command of the troop talk briefly to the Palmer brothers, then wave them forward and stop Jed, who was riding between the two sledges. To her surprise, he seemed to spend longer with Jed than with the Palmers but finally let him go and came back to where they waited.

"Morning, ma'am." The sergeant's tone was friendly. "I hear you've done us a favour, wounded a couple of the Bartram brothers, they tell me, you and that young brother of yours. Good shooting, ma'am. What was the name? You're all travelling together, Mr. Palmer tells me."

"Mrs. Purchis." Should she explain that Brisson was only a chance-met companion?

"Purchis?" The sergeant looked startled. "No kin to Captain Purchis of the *Georgia*, I hope?"

"His wife?" Her voice shook. "Why?"

"Bad news, I'm afraid, ma'am. In *Rivington's Gazette.* We took a man with a copy just yesterday. I'm sorry to have to tell you." He paused, searching for words.

"He's dead?" She swayed where she sat. "My husband's dead?"

"No, no. I'm sorry, ma'am. Stupid of me. No, but it's bad just the same. His mother is. And his aunt. They tried to get up from Savannah to Charleston. Too small a party. The Scopholites got them. The British are making a big story of it, a warning to others that they're safer in British hands."

"Oh, dear God." She put a cold hand to her brow. Poor, kind Mrs. Purchis; poor Mrs. Mayfield. But what about their niece? What of Abigail? "Just the two of them?" It was an effort to keep her voice steady.

"So far as I know, ma'am. A nasty business, I'm afraid. Those Scopholites are little better than animals."

"Stop it," said Charles Brisson. "Don't tell her!"

But she had heard too much already. "Mrs. Purchis," she said. "Anne Mayfield." The world was spinning round her. "I am so sorry." She clung with cold hands to the seat of the sledge. "But I think I am going to faint."

"I'm sorry." She heard herself saying it again as she came reluctantly back to consciousness.

"No need." Brisson had found the smelling salts she used for Ruth and was holding them under her nose. "You have been so very brave, always, madame, but that bad news was too much for anyone."

"My poor husband. His mother and his aunt. Oh, the poor things." She would not think about it. "Have the soldiers gone?"

"Yes. With a thousand apologies from that dolt of a sergeant for breaking it to you so crudely."

"There was no other way," she said. If she only knew what had happened to Abigail. No time for that now. "We must get on. The Palmers will be wondering what has become of us. If you would be so good as to drive, monsieur?"

"I wish you would call me Charles," he said. And then, sensing her reaction: "Forgive me. I know it is presumptuous. But I really do not wish to be known as a Frenchman. My business is most confidential."

They found the Palmers and Jed anxiously awaiting them at a place where the road forked. "We were beginning to be afraid you'd had trouble with those soldiers after all," said George Palmer. "I'd told them all about you. I was sure there would be no difficulty, or we would have waited for you."

"No trouble," said Mercy. "But they gave me terrible news. My mother-in-law and her sister . . ." She could not go on and was deeply grateful when Brisson intervened to explain, as briefly as possible.

After the inevitable exclamations of horror and sympathy she managed to explain her gnawing anxiety about Abigail, and it was soon decided that they would push on through Princeton to Bristol and hope to reach Philadelphia late next day. "You should get news there, and let us hope it will be good," said George Palmer. "I really think we could get another stage even out of your horses, so long as we make sure they are extra well fed at night. And to tell truth, it would suit us very well, ma'am."

That night, as they were getting ready for bed in a tiny room that they actually had to themselves, Ruth suddenly stretched out a hand to Mercy. "Poor Hart," she said. "How he will mind. And poor Mercy. I am so sorry."

"Why, Ruth!" The tears Mercy had controlled all day suddenly flowed fast and free. "Why, thank you!" She pulled her close for a long, warm kiss. "You love Hart, too, don't you?" Suddenly she was glad she had assumed what had seemed the burden of Ruth and reproached herself for her previous doubts. "Maybe this sad news will bring him home." She was ashamed to hope it. "And surely there will be news of Abigail in Philadelphia."

"My cousin Abigail," said Ruth.

Next day the sun shone, at last, a brilliant change from grey, snow-laden skies, and from time to time, passing under trees, Mercy would hear the drip of water, as icicles began to thaw. The sun was actually warm on her face, and she felt a strange little leap of hope and began to think about spring—and Hart. Disgusting. And yet it did seem possible that the deaths of his mother and aunt would make it necessary for him to come home, if only to make arrangements about the Mayfield house in Charleston. Besides, he, too, would be racked by anxiety about Abigail. She herself was beginning to hope that Abigail had stayed in Savannah. After all, she had always been Loyalist in her sympathies and was in love with another Loyalist, Giles Habersham, who was overseas somewhere, serving with the British. What a strange, horrible business it all was. More than anything else that had happened to her in the long, sad years of the war, the deaths of Mrs. Purchis and Mrs. Mayfield had brought home to her the savagery of this fight between friends.

She was driving, and glad of the distraction, when they caught up with the Palmers, who had stopped by the side of the road to mend a broken piece of harness. "I'll go on," she told them. "The road's clear enough now; I'm sure I can find the way. We'll see you at the inn in Bristol."

Driving on, she found her mind kept coming back to Mrs. Purchis and Mrs. Mayfield. The Scopholites, followers of the illiterate Loyalist Colonel Scophol, were known for their barbarous cruelty. What horrors had the two elderly ladies endured before they died? Plagued with these thoughts, she had been letting the horses take their own reliable way downhill along the well-used road when an exclamation from Brisson brought her attention back with a jerk. She had thought the road unusually smooth as it reached level ground and now realised that they were crossing a river on the ice. She could hear the rush of water. But that was all wrong. That was horribly dangerous. And on the thought, one of the horses plunged suddenly through the ice.

"Dear God!" said Brisson. "Stay where you are, madame. The sledge should be safe enough." He was out already, struggling to free the horse from the sledge, before she remembered his bad shoulder. He would never manage by himself.

"Stay here, Ruth," she commanded. "Here, take the reins, hold the other horse steady. Please God he doesn't go through too." The broad-based sledge really did seem safe enough, but as she spoke, the second horse also let out a snort of fright and plunged through the ice. "Let go the reins, Ruth," she urged. "It's our only hope, even if we lose them both." She was out on the ice now, beside the sledge, frantically trying to push it back to safety, desperately aware of the struggling, panicked horses, dangerously close. Then, horribly, she felt the ice give under her. Plunging into freezing water, she felt, with despair, the unexpected strength of the current and was fighting for her life, trying to get a grip on ice that crumbled away as she clutched at it.

How long did she struggle there? The cold was numbing; her hands and feet would no longer obey her; her skirts had become a clinging shroud; she felt herself begin to give up, to let go. Cold . . . cold . . .

Life, coming back, was thrillingly painful. Someone was chafing her hands. She could hear shouting. Then: "Mercy! Mercy!" Ruth's voice. "Dear Mercy, be better."

She was in the sledge, soaking wet, wrapped in all the rugs. Ruth was bending over her, smelling salts in hand. "You are better." Smiling, Ruth was suddenly beautiful. Life was beautiful. To be alive was a miracle.

"What happened?" Mercy saw that the sledge was safe on the other side of the river.

"Mr. Brisson saved your life. He got you to the bank before the Palmers caught up. I don't know how they got the horses out. I was looking after you. Oh, Mercy, I was afraid you were dead."

"Not a bit of it." Mercy was amazed at the change in Ruth. "And the horses?"

"Will be all right tomorrow, they say. We have to spend the night at the inn here."

That night it was Ruth who insisted that Mercy must go straight to bed and persuaded the landlady of the little inn to make her a great bowlful of steaming soup. "You must get warm." She brought her a hot brick. "You keep shivering, dear Mercy. You must not think about poor Mrs. Purchis and Mrs. Mayfield. You must have loved them very much."

"Well." Mercy thought about it. "They were good to me. In their way." It was true, at least, of Mrs. Purchis. Anne Mayfield had never been her friend. But what difference did that make now? "I can't stop thinking about Abigail," she said. "Pray God those devils of Scopholites have not carried her off." It did not bear thinking of, and she could not stop.

"You must sleep." Ruth took the empty bowl. "Mr. Brisson said to tell you the horses will be fit to travel in the morning, if you are."

"I shall be," said Mercy.

# VII ⊱⦁–

"Your England's beautiful, Cousin." Hart and Dick
Purchas were driving swiftly through high green Devon
lanes. "It all seems like a dream. I don't know how to
thank you. To be free, to be coming home with you like
this." But was it dream or nightmare? On the face of it,
he had been incredibly lucky. Dick Purchas had stood
his friend indeed. His report to the Admiralty had not
spoken of the conspiracy to seize the *Sparrow*. Instead of
figuring as the two-faced wretch he felt himself, Hart was
the hero who had caught a madman trying to fire the
*Sparrow* and saved the ship at the risk of his own life.
As a result, he had been paroled to his cousin's custody,
and they were on their way to the Purchas home, Denton
Hall in Sussex, while the *Sparrow* refitted at Plymouth.

"No need for thanks," said Dick Purchas. "You saved
my ship." He leaned forward to look out of the post chaise.
"It's a late spring. Here it is May, and the blackthorn's
still out. If only I could have got home for the last of the
ploughing. And the spring planting . . . I do look forward
to showing you my home, Cousin Hart, and having you
meet my family. Remarkable that Julia has still not married." He had found letters awaiting him at Plymouth, but
as they themselves had brought the latest news from
America, there was no knowing how long Hart might
have to wait for word from Mercy and his mother. It

was small comfort to have learnt, on board the *Sparrow*, that an English fleet had sailed from New York in December to launch the attack on Charleston that Mercy had predicted. That was another thing. Now that he had lived on such friendly terms with the officers of the *Sparrow*, he found he did not altogether like to remember Mercy's activities as a spy in Savannah.

That was part of the nightmare, and so were the expressions on the faces of the Georgians when he had said good-bye to them. Whatever Dick had told the Admiralty, they must know the truth, must know that he had foiled Grant in his attempt to fire the *Sparrow* and perhaps free them. He fought that savage battle over and over again in his dreams. At the time his captain's instinct to save a threatened ship had sent him straight into combat with Grant. And looking back, he did not see what else he could have done, but the fact remained that however publicly acclaimed, he cut a sorry figure in his own eyes. He had saved an enemy ship and owed the shreds of his reputation to his cousin's glossing of the story, but felt in his heart that it could not last. Some of the members of the *Georgia*'s crew must have known what Grant had planned. Or must they? Might Grant not have seized the sudden chance offered by the fog, relying on his fellow conspirators to back him up in the confusion caused by the fire?

A forlorn hope, but he clung to it. The Georgians' black looks, after all, were understandable enough. He had given his word not to try to escape and he was going free, to a life of luxury, while they must endure the captivity of service either in the British navy or, the still worse kind, in prison at Mill Hill. He had hopes of hearing from his wife and family sooner or later; they had none, so long as the war lasted. And that began to seem like forever. Dick Purchas's hopes that they would arrive to find the peace party in power had proved vain despite the fact that Lord North's government had actually been defeated by eighteen votes in the House of Commons on Mr. Dunning's motion: "The influence of the crown has increased, is increasing and ought to be diminished." Petitions against the war from counties and towns had been heaped on the table in the House, but nothing had come of it.

"We Whigs have no real leader; that's our trouble."

Dick Purchas had been thinking on the same lines. "If only Charles Fox had more bottom. A brilliant man, Cousin, but unstable . . . So brilliant that no one else can lead . . . So rash he is not fit to lead himself. And anyway, the King would never have him. I am afraid you had best resign yourself to spending some time at Denton Hall, though I am sure we will be able to arrange an exchange for you in the end. Now Parliament has passed an act allowing the exchange of naval prisoners, it should be no problem. Just a matter of time."

"Which I shall be happy to spend with you. I can't tell you how grateful I am to you, Cousin. I know it's thanks to you that it's to be Denton Hall for me and not Mill Hill. I do hope I did right in giving my word not to try to escape."

"Of course you did." It was a measure of the growing friendship between them that Hart was able to discuss his gnawing anxiety about this with his newfound cousin. "As I have said before," Dick went on, "I am sure that you can do more for the American cause and the cause of peace by mixing in society here in England than by rotting in prison."

"And God knows there's no future for me now as a privateer captain," said Hart grimly. They had passed a file of chained prisoners earlier in the day, and it was not a sight he would forget in a hurry. It was, in fact, the only sign of war he had seen as they drove swiftly through a countryside of neat fields, prosperous houses, and comfortable inns.

"I think that's just the trouble," said Dick Purchas when Hart remarked on this over an excellent dinner at the Dolphin Inn at Southampton. "Most of the time this war hits people here in England only in their purses. Unless they've a relative involved, that is. From time to time something happens to bring it home to the country at large: the invasion scare last summer, for instance, or your John Paul Jones's forays along our coast. Then the cry is all for peace. . . . But when the immediate crisis is past, people forget again. America is a long way off."

"It is indeed." Even with favourable westerlies most of the way, the voyage had seemed endless to Hart, the thin thread of love that bound him to wife and family and America stretching and stretching over the long sea miles.

"But what of France and Spain?" He pushed away the memory of Mercy. "And now this armed neutrality of the northern powers that the Empress of Russia is forming?" He and Dick both spent their evenings passionately reading English newspapers.

"More words than deeds, if you ask me," said Dick Purchas. "The northern powers care only about their trade, Spain's rotten to the core, and as for the French . . . Well, you saw, did you not, that their Admiral d'Estaing is back home, licking his wounds, after his defeat at Savannah." He poured wine for them both. "Let's not talk of the war, Cousin. Let's drink to your wife and the good news I hope you will have of her soon."

They reached Denton Hall next afternoon, and Hart was amazed all over again at the sheer size of English houses. He had thought his beloved lost plantation house at Winchelsea large and luxurious enough, but it seemed, in retrospect, a mere cottage compared with Denton Hall as they rounded a bend in the carriage drive and saw it lying in its hollow of the hills, rambling red brick glowing in the afternoon sun. "It's a palace, Cousin!" he exclaimed.

"Nonsense! You've seen Petworth House and can say that! But it's home, thank God. And there's Julia. I knew she'd be here to give us the meeting." He opened the carriage door and jumped out before it had even stopped. "Julia!" He took the steps at a bound and threw his arms round the girl who waited at the top. "I knew you'd be here! And Mother?"

"Here, too. She awaits you in the small saloon." She pulled away a little to look up at her brother, and Hart, alighting from the coach, thought her the most beautiful woman he had ever seen. Small, dark, and animated, she looked even lovelier as she made a little face of disgust and explained, "No London this season. We're retrenching, Dick. Economy's the cry."

"George in debt again?"

"In debt! He's drowned in it. Cards . . . cocking . . . horses . . ." A defiant smile. "Women! You'll have to speak to Father, Dick. He won't see him in London, won't let him come here. It's worse than when he joined the Mohawks. Of course, he's going from bad to worse, poor George. Oh, Dick, I'm glad you're home."

"So am I." He turned, with a smile of apology, to

where Hart had stood, an embarrassed audience, at the foot of the steps. "You must meet our cousin Hart Purchis. Hart, my sister Julia. Forgive the family gossip."

"I envy you," said Hart, with truth. "Your most humble servant, Miss Purchas."

"Oh, call me Julia," she said, "since we are to be cousins. Welcome to Denton Hall, Cousin Hart." She held out a tiny, elegant, gloved hand, and Hart, admiring her from neat kid shoes to exquisitely curling unpowdered hair, longed for the expertise to kiss it but dared not venture.

"Come and meet Mamma." She kept hold of his hand to lead him indoors. "She longs to see you, Dick."

"In the vapours?"

"Badly hipped." She was walking between the two men, her arm in Dick's while she still held Hart's hand, and he admired the wide double doors and spacious hall that made this possible. "You know, Dick," she went on, "for Mamma, the sun has always risen and set in George. To have him forbidden the house . . . Oh, I am glad you're home, nice Brother. Now we shall all be to rights again. You'll talk to Father. You were always the wise one."

Dick laughed, a little ruefully, Hart thought. "Younger brothers need to cultivate sense," he said. "I'm glad you're family, Cousin Hart, or you would think this a strange welcome. But come and meet my mother." Anticipating a footman, he threw open a door at the back of the wide, light hall and revealed a small sitting room where afternoon sunshine glowed on rose-pink furniture.

"Richard! At last! Now we shall be comfortable again!" Like her daughter, Mrs. Purchas was tiny and elegant beyond belief, but a small habitual frown marred her still exquisite features, and Hart was oddly reminded of his aunt Mayfield. As she reached up to accept Dick's kiss, Hart had a sudden vision of Mercy, strong, and brown, and golden from the sun, where these Englishwomen were pale and exquisite as hothouse lilies. "Cousin Hart!" Mrs. Purchas detached herself from Dick's embrace and held out a hand. "Welcome to your English home. And God bless you for saving the *Sparrow* and Richard's life." She put a tiny lace-trimmed handkerchief to dry eyes. "We owe you more than we can ever repay." And then, on a totally different note and with a glance at the ormolu clock on the chimneypiece: "We dine at five, Richard. Country hours. Julia, my love, will you have your cousin shown to his room? You see, Cousin Hart, we do not mean to stand on ceremony with you."

"I'm delighted." She obviously wanted to be alone with her son. Well, that was natural enough. As he and Julia left the room, he heard Mrs. Purchas's eager question: "And the prize money, Richard. How much?"

Prize money. The *Georgia*. But she had sunk. "I beg your pardon?" Julia Purchas had said something.

"You must bear with my mother," she said. "We have been all to pieces since this last news of poor George. But Dick will bring all about again. He always does, our good, hardworking Dick." She smiled up at him, black brows exquisitely arched. "Tell truth, Cousin Hart, you are wishing our family problems at Jericho and longing for a little peace and quietness. But let me just say, 'Welcome to your new home, Cousin.' Soames—" she addressed a formidable, liveried figure—"have someone take Mr. Purchis to his room. We meet before dinner in the small saloon, Cousin, when it is just the family. At five to five? Mamma is a perfect dragon for punctuality." A grandfather clock in the hall chimed the half hour. "My stars!" She lifted flowing skirts to run nimbly up the stair, then turned at the top to smile down at him. "I do hope you are not a dandy, Cousin. My maid will be at her wits' end to dress me in time."

Following more slowly in the wake of a diminutive page, Hart thought ruefully of the borrowed evening dress that had seemed only just good enough for the captain's cabin of the *Sparrow*. What a wretched figure he would cut in this elegant household, where the talk was all of debt and retrenchment, and the living luxurious beyond his imagining. So far Mrs. Purchas and her daughter had been kindness itself, but what would they say when he presented himself for dinner in Dick's ill-fitting second best?

"Your room, sir." Did the page expect to be tipped? What was the English word? Vails, Dick had said, handing them out at the inns where they had stayed. He looked round the luxurious bedroom, which, like the small saloon, faced west and was full of warm afternoon light. Though it had seemed so snugly tucked away among the rolling hills that Dick had told him were called downs, he now saw that Denton Hall was, in fact, on a low outlying spur, so that even this window at the back of the house commanded a wide, rising view of rolling hillside and grazing sheep. It was all incredibly beautiful, incredibly peaceful. Stable noises came from somewhere to his right, pigeons cooed, and then, down the valley, a clock chimed the three quarters.

It brought him back with a start to the present and the borrowed dress coat and knee breeches laid ready for him on the big four-poster bed. He was running a comb through his hair when a tap on the door heralded a neat black-clad manservant who announced himself as Price, Mr. Richard's man, and looked him over with a reproachful eye. "The ladies are already in the small saloon," he said at last, apparently giving up hope of making a bad job any better. "Mr. Richard sent me to see if you needed any help."

"No, thanks." He adjusted his borrowed cravat, shook out the ruffles at his wrists, and almost found himself wishing he was in Mill Prison.

"Then let me show you your way, sir. It's easy to get lost in this old house, but you'll get the hang of it soon enough. You're in the west wing, see." He opened the panelled door and ushered Hart out into the wide hall. "The east wing's shut up," he explained. "Mr. George's rooms are there." Closed doors to right and left suggested other bedrooms, and Hart wondered how many the house could sleep. They went up a step, and down two, and rounded a corner to see the wide main staircase up which Hart had come. "There you are, sir," said Price. "You'll find the ladies in the small saloon where they was before."

"Thank you, Price." He must ask Dick about tipping. But then what was he going to do about money? The little supply he had rescued from the *Georgia* was almost exhausted now. What would have become of him if he had not met his kind cousin Dick, who had insisted on paying the expenses of the journey? Now that he had learnt that Dick's family were in financial straits, he felt more unhappy than ever about being unable to repay him.

If he had thought Julia Purchas and her mother elegant before, he found them overwhelming in their low-cut evening silks. Julia was in deep red and was being teased about it by her brother, who looked even better, Hart thought, in civilian evening dress than he had in uniform.

"I'm no bread-and-butter miss, to be wearing white muslin." Julia turned from Dick as Hart entered the room and gave him a glance of amused commiseration. "Oh, poor Cousin Hart." He liked the way she used his first name. "Dick, you must positively take our cousin to London and get Knill to rig him out. You'll have to go, anyway, to see Father."

"Not to mention the Lords of the Admiralty," said her brother. "Since things are in such a bad way here, I must lose no time in getting another ship. And you will like to see something of London, Cousin, I have no doubt. Who knows, I may even be able to arrange a meeting for you with your hero, Dr. Johnson, though I should warn you that he is a diehard Tory and hates the very word 'American.' "

"All the more reason to meet him and try to convince him that we are not all quite barbarians," said Hart. "But, Cousin"—he hated to say it, and yet it must be said— "you know, I am head over ears in your debt already. I think if Mrs. and Miss Purchas will be so kind as to let me, I too must stay in the country on a repairing lease." He bowed to Julia as he quoted her own words.

She laughed. "Dipped like the rest of us? That's friendly! But no need for you to fret. We know all the moneylenders in town. Who better, with George in our family? Dick will find someone to lend you what you need on the security of your American estates, I am sure."

"But . . ." He was trying to think how tactfully to explain that everything belonged to his mother, while Winchelsea, the greater part of his inheritance, had been sequestered by the British, when Soames, the butler, appeared to announce that dinner was served.

"No buts for now," said Julia gaily, putting her hand through his arm. "Food comes first. But I warn you, Cousin, I shall not leave teasing you until you have got yourself suitably fitted out. If you look so very much the thing in Dick's castoffs, you will be the talk of the county when Knill has done his best for you. And you must know, since we have to rusticate, we mean to entertain down here this summer. It is our duty to Papa, of course, as a Member of Parliament. I hope you will find our life here not too tedious, even if it is in the country."

"I like the country," said Hart. "Particularly since you are here, Cousin Julia. Though it is true that I do long to see London."

"Oh, Cousin!" Julia laughed up at him. "How could you so spoil your charming compliment!"

"Of course, you must see London." Dick Purchas was seating his mother at the head of the table. "Julia's right, you'll have no problem about funds. We'll go to town just as soon as I have seen Glubb, the bailiff, and can report to my father on how things go on down here. I must see George and find out just how badly he is in debt. He is in London, I take it?"

"Where else?" said his sister. "Playing deep at the Cocoa Tree as usual. You'll have no trouble finding him. Just go where the play is deepest; he'll be there."

"That's quite enough about my poor George," said Mrs. Purchas pettishly. "It gives me the vapours even to think of him." She turned to Hart. "Tell us of your home, Cousin, and of all the adventures you must have had in the course of this terrible war."

"It's a long story, ma'am." From her bored tone, Hart was sure that it was one she did not in the least want to hear.

"And a fascinating one, I'll be bound," said Julia. "But we'll spare you for tonight, Cousin, for indeed, it must be painful for you to remember. Time enough when you get back from London for the story of your accidents of war. Then I'll play Desdemona to your Othello willingly enough." And then, an afterthought: "Do you read Mr. Shakespeare's plays in Georgia, Cousin?"

"Yes, and act them too. We are not quite barbarians, you know." He had a sudden vision of Mercy "rehearsing" with his cousin Francis that night when he had acted as unwilling spy on his own house. What play was it that had given Francis the pretext for that snatched kiss? He had never asked Mercy. Never dared to? "My wife." It was an effort to say it, but an effort he had been intending to make. It had begun to seem strange to him that no one had spoken of her. "My wife is an admirable actress. She learned from Mr. Garrick himself."

"Ah, poor Mr. Garrick." Mrs. Purchas sighed. "We

miss him sadly. Even I—poor invalid that I am—when I can get there, find the London theatre sadly gone off since his death last year."

"I shall hardly be in a position to judge," said Hart. "I am afraid our attempts at drama in Savannah have always been of the most amateurish kind."

"But you can act, I am sure, Cousin," said Julia. "I have it! Since we must do penance here for George's extravagance, why should we not stage our own play? Dick, you were always spouting Shakespeare when we were young. Have you forgot it all?"

"No, not I. I can still play Hamlet to your Ophelia if you so wish."

"Oh, pish." Julia made her expressive little face at him. "Shakespeare is all very well, Dick, but surely we can find something a little more up to the minute for Hart here to make his debut. Will you play hero to my heroine, Cousin Hart?"

"Gladly." It was only later, getting ready for bed, that he remembered how the conversation had seemed to slide away from the subject of Mercy. No doubt his kind cousins were trying to spare him from unhappy reflections, but he would rather they had talked about her. Climbing into the vast bed, he wondered how she was getting on with the Pastons. Judging by the New Englanders he had met when he was at Harvard, he could not help feeling that she might come as something of a surprise to Puritan Boston and found himself hoping that she had been able to adjust her ways to those of her hosts. As to that story Bill had told him of her being thought a Jonah by his crew, he had long since stopped worrying about it. Mrs. Paston would have laughed it to scorn easily enough, even if it should have got out to Farnham. She and Mercy would be friends at once, he thought, two strong-minded women.

He blew out his candle. Lord, what a lifetime it seemed since he had rescued Mercy from the mob that had killed her father. She had been a timid child then. Now she was a beautiful woman, and a formidable one. His wife, in law, if not in fact. As always, memory of the frustrations of that crowded voyage on the Georgia brought hot colour flooding to his face, even here in this unbelievably quiet, comfortable English bedroom. When they next met, it would all be different. He would be master. Master? What in the world had made him think that? And curiously, he had a vision of his newfound cousin Julia, looking up at him with those sparkling dark eyes that somehow seemed to hint at sadness, at dark depths, and asking if he would play hero to her heroine. Harmless enough, between cousins. Of course, he would do so and maybe, somehow, in doing so, would become the man he meant to be.

# VIII ⚜

I've chosen our play, Cousin." Julia was pouring Hart's tea at their ten o'clock breakfast, and he thought her even more entrancing in today's country chintz than in last night's red silk. *"All for Love,* Mr. Dryden's improvement on *Antony and Cleopatra.* Do you know it?"

"No," he confessed. "You will think me an American boor, I am afraid."

"Never that. You have been too busy making life awkward for Dick and his naval friends to have had much time for reading. But it's just the play for us, I promise you. *All for Love, or The World Well Lost.* Is that not an admirable title? And as for the speeches . . . we will have the whole county at our feet."

"You mean to perform for the whole county?" Dick had just joined them from the estate office where he had been closeted with Glubb, the bailiff.

"If they will come." She arched elegant brows at him. "And I see no reason why they should not. Admit, kind brother, that it is the least expensive form of entertainment we could possibly think of. Now Mamma, you must know, wants to give a breakfast or a *fête champêtre.* Just imagine what that would cost! After a play we need merely serve light refreshments. It should suit your starched notions admirably."

"Dear Julia." Dick sighed and poured coffee. "You must know this retrenchment is no wish of mine."

"Nor any of your fault. I know it only too well. And am doing my best to help you. After all, we have this American lion of a cousin. Shall we not make the most of him? You will not mind, Cousin Hart?" Her glance for him was appealing.

"Anything to be of service to you." He spoke with feeling. "I owe Dick more than I can ever repay. But I am afraid," he went on ruefully, "I am the very smallest possible kind of lion."

"Wait and see," she said. "We Purchases may be in opposition, but we have friends just the same. I think we will find you quite a king of beasts when our newspapers have had their say about you. Don't you see what a point it is? Cousins meeting in this bloody war that should never have happened. Saving each other. Why, you'll be the Damon and Pythias of the age." And then, with a hand held up as it were in self-defence: "Don't say it, Cousin. I plead guilty. My father would have me educated with the boys. I cannot help it if I am something of a bluestocking."

"The most beautiful one I ever imagined," said Hart.

"Imagined bluestockings!" Now she was laughing at him. "What else do you imagine, Cousin Hart?"

What indeed? He felt the hot colour rise to his face and was saved by the entrance of Mrs. Purchas, who bade them all a somewhat fretful good morning, described her sleepless night, and applied herself to chocolate with a will.

After breakfast Dick invited Hart to ride round the estate with him, and he accepted with enthusiasm. "I just hope I shall be able to handle one of your highbred English horses with this weak arm of mine."

"You shall have the gentlest beast in the stables for this first time," Dick promised, and in fact, when he mounted the plump black mare that had been led out for him, Hart was surprised to find how much better his arm was. Rest and sea air had done their work well, and now, recollecting, he knew that before the voyage he would not have stood a chance against Grant in that savage, silent fight.

"I owe you more than my freedom, Cousin," he said

as they set forth down the drive together. "I seem to owe you the use of my right arm, too."

"I noticed you are using it more freely," said Dick. "I'm glad." He was silent for a while, preoccupied, Hart thought, with the bad news he had found awaiting him. "We'll go up to the top of the downs," he said when they turned from the drive into a deep, chalk-white lane. "I need to decide which fields we should sell."

"As bad as that? I'm sorry."

"As bad as possible. Glubb greeted me almost in tears. In the years I've been away, things have gone from bad to worse. Well, my father has his life in Parliament, in London. . . . He has never interested himself much in the place except as a source of income. He was a younger brother, you know, not brought up to the responsibilities of property. And as for George . . . since he did his grand tour, he has never thought of anything but pleasure. Well, how should he care about the place when he had my father's example always before him?"

"You seem to," said Hart.

"Ah, I love it. I grew up here, you see. There are ten years between George and me. When he was a boy, my uncle was still alive. This house was his, and we lived in London. George is a Londoner; I'm a countryman. It's as simple as that. My mother's a Londoner, too, at heart. It's hard on her to have to ruralise down here. And as for poor Julia." He paused for a moment as the horses laboured up a particularly steep slope of the now grassy lane. "They've lost her dowry among them," he said angrily. "I could not imagine why she had not married long since. Now I understand. She was refusing offers to right and left when I went to sea. My mother thought she was holding out for a coronet at the least of it. You will think us a cold-blooded set, I am afraid."

Hart had been thinking that very thing but said, "No doubt she was waiting to find someone she could really love." Mrs. Purchas might be a cold-blooded fortune hunter on her daughter's behalf; he was very sure that Julia, so friendly to a penniless cousin, was nothing of the kind.

"Very likely," said Dick, and set his horse to the last steep bend of the track. At the top he stopped again. "Look!" He pointed with his whip. "A fair inheritance, is it not? When my father succeeded, the Purchas lands stretched from that winding river in the valley there clear over to that line of woods. Good land, too. It could have been made to pay for all. I begged my father to let me run the place for him, try improvements, like Turnip Townshend, or Rockingham in the north. He would have none of it. Thought a farmer son would be a disgrace. And with Farmer George for our king! As a result, the estate has dwindled to the land between those lanes." Again the whip pointed. "And I must decide what next to sell, so poor Julia can have her chance at last. It's a pity we sank your *Georgia*. The prize money would make a deal of difference." And then: "Forgive me!"

"No need. But surely you must have taken other prizes?"

"There are two kinds of captains, Cousin, in our navy: the ones who look for prizes and the ones who consider their country's good. And there's another thing. I have taken prizes in my time and found the profits from them so whittled away by prize courts that I have even found myself having to pay out lest my men suffer." He drew in a deep breath of sweet-smelling downland air. "If we were not at war, I would send in my papers tomorrow. I never liked the navy. Never wanted to join it. But in the navy the Purchas family has influence. So—it was the navy for me. It's a horrible life, cruelty from start to finish. I would not treat a beast on my land the way I was treated as a midshipman. And then, as captain, to know that the same things are happening to the young creatures in one's charge and to be powerless to help them. Horrible! Do you know when I first really liked you, Cousin?"

"No?"

"When we had to flog the man Grant. You looked the way I felt. Sick. But what can one do? It's the law."

"A bad one," said Hart. "God knows, I had trouble enough with my crew, but you almost make me feel that our way is better."

"Do you know, I am beginning to wonder if it is. And that's why, in the end, I think you will beat us, whatever the wiseacres say. I just wish it would be soon, for all our sakes. In the meantime, which would you sell? The fields to the east or those to the west?"

"Must it be so many?"

"If Julia is to have another season and a dowry at the end of it. Yes, it must."

"First tell me about your agriculture here. I'm a farmer myself, remember, though you can hardly imagine anything more different than our land." He was ashamed to feel a blurring of his eyes as a vision of the flat green rice fields at Winchelsea and the great sweep of the Savannah River imposed itself over his neat prospect of field and coppice and hill.

"Gladly." If Dick noticed, he gave no sign of it but plunged into a technical description of the problems of Sussex agriculture, of fallowing, and root crops, and the new machinery that was causing trouble among agricultural labourers.

They returned home late in the afternoon in great charity with each other, having replanned the entire economy of the Denton Hall estate. "And then turnips," Dick was saying as they rounded the curve of the drive to see the hall, as they had the day before, mellow in afternoon sunshine. "Do you really think I might pay our way without selling, Cousin?"

"With luck and the way agricultural prices are rising? I don't see why not. Mad to sell land at the moment. And surely anyone who truly loved your sister must be prepared to wait more than a year for her hand."

"Maybe," said Dick. "But would Julia?" And then: "Look, there she is."

Once again Julia had appeared at the top of the steps to greet them. But this time it seemed to be Hart who had all her attention. "Hart!" She came down the steps as they dismounted. "Oh, my poor Cousin!"

"What is it, Julia? Why the long face?" Dick sounded almost impatient.

Julia ignored him, holding out her hand to Hart. "Come indoors, Cousin. I've . . . I've bad news for you."

"News?" He gave the reins to the groom. "But how?"

"That bundle of New York papers you brought home, Dick." She turned to her brother. "Price has just unpacked them. You had never looked at them, I collect?"

"No chance," he told her. "I don't even know where they got stowed in the end. Just some duplicate copies; the others must be at the Admiralty by now. But why the amazement, Julia?"

"News from New York?" Hart's voice shook. "My wife? What is it? Tell me!"

"Come in here." She took his hand and led him into an empty book-lined room. "My mother's in the morning room." She turned to face him. "Not your wife, my poor cousin. Your mother and aunt."

"My mother? Savannah?"

"No." Still gazing at him with huge, pitiful eyes, she picked up a ragged copy of *Rivington's Gazette* from the study table. "Read it, Cousin. I can't. I'm so very sorry . . . I'll leave you. Come, Dick. Hart will want to be alone." The door closed softly behind them as Hart began to read.

When he put the paper down, his eyes were full of tears. Both his mother and his aunt. Dead. Horribly dead. The article in the Loyalist paper was obviously not the first report of the disaster and did not go into details, but its implications were clear. The grim story was used as an argument for a swift, just peace. Mrs. Purchis and Mrs. Mayfield were innocent victims, the anonymous writer said, of the savagery of what amounted to civil war. They had decided to flee the safety of British-held Savannah for the hazards of life in American Charleston. Their little party had never got there; their mutilated bodies had been found by a band of Tory soldiers and given decent burial. Mrs. Purchis was the mother of a well-known privateer captain. Every thinking person must feel for him and hope that this personal disaster would bring home to him the folly of fighting against his king and country.

Horrible. He stared blindly at the paper. Had it been Scopholites, up from St. Augustine, or those other savages, the King's Rangers, who followed the embittered Tory leader, Thomas Brown? It could even have been Indians. Unspeakable. And his cousin Abigail? No mention of her. Had she been with them and carried off to endure a slower, more horrible fate? He would not believe it. Turning the page with a shaking hand, he found a further paragraph. Sir James Wright, British Governor of Savannah, who had reported the sad news to New York, had written that he had done his best to persuade the two ladies not to leave the safety of Savannah and risk the dangerous journey north to rebel-held Charleston. They had stolen away, in the end, without his permission and in too small a party for safety. It was one of war's tragedies, and they were mourned by their niece, Miss Purchis, a devoted Loyalist, who had wisely refused to go with them.

Ah, poor Abigail, he thought, all alone in the house in Oglethorpe Square, mourning the aunts who had brought her up. Why had they gone? And in too small a party for safety? What had been happening in Savannah, since the unsuccessful French and American siege, to make them embark on so desperate a venture? But he was afraid he knew. The disgrace of Mercy's activities as the Rebel Pamphleteer must have been too much for them. They had loved their social life, enjoyed acting as hostesses to the British officers who visited Mercy's club. If they had found themselves suddenly ostracised, it would have been painful indeed. So—all Mercy's fault?

He must not think like that. She was a heroine, had risked her life over and over again for the American cause. It was sheer chance that it was not her own life that had been lost, but those of the two elderly ladies who had been good to her. It was all horrible . . . too horrible to be borne. Absurd. It must be borne. Vengeance? What use was that? He had a sudden, mad vision of himself attacking Dick's mother because she was English. Attacking Julia?

A little scratching at the door. "Hart? Cousin Hart, may I come in?" Julia's big eyes were full of tears as she held out both hands to him. "You must not stay alone any longer. It is too much to bear alone."

"Thank you." He pressed her hands in his and raised them to his lips. "That is just what I was thinking. It is like you to have thought of it."

"You must talk about them," she said. "Tell me about them. It will make you feel better, I promise you. Come into the garden, Cousin."

She was right. It did do him good to talk about them, sitting beside his newfound cousin in the little Gothic summer house that looked across parkland to the downs. Extraordinary to sit here, in peaceful England, and try to explain about the Scopholites, about the appalling savagery of the war in the southern states.

"And they are fighting on the British side, these savages?" she asked. "It's horrible, Cousin. It makes one ashamed. . . . We should have worked harder to make an end of this wicked war." She turned her big, tear-dimmed eyes full on him. "I am afraid we must face it that our opposition papers will make the most of this sad story. The copies of the New York papers that Dick sent to the Admiralty will have been read by now; the news will be out. You must resign yourself to being very much in the limelight for a while, my poor Hart." And then, as he continued silent: "Oh, Cousin, I do hope you have not been thinking about vengeance for this tragedy."

"How can I, when you are all so good to me?" he said.

"I am so glad you feel like that." She reached out an impulsive hand to take his. "Thank God Dick never looked at those papers, that you were here, among friends, before you heard the news. Otherwise, it might well have made you mad. As it is, I am sure you will see that it gives you a duty to do everything you can to work for peace."

"Peace and liberty," he said.

"But that's of course. Only, dear Hart, now you must see that peace can be worked for only by peaceful means. By honest ones. Not"—she hesitated—"not underhand, hole-in-corner . . . You will be a public figure," she went on quickly. "You must speak out. Tell of your own trage-dy, to help avoid others. You will be happier, doing that."

"Not at once," he said. "First I must mourn my dead."

"But not alone." She rose to her feet and put on the big chip hat she had been carrying. "Come for a walk with me, Cousin. I have an old woman I visit most days, an old servant, pensioned off, who thinks the sun rises and sets in our family. She will be longing for news of Dick, and to tell truth, he is sure to be too busy to visit her. Will you come with me and get a glimpse of how our people live? It will distract you, a little, if anything can."

"I'd like that. Thank you." Anything to stop thinking about his mother, about Aunt Anne, horribly dead. But what had Julia meant when she spoke of underhand activi-ties, hole-in-corner? Could she have known of Mercy's work as a spy? Impossible. The British themselves had hushed it up. It was just his morbid imagination that had applied the words to Mercy. Mercy, who had risked her life over and over again for the cause of liberty. Would she be wondering if that rash journey might have been partly her fault? How wretched she must be feeling if so.

He longed to be with her, to comfort her, and thought with horror of the wide waters of the Atlantic, stretching between them.

"You must not mind it so much, Cousin." Julia put a gentle hand on his arm. "It is all over, all done with. And here we are. You must smile, please, and be good to my old lady."

Granny Penfold lived in a tiny thatched cottage close to the lodge gates at the end of the drive. Approaching it by a shortcut across the park, they came on her in her garden, feeding hens. "Miss Julia." She bobbed a quick curtsy and surveyed them with bright eyes. "This is a sight to cure blindness, and no mistake. Come in, you and the foreign gentleman, and taste a drop of my cowslip wine."

"Not foreign," said Julia. "American, Granny, and our cousin."

"Course I know that." She was wrinkled and withered like a last year's apple, but her eyes were sharp with intelligence. "Everyone in Denton knows about the captain and how he saved my Dick's life, God bless him." To Hart's surprise, she seized his hand and kissed it with dry old lips. "Dick was my baby," she explained. "Did Miss not tell you? I fostered him after mine died. He's the only son I'll ever have. And you saved him for me, sir. He says you're a right one, and no mistake."

"You've seen him?" Hart glanced in quick surprise at Julia, but she had turned away to listen to the chiming of the village clock.

"Jimini," she said. "It's four o'clock. We must be on our way, Cousin, or we will be late for dinner. We'll taste your cowslip wine another day, Granny."

Julia proved right. The two items of news, simultaneously received in London, of Hart's saving of the *Sparrow* and his mother's death, became a nine days' wonder. As she had predicted, the Whig newspapers seized on it as typifying the savagery of what they described as an unnecessary war. Even the government papers were friendly in their references to Hart and sympathetic in reporting the deaths of his mother and aunt. To his deep, unspoken relief, there was no reference to Mercy's identity as the Rebel Pamphleteer. In their fury at having been duped by a woman, the British in Savannah had kept her secret well. But he could not forget it. What had Mercy gained for the American side by her activities as spy and pamphleteer that could possibly make up for this personal disaster?

He had spent the morning after he learned of his mother's and aunt's deaths in trying to write to Mercy and found it even more difficult than the long diary letter he had written her on board the *Sparrow*. Would she ever get that? Dick had laughed, promised to find a smuggler in Plymouth to start it on its hazardous way to America by way of France, and said, with a note of apology, that he would have to read it. It had not made its writing any easier.

This one, still more difficult, was to go under cover to the British commander in New York, and it, too, must be read by Dick and, no doubt, in New York too. "God knows whether it will ever get to your wife," Dick had said. "But put it in the post bag in the hall, and pray to God."

Trying to write words of comfort to Mercy, Hart found himself wondering again how she would feel when she heard the news. Since it was in *Rivington's Gazette*, it was bound to be picked up by the Boston papers. What would she do? Would she go down to Savannah, perhaps, and claim the house in Oglethorpe Square on his behalf? And what would she and Abigail have to say to each other if she did? And, perhaps worst of all, how could he bear the fact that his mother's death, so publicly reported, had gone far to solve his own financial problems?

Dick had been surprised to learn that Hart's mother had in fact owned the Savannah property but urged that they go to London as soon as Hart could bear to. "I think, properly handled, this news might earn you your freedom," he explained. "It's painful for you, I know, but you must take some thought for the future. There is your wife to be considered, Hart, and, who knows, there may be an heir in prospect."

"An heir? Oh." Hart controlled the mad impulse to say, "Impossible." The knowledge that there was no chance that Mercy could be carrying his child was most entirely his secret. And hers, he thought, and was appalled to find himself almost glad that she could not be bearing his child. No real record existed of that mad marriage of theirs on board Captain Bougainville's ship. The paper

Bill had risked his life to save was so spoiled by sea-water as to be worthless. And Bill, the only American wit-ness of the marriage, was dead. The Frenchmen must be scattered to the four winds by now. Suppose . . . just sup-pose that Mercy were to find someone else, some thriving Boston merchant, some teacher at Harvard College . . . And thinking this, he was appalled at an inward vision of Julia, dark eyes full of sympathetic tears. Julia, who some-how never mentioned Mercy . . .

He must not think like this. Horrified at himself, he surprised Dick by agreeing readily to his proposal that they leave for London at once.

"You can buy your mourning there," said Dick, "and the sooner you put in your claim for the Savannah prop-erty, the better."

"I doubt there is anything I can do about the property this side of the Atlantic," said Hart. "But I know Sir James Wright will stand my friend." He could only hope he was right. Once again he was confronted by the in-tractable problem of Mercy, spy and Rebel Pamphleteer. However carefully the British had kept her secret, there could be no question but that Sir James Wright knew how she had worked against the British. Would he let it influence him? He rather thought not, but there was no way he could be sure. Nor did he know how his aunt Mayfield's estate stood, and he was angry with himself for wondering if she had made a will after her son Francis's death.

"Your aunt." Dick must have been thinking on similar lines. "She died childless, did she not?"

"Yes. Her son was killed in the attack on Savannah." It was the generally accepted version of Francis's death, and he smiled grimly to himself as he remembered the facts, the silent, swaying struggle on the rotten wharf across the river from Savannah and Francis's horrible, well-earned death among the alligators.

"She was a woman of property too? It was her house in Charleston to which they were going, poor things?"

"Yes." Impossible to mind Dick's frank curiosity. "I very much hope she will have willed it to my Cousin Abigail after Francis's death." Poetic justice if she had. It was Francis who had contrived to "lose" Abigail's dowry and so make it impossible for her to marry her Loyalist lover, Giles Habersham.

"If she made a will," said Dick. "If not . . . ?"

"I suppose I would inherit," said Hart reluctantly. "But we're talking of shadows, Cousin. The British may well have taken Charleston by now, and I've no friends there."

"Then we must find you some in London," said Dick.

Julia greeted the news of their imminent departure with approval. "We shall miss you two sadly, Mamma and I," she told Hart, "but I am sure you are right to go. The sight of London will be a distraction for you, and besides, I long to see you a free man indeed. I only hope these anti-Catholic activities of Lord George Gordon's will not make things harder for you. I am afraid that he is known as a supporter of you Americans as well as a Catholic hater," and then, seeing him look puzzled: "How stupid I am! Of course, you know nothing about him. How should you? He's a mad Scots Protestant lord, Cousin, who is making a great fuss and botheration about an act for Catholic relief that Parliament passed two years ago. He even went and read the poor King a great lecture about it this winter, they say, and has not been let across the threshold of St. James's Palace since. But what's that to the purpose, when he has a seat in the House of Commons, and his crazy Protestant associations all over the country? They are collecting signatures for a monster petition to the House. Someone actually came here canvassing, but I sent him away with a flea in his ear."

"I should hope so," said Dick. "But, Julia, I hardly see why mad George Gordon's activities should affect Hart's affairs. When I was last home, they were saying at Brooks's that there were three parties: government, opposition, and Lord George Gordon, he had so little support in the House."

"In the House, yes, but the country is another matter. And the trouble is he claims that the Catholic Relief Act was mainly intended to make it easier to enlist Catholics for the war against America. He's a great friend to you Americans, Cousin Hart, but not the kind that will do you much good, I'm afraid."

"Dear Julia." Dick was looking at her with some surprise. "What a politician you have become, to be sure. I hardly recognise the giddy girl I left behind."

She laughed and picked up her tapestry frame. "You think I should mind my needle like a good girl and leave politics to you men. But you know, Dick, this fine useless work always bored me to distraction, and buried here in the country, one must read the newspapers or go melancholy mad." She put out a quick hand to touch Hart's sleeve. "Dear Hart, I am so sorry. For a moment I quite forgot. You are being so brave it is hard always to remember just what you must be suffering. You'll be glad to be safe away from a rattlepate like me."

"On the contrary," said Hart. "Your lively spirits do me more good than anything. I only wish you were coming to London, too." Now why in the world had he said that when his every instinct warned him to get away from this dangerously attractive cousin as fast as possible?

"Oh, so do I!" exclaimed Julia. "If only we could, Mamma and I, just to help keep your spirits up. Well"— she put down the tapestry frame with a look of dislike— "maybe we will surprise you yet. I know how sad Mamma has felt at being unable even to send in her name at the Queen's House on the occasion of the King's Birthday next month. Oh, Dick!" She stifled a gurgle of laughter. "If you could but see your own face! You are imagining Birthday dresses and all kinds of extravagant fripperies! As if I had not long outgrown such girlish nonsense. I would just like to show our poor cousin a little of London. To take him to see the exhibition of pictures, perhaps, in the new rooms at Somerset House, where he will find his compatriot Mr. West well represented, I am sure. There could be no harm in that, however deep our mourning. Our coming to London would be almost an economy, Dick, since it means the servants here can be put on board wages, and you know what it costs to keep up two households. And of course, there will be no gadding, no theatregoing, though we might perhaps take our cousin to a concert of Mr. Handel's sacred music. Say you would really like us to join you in town, Cousin Hart!"

"Indeed I would." What else could he say? Besides, he knew with shame how completely he meant it.

Dick, apologising for having no kind of sporting vehicle, no curricle or high-perch phaeton in which to drive to London, had suggested that they ride there instead, sending a servant ahead on the waggon with their baggage.

"My father keeps his carriage in town, of course," he explained, and Hart felt a sudden qualm of anxiety at the thought of meeting this unknown relative.

"I hope he won't mind my coming," he said.

"Mind? I just hope he won't try to make political capital of you. It's his life, you know, politics, and I'm afraid a disappointing one. He has never had the gift of holding the House with a speech, and somehow office has always eluded him. But of course, he will be delighted to see you. He wrote in the warmest terms about your saving the *Sparrow*."

"Good of him." Hart had noticed that Dick always spoke of his father with a touch of reserve and wondered a little just what Mr. Purchas, Senior, was like.

They set off betimes next morning, Hart almost dizzy with fatigue after yet another night divided between wakefulness and nightmare. Hard to decide which had been worse, the waking memory of his mother and aunt or the horribly vivid dreams about their deaths. And in some ways worse still, there had been other dreams, dreams with Mercy and Julia changing faces, changing bodies. He was ashamed to remember them.

"Ah, poor Cousin Hart." Julia had got up early to see them off. "You look as if you had not slept at all. Should you put off your journey till tomorrow, do you think?"

"No!" It came out more strongly than he intended and earned him a quick, enquiring glance from those perceptive dark eyes.

"You're right, of course." Her smile was understanding. "The change will help, I am sure. I like you for loving your mother so much, Cousin Hart." She was all in black this morning, and it made her look incredibly slender, as if the merest breath of wind would blow her away as she stood on the steps to watch them mount. "Take care of him, Dick. And give my loving respects to Father. I shall pray for you, Hart." She came down the steps to say it to him alone.

"Thank you." Miserably inadequate phrase for all that he was feeling.

# IX ❧—

Are you sure you are well enough to travel, Mrs. Purchis?" Charles Brisson looked anxiously at Mercy across the breakfast table of Mr. Williams's inn at Trenton.

"Of course I am." Mercy brought out the lie as robustly as she could and combined it with a quelling look for Ruth, who had shared her bed and must know how she had shivered and sweated all night long after the icy shock of her near drowning the day before. She drank tea with a hand that would shake. "The air will do me good," she said.

"I hope so." Brisson sounded so doubtful that she was afraid she must look as ill as she felt. "But you must let me drive all the way," he went on. "My shoulder is wonderfully better this morning, and your horses are so worn out they won't give me any trouble."

"Just so long as they get us there," said Mercy. "But it won't be a long day, will it?"

"No indeed." George Palmer helped himself to more ham. "A mere nothing compared with the distances you have covered, Mrs. Purchis. I am sure you are best making the effort and getting to Philadelphia today. You'll be much more comfortable in our house on Front Street than pigging it here in this damned expensive inn."

"Your house?" she asked, surprised.

"Why, yes. Did you not know that we are Philadelphians, my brother and I? Have been since the damned British took New York and threw us out of town with nothing but what we stood up in. It's of course that you and Miss Paston will stay with us until you find your own friends. I have sent Sam on already to give orders for our reception. One more cold day's journey, ma'am, and I think I can promise you all the comforts of home."

"Oh, thank you!" It seemed like an answer to prayer, and she forced down some thick bread and butter, despite the soreness of her throat and the throbbing of her head. She had been too tired and shaken to bargain with the landlord the night before, and the price he had quoted would nearly exhaust her funds. Now, miraculously, her little party would be lodged free in Philadelphia, at least for a while.

"And you too." George Palmer turned to Brisson. "With the Congress in session, Philadelphia will be as full of people as it can hold. You'll be a deal more comfortable with us. And it's time our lazy dogs of servants had something to do with themselves, after all these months on board wages while we've been at the North." He pulled out a huge gold turnip watch. "I suggest we start as soon as possible. I quite long to be home, and Mrs. Purchis will be better avoiding the chill of evening."

"Yes, thank you." It hurt horribly to speak. Mercy swallowed more tea. "We will be ready directly. Are you sure you are fit to drive, Mr. Brisson?"

"I'd rather drive than ride," he told her. "You are doing me a real kindness in letting me. And I know the boy will enjoy another day on my horse."

"Yes, sir." Jed was looking anxious, and Mercy wondered if the Palmers' invitation had been intended to include him. Time enough to worry about that when they reached Philadelphia. For the moment it took every ounce of her strength to help Ruth pack their portmanteau and settle the reckoning with the landlord. He overcharged her, and she knew it, but let it go. It hurt too much to speak.

The Palmers insisted on lending her their warmest fur rug, and Ruth tucked it anxiously round her, but the seat of the sledge felt ice-cold, and she was gradually becoming aware that her heavy coat, which the landlady had reluctantly agreed to dry for her by the kitchen fire, was still damp. Madness to have agreed to travel today, but it had been obvious that Brisson and the Palmers meant to go on whatever she decided. Even the invitation to stay might have depended on her party's accompanying them. And that was odd somehow.

But then everything was odd today. Her mind was playing the strangest tricks on her. For a moment she was sure that Ruth, sitting beside her on the cold seat of the sledge, was Abigail, that she was about to turn and reproach her for the deaths of Mrs. Purchis and Mrs. Mayfield. How long since she had heard of those horrible deaths? Two days? Two years? A lifetime?

"You made them go," said Abigail. "You sent them to their deaths."

"No!" she exclaimed. "No! It's not true!"

"What's the matter, Mercy dear?" Ruth—it was Ruth after all—reached out a cold, anxious hand to touch her face.

"Nothing. I was imagining things. Stupid." They had left the little town of Trenton, the sledge moving easily on the packed snow of a well-used road. And now, all about them, were the signs of the British attack on and final retreat from Philadelphia. Skeletons of burnt houses and barns loomed stark against the snow. Picket fences had great ragged gaps; trees flung broken branches at the sky, witnesses to savage gunfire.

And behind them lurked the ghosts. Mrs. Purchis and Mrs. Mayfield peered out here from over a blackened wall, there from a savaged tree, smiling horribly, beckoning. What were they saying? How could she bear it? How could she not? "Come and join us," they called. "It's cold, in the snow, where we lie. You killed us, come and join us in our cold grave."

"No!" Fighting her way back to sanity, she found she was clutching Ruth's hand. "No, of course, we should go on." By what miracle had she understood what Ruth had just said? "I'll be better when we get there." Better? Or dead? Quiet in the cold, like the two women she had killed. Face it. She almost certainly had. And Abigail? Abigail, who had been beside her just now. Was she dead, too, also a victim of her own activities as spy and Rebel Pamphleteer? How proud she had felt, back in Savannah, dressed out in satin and emeralds, smiling and smiling at bemused British officers, tricking them into telling her little, trivial-seeming, possibly vital bits of information. Had any of it really helped the American cause? Had any member of the harassed Georgian government in exile paused to read the reports she had penned so carefully, smuggled out so secretly? She doubted it now. There were two rival exiled governments, she knew, in the west of Georgia, feuding bitterly between themselves. How should they have time for the information she sent them at such risk?

Not her own risk. She had escaped. She had married and lived happily ever after. Happily! A dry, bitter little laugh shook her and drew an anxious glance from Ruth. Happily ever after. What would Hart think when he learned that she had killed his mother and aunt? He had never really liked her activities as a spy, even when he had finally come to believe in them. Better, in his eyes, just better to be a spy than the loose woman he had thought her at first? Maybe he had thought so then, but now, with the consequences written in blood on his family? What would Hart think now? What would he feel? Would he be glad that their marriage was still one in name only? And if he was, could she blame him?

Where was Hart now? If only she could see him, tell him, ask his forgiveness. Eagerly scanning the dog-eared newspapers usually available in the taverns where they spent the night, she had found no reference to the *Georgia* and made herself believe that no news was good news. But was it in this case? A prize would have been news and she was afraid that Hart badly needed a prize to settle the allegiance of his disaffected crew. But, she had told herself over and over again, the papers she had seen were inevitably old ones. In Philadelphia there would be up-to-date news. And what kind of welcome for Hart's wife, his mother's murderer?

"You're tired, ma'am." Charles Brisson turned to tuck the fur more closely round her. "And no wonder after yesterday's adventure. But keep your brave heart up; it's not long now. On a good day I believe we could see the steeple of Independence Hall by now."

"You've been to Philadelphia before?" Somehow she had thought this his first visit to America.

"Oh, yes. In happier times. It makes a man mad to see the damage done by the British." He pointed with his whip to the blackened shell of a farmhouse, bleak against the snow. "It's starting to snow again. I wish the Palmers had made an earlier start. At this rate it will be dark before we get to town, and cold with it, I am afraid. So much for that thaw that nearly cost you your life. I wish you were safe in your bed, with a hot brick at your feet."

"Not half so much as I do." A mistake to speak. Cold air and a whisper of snow blew into her mouth and hurt her throat. Her teeth would not close again; she felt them rattling together. She had never believed that one's teeth could really chatter. "I'm cold," she managed. "I don't think . . . I don't know . . ." The chattering was worse, uncontrollable now.

"Ruth." Brisson's voice came from far off. "Mrs. Purchis is ill. Pile more rugs on her, everything there is; it doesn't matter about us; we must keep her warm."

"Oh, poor Mercy. Should we not stop? There are lights in that house over there." As she spoke, Ruth folded her own rug over Mercy, who merely felt colder under its weight and was now shivering in great, involuntary spasms.

"No, no. Much best get her to town: the chance of a doctor, the Palmers' house. Hardly half an hour, I think, and then you will be warm, Mrs. Purchis." He had called Ruth by her first name. How very odd. How very cold. How many miles to Babylon? I am freezing to death, and this cold hell is the one I have earned by all my cleverness. "Did Mrs. Purchis and Mrs. Mayfield die cold, too?" She had not known she had spoken aloud until Brisson answered her.

"Don't think of that. Don't think of dying. Think of a fire, and food, and light. Keep up that brave heart of yours."

"Hart," she heard herself say. "He'll never forgive me. How could he? His mother, his aunt, all my fault. All . . . all my fault. Playing at heroines . . . It's dark," she said. "It's so dark."

"Give her this; make her drink it."

"I'll try." Ruth's anxious voice. Ruth's cold hands, fumbling with something; then the sting of fiery liquid in her cold mouth.

"Rum," she said. "Like Mrs. Paston. I shall die like her,

in the dark. Lay me beside her, Ruth, till the spring comes, and the worms. It's all I'm good for. Murderer . . . Are they lying in the cold still? Mrs. Purchis, Mrs. Mayfield . . . Waiting . . . waiting for me? I had no idea hell would be so cold. Oh!" Her mouth was filled with another dram of the fiery rum, and this time she felt its warmth all through her.

"I think she's asleep." Ruth's voice.

"Thank God for that. Hold her tight; keep her warm if you can. We're almost there."

Blur of lights; a new movement of the sledge; voices. Asleep? Awake? Did it matter? "Poor Mercy." Ruth's voice again. "Let me." Ruth's cold hands helping lift her. Ruth's voice so different. What was it?

"Love," Mercy said, and slept at last.

How long? Dream and nightmare; light and darkness; warmth. And always Ruth's loving hands. Ruth lifting her, helping her drink, feeding her mouthfuls of hot gruel, talking to her. "Don't die, Mercy, please don't die. You're all I've got. You and Jed. You're my family. Please, Mercy."

Too tired to speak. Family: Hart. Something warm was running down her cheeks. Tears? What a waste of time. With an immense effort she managed to turn away from the light, towards the wall, towards darkness, towards death.

Screams. Ruth? Daylight now, and Ruth screaming, somewhere quite close by. Screaming . . . screaming . . . screaming. "I can't bear it." Very slowly, with immense effort, she sat up in bed, pushed away the heavy feather quilt, and stood up, groggily, leaning against the bedhead, her heavy nightgown warm about her. A tiny room, a cupboard really, opening from another one. And from there, the screams, still horribly resounding. "Ruth!" But her voice did not obey her, came out merely as a croak. The screaming grew wilder, more desperate, intolerable. She swayed away from the bed and grabbed at the doorway.

A larger room. Sunlight in it. A bed. Ruth sitting on it, hunched together, drawing breath for yet another scream.

"Ruth!" This time it came out, the thread of a whisper. "Ruth, don't!"

"Mercy!" She was on her feet, taller, thinner, very white, holding out loving arms to catch Mercy as she swayed and fell.


"Found them in bed together, snug as you please." A strange voice, a woman's, self-excusing? "I only ran out round the corner for a moment, for a cup of flour. Left that dratted boy to take care of things. Where is he anyway? But they're none the worse, surely, Doctor?"

"Two patients instead of one?" A cool hand picked up Mercy's and felt her pulse. "This one's much better. I should have seen the girl was wearing herself out nursing her. So should you, come to that, Mrs. Peabody."

"Maybe I did. But no business of mine. Me with my gentlemen to look after, *and* that guest of theirs. No part of my job to be looking after a sick young lady. Or two of them!"

"A heroine of the Revolution, Mrs. Peabody."

"A fiddlestick, Dr. Marston. What kind of heroine gets her ma-in-law killed, that's what I want to know? Ask me, all that's happened serves her richly right, and so I shall tell her, soon as I get the chance."

Mercy opened heavy eyes. "What has happened to me?" she asked.

"You've been very ill, Mrs. Purchis," said the doctor. "For a while I was afraid we were going to lose you. I think you owe your life to this child here"—he was feeling Ruth's pulse—"who has worn herself out, I am afraid, looking after you." He sounded anxious now. "She's very fast asleep."

"She does that after one of her screaming fits."

"Screaming?"

"That's what roused me. She saw her twin sister killed by Indians. Sometimes she remembers . . . Oh, my God!" It brought it all back. "Mrs. Purchis. Mrs. Mayfield. Is there any news of my husband, Doctor? Letters from him?"

"I'm afraid not, ma'am. Now you are not to distress yourself; the worst possible thing for you. Naturally no news is good news, but the fact is there has been none of your husband and the *Georgia* since he landed you near Boston."

"He had stores for three months," she said. "If he had taken a prize, though, he would have brought her in—or sent her."

"She might have been retaken."

"Anything could have happened. His crew were disaffected."

"You knew?" He sounded surprised. "Yes, there have been rumours, down from Boston. Shameful the way they treated you there, you and Miss Paston."

"You've heard about that?"

"Everyone has. You must resign yourself to being the toast of the town, Mrs. Purchis. What with the boy Jed's stories of your courage up at Farnham and the way the Palmers and Mr. Brisson sing your praises for what you did to the Bartram brothers you are quite the lioness of the hour. Now you are better, I can see I must forbid visitors for a while, or you will be worn out all over again."

"But, Doctor . . ." She had to ask it. "Mrs. Purchis. Mrs. Mayfield. People must know about their deaths, too."

"A terrible thing," he said gravely. "But, my dear Mrs. Purchis, you must not be blaming yourself. I know how you feel; you have talked, a great deal, while you have been ill. No, no." He held up a friendly hand, seeing hot colour flood her pale face. "No need to fret. Secrets of the sick chamber. No one knows but that good child there and me. I don't think she understood half of what you were saying. And I have forgotten it. But so far as those two poor ladies are concerned, you must not let yourself feel that their terrible death was your fault. Oh, yes, things may have been said in the first shock of their deaths . . . best ignored, forgotten. There is a letter for you, from Miss Purchis. I hope it will do you more good than anything I can say to you. She has been most generous and most particular in what she has said in public."

"Oh, thank God! Abigail's alive!"

"Indeed she is, and blames that disastrous journey of her aunts' squarely on Mrs. Mayfield, who was afraid that her house in Charleston would be destroyed while the town was being fortified against the expected British attack."

"They knew about that? And still went?"

"Dear me, yes. Everyone knows. For a while, with the

weather so stormy, we all hoped Clinton's fleet had been dispersed. They certainly took long enough on their way south. But then, just when everyone's hopes were up, they turned up at Savannah itself to refit after their rough voyage. That was what sent those poor ladies hurrying north."

"Madness," said Mercy, "to go to a town that was expecting a siege."

"But nobody expects the British to succeed," said the doctor comfortably. "General Clinton has more enemies than friends; there are even rumours that he has resigned his command. And you know what happened last time the British attacked Charleston. Moultrie and his friends soon sent them to the right-about. And of course, poor Mrs. Mayfield had another reason to be anxious about her house."

"Oh?"

"I have no doubt that Miss Abigail Purchis will have mentioned it in her letter. It is common knowledge now that Mrs. Mayfield's son Francis was playing a double game, pretending to be an ardent Patriot, but in fact siding with the British. You must have known that."

"I certainly did." Mercy shivered, remembering how nearly Francis had been her death.

"Well, naturally, when the Patriots in Charleston heard about that, there was talk of confiscating the Mayfield house. Which, I understand, is most admirably situated, for either military or trade purposes. A most valuable property. Mrs. Mayfield hoped to save it by showing her Patriot sympathies in that dangerous journey north. She made various statements, before she left, about how she had supported you in your activities as the Rebel Pamphleteer."

"Good gracious!" said Mercy. "Just fancy that!" And then, "So you know about that too?"

"My dear Mrs. Purchis, here in Philadelphia we are at the centre of things, we know everything. And one thing I can tell you, you will have no trouble in establishing your and your husband's claim to the Charleston house."

"Our claim?"

"Mrs. Mayfield left no will. As her nephew your husband is her natural heir. And to his mother's property in

Savannah, of course, though for the moment Sir James Wright has granted that to Miss Abigail Purchis, as the only Loyalist in the family. I have no doubt she has written to you about that in her letter, which I will fetch and leave you in peace. You must rest, Mrs. Purchis. Your recovery is little short of a miracle; you have my orders not to leave your room until I give you permission."

"But the Mr. Palmers! How can I continue to impose on them so?"

"Nothing of the kind. They are proud to be caring for a heroine of the Revolution. And you are not to be worrying about being a charge on them either. It is unfortunate, of course, that there are no representatives from Georgia here in Philadelphia at present, but there is talk of Governor Howley's coming north, and I am sure he will do something for you when he gets here. And besides, your husband may sail up the Delaware any day, with prize money and to spare."

"If only there would be news of him," said Mercy.

"I'm sure there will be soon." He handed her the letter he had taken out of a bureau drawer. "I'll leave you to rest now if you are sure Miss Paston will be herself when she wakes."

"Oh, yes, I have seen her in these fits before."

"And seen her through them, I have no doubt. May I say what a remarkable young lady I think you, Mrs. Purchis?"

"Young?" she said. "I feel a thousand years old."

"Well, I have news for you." He picked up a hand glass and gave it to her. "You most certainly do not look it. I had been wondering how to break it to you about your hair!"

"My hair? Good God!" The face that looked back at her from the glass was a stranger's. No, stranger than that. It was the face she remembered from that first day at Winchelsea, when Hart had rescued her from the mob that killed her father. A thin, pale face, oddly young, with dark hair cut short around it, so different, so strangely different from the golden tan and henna-tinted hair that had ensnared young British officers in Savannah.

"We had to cut it," said the doctor. "I wouldn't be surprised if you set a new style. And a fine change it

would be from the monstrous high heads Philadelphia
ladies wear these days."

"Philadelphia," she said. "I'm in Philadelphia."

Abigail's letter was short, hurriedly written, and very
much to the point:

> *Dearest Mercy,*
> *I have just heard the things people are saying. You*
> *are not to believe any of them. My aunt Mayfield*
> *would go to Charleston. She had heard that the*
> *Patriots meant to confiscate her house. You know how*
> *she felt about that house. My poor aunt Purchis didn't*
> *want to go with her above half, but she had some mad*
> *hope that she would find Hart there, or that he would*
> *be able to find her. It had nothing whatever to do*
> *with you, Mercy dear, or with anything you had done,*
> *and you must let nothing make you think otherwise.*
> *I am writing Hart today, though God knows when*
> *he will get the letter, and am also telling him, as I*
> *do you, that I am merely holding the house in Ogle-*
> *thorpe Square for him, and for you, and for your*
> *children. Dear Mercy, I am so happy for you both.*

For your children. Warm, gentle, relieving tears poured
down her face. She should have known that Abigail would
stand her friend. Whatever happened, Abigail would hold
the house in Oglethorpe Square for Hart and for her. And
their children! Abigail believed them happily married.
Poor Abigail, whose own lover was somewhere in Europe,
serving in the British army. How much more hope for her
and Hart than for Abigail and Giles Habersham. What a
selfish wretch she had been, thinking only of her own
troubles.

Beside her, Ruth stirred, someone else who had more
troubles than hers. "Mercy!" She looked up and saw
Mercy bending over her. "You're better! You're really
better?"

"Really and truly." Mercy smiled down at her. "And
all thanks to you, the doctor says. You saved my life,
Ruth dear, with your love and your nursing."

"I'm glad." Ruth reached out a hand to take Mercy's
white one, and Mercy felt how chapped and sore it was.

"You've looked after me all by yourself?"

Ruth actually laughed. "I should rather think I had. Mrs. Peabody, the housekeeper, doesn't reckon much to us, I'm afraid. But I've been glad to help out in the kitchen, so long as it meant she didn't fuss about your being ill. And Jed's been worth his weight in gold in the yard, so she hasn't really been able to make much of it."

"But surely, the Palmers . . . Mr. Brisson . . ."

"Oh, Mr. Brisson went away quite soon, and as to the Palmers, I don't really think they notice what goes on in the house, so long as they get their meals on time. They're down at the countinghouse mostly. I wish we could get a house of our own, Mercy. I know it's ungrateful of me, but I don't somehow like those Palmers."

"Why, Ruth!" Mercy was amazed at the change in the girl. It was almost worth having been so ill herself if it had wrought this amazing improvement in Ruth's condition. But, she remembered, there had been that screaming fit that had shaken her out of her own lethargy. "Ruth." She wondered if she dared ask it. "Do you remember screaming just now?"

"Yes. I'm ashamed. It's the first time, Mercy, since you got ill."

"Do you know what started it?"

"Started?" Ruth looked at her surprised. They had never discussed her screaming fits before. "Why, yes. I was afraid I was going to lose you too, like my mother, like poor sister Naomi. Oh, Mercy, poor Naomi." Now she was crying, but crying easily, as Mercy herself had done earlier.

"We're going to be better now," said Mercy. "Both of us. And we're going to find somewhere else to live, where they don't treat you like a servant, Ruth dear."

"I don't mind," said Ruth. "Not if it's for you."

# X

Coming home for their five o'clock dinner, George and Henry Palmer found Mercy up and dressed to receive them. "Why, Mrs. Purchis, this is a famous surprise." George Palmer took her hand in his moist one. "But are you sure you should be up so soon?"

"So soon?" She looked from him to his brother, thinking how very little she knew about these chance-met journey companions. "I am only ashamed to have trespassed so on your hospitality. I hope it will not be long before I am able to take myself and my two young friends off your hands." She had given up the pretence that the three of them were brother and sisters.

"Off our hands!" exclaimed Henry Palmer, who, like his brother, was very plainly dressed in black broadcloth, with the whitest possible linen. "But thee must not be thinking of such a thing, Mrs. Purchis."

"You're Quakers!" she exclaimed. "I had no idea." But of course, Philadelphia was a Quaker city.

"Not very good ones, I am afraid." George Palmer had a fulminating glance for his younger brother. "You will have noticed that I have found it best, for many reasons, to abandon the sect's mannerisms of speech. I only wish I could persuade my brother to do likewise. As you surely know, Mrs. Purchis, such a politician as you are, the Quakers here in Philadelphia are deeply tainted with

Loyalism. Absurd of them. I cannot imagine why having come here for religious reasons, they think they will be safe or happy under the bigoted government of George the Third and his Parliament. That is why I, personally, have ceased all connection with the sect. But my brother is an obstinate man, Mrs. Purchis, and one must respect him for sticking to his religious principles."

"Indeed one must." Mercy looked from one jowled, prosperous face to the other. They did not look as if they had let their principles stand very seriously in the way of their business. Would Mr. Golding look something like this, she wondered, if she ever met him? Another prosperous businessman making a profit out of this war, regardless of principle. "I owe you more than I can ever repay," she said. And then, watching their faces with amusement, "In kindness, I mean. Of course, what my young friends and I owe you for board and lodging will be repaid just as soon as I can arrange funds from my family. I have had the kindest possible letter from my cousin Miss Abigail Purchis, in Savannah, who is holding the family house there for my husband and myself. It is, therefore, but a matter of time before I can repay you, but for the present I must really arrange to cease burdening your household with our party."

"But, Mrs. Purchis, thee cannot be serious," said Henry Palmer.

"You must let us persuade you to think again of this," interrupted his brother. "We have looked forward so much to the pleasure of introducing you to Philadelphia society. And indeed, Mrs. Purchis, I fear I should warn you not to entertain too high hopes of help from Georgia. You must know, I am sure, as well as I do, how sadly divided their councils are down there. I am afraid we have to face it that the Continental Congress is hesitant about throwing good money after bad in that direction. Lachlan McIntosh is a friend of your husband's—is he not?—and you must have followed this whole deplorable business of the forged letter about him. What with that and the savage duel in which James Jackson killed George Wells out in the wild west of Georgia somewhere, the Continental Congress thinks it better to send any funds it can spare to General Lincoln, who commands the Continental forces in the South, and to Joseph Clay, the Paymaster General. I

doubt even Governor Howley—if he still is governor—
will be in a position to do much for you."

"Whereas we," said his brother, "are willing, are eager
to present thee to society as our friend and honoured guest.
There is to be a ball at the French Minister's next week—
the Chevalier de la Luzerne. All of Philadelphia will be
there. Naturally you were invited, as our guest, but we
were not able to hold out much hope of your being able to
attend. But now, perhaps?" He saw her hesitate. "Your
friend Mr. Brisson will be there, I know. He intends to
return in time for the party. It will be quite an occasion,
Mrs. Purchis, and one at which I think you would be
wise to be present. General Washington has accepted, I
believe, and so have General Arnold and his wife."

"Benedict Arnold? But I thought there was some trouble
about corruption during the time he was military commander here after the British evacuation."

"What a well-informed young lady you are to be sure,"
said George Palmer. "But that's all over and done with.
He was tried this January on a set of trumped-up charges
and dismissed without a stain on his character. This
party will put the final touch on his position. You should
most certainly come, Mrs. Purchis."

"But—my mother-in-law—my husband's aunt—I'm in
the deepest mourning."

"My dear Mrs. Purchis, if everyone who was in mourning stayed home these days, there would be no parties.
Wear your blacks, of course, but come."

"I would certainly like to meet General Washington,"
she said. And then, remembering. "This invitation, I hope
it extends to Miss Paston, too? After all, her brother was
a hero of the Revolution if ever there was one."

"Ah, Miss Paston." George Palmer looked unhappy.
"Mrs. Peabody tells me she had a screaming fit yesterday.
Not perhaps the ideal guest for a social event?"

"Mr. Palmer, have you looked at Miss Paston's hands
lately?"

"Her hands?"

"Yes. She has been working in your kitchen like a
drudge and nursing me, which it seems was beneath your
Mrs. Peabody's dignity. No wonder if she grew hysterical,
with so much responsibility on her shoulders. Dr. Marston
says I owe her my life, and I believe him. It is good of

you to ask me to stay on with you, to wish me to accompany you to this party of the French Minister's. If I do either, it is on the understanding that Ruth Paston is treated as I am."

"And the boy, Jed?" George Palmer sounded different, suddenly, formidable. "I suppose I am to invite him into the parlour?"

"No, no." Mercy gave him a very straight look. "You know as well as I do that he would be miserable. But I see no reason why you should not pay him for all the work he seems to be doing about the place."

"But of course." His tone was ingratiating again. "Stupid of me to have let it slip my mind. I will make arrangements at once, and you and Miss Paston will come to the French Minister's ball?"

"Yes," said Mercy, aware of a tacit bargain struck. "Yes, I think we will. And now, if you will excuse me, I must write to my husband."

"You have had news then?"

"Alas, no. But he promised to look for me in Farnham when he could. There must be a letter waiting for him there."

"Write by all means, Mrs. Purchis." His tone was sceptical. "We can most certainly send the letter to Farnham for you."

The French Legation occupied what had been the John Dickinson House on Chestnut Street between Sixth and Seventh streets. A handsome house, it was set by itself in grounds that had been used as a graveyard when it was a military hospital before the British capture of Philadelphia. But under the new Minister, Luzerne, the house had been entirely renovated and the gardens restocked. "You should see it in the spring," said George Palmer, helping Mercy out of his sledge onto steps swept clean of snow. "The gardens are a perfect feast of blossom in May."

"Concealing graves?" Mercy could not help a shudder.

"Mrs. Purchis!" Angrily. "This is a party, given by our gallant allies, in the first foreign legation to be opened in our country. It is no time to be refining on such thoughts."

"You're right. I'm sorry." She was glad to leave him and take off her warm coat in the well-heated boudoir set aside for lady guests. Surveying her neat black self in the glass, she could not help a wry comparison with the groups of exquisitely clad Philadelphia belles around her. One particularly caught her eye, a conscious beauty in a pink dress over a gauze petticoat and with five white plumes nodding over her high-piled hair. As Palmer had said, all the ladies' heads were dressed immensely high, so that she felt a positive freak with her own short-cropped, closely curling hair.

Best get it over with. Following the beauty out into the main hall where the Palmer brothers were awaiting her, she heard them greet her effusively as Mrs. Arnold. "But I do not see your husband, ma'am," said George Palmer.

"No. Too tedious." She shrugged bare, beautiful shoulders. "Some legal business or other, but he hopes to look in for a moment later on."

"No fear that you will lack for cavaliers in the meanwhile," said George Palmer, heavily gallant, then paused, seeing Mercy where she stood behind Mrs. Arnold. "Ah, my dear Mrs. Purchis, you must let me make you known to Mrs. Benedict Arnold."

"Delighted, I am sure." Mrs. Arnold swept a deep, faintly mocking curtsy, and Mercy remembered that she had been known for her Tory sympathies before her surprise marriage to the famous American general so much older than herself. Returning the curtsy with a rustle of black bombasine, she thought that there might well be truth in the rumour that Mrs. Arnold's extravagance had had something to do with the accusations that her husband had taken advantage of his position as military governor of Philadelphia to feather his own nest. Or pay for his wife's imported French hats?

"The heroine of the hour," said Mrs. Arnold. "But I must condole with you on the deaths of your mother-in-law and her sister, Mrs. Purchis. I trust you have comfortable news of your husband, ma'am."

"None, I am sorry to say." Mercy was glad now that she had reluctantly agreed to Ruth's plea to stay at home. This party was no place for her. She turned at a touch on her arm and was delighted to see Charles Brisson.

"Mrs. Purchis." He took her hand and kissed it. "I cannot tell you how happy it makes me to see you here." He sketched a bow for Mrs. Arnold and the Palmers, tucked her hand firmly under his arm, and had her half across the crowded room before she had time to return his greeting. "That bitch," he said, smiling down at her with eyes that seemed to understand everything she felt. "I am surprised the Palmers let you be exposed to her."

"They could hardly help it, but I do thank you for my rescue, monsieur."

"Charles." Pronounced English fashion, it was accompanied by a warning pressure on her arm. "I wish you would call me Charles," he went on, on a lighter note. "After all, we are old friends, old allies. I must be allowed to claim my position with regard to the belle of the evening."

"The belle!" She flashed him a mocking glance. "Thank you for nothing, Mr. Brisson. I have eyes; I know what I look like. I know how I stand out in this bevy of graces, like a crow among—"

"Pigeons." He finished it for her as she looked for the right word for the diaphanous beauties around them. "Pouter pigeons, Mrs. Purchis—if I must call you Mrs. Purchis. Dressed to kill—or be killed. But I think you do not quite understand your position here tonight. Let me make you known to your host, and then, perhaps, you will see." He led her through a wide archway into a brilliantly lighted saloon where music was playing quietly and a crowd had gathered around the evening's host, the Chevalier de la Luzerne.

"Monsieur Otto." Brisson addressed a handsome, willowy young man with a faintly melancholy, almost poetic cast of feature, who was talking with animation to a very young, very beautiful lady in white. "May I have the pleasure of making you known to Mrs. Purchis?"

"Our heroine!" Otto took Mercy's hand and kissed it. "May I present my good friend Miss Nancy Shippen before I do my duty and take you to our Minister, who I know quite longs to meet you." His English was as fluent as Brisson's but more heavily accented.

"Mrs. Purchis!" Miss Shippen surprised Mercy by impulsively reaching up to kiss her. "Let me be the first to welcome you to Philadelphia and say how truly my parents and I hope to be your friends while you are here. We live just across the way, you know, in Locust Street. We shall hope to see you there often." She looked unhappy for a moment. "I am afraid my mamma will not permit me to call in Front Street, but do, pray, come to us. We are always at home to our friends. But I am running on, and I know Monsieur Otto wishes to present you to the Minister."

Borne away on Otto's arm, Mercy was surprised to find a way opening for them through the crowd around the Minister. He turned, saw her, and came forward, hands outstretched. "Mrs. Purchis! Welcome to this little piece of France. My country and I are eternally indebted both to you and to your brave husband for all the help he gave to the Comte d'Estaing in that unlucky business down at Savannah. You have news of him, I hope?"

"Not yet, I am sorry to say." For a moment, she was afraid the unexpected, kind reference to Hart would reduce her to tears, but she mastered them as Otto presented Brisson in his turn to the Minister, who seemed not to know him. His mission must be a secret one indeed, she thought, almost mechanically receiving the Minister's condolences on the deaths of Mrs. Purchis and Mrs. Mayfield.

"You do not dance, of course," Luzerne went on, "but as our guest of honour, you must allow me to present you to our other most honoured guest General Washington."

Guest of honour. She went through the introduction to the tall, gangling general, who held the fortunes of the rebellious colonies in his strong brown hands, almost in a daze. It was a far cry indeed from the desperate, ice-cold days of the journey south. And now Otto had taken her a little aside and was saying something, very quietly, very courteously, about her finances, about a pension from the French. "We would wish you to be independent here in Philadelphia," he said. "The Minister asked me to tell you that he would be happy to help you set up your own establishment. It is not fitting that you should be living with those Palmers."

"Oh?"

"We thought you did not know. They are gravely suspect of traffic with the British. If it had not been for your presence in their house, they would not have been invited tonight."

"I see." Indeed, it explained a great deal. "Frankly," she went on, "I would be delighted to leave their house, but, Monsieur Otto, I am penniless and deeply in their debt."

"That is just what the Minister thought. There is a little house, madame, further down Chestnut Street, that belongs to the legation. He asked me to tell you that he would take it as a personal favour if you would move there. No question of rent, of course. With your living free and the small pension he wishes to give you, you should be able to manage until you hear from your husband and your friends in Georgia."

"It's too kind!"

"On the contrary, madame, the Minister asked me to tell you that it is mere policy. An acute observer like you will find Philadelphia full of dangerous crosscurrents. We cannot afford to have so good a friend living in the house of known enemies."

"Known?"

"Nothing provable, but yes, known. For your ears only." He smiled at her, and she thought what an attractive young man he was, and was angry with herself for thinking it. "We, who know and admire your activities in Savannah feel quite safe in trusting you with a small secret like this one."

"Oh, thank you for saying that. I was beginning to feel that it had all been for nothing. That I had killed those two poor ladies, which, in effect, I did, for nothing."

"Never think that. It is people like you and your husband, with the courage of their convictions, who helped convince my government that yours was a cause worth aiding. I beg you, do not undervalue yourself, madame, or what you have done for the cause of liberty. And—may I tell the Minister that you will accept the house? And the pension?"

"Oh, *yes*. With my deepest thanks."

"He will be delighted. And so am I." He turned as Charles Brisson rejoined them with Miss Shippen on his arm.

"It is time to be taking the ladies to supper," said Brisson. "And I am sure you will agree that fair exchange is no robbery, monsieur." He made the pronunciation curiously English, and Mercy thought once again that his disguise must go deep indeed.

Extraordinary to be eating a delicious European-style

meal, washed down with real champagne. "I feel as if
I was in a dream," Mercy told Charles Brisson, who had
found them a quiet corner away from the brilliance of the
chandeliers.

"A happy one, I hope."

"Well." She thought about it. "Less unhappy, at least."
It was both odd and comforting to feel she could talk to
him as to an old friend. "But what a strange occasion this
is." She looked around the crowded room. "There must
be three or four men to every woman."

"This is Philadelphia, ma'am. Do your Georgian representatives bring their wives on the dangerous journey to
attend the Continental Congress?"

"No, of course not. Stupid of me. So these are the men
who hold our fate in their hands." She looked about her,
a little doubtfully.

"Well, yes. Some worthy of the trust. Some perhaps
less so. As no doubt you know, there are no delegates
at the moment from Georgia, owing to the desperate state
of affairs down there, so I am afraid you will have no
friends here. But there is someone who might interest you:
Mr. Lovell from Massachusetts. A most faithful member.
He has not been home to his wife since he took his seat
here in '77. Now *he* might be of assistance to you, granted
your New England connection. He's a powerful man, and
close friend to John Adams, who is in Europe on congres-
sional business. Would you wish me to introduce him to
you?"

"Not tonight, I think." For some reason she did not
like the look of the black-clad New Englander. "Besides,
I really believe some of my troubles are over. The French
Minister is most kindly giving me a little house and a
pension. He does not seem to like my living with the
Palmers."

"Oh?"

"Well, no more do I." She remembered Otto's charge
of secrecy and was ashamed of herself. "Do you know
they have been letting poor Ruth work as a perfect drudge
in their kitchen, and Jed, for nothing, in their yard. I
shall be glad to leave them."

"I'm delighted to hear that you can. I was shocked
to see them making you known to that Tory bitch Peggy
Arnold. And I am afraid she put her claws into you too.

You would never think she and Miss Nancy Shippen were cousins."

"Are they indeed?"

"Yes, but of very different political complexions. Dr. Shippen, Miss Nancy's father, is chief physician to the Continental Army, a notable man, though like so many others, he is under fire in the Congress. I sometimes think you Americans do not have the gift of trusting each other in high office. There seem to be constant accusations flying to and fro, as with that nonsensical one against General Arnold, who is one of the Revolution's heroes, even if he did fall in love with a Tory beauty and marry her out of hand. Now Nancy Shippen is something quite else again. I think it will be a case between her and young Otto of the legation here. Indeed, if I had not thought that, I should have been quite jealous of the time Otto spent with you tonight."

"Jealous?" she said. "What an absurd thing to say." But it was difficult not to find it a little heartwarming. How long was it since she had enjoyed this kind of masculine admiration? And on the thought: Oh, Hart, she said to herself. Dear Hart, where are you now?

Brisson must have seen the shadow cross her face. "Come"—he took her hand—"let me have the pleasure of introducing you to the cream of Philadelphia society."

"Enjoy it?" she said later to Ruth, who had stayed up for her. "Yes, I suppose so. I don't know which is more awkward, to be treated as a heroine, as I was by the men, or as a freak, as by the women. If it had not been for Mr. Brisson and Miss Shippen, I fear I would have had a sad enough time of it. Oh, Ruth, I wish I would hear from Hart."

"So do I." Ruth looked as if she would have liked to say more, but did not.

It was a pleasure, next morning, to announce to the Palmer brothers that she would be moving in a day or so to the house on Chestnut Street. "And as soon as funds come through from Georgia, I will pay you what I owe you for our lodging," she concluded. "Perhaps you will let me have the figure?"

The house on Chestnut Street was a delight. It must have been built by the Dickinsons, she thought, for a widowed

mother or maiden aunt, and had just accommodation
enough for her little party and the young maidservant the
French Minister insisted on providing. Brick-built like
most Philadelphia houses, it reminded her of the English
cottage she had lived in as a child, and if the move there
did not bring a child's instant happiness, it brought at least
the next best thing, content. The French pension would
pay their quiet way. Presently she would hear from Hart,
receive funds from Abigail to pay the debt to the Palmers
that weighed heavily on her . . . And in the meanwhile,
"It's like playing house," she told Ruth, who had bloomed
into almost a glow of girlhood since their move.

"A very busy house," said Ruth.

It was true. Whereas the only callers at the Palmer house
had been serious businessmen, Mercy and Ruth now found
themselves entertaining Philadelphia Society. Nancy Shippen was their first caller and was followed by all the
other Philadelphia ladies of quality, by rich Mrs. Morris,
handsome Mrs. Bingham, and a crowd of younger ladies
all longing to be friends. Best of all, Mercy and Ruth
had received cards notifying them that their names had
been added to the list of the elite Philadelphia Assembly,
and Nancy Shippen, already their good friend, had explained just what an honour this was. "You must certainly
come to the next ball," she told them, "even if you do
not choose to dance. It will settle the question of your
place here in Philadelphia. There was a little talk, you
know, about your staying with those Palmers."

"I think they saved my life." Now that she was safe
away from their house, Mercy felt rather guilty about the
Palmers. Besides, though she found Nancy Shippen charming, she could not get used to the frivolous tone of Philadelphia society—at least the female side of it. Listening as
their morning callers discussed the latest Paris fashions,
the cut of a sleeve or the set of a cap, as if their lives
depended on getting them right, it was strange to remember the savage war still being fought in Georgia, the
British siege lines creeping closer and closer to beleaguered
Charleston.

"They make me feel a million years old," she confided
to Ruth after a particularly long morning of calls.

"You don't look it, Mercy dear." Ruth smoothed a fold
of her white muslin dress. "I'm glad you agreed with Miss

Shippen that we should wear white. It makes one feel alive again somehow."

"Dear Ruth!" Mercy stretched out an impulsive hand to press hers. "I don't know how I would have managed without you. Yes, I think Miss Shippen was right about our blacks. There's not much she doesn't know about the way to go on in Philadelphia." She looked thoughtfully down at her own white dress, remembering how she had longed, back in '74, to wear black for her father and how Hart had insisted that she must bow to the government decree that mourning was unpatriotic. He had given her the ebony mourning locket with a piece of her father's hair that she was wearing now, the one piece of jewelry she had not lost in that desperate flight from Savannah, since she never took it off. But now it held Hart's hair.

"If only we'd hear from him," she said.

"Hart?" Ruth understood her at once. "I know. It is strange. What can have happened to him, Mercy?" It was spring now, with the wide Philadelphia streets all awash with melting snow, and still there had been no word from Hart or about the *Georgia*.

The news came at last in a letter from Abigail that had taken an inordinate time on its smuggled way from British-held Savannah north through the chaos of Georgia and South Carolina. The dirty, dog-eared missive enclosed one from Hart to his mother, which, in its turn, had been enclosed to Sir James Wright.

"I am so sorry," wrote Abigail. "I expect you have heard from Hart himself but thought you should have this at once. Dear Mercy, what can I say?"

Hart's letter to his mother, brief, scrawled, almost illegible by now, told of his capture by the British ship *Sparrow*, of the good fortune that her captain was his cousin, and then the black news: He was on his way to England.

"He wrote his mother." Mercy handed the letter to Ruth. "And did not trouble to write to me."

"But, Mercy," Ruth protested, "he would have written to Farnham."

"And the letter would be here by now," said Mercy bleakly. "Since I paid that man Golding for his horses, he would have no reason for not sending it on to me, and you know that in the main the posts between here and Boston are reliable."

"It might have been seized by the British." Ruth was grasping at straws.

"Or it might not have been written," said Mercy. "He doubtless began with his mother and then had no time for me." She looked again at the date on Hart's letter. "So long ago," she said. "I am surprised we have not had news from New York, by way of *Rivington's Gazette.*" She paused at the sound of a knock on the door. "It's not the hour for callers." She listened as their young maid went running to the front door. "Who can it be?"

"It's Mr. Brisson, ma'am." The girl, Betsy, dropped a quick curtsy. "He makes his apologies and says it's urgent."

"Show him in, Betsy." Brisson had been away for a few weeks, and Mercy had been surprised to find how much she missed his friendly, reliable support among the pitfalls of Philadelphia society.

"Mrs. Purchis, Miss Paston." Charles Brisson was splashed with mud as if he had just arrived in town. "Forgive me for coming to you like this, but I thought I must tell you at once, break it to you—" He stopped, looked at Mercy. "But I see you know. You have heard already?"

"About my husband? That he is a prisoner. Yes, I have just heard this moment."

"From him? Oh, I am *glad.*" And then, on a different note: "That you have heard from him, I mean. The news itself is terrible; I had hoped to break it to you more gently. That he should be carried to England! Please God they are not too hard on him there. But what does he say, ma'am, if I may ask?"

"Not much," said Mercy. "He wrote his mother. My cousin Miss Purchis has sent it on to me. But how did you hear of it, Mr. Brisson?"

"I've been at the North," he explained. "I picked up a copy of *Rivington's Gazette* in a tavern on the way back. Of course, you can trust the New York Tories to make the most of such a piece of news. They know all about your husband's activities during the attack on Savannah, I'm sorry to have to tell you, ma'am. But nothing, thank God, of yours." He reached into the pocket of his greatcoat and handed her a dog-eared newspaper. "I paid the landlord of the inn a small fortune for this. I thought you would wish to see it yourself."

"Oh, thank you!" She took the paper and moved over to the window to read the smeared print of the broadsheet, half-hearing Charles Brisson engage in his usual friendly, almost brotherly chat with Ruth. The report was short and to the point. The British frigate *Sparrow,* Captain Richard Purchas, had outfought and sunk the privateer *Georgia* and had made a prisoner of her notorious captain, Hart Purchis, known for his activities during the attack on Savannah. Since the *Sparrow* was on her way to England with despatches, the pirate Purchis would no doubt meet the fate he deserved when he got there.

"You must not take it too hard." Brisson joined her at the window. "They are not barbarians, the British. He doubtless had his letters of marque. He will be treated as a prisoner merely. I am sure of it."

"Thank you." She looked up at him, tears in her eyes. "If only I had heard from him."

"It is strange. But as Miss Paston says, he would most certainly have written to you at Farnham."

"And I have not had the letter after all this time? How long did it take you to come down from Boston, Mr. Brisson?"

"Much longer than it took you from Farnham. Now the thaw has begun, the roads are terrible. You must be patient, ma'am, and hope the best."

It was not easy. Her gnawing anxiety was exacerbated by a stream of callers whose sympathetic amazement that she had not heard from Hart was merely a last straw. A week passed, another, and still no word came from Farnham. Instead, there was a further report in *Rivington's Gazette*—an issue brought her this time by George Palmer. There were rumours, according to the *Gazette,* that the capture of Captain Purchis's *Georgia* had been made easier by disaffection among her crew.

"All my fault!" she told Ruth. "They thought me a Jonah. No wonder he did not write to me."

"I am sure he did," said Ruth.

"You're a good friend, Ruth dear. To both of us."

# XI

It was already evening when Hart and Dick rode into London across Westminster Bridge. The big lighted building ahead was Parliament itself, Dick told Hart. Lights moving on the wide river below them were on boats, probably taking parties to the pleasure gardens at Vauxhall and Ranelagh. "I'm sorry you won't get your first view of the city by daylight."

"No matter." Hart tried to sound as if he cared. But how should he when his thoughts were so horribly divided between his dead mother and his living cousin? It had been more than high time to get away from Denton Hall. When he said good-bye to Julia, he had suddenly found himself wondering whether she was not aware of his growing, uncontrollable feeling for her. Vain fool that he was, as she smiled up at him, he had almost found himself imagining that she shared it.

"Not long now." Aware of his companion's dark mood, Dick kept his voice determinedly cheerful. "And a hot supper waiting. Lucky for us Parliament hasn't risen yet, or we'd be thronged with carriages this side the bridge. My father will be still in the House, of course." Was there a hint of relief in his voice? "Here we are," he said at last. "St. James's Square, and this is Charles Street, and the house illuminated for us, so they have had my message. You'll be glad to get to your bed, Cousin."

"Forgive me," said Hart as they dismounted. "I've been wretched company."

"And I like you the better for it. One must mourn. . . . Ah—" The door of the high, narrow house had swung open. "Here's Jones to make us welcome. You got my message, I see." He turned to address the tall man in livery who trod down the steps towards them.

"Yes, sir, and thanked God for it, Mr. Richard. Your father's at home, sir, and Mr. George."

"George!" Dick handed his reins to a boy and hurried up the steps, beckoning Hart to follow him.

A lighted hall; more servants in livery; the sound of furious voices. No wonder the footmen looked scared, Hart thought, as Dick strode across the hall and threw open a door.

"Not another penny, sir!" The speaker swung round as the door opened behind him, and Hart saw a red face clotted with anger under the bag-wig. "Dick," Mr. Purchas greeted his younger son. "You're just in time to stop me giving your brother the horsewhipping he deserves. Gad, sir." He swung back to face the tall young man who leant negligently against the chimneypiece. "If I could only break the entail, I'd cut you off this minute in Dick's favour."

"Yes, but you can't, can you?" George Purchas wore his own hair in elegant confusion round a handsome face very like Julia's, but marred by obvious marks of dissipation. "I know you'd like to cut me out in favour of good little Dick here, but as you can't, had we not best put our heads together and think how best we can pay these honourable debts of mine? It won't help Dick's promotion in the navy, nor yet Julia's slender chances of marriage, if I'm known to be languishing in the King's Bench Prison. You should have seen me sooner, Father dear, not let me get to this extremity."

"I'll see you in hell before I pay your debts again," said his father. "Haven't you done enough harm already? Julia's dowry—" He stopped short, seeing Hart for the first time. "We're forgetting ourselves. Dick, present your American cousin. As for you, sir." He rounded once more on his elder son. "Think yourself lucky that I let you spend the night here. We will talk more in the morning."

"And to more effect, I devoutly hope. Cousin Hart"—

he moved languidly forward, smiling a smile of immense charm and holding out a hand—"welcome to England. You see, we treat you quite as family."

"Family be damned," said his father. "Get to your room, sir, and don't try your wheedling on your cousin. Now go!"

For a moment, looking from one to the other, Hart thought George Purchas was going to defy his father. Then, smiling lazily, he made them all a sardonic, graceful bow. "Your most obedient." The mocking tone belied the words, and he swept them with one last impartial, challenging glance before he turned and left the room.

"God give me patience!" Mr. Purchas pushed both knuckles against his forehead as if to keep it from bursting open. Then he took a deep breath and turned to Hart. "Welcome to London, Cousin, and my deepest condolences. You must let us be your family now."

"Why, thank you, sir." Hart was touched that the older man had remembered his loss through all his own rage. "You're all so kind. Mrs. Purchas, Miss Julia . . ."

"My Julia." The frowning face relaxed. "She's worth ten of her brothers. More sense in her little finger . . ." He turned to Dick. "I've sent for Busby to come first thing in the morning. This is a bad business of George's, and of course, he's right, damn him. Dearly though I'd like to, we can't let him rot in the King's Bench Prison."

"Is it really as bad as that?" asked Dick.

"As bad as possible. He lost ten thousand to that adventurer O'Brien at the Cocoa Tree the other night. And God knows what else he owes besides. . . ." He turned with an attempt at a smile to Hart. "You see we are treating you quite as one of ourselves. And that reminds me—your sad loss—you'll need, I have no doubt, to be thinking, however reluctantly, about your own position. I cannot recommend our Mr. Busby too highly if you should need professional advice. I can tell you, he knows more about our family than I ever shall. I spoke of you to him—I trust you will not mind it—and he actually brought out a map of your estates at Winchelsea in the Savannah."

"It's more than I have ever seen," said Hart. "But of course, those estates are in British hands now."

"A terrible war," said Mr. Purchas. "Cousin against

cousin, brother against brother. We Whigs have been against it from the start. Let us drink to a speedy end to it."

"With all my heart," said Hart.

He slept late next morning and was waked by Dick's man, Price, with an armful of Dick's clothes. "Mr. Dick sent you these, sir. London togs, to keep you going until you're fitted out with your own mourning. And he says to tell you that Mr. Busby is here and should be ready for you when you've had your breakfast. Mr. Purchas and Mr. Dick have been with Busby since nine o'clock," he confided.

"And Mr. George?"

"Left in the night, sir. Said the bed was too hard. 'If you should need me,' he says to the footman, cool as a cucumber, 'my club will find me.' "

"His club?"

"The Cocoa Tree, sir."

Mr. Busby was a neat little man in shiny black and a tie-wig. He looked exhausted from his long session with Mr. Purchas and Dick but greeted Hart with enthusiasm. "The American heir," he said. "It's a pleasure to meet you, Mr. Purchis, and I trust you will let me serve you in every way I can. It's a question, I understand from Mr. Dick of . . . er . . . funds?"

"Precisely so," said Hart. "You call me the American heir, Mr. Busby, but I must tell you that the greater part of the American estate—the plantation and house at Winchelsea—has been sequestered by you British. And for all I know, the house in Savannah as well."

"Unfortunate." Mr. Busby put his hands together and looked severely at the fingertips. "Most unfortunate. But there is, I understand, also a question of a house in Charleston?"

"Which may also be in British hands by now," said Hart.

"So an accommodation with the authorities is of the first importance." Mr. Busby summed it up. "Mr. Dick seems hopeful of the result, and you will be well advised, I think, to leave the matter in his hands. The family is not without influence, as I am sure you must be aware. In the meantime, I think I can assure you that there will be no problem about funds. With your expectations, Mr. Purchis, we will be able to stretch things just a little. You will draw on me, of course, while I investigate the various channels open to us."

"But are there any channels? Surely, with a war on . . ."

Busby quelled the protest with a wave of one thin hand. "War or no war, Mr. Purchis, trade must go on. Leave matters of business to me, I beg. Oh, one other thing. I understand from Mr. Dick that you are on the best of terms with your cousin Abigail Purchis, the only other possible heir to the Charleston house."

"Yes, of course. I hope she *is* the heir. I certainly think it most likely that she has been granted the Savannah house and maybe even Winchelsea too."

"Yes, a confirmed Loyalist, I understand. There has never, I suppose, been any question of . . . er . . . of a romance between you and Miss Purchis?"

"Romance? Good God, no. First cousins and brought up together! Besides, as you well know, Mr. Busby, I am a married man." As before, down in Sussex, he had been puzzled by Busby's failure to mention Mercy.

"Well, yes and, if I may say so, no, Mr. Purchis. A marriage made in haste, on a French ship, the witnesses scattered to the winds, very likely dead by this time . . . And the documents, I understand, very much the worse for seawater."

"I'm married just the same," said Hart.

"Yes, yes, of course you are. In the eyes of God, Mr. Purchis, in the eyes of God. Well"—he reached out to neaten the piles of papers on the desk before him—"I believe I need not take up any more of your valuable time, Mr. Purchis. You will draw on me at Drummond's to any extent you please. You will be wishing to buy yourself mourning, of course, and Mr. Dick will tell you that you should make at least some appearance in society. You will find sympathisers in plenty, with your romantic story, and I am sure I do not need to warn you to have a care what you say. The English branch of the family has troubles enough without your adding to them by any rash republican statements. I have urged Mr. Purchas to send for Miss Julia from the country, by the way. She's the level-headed one of the family; she'll bring them about if anyone can. A great pity she's not a boy and the eldest."

Hart laughed and surprised the man of business by shaking him warmly by the hand. "I'm glad Miss Julia's coming," he said. "She will do us all good. Mr. Busby"—he paused, uncertain how to phrase the question—"if there was something I could do to help my relatives?"

"I should most certainly tell you of it," said Busby. "I'm delighted to hear you say that, Mr. Purchis. For the moment, I think the fact of your staying with them, the whole romantic story, the American heir—"

"I wish you would not call me that," protested Hart. "I've explained to you about the sequestration. . . ."

"Yes, yes, I know." Once again Busby raised that gentle, quelling hand. "But the papers won't. You might as well resign yourself to the title, Mr. Purchis, and to being a nine days' wonder. And since you ask, the one kindness you *can* do your English cousins is to let the story pass. Credit is a strange thing, as I am sure you must know, a man of the world like yourself. . . . The stories about your fabulous plantation at Winchelsea are just what the family needs just now. Don't go out of your way to deny them, however absurd they strike you as being. It might just make all the difference."

"I see," said Hart reluctantly. This was not exactly the kind of help he had had in mind, but having made the offer, he felt in honour bound to stick to it.

Julia made it easier. She and her mother reached London a few days later, and she greeted Hart with affectionate amusement as "our American nabob. Our country neighbours are cross as patch with me," she went on, "for having had such a paragon in the house and not letting them see him. You will have to come back to Sussex at the end of the season, Cousin Hart, so that I may make amends. You'll have all the matchmaking mammas in the country at your heels."

"What a fortunate thing for me that I am a married man," said Hart.

"Is it not?" she agreed. "It makes it proper, you know, for me to take you about and introduce you to all my friends as my respectable married cousin. You will come, won't you, Cousin Hart? I hardly like to ask it of you, so recent as your mourning is and for so sad a cause, but it will be of the utmost importance for us that you should be seen to be on family terms with us."

"I can think of nothing that would give me greater

happiness than to be of use to you, Cousin Julia," said
Hart, relieved that Julia, at least, recognised his married
state.

"Gallant as always." She flashed him the smile that was
so like her elder brother's. "And may I congratulate you
on your turnout, Cousin? Black becomes you to a marvel,
and I can see Knill has exerted himself to the limit for
you."

"I'm grateful to Dick for the recommendation." He
smiled ruefully. "Since those extravagant reports in the
papers, I have been inundated with offers of service. I
shall be a regular Bond Street lounger if I don't take
care."

"Oh, we can do better for you than that. You must
accompany me to Lady Garrard's rout tonight. She's one
of our leading Whig hostesses, and I can think of no
better house for you to make your bow to society. The
Duchess of Devonshire is a dear friend of hers, and I
have no doubt Fox will look in on the way home from
the House."

"I should like above all things to meet him," said Hart.

In fact, he found the rout party a dead bore. It took
him and Julia fifteen minutes just to get up the ornate stair
to where Lady Garrard, greeting her guests, gave him a
limp hand and said something polite but unintelligible.
"Lady Garrard is almost too popular," explained Julia as
they worked their way into a high-ceilinged salon so
crowded with people that it was hard for him to hear her.
"Her parties are always the most tremendous squeeze.
There's the Duchess of Devonshire." She pointed with her
fan to a far corner of the huge room, where he could
see the top of an outrageously high-dressed head, crowned
with a plume of feathers. "She's talking to General Con-
way. He's quite one of our Whig heroes. I must make you
known to him."

"If we ever get so far," said Hart ruefully, doing his
best to avoid the voluminous skirts of a tall woman in
blue who was standing with her back to him and talking
in a very loud voice about "George Gordon and his mad
Protestants."

"You'll get used to it," said Julia, and then: "Why,
George! This is a pleasant surprise. And Mordaunt, too.

What in the world are you doing so far from the Cocoa Tree?"

"Retrenching," said George Purchas succinctly. "My friend Mordaunt"—he introduced them—"my cousin Purchis." And then, as Hart exchanged bows with his sullen-looking companion: "Lady Peterborough—his mother—has cut up rough just like the old man. So here we are, a pair of involuntary reformed characters."

"I'm delighted to hear it," said Julia. "But what a squeeze. I had meant to present our cousin to the Duchess of Devonshire and her set, but there's not a chance of getting across the room to them."

"Not if you value that silk of yours," said her brother. "It took us all our good manners to find you, didn't it, Henry?"

"Your manners," growled his companion. "I've none, as you well know. And this room is insufferably hot. Let's make a bolt for it and go on to Cornelys's Rooms; there'll be air to breathe there."

"An excellent notion," said George Purchas. "Who knows? We may find the Duchess of Devonshire there, too."

"Or the Duchess of Portland," said Mordaunt with the odd sort of snarl that seemed the nearest he could get to a smile.

Mrs. Cornelys's Rooms in Soho Square were not quite what Hart had imagined. He had expected another private house, but this appeared to be a place of public entertainment, and many of the richly dressed crowd that thronged the spacious saloons wore dominoes and masks. "This is a public place?" he asked Julia. "I'm not sure—" It was one thing to visit a private party when in deep mourning, but this was something else again.

"It's all the rage," said Julia. "We won't stay long, Cousin, if you had rather not. Just take a turn about the rooms, to see who is here, then maybe a glass of something, and so home to our virtuous beds. You'll not deny me this pleasure on my first night out in London?" She raised big, pleading eyes to his. "It seems forever that I've been cooped up at Denton Hall. Oh, look! There's Lady Garrard's son. He must have done a bolt, too. He's quite a rising man in government. I'll make you known to him. Piers." She reached out with her fan and touched an elegant dark green shoulder. "You're quite ignoring me."

"Julia, by all that's wonderful!" The young man swung round and took both her hands. "When did you escape from your durance vile? And by God, this must be the American heir. Delighted to meet you, Mr. Purchis." He let go of Julia's hand and held out his white one to Hart. "You're quite the man of the hour, you know. Someone was asking me about you just yesterday, someone who must be nameless, you understand. I shall be able to tell him you are most completely the thing. As was to be expected, lucky dog, with our angel Julia for cousin and mentor. But come, why are we standing here? Let us find a box and have a drink and a proper chat. I've not seen you, blessed Julia, since—"

"Too long," Julia interrupted him. "Yes, do let us find a box. I am quite parched with thirst." And then, taking Hart's arm to follow her friend, she explained in a low voice. "Piers Blanding is the very man you need. The secretary's office . . . So much influence, so much style . . . And I can see you have made a great impression on him already."

Settling himself beside her in the luxurious box that commanded an admirable view of the crowded rooms, Hart wished that he could share her enthusiasm about Piers Blanding, who seemed to him the epitome of the creature he had heard described as a Bond Street beau. From striped waistcoat to ivory-topped cane, everything about him was just slightly too good to be true, Hart thought, and then thought, angrily, that it was merely his own ignorance that made him think so. Or—a horrid flash of self-knowledge—he could not be jealous of this man to whom Julia spoke so familiarly by his first name?

Piers Blanding had given his orders to a liveried man who hovered outside the box, and they were soon eating a luxurious cold collation washed down with what seemed to Hart a great deal of claret. "You wouldn't like something . . . something lighter?" he asked as Blanding refilled Julia's glass.

"Lighter?" She looked at him for a moment in entrancing puzzlement, then gave her delicious little laugh. "Oh, dear Cousin Hart, you think I would rather have orgeat or even lemonade as at stuffy old Almack's! No, I thank you, the ladies of our family have always drunk their glass with the gentlemen, and I hope we always will. They do things otherwise in your American colonies, I suppose?"

"Not colonies, Cousin," he said, suddenly stiff. "Independent states, if you please."

"I stand corrected." She raised her glass in silent toast. "Ah, here come the others." She turned to greet George and Mordaunt, who each now had a ravishing young lady on his arm. To Hart's surprise, no formal introductions were made, though he soon learned that the ladies were Mrs. Barry and Mrs. Warren, or, mostly, Charlotte and Emily. He understood, now, why Blanding had ordered for so many and was not entirely surprised, when they came at last to leave, that he seemed to be expected to pay for all of them.

"Dear Hart," said Julia, pressing his arm as he led her down to the waiting carriage. "I do thank you for my happy evening. And for keeping my bad brother out of mischief for once. Just think what he might have been losing at the Cocoa Tree."

"Yes, indeed," said Hart dutifully, and told himself that he had best pay another call on Drummond's Bank in the morning.

Next day the papers spoke hopefully of a probable early end to General Clinton's siege of Charleston. "It seems extraordinary." Hart put down the *Public Ledger*.

"Extraordinary?"

"That I should be free to enjoy myself here in London while men on both sides are fighting and dying at Charleston."

"Let us hope that they are not," said Dick. "It does look as if Clinton's force was overwhelming. Your General Lincoln must surely see reason and surrender. Then, perhaps, it will be possible for us to negotiate a peace with honour to all sides."

"I wish I could believe it," said Hart.

"Well," Dick said bracingly, "believe it or not, there is nothing in the world you can do about it, so let us put on our leathers and take Julia for the ride in the park she longs for. She's right, you know." He had seen Hart hesitate. "It can do you nothing but good to be seen to be behaving like a reasonable man. You must see that any excessive exhibition of mourning might be misconstrued. You cannot possibly go wrong if you stay close to Julia, who is universally loved, and with cause."

"I should think so," said Hart warmly.

It was extraordinary to have escaped from so much danger, to be still under threat of imprisonment, and to find himself in fact involved in the whole pleasant whirl of London society. Protesting less and less, he rode with Julia in the park, squired her to the exhibition of paintings at Somerset House, and let her make up parties to see Mr. Sheridan's *School for Scandal* and Lady Craven's comedy, *The Miniature Picture,* with Perdita Robinson, the young actress who was rumoured to be the Prince of Wales's mistress. Julia seemed to know just whom to ask on these occasions and made everything easy for him, even down to the paying, which was, of course, his affair.

He had not actually met Mr. Fox or Mr. Burke yet, though he had seen them often enough at the parties to which he squired Julia, and, what concerned him even more, there had so far been no response to his request for an exchange. But as Dick and Julia both said, it was early yet. Two or three weeks were nothing when it was a question of the grinding of the mills of power. "And there could be nothing more fatal than to seem too pressing," said Julia in reply to one of his anxious speeches. "Just keep on as you have been, Cousin, and I am sure we will see a happy ending soon enough. In the meantime, you must arbitrate between Dick and me. We have quite come to cuts as to what we should do this evening. I say Vauxhall, and he says Ranelagh, so you must decide for us."

"On the contrary," said Hart, "you must decide, Cousin. But," he went on, puzzled, "is there not a ball at Devonshire House tonight?" Here would be his chance for a meeting with Fox, who surely would not be dancing.

"A ball! Why, Cousin Hart, I am surprised at you." Julia made him a little face of shocked surprise. "You in such deep mourning to be talking of balls! You must understand, dear Cousin, that breakfasts and routs are one thing, balls quite another. Lord, it's lucky for you that you have me to school you, or I hate to think what trouble you would be getting into! As it is, I give my voice for Vauxhall. Dick, you must command one of Mr. Roberts's boats. The one with eight oars, and shall we have music?" She turned with a pretty hesitation to Hart. "It's charming to be rowed upstream from the Whitehall Steps with one's attendant band of horns and trumpets playing Mr. Handel's *Water Music*."

"It sounds delightful," said Hart.

It would have been still more so, he thought, later, ensconced in a snug box, with burnt champagne and the expensive, thin-sliced ham for which Vauxhall was famous, if their party had been a more interesting one. He was getting a little tired of Mordaunt and Blanding and their attendant ladies and began to find himself surprised that Julia continued to enjoy their company and their endless talk of parties of pleasure and, in the ladies' case, dress. The gentlemen talked about this too, about waistcoats and snuff boxes and boot polish, in the intervals of their interminable talk of racing and of bets won and lost.

"Look!" Could Julia have read his mind, as she sometimes seemed to do? "Now there is a party that will interest you, Hart. There is Dr. Johnson's friend Miss Burney, the daughter of the musician, you know, with Mr. Thrale and his wife and daughter. I quite thought they were at Bath."

"Is Dr. Johnson there?" asked Hart. "I would dearly love to meet him."

"And get one of his famous setdowns, for being that lowest of God's creatures, an American? No, I am sorry to have to disappoint you, but I doubt this is the kind of place he frequents. Or at least not when his toady Boswell is at home ruralising with his Scotch wife and all those children. And anyway," Julia finished with some finality, "Mr. and Mrs. Thrale are very good sort of people, I am sure, but not quite the kind that I would wish you to be associating with. And I am your mentor, do not forget."

"And the most delightful one a man could have. But pray, wise mentor, since so you are, when am I to see Mr. Walpole's Strawberry Hill? I have read of the wonders he has done with the place—of his fountains and grottoes, as far off as America, and I do dearly long to see it."

"Stupid of me!" said Julia. "I had quite forgot. Dear Mr. Walpole, he is an old man, though he would rather die than admit it, and I really believe he must have overlooked my letter. He is nice, you know, about whom he admits to his beloved Strawberry. I will write again in the morning."

# XII ⚜

Dick and Hart both had business in the City next morning, Dick with Mr. Busby and Hart once more at Drummond's Bank. Meeting Hart outside St. Paul's, Dick proposed that they should stay in the City for a while. "Busby tells me that some of Gordon's people from his great meeting in St. George's Fields are to march to Parliament by way of the City this morning and then up Fleet Street and the Strand. It would be interesting to see what kind of crowd he has stirred up by this strange campaign of his against the Roman Catholics. Nothing will come of it, of course. Everyone knows that the Relief Act of '78 was a measure of simple justice. Now, by taking the oath of allegiance, a Roman Catholic can actually inherit an estate—or serve his King as an officer in the army. Between ourselves, we Whigs always thought that was part of the purpose of the act: to help recruitment for service against you rebel Americans." A smile for Hart deprived this of its sting. "It all passed off so quietly at the time that it's hard to understand why Gordon is making such a to-do about it now. But everyone knows him for something of a wild man. He'll never get anywhere with his petition, but let us see what sort of numbers he has contrived to assemble."

Hart agreed. "I'll send the curricle back to Fozard's, and let us walk back to Charles Street. Now this hot weather has dried up the mud in the roads, I immensely enjoy walking in your great city."

Dick laughed. "A most unfashionable pastime, but so do I." He was silent for a moment, then smiled rather ruefully at Hart. "The truth of the matter is, I'm no Londoner, never have been. A few weeks on the gad here are enough for me. Frankly, I wish your business was happily settled and we could go home to Denton."

"Are you waiting for me?" This was news to Hart. "I thought you, too, were waiting for news of a ship."

Dick looked unhappy now. "They don't hold out much hope at the Admiralty. To tell truth, Hart, I do not quite understand what is going on there. There's a feeling . . . oh, it's nothing. London always gives me the blue devils."

"I'm sorry. And sorrier still that you have to stay on my account. And were it not for the pleasure of Julia's company, I would be inclined to agree with you about London. I was never a great one for society either. . . . That reminds me, Dick, who are the Mohawks?"

"The Mohawks?" Surprised. "Why, a very wild gang of young men indeed. They took their name from the Indian tribe, and a good many of their habits, by what one hears. What makes you ask about them?"

"Something Julia said"—Hart wished now that he had not raised the subject—"about George . . ."

"George? Was he mixed up with them? I do hope not! It's terrible to have been away for so long. Sometime I feel I hardly know my own brother and sister anymore. I worry about them, Hart."

"Surely no need to worry about Julia," said Hart.

"No . . . no, of course not." He turned to look down Cheapside, listening. They could hear the buzzing murmur of many voices, now, and an occasional burst of singing. "Hymns, I think. They sound quiet enough."

"But a great many of them." Hart had heard the noise of a mob too often at home in Savannah, and though this did indeed sound like an unusually peaceful one, he could not help a slight chilling of the blood. "What are your English mobs like?" he asked.

"Like all mobs: frightening," said Dick. "I was in town during the Wilkes and Liberty riots in '69 and don't much want to see anything like that again. Mind you, John Wilkes had some right on his side, as you must know, such a friend to you Americans as he is. But there was the devil to pay for a while. The case today is quite other, of course. If mad Lord George should stir up trouble, which I do not expect, it needs only a magistrate with the courage to read the Riot Act and a few soldiers ready to do their duty, and it's over in a trice. It's true"—he looked up at the cloudless sky of yet another brilliantly fine day—"this hot weather may mean greater numbers, perhaps a bit of trouble as a result, but nothing to signify, I am sure. Government have known about the meeting in St. George's Fields and the planned marches to Parliament for some time; they will undoubtedly have made their preparations. Look, there the marchers come. You see, a very decent-looking lot of men."

"And women," said Hart in surprise. "It looks almost like a family outing. And so many of them in black, too. Yes, I agree with you, Dick, they do look a sober lot. But, Lord, what a number of them! And this is only one of three processions, you say?"

"So Busby says. Hark at that!" The leaders of the procession had reached St. Paul's now and had broken out into three deep, echoing cheers for the cathedral. "You see; they are men of God, they respect the church."

"You think cheering a sign of respect? I wonder." The marchers were filing past now, cheering as they came, and Hart saw that most of them wore blue cockades in their hats, while some carried banners, with the legend "No Popery!" He also noticed that the procession was being quietly joined by people who came out of the small side streets and that many of these were of quite another stamp from the respectable black-clad leaders. He pointed this out to Dick, who agreed.

"Yes, the inevitable crowd of hangers-on, pickpockets and petty thieves, and discontented 'prentices. You'd best watch your pockets. . . . What do you say we cut across the fields and rejoin the procession when it gets to the Strand? It is moving slowly enough, in all conscience."

"And is long enough. It sounds like the sea," Hart went on as they turned away into the shabby open country round the Fleet Ditch. When they rejoined the procession, near Temple Bar, he thought that the raffish element in it had increased considerably. "And listen to that!" he exclaimed

as a great shout of "No Popery!" came reverberating back
down the long procession.

"They must be passing near one of the Catholic
chapels," said Dick. "Oh, well, harmless enough, I suppose.
Let them shout away their feelings and be done with it."

"If it's only that," said Hart. "I think we should hurry
home, Dick, and warn your father to be ready for trouble
when he goes down to the House today."

"Nonsense," said Dick cheerfully. "But let us by all
means go home; we promised Julia a ride in the park. I'm
surprised you should have forgotten."

Hart had not in fact done so but, as so often these
days, had been trying to bridle his eagerness to see Julia,
to be with her, to touch her hand while helping her to
mount her horse. It was horrible that he should feel like
this; he was ashamed; he fought it as best he could; and in
the end, he could not help himself. To see her daily, many
times every day, to have to live in the same house with her
and pretend, always, that he felt for her only what a cousin
should, was horrible, was more than he could bear. But it
must be borne. He knew he should move away, into
lodgings, free from this daily, hourly temptation, but the
terms of his parole tied him to Dick, and besides, he had
promised Busby that he would stand by the Purchases.

If only he would hear from Mercy. Then perhaps she
would become real to him again instead of seeming more
and more shadowy and remote, his wife in name only.
The cold salt width of the Atlantic lay between them,
dulling memory, chilling the heart. Two more lines of the
ballad his mother used to sing came suddenly back to him,
giving him the whole first verse:

> *Oh, wide is the water, I cannot get o'er,*
> *The water lies wide twixt my true love and me,*
> *I stand alone on a stranger shore*
> *And never more my true love shall see.*

His true love. Mercy? Mercy, who had caused his mother's
death. And still had sent no word of comfort, of apology . . . Busby had explained, pitying his ignorance, that
there was a lively traffic in smuggled American mail by
way of Holland. Mercy must have seen the news both
of his capture and of his mother's death in *Rivington's*

*Gazette,* which was freely circulated among the rebels. Rebels? He pulled himself up. He meant, of course, the free Americans.

They found Julia impatiently awaiting them, very elegant in a new dark green riding habit with gold frogging.

"You're very fine, Julia," said Dick.

She pulled one of her expressive faces. "Since revered Papa decrees that my mother and I may not go to the Birthday, and therefore do not have the expense of hoops and feathers, she has the vapours, and I have treated myself to the consolation of one whole new habit. Anyway"—brightening up—"the Birthday would be small pleasure without the benefit of my favourite escort." She gave her rich little laugh. "I would just like to see Farmer George's face if we were so bold as to confront him with one of his rebellious Americans. And that starchy Queen of his, too, and all those sad princesses. But instead, I have arranged a party of pleasure for us, of which I do hope you will approve, Cousin Hart. Mordaunt and George and you and I are all to hire one of Mr. Roberts's boats and make a night of it at Vauxhall. Monday, of course, since the Birthday will be celebrated then. You shall come, too, Dick, if you can find yourself a young lady. I am not to be troubling with you if I have Hart to gallant me, as I trust I will." With a ravishing upward sweep of dark eyes.

The park was unusually full of people, even for a Friday, and Julia was soon surrounded by her usual crowd of devoted cavaliers. Hart always enjoyed watching her hold court like this, and enjoyed it the more because of the sparkling, special look she saved for him. There were never any women in her company, he had noticed and could only suppose that her rivals could not bear to be outshone.

They were joined, after a while, by George Purchas and Mordaunt. "There's the devil to pay at Westminster," said George with evident pleasure. "Members being jostled and tousled and made to swear 'No Popery' before they are so much as allowed into the House. Chief justices without their wigs; bishops without their gowns, and Lord Boston's very life in danger. Don't I just hope some disaster may strike our revered parent. Nothing too serious, you understand, just death."

"George!" said Julia. "It's no subject for your jokes!"

"Who said I was joking? But we are shocking our American cousin. Surely you are used to the antics of the mob on your republican shores, Cousin Purchis."

"I am afraid so," said Hart gravely. "And very much ashamed of them. But are things really so serious down at Westminster? Should we not go there and try to help Mr. Purchas?"

"Quite impossible," said Mordaunt. "I am but now come from there, and I tell you you might as well look for a hot coal in hell as one man in that scrimmage. If Mr. Purchas has his wits about him, as, to give the devil his due, he mainly has, he is snug at home by this time, having given his coachman the office to turn tail at sight of the mob."

"I expect you are right," said Dick. "But I think we should go home and make sure."

George gave his rather brutal laugh. "You may do so, good little brother, since his life is undoubtedly of some value to you. But I will spare you my company, though it's true there is always the chance that the sight of me might bring on an apoplexy where the mob had failed to do so. Come, Mordaunt, let's go and see what the rascals are up to now."

As the other three turned their horses' heads towards Piccadilly and home, Julia put out a quick hand to touch Hart's where it lay on his bridle. "You must not take my naughty George seriously," she said. "His tongue was always his worst enemy. You will grow to love him as you know him better. I wish you would help me make him and my father better friends. Father thinks the world of you, I know. You won't trouble him with the foolish things George has been saying?"

"I should think not," said Hart.

Reaching the house in Charles Street they found that Mr. Purchas had indeed turned homeward on sight of the mob around Parliament. He had been badly frightened by what he had seen and poured it all out to them. Lord Ashburnham had been mobbed and dragged into the House half-conscious, Welbore Ellis had escaped over the roofs from Guildhall, Lord North himself had been insulted and his hat snatched from his head. "We Whigs would have managed things better. If there's no one killed," Purchas concluded, "it will be a miracle. And that madman Gordon rushing in and out of the lobby to egg his followers on. I hope to see him hang for high treason before I am very much older."

"High treason!" exclaimed Dick. "As serious as that?"

"As serious as possible," said his father. "I cannot understand, since government knew what Lord George was planning, why they did not make arrangements with the magistrates and the Lord Mayor ahead of time."

Julia gave her silvery laugh. "Someone told me," she said, "that Lord North meant to send a message and forgot."

"It would be like him," said her father. "Just one more Tory blunder. Now if we Whigs were in power . . ."

"Yes, Papa," said his two children at once.

Julia took Hart to a small party at the house of an old friend of hers that night. "Quite a simple affair," she explained. "But it will take our minds off the trouble today. You will not mind it being quite quiet, I know. I have known Susan forever, and she longs to meet the American cousin of whom I have spoken so much. Mr. Bond is quite in a thriving way in the city, though I do not rightly understand what it is that he does. They have a good enough house in Lincoln's Inn Fields and live in the simplest possible way, which you, with your ideas of equality, must approve."

"I am sure I shall be more than delighted to meet any friends of yours." And yet Hart was slightly puzzled. Julia had refused to introduce him to Mr. and Mrs. Thrale and their friend Fanny Burney, the famous author of *Evelina*, because she did not consider the brewer, Thrale, her social equal. And yet Thrale was the friend of the great Dr. Johnson himself. But it was all part of Julia's charming, impulsive, baffling character. Naturally she would never desert an old school friend.

When the carriage came round to take them to Lincoln's Inn Fields, Hart asked at once if there was news from Parliament. "Oh, yes, bless you, sir," said the coachman. "All's right and tight again. The Guards were called out in the end and gave the crowd a good fright, rode over some of them, by what I hear, no one hurt, or not much; then Justice Addington told them to go home, and they gave him three cheers and went. Mind you, it did look nasty early on, when I was down there with the master, but all's over now; they've had their bit of fun and gig and gone home to bed."

"That's good." Hart helped Julia into the carriage and felt the familiar, intolerable ecstasy of her hand on his. "I'm glad it is all so well over."

She laughed up at him. "Anyone would think you were a Catholic yourself, Cousin Hart, so anxious as you are about it all."

"I've seen mobs at work," he told her, and had a sudden vision of Mercy that first night they met, desperately trying to quench the flames of her burning home. Mercy sewing shirts for him before he went to Harvard. The strong brown hands always so busy. Busy? She had reached out her hand and saved him from the living death on the prison hulk in New York Harbour. She had saved him again, despite himself, when the British had taken Savannah and Francis Mayfield had come to kill him. Was it just because he owed her so much that he had been such a wretched failure as a husband? And was it because of that very failure that she had not written to him? Did she, too, feel that their marriage had ended . . . had never really begun?

"Hart Purchis!" said Julia's teasing voice. "I vow you've not listened to a word I said."

"Forgive me. I was thinking about mobs." He was ashamed of the lie as he spoke it.

He took an instant liking to the Bonds, though he was surprised at how much older Mrs. Bond seemed than her friend. But Julia had warned him of this. "She has quite gone off, poor love, with all the childbearing. Four in three years. Twins, you see; quite barbarous!"

But Hart, taken up to the nursery at his own request, did not find it barbarous at all and liked Mrs. Bond better still for her obvious devotion to her thriving little family. He was surprised to find that the twin boys were old enough to ask a flood of questions that reminded him suddenly and painfully of his first meeting with the Paston girls. Yes, indeed, he told George and Harry Bond, he had seen a Red Indian, had, in fact, seen a great many, and, on being pressed, gave a very creditable imitation of a war whoop, which put the seal of success on the nursery visit.

"How old are they?" he asked as Mrs. Bond shut the nursery door behind them.

"The boys?" She smiled at him. "Old enough to be great little tyrants. Mr. Purchis"—she put out a hand to detain him for a moment on the upper landing—"I am so glad to have this chance to speak to you. I love Julia so dearly . . . she was quite my little pet at school. I'm—older than she is, of course. Being so happy myself, I . . . I find myself anxious about her sometimes. I am so glad you are come, and her brother Dick home, too. I do not . . . I cannot think George Purchas a good influence. Nor yet his friends."

"She has a good friend in you, I can see," said Hart, but felt faintly relieved when she turned to lead the way back downstairs. What exactly did Mrs. Bond expect him to do for Julia?

It was a lively romp of a party, with games of brag and speculation for the younger members and whist for the chaperones, and it was only when Mrs. Bond called for silence so that Julia could sing for the company that Hart heard another sound, beyond and behind the suddenly suspended flow of cheerful chatter.

He rose to his feet and moved across to pull aside the velvet curtain from one of the high windows.

"You heard it, too?" Mr. Bond had crossed the room to join him and now pulled the curtain together behind them, so that they stood isolated in the window embrasure. "Dear God!" He looked, as Hart was, in silent horror out at the square below, which was filling rapidly with people. Here and there a torch, carried high, illuminated a group of faces, blue cockades, a "No Popery" banner. "They're carrying tools." He turned to Hart. "Look! Spades . . . pick-axes . . . crowbars."

"They are all men now," said Hart, "by the look of it. I suppose one should thank God for that. But what's their aim, do you think?"

"I'm afraid"—Bond was peering out of the window as the crowd went on pouring into the square from the direction of Great Queen Street—"I am very much afraid it must be the chapel of the Sardinian Ambassador. It's over there"—he pointed—"in Duke Street."

"We must get help," said Hart. "But how?" The square was now entirely filled by the mob.

"Madame Cordon, the Ambassador's wife, is expecting a child," said Bond. "They live next door to the chapel. I'll send a man out the back way, to Sir John Fielding's, and to Alderman Kennet, the Lord Mayor. We need the military here, and the Riot Act read. Listen!"

The crowd had clotted now on the far side of the square, and Hart could hear the shatter of glass and the heavy sound of battering against the chapel doors. The shouts of "No Popery" had increased, and the mob sounded more like an enormous, raging beehive than ever. "You calm the ladies," said Bond, "while I send for help."

"What is it?" Julia drew aside the curtain to join them. "What are you two being so private about?" And then: "Oh, jimini!" She leaned against Hart to look out. "The mob! What a stroke of luck!"

"Luck?"

She pulled a face at him. "Oh, yes, of course, it is terrible, and dear knows how we are going to get home, but just look! See what a fine view we have of everything that goes on. Hark!"

"The chapel door is down," said Hart grimly as the mob suddenly surged into the dark building and torchlight began to flicker at its windows. "I hope to God Mr. Bond can get help in time." Now by the uncertain light of the torches he could see pieces of furniture, books, hassocks, plates tossed out from hand to hand over the heads of the crowd that still seethed in the square.

"Of course there will be help," she said impatiently. "Why, Madame Cordon, the Ambassador's wife, is a dear friend of the Walpoles. No need to be anxious for her! No doubt she is sitting snug by the fire this moment in Thomas Walpole's house over there. The *ton* take care of their own. Oh, look, they are starting a fire!" In the middle of the square a small flicker of flame was rapidly growing into a raging bonfire as it was fed with the chapel's furnishings. "Hart." An anxious hand on his sleeve. "How in the world are we going to get home?"

"God knows. I wish Dick were here." Dick had been summoned to the Admiralty that afternoon, and he hoped it might mean news of a ship at last. But he had been puzzled that Julia had not suggested that Dick join them at the Bonds' and tell them his news. They were a strange family, the Purchases. Mrs. Purchas was always ailing, yet never exactly ill; Mr. Purchas was always talking about "we Whigs," yet seemed to play no active part in politics. And George . . . George was the greatest enigma of all. On the surface, he seemed the complete young man-about-town, but under the veneer, Hart sometimes caught a glimpse of savage strength that reminded him of the first day they had met. But why should he think to understand the Purchases when he understood so little of English society?

"Poor Dick." Julia shrugged elegant, bare shoulders. "He was mad for Susan, you know, when we were all children together, but of course, it was quite hopeless. A younger son, with his way to make, and in the navy! And Dick never has had much gift for getting prize money. Oh—" she clutched his arm, sending yet another uncontrollable, shameful thrill through him—"they've fired the chapel!"

"The foot guards are coming." Mr. Bond rejoined them. "And the fire engines, but there's no sign of a magistrate." He watched with them as the foot guards marched into the square, fixed bayonets, gleaming in the firelight, and formed a ring of steel around the mob at the chapel doors. "But they'll be able to do nothing without the Riot Act read," he said gloomily. "Look! The mob aren't letting the fire engines at the chapel. It will be burnt to the ground, and its neighbours with it. And built by Inigo Jones!"

"I don't think the soldiers are really trying," said Hart.

"No," Bond agreed. "I've heard that many of them are anti-Catholic. It's a bad business, Mr. Purchis, a frightening, bad business. Ah, they're letting the fire engines at the other houses."

"Yes," said Hart. "The mob are, not the soldiers." He turned as Julia, who had left them for a moment, came back and put a confiding hand on his arm.

"Hart," she said, "Susan urges that we stay here for the night. She will send a message, the back way, to Charles Street, so my parents are not anxious."

Bond looked doubtful. "Delighted to have you, naturally, but, Miss Purchas, do you really think—"

"Susan and I have it all settled," said Julia. "There is talk of other fires between here and Charles Street. They

say the Bavarian Ambassador's chapel is in flames too.
And serve him right," she added, "for an arrant old
smuggler that he is. But, Hart, would you think me a
coward if I urged that we do stay here? It is all very well
for the Bonds' other friends; they have not so far to go.
But I'm told the whole sky is red with fire; God knows
what other mobs we might not encounter between here
and home."

Susan Bond, joining them at this point, added her en-
treaties to Julia's, and Hart was relieved to agree. "Things
will seem better in the morning."

"They could hardly seem worse," said Bond. "Do you
know the Lord Mayor flatly refused to do anything at all?
I always knew him for a cipher, but this is the outside
of enough. It almost makes one wonder if he does not
sympathise with the mob."

"You cannot mean he hopes for a revolution!" exclaimed Hart.

Bond passed a weary hand across his face. "To tell
truth, I do not rightly know what I mean," he said.

By the time they were ready for bed the square was
quiet at last, and Hart almost wished he had insisted that
they wait and return to Charles Street, but there was
nothing for it now but to make the best of things.

Morning brought Dick, grey-faced. "The carriage is
below." He had found them all at the breakfast table,
a most unusual appearance for Julia, and had made his
greetings so brief as to be uncivil. "Fetch your shawl,
Julia. The streets are crowded with sightseers already.
Hart, I am going to ask you to walk home. You must not
be seen with Julia in your evening dress."

"But surely—" Hart began a protest, then abandoned
it. In the very real danger of the night before, he had
never given a thought to the nice rules of London society
but still could see nothing wrong about their spending
the night at the Bonds'. Now, with Dick lowering beside
him, he made his farewells at once as warm and as brief
as possible and found himself downstairs and in the street
before Julia had returned with her shawl.

"Here!" Dick handed him a greatcoat, unsuitably warm
for the time of year. "Can you find your way back through
side streets? I'd as lief you saw no one we know. God,
Hart, of all the scatterbrained starts . . ."

"I don't understand you," said Hart, angry at last. "I'd rather die than harm Julia, but, Dick, if you had seen the crowd last night . . . And to stay with an old friend, a married lady . . ."

"Married?" said Dick. "Who said they were married?"

Striding home, Hart did not notice the signs of last night's rioting in the shabby slum streets or the sodden, gin-soaked beggars who caught at the skirts of his great-coat. Susan and Bond were not married. Julia had taken him to their house . . . Julia had let him fatally compromise her, and there was nothing in the world he could do about it.

"I'm sorry." He confronted Mr. Purchas across his study table. "I cannot begin to tell you how sorry I am. I only hope you will believe that I had no idea. If Julia had only told me . . ."

"Spilt milk," said Mr. Purchas. "The question is, what's to do now? It would be Saturday, but I wager no one will have left town. I am sure I can find either the Bishop of Lincoln or of Lichfield. One of them should be able and willing to do our business if it's put to them in the proper light."

"Our business?"

"Marry you and Julia, of course. What else are we discussing? It's not what I'd hoped for her, but—"

"Mr. Purchas," Hart interrupted him with the courage of desperation, "you are forgetting. I am a married man."

"*Tchah,*" said Purchas. "Too late in the day to be remembering that now. You've escorted Julia everywhere, set tongues wagging about her, and now this last folly . . . It was when she first came to London that you should have remembered you were a married man. But no need to look so down in the mouth, man. I've talked this over with Busby. Did so as soon as I saw how the land lay between you and Julia. What kind of father would you think me otherwise? Busby sees no problem, or none that cannot be surmounted. A nullity, of course. A rash attempt at a marriage, performed by a Catholic sea captain, an enemy of the country; no documents; no surviving witnesses, or none we know of. It's a mere farce, cousin—" he corrected himself—"son Hart."

A nullity. Hart had felt his face flush scarlet in the course of this remarkable speech. It was what he had

sometimes thought himself. What he had wanted? He
could not do it. "I'm a witness," he said. "I and my wife
are both witnesses."

"Your wife! Your whore! Do you know where she is
now, this so-called wife of yours? She's the belle of
Philadelphia."

"Philadelphia?"

"Thought that would surprise you. Left her near
Boston, didn't you, to be looked after by relatives? She
seems to have cut and run from there soon enough. Not
luxurious enough maybe for a lady used to being the
toast of Savannah? Piers Blanding brought me the report
just last night."

"Report?"

"From New York. They've ways and means there of
knowing what goes on among the American rebels. Now,
understand me, Hart Purchis, I'm as good a friend of you
Americans as you could wish, but our old enemies the
French are another matter."

"The French?"

"The lady who passes for your wife has been set up
in a house in Philadelphia by the French Minister there,
by Luzerne himself. Now what have you to say to that?
I don't know whether she repays him by spying, or by—
other favours, but it hardly seems, does it, as if she
looked on herself or was behaving as your lawful wedded
wife?"

"I must see the report." Hart felt he was clutching at
straws.

"Impossible. It was most secret. Young Blanding merely
let me glance at it. But you have my word for it. Julia's
father's word. Hush!" He held up a hand. "There's the
carriage now. You won't want to see Julia yet. Hart"—
he held out a friendly hand—"I'm sorry it had to happen
this way, but glad, truly glad, to have you for a son. Your
very staunchness in defence of that worthless wife of yours
does you credit. But go to your room; think it over. We've
a little time yet, specially with this mob in the streets,
drawing all eyes. Sleep on it, if you must, but let me
have the word I need just as soon as you can. For Julia's
sake. For all our sakes."

"Thank you, sir." He found his way to his room like a
blind man, tore off his evening dress, and threw himself

flat on his bed. Mercy. He had thought he had forgotten
her. Mercy and a Frenchman. Luzerne. The French Minister in Philadelphia. What in the name of God was Mercy
doing in Philadelphia? Forgotten her? Why should it
come back to him now, that exacerbating vision of Mercy
in her low-cut bronze dress, laughing and flirting with
British officers, with Francis, wooing them, blinding them
with her charms, smiling and smiling and letting them tell
her the secrets she would use against them as the Rebel
Pamphleteer? He had suspected her then, fiercely, jealously, horribly suspected her, and very nearly been her destruction as a result.

He got slowly up from the bed and moved over to look
at his grey face in the glass. He had thought the worst
of Mercy, back in Savannah, and been wrong. However
great the temptation, he would not do it again. And curiously enough, now that he was really remembering Mercy,
the temptation did not seem so great as all that. How
strange. Only this morning the sight of Julia across the
breakfast table had been enough to set his pulses stirring.
And now? Now he could think only of Mercy.

"I'm sorry, sir." He sought out Mr. Purchas late that
afternoon. "I cannot do it. I'm a married man." He repeated it as one might a spell.

"You're a young idiot. Take twenty-four hours. Keep
yourself to yourself. Think it over. Sunday tomorrow. I'll
have your meals sent to your room."

# XIII ❧

Anxiously reading and rereading the reports of Hart's capture by the British, Mercy consoled herself as best she might with the fact that there was no reference to her. "Dare I hope, do you think, that word of what I did in Savannah has not reached England?" she asked Charles Brisson one fine May morning when he had found her and Ruth hemming sheets in their blossom-filled garden.

"One should always hope," said Charles Brisson. "It is better for the soul than despairing. But one should also be a little realistic, madame."

"What do you mean?"

"That I am afraid word of your reception here in Philadelphia is bound to reach the British in New York. You know how it is. There is constant traffic across the debatable ground between the two armies. Sooner or later they will hear in New York that you are living here, that you have been welcomed, feted. . . . And how rightly so! But from the point of view of your husband, it can only be unfortunate. News that reaches New York reaches England in the end. I would not be your friend if I did not admit to you that it can only prejudice his position when he stands trial."

"Trial? You think it will come to that?"

"It will be a miracle if it does not. A known privateer . . . and with, forgive me, a known spy for his wife . . .

154

What he did at Savannah is one thing; then he might be considered a part of the American navy . . . though, mind you, even that is not necessarily a protection. You know as well as I do that General Washington, General Arnold, all of them lead their lives with the feel of the noose about their throats. What do you think Charles Lee expected when he was captured in '76."

"Death?" The needle dropped from her cold fingers. "Mr. Brisson, you can't think . . . they wouldn't, the British? They are civilised people." It was so exactly what she had secretly feared that she could hardly forgive him for putting it into words.

"Civilised? Who is really so when it comes to the point? Face it, madame. From all one hears, the antiwar party is growing daily in strength, over there in London, and the government may be pushed to desperate measures to whip up support for the war. What more effective than a show trial? You know what feelings were roused by John Paul Jones's ravages round the British coasts last year. I would not wish to see your husband made scapegoat for his exploits, madame."

"Oh, God!" She dropped the sheet on the grass. "What shall I do? You're the only person I really trust, here in Philadelphia. You and Ruth, of course." She reached out a quick hand to press Ruth's, which had also fallen listless on to her sewing as she listened to them.

"I am glad you say so." He glanced quickly round the sunny garden. "Ruth, would you be so good as to make sure we cannot be disturbed? There is something I very much want to say to Mrs. Purchis."

"Yes, of course." Ruth jumped to her feet. "I won't let anyone past the back door. You can count on me, Mercy."

"I know I can." Mercy watched her with great affection as she hurried away through the neat garden. Wonderful how much better she was, and strange that Charles Brisson used her first name so freely while he always called her madame or Mrs. Purchis. He had visited them constantly, too, since he had been back in Philadelphia. Could there be something in it . . . between him and Ruth? What a strange thought. She smiled up at Brisson. "You wished to speak to me?"

"Madame, you ask my advice. I have longed to give it to you. I think you should go to England."

"To England? Have you taken leave of your senses?"

He had stood up when Ruth left them, now sat down again on the close cropped grass at her feet. "I often think so." He smiled up at her. Then, very grave all of a sudden: "Madame, I am about to put my life in your hands. Can I trust you, those little hands of yours?"

"Of course you can." She looked down at them, puzzled.

"Well, then. Give me your solemn promise of secrecy, and I think I can help you get to England. Or, to be precise, to France, whence, as I have no doubt you know, one can always find a friendly smuggler to take one across to England. This is a strange war and makes for strange friendships."

"But what would I do in England?"

"Speak up for your husband. Plead for him in court. They are great sentimentalists, the English. It will be very bad for your husband if the prosecutor can describe you at his trial—his wife—as a spy against England, living in luxury here in Philadelphia, the protégée of the French. Ah, you had not thought of that? It will be said; it is bound to be said. And you know as well as I do that though the British are impatient with you Americans, they hate the French. With you, it is a family quarrel, to be laughed off in the end, forgiven. . . . With the French—with us—it is quite other. We are old enemies."

"You mean"—she looked at him with horror—"everything I have done is harmful to Hart. I have killed his mother and aunt, and now, just by being here, by living in this house, I am endangering his life."

"I very much fear so." He met her eyes squarely. "And that is why I made you this offer. I feel responsible, you see. It was I who made you known to the French here, to the Chevalier de la Luzerne. Everything else has followed from that. I could not bear the hatred you would feel for me, madame, if your husband's death should be the result of the help I have tried to give you."

"But what shall I do? Could you really help me get to France?"

"Yes, that I can do. I am going myself, you see. But secretly, most secretly. If you wish to come, you must be ready to leave on the instant and without a word to anyone. Will you trust me so far?"

"Oh, yes, of course, I trust you!" And yet how strange it

was that she did so. "But Ruth?" she asked. "I cannot leave Ruth."

"Naturally not. I would very much prefer that you bring her. You should not be alone, the only woman, on such a journey. But, madame, if you value your life—and mine —you must tell her nothing. Not until the moment comes. Can you do that?"

"Dear Ruth. She would go anywhere with me. But the French minister . . . this house . . . I should say something to him?"

"Leave all that to me. Just live as you always do, in full sight of the world, and be ready, with the smallest possible baggage, for when I give the word. It may be very sudden, very strange, not the kind of message you expect at all. But if it is from me, you will know what it means." He thought for a moment. "And just to be sure that it is from me," he went on, "if I cannot come for you myself, my messenger will announce himself as Mr. Jones."

"Mr. Jones." It took her back to what he had said earlier. "Would they really hang Hart for what John Paul Jones did?"

"In war anything can happen. You will risk imprisonment yourself with every step of this dangerous journey. I would not be your friend if I did not remind you of that, but they are chivalrous, the British. I am sure as I am of anything that if you deliver yourself into their hands, young and beautiful as you are, they will make a heroine of you, just the way the French have here."

"But not the Americans." She smiled at him, her heart warmed by the compliment. "Do you know, I'd be glad to get away from here? Only—I wish I had heard from Hart —from my husband. It is so strange that he has not written. Suppose he did not want me to come?"

"Impossible. Except, of course, that he might be anxious for your safety, but truly I do not think you would have anything to fear. It was embarrassing enough for the British to have you—a woman—fool them so roundly in Savannah. I am sure they will not want to make the fact more public than they must. No, I think once you are there, you should be safe enough, but the journey will be both dangerous and uncomfortable. I am in honour bound to prepare you for that."

"Oh, that's nothing. I am more grateful to you than I

can say for making it possible. Will it be soon, do you think?"

"I very much hope so. Remember, madame, not a word to anyone, and wait for a message from Mr. Jones. But first, I must ask for your solemn vow of secrecy. I am putting my life in your hands with this offer. Will you promise me, by whatever you hold most dear—by the husband you go to—that whatever happens you will say nothing about what I have told you."

"You mean about your working for the French?"

"About that, about our first meeting, about anything that seems strange in my life."

"So much seems strange. It is a great deal to ask."

"I must ask it."

Their eyes met and held for a long moment. Then, "I promise," she said. "By all that I hold most dear."

"Thank you." He took her hand and bent to kiss it. "Here comes Miss Paston. Nothing to her."

"Miss Shippen has come to call," said Ruth. "And Monsieur Otto with her. I have asked them to wait in the parlour."

"Did you say I was here?" asked Brisson.

"No. Should I have?"

"You are a most admirable girl. If I may"—he turned back to Mercy—"I will take French leave, over the hedge."

"If you wish." Was she mad, she wondered, gathering up her sewing to go indoors and join her new guests, to trust this mysterious young man about whom she knew so little? She had liked him instinctively from their first dramatic meeting, and since then he had saved her life, helped her to her present happy position in Philadelphia society, and been a constant support against the quiet barbs of people like Mrs. Arnold. No wonder if she was fond of him. He's like a brother to me, she thought and, thinking this, found her thoughts flash to Hart. Incredible, unbearable that she had still not heard from him.

Greeting Otto and Nancy Shippen, she was tempted for a moment to bring Brisson's name casually into the conversation, just to see what Otto would say about him. But she knew she must resist the temptation and was glad she had done so when they had left and Ruth said, on a very tentative note, "Mercy?"

"Yes, dear."

"Mercy, forgive me. I am so ignorant . . . I am sure it is my stupidity, but I think . . . I think mother would have said . . ."

"Yes?" Mercy prompted as she came to a standstill.

"Should you talk alone with young men?" Ruth got it all out in one hurried breath.

"No, dear, you are quite right, and your mother would have said so. But you must take my word for it that in this case there is an overriding reason for my talking with Charles Brisson. You will know all about it soon enough, and in the meanwhile I am most grateful for what you have said. Mind you," she smiled teasingly at Ruth, "what about Monsieur Otto and Miss Shippen? You left them alone in the parlour. And she is not even a married lady."

"No indeed," said Ruth. And then, "Ah, the poor things."

"Poor?"

"Did you not know? There is a Colonel Livingston her parents want her to marry. An older man; very rich. Only —she and young Monsieur Otto . . ."

"A case? Ruth, you keep surprising me. How did you learn all this?"

Ruth laughed, and Mercy thought what a pleasure it was to hear. "They're all so scared of you, Mercy dear. They think a heroine of the Revolution is quite above their touch. And they're quite right too," she added loyally. "You are all that, and so much more. But they talk to me, at the sewing parties. I'm just a silly girl. They're not afraid of me. And I do enjoy it. It almost makes me forget . . . Mercy?"

"Yes." A new note in Ruth's voice caught Mercy's full attention.

"You've been so good to me. May I—please, may I tell you something, and will you try and go on loving me? You've been so good," she explained, "so wonderfully good. Am I wicked to think you must love me?"

"Not wicked at all." Mercy took her hand. "Of course I love you, Ruth dear, and always shall. We need each other, you and I."

"Oh, I'm glad you said that. But, just the same, I want to tell you . . . I must tell you, even if you never speak to me again. Mercy, that day—" The hand in Mercy's writhed like a suffering thing. "That terrible day. When I saw Naomi . . . when I saw . . . when I saw. Mercy! For a moment, just for a moment, I was glad. I thought, 'Serve her right! Why should she have had George, not me?' Oh, Mercy, I'll never forgive myself. You'll never forgive me. Why should anyone?"

"You mean?" Mercy thought about it, horror-struck. "You were twins. You and Naomi. You loved George too?"

"Of course I loved him. Who could help it? And, Mercy, he loved me first. He *met* me first. Oh, Mercy, will God ever forgive me? I was *glad!*"

"And now you are as sorry as you can be." Mercy reached out to pull her down beside her and stroke her hair. "You've always been sorry, and you know it. You loved them both, that's all. What's wrong with love?"

"Selfish love." Ruth looked up at her, clear-eyed through her tears. "I've been punished, Mercy. God has punished me. Is that enough, do you think? Will you forgive me? Can you forgive me?"

"Forgive?" asked Mercy. "Dear Ruth, I'm not God. I see nothing to forgive. You saved my life, remember? We're friends, Ruth; we'll always be friends. It's better than love, I begin to think." And thought to herself that Brisson was a friend.

"I wish I knew what you meant." Ruth looked at her, puzzled. But after that tear-drenched confession she never screamed in the night again.

The message from Mr. Jones came ten days later. It was not at all what Mercy had expected. She and Ruth had been invited by Nancy Shippen to join in a party of pleasure she and her cousin Mrs. Benedict Arnold were making up to drive out and dine at Mr. Benezet's inn at Bristol, and her first instinct had been to refuse. Nancy Shippen, extending the invitation, had explained that there could be no fear of molestation from the British since everyone knew that the garrison of New York had been cut to the bone in order to provide troops for the attack on Charleston, about which anxiety was mounting daily.

But Mercy persisted in her refusal. She could not quite like either General Arnold or his pretty, frivolous new wife, whose rudeness, the first time they met, had made a lasting impression on her. When Nancy Shippen called a second time to urge that she and Ruth join the party, she made their excuses, explaining that she did not feel like joining parties of pleasure when she still had no news of how her husband fared in England.

"I do understand," said Nancy Shippen. "And respect you for it. But, dear Mrs. Purchis, your husband would not wish you to deny yourself all pleasure, and there is Ruth to be considered too. She is vastly better, is she not?"

"Yes, I am happy to say."

"And the reason not far to seek," said Nancy with a twinkle. "I have prevailed upon Mr. Brisson to be of our party. He says he wants above all to visit Germantown, where General Washington almost beat the English in '77. He has asked if he may bring a friend of his, a Mr. Jones from Boston, who, he says, is particularly interested in the strategy of that day. So we will not lack for cavaliers, and Mr. Benezet's inn is famous for its dinners. It will do us all good to get out of town and take a look at the countryside. Do change your mind and come, Mrs. Purchis. I know Ruth longs to do so."

"Do you know, I believe I will," said Mercy, alerted by the mention of Mr. Jones.

"That's right. I know you will not regret it. And now that is so comfortably settled, we can get to the strategy of the occasion, as Monsieur Otto would say. Mr. Brisson begs the pleasure of conveying you two in his carriage. We are all to start very early in the morning, so that we can visit the battlefield at Germantown and then drive on to Bristol for our dinner. You will be delighted with the view of the river that one gets from Mr. Benezet's inn. Oh, but I quite forgot; you must have come that way on that adventurous journey of yours from Boston."

"Yes, but I was ill at the time." Was this, perhaps, why she had felt so reluctant to join the pleasure party? She would never forget that nightmare drive from Trenton, haunted by memories of Mrs. Purchis and Anne Mayfield. "And besides," she went on, "it was winter."

"And what a winter! You will be amazed how beautiful the road is with the orchards in bloom. That's settled, then, and I am delighted." She rose to her feet. "And there, if I am not mistaken, is Colonel Livingston's carriage for me. No, I won't let him come in. I've taken quite enough of your time already."

Mercy was glad to let her go. She liked Colonel Livingston very much less even than she did General Arnold.

He had a way of looking at women that sent shivers down her spine. And what kind of soldier was it who gave up his command in order to dangle after a young woman who was as evidently in love with someone else as Nancy Shippen was with Monsieur Otto?

But that was no affair of hers. She turned her mind to the problems of how she was to get the portmanteau she had packed for herself and Ruth into Brisson's carriage. It would be so much easier if she could tell Ruth, but she knew that Brisson was right in forbidding it. Ruth was wonderfully better since that disturbing confession of hers, but her face was too open for secrets.

In the end, as she might have expected, Brisson himself solved the problem for her. He called two days before the projected party to say that his friend Mr. Jones would not after all be accompanying them. "Will you ladies resign yourself to just one escort between you," he asked, "if I promise to make up in assiduity for what I lack in numbers?"

Mercy laughed. "Of course we will," she said. "It will be quite a change, here in Philadelphia, to see the men outnumbered for once. If I were a congressman's wife, I think I would insist on spending at least some of the year at my husband's side. It is not good for men to be too much alone."

"You should meet the redoubtable Mrs. John Adams, who shares your views," said Brisson. "I had that pleasure when I landed in Boston, and I believe you and she would deal wonderfully together. She is quite in the Roman line. Calls herself Portia, I believe, in her letters."

"A bluestocking?" asked Mercy. "Her husband's in France, is he not? Have you met him?"

"No, I have not been so fortunate." He changed the subject. "To return to our outing. May I be so bold as to suggest that you two ladies bring whatever you might need for a night at Mr. Benezet's inn? I know you for a couple of experienced campaigners, and I am sure I do not need to explain that though Mrs. Arnold and Miss Shippen intend that their party should start off betimes, they may not contrive to do so."

"No, indeed," said Mercy. "It is well thought of Mr. Brisson. We will most certainly do as you suggest."

The day of the outing dawned brilliantly fine, and Mercy

and Ruth, at least, were ready when Brisson called for them. If Ruth had been slightly surprised by the extent of Mercy's packing, she said nothing about it. Mercy's whim was law to her.

"That's good. You remembered." Brisson handed the portmanteau to his groom. "If you will take my advice, ladies, we will not set off for a while. I took a turn by the Arnold house on my way here, and Mrs. Arnold will not be ready this hour or more. Her husband has business to see to before they set forward."

"He is coming too?" Mercy was surprised to find how much she had hoped that General Arnold would find himself too busy to join the party.

"Oh, yes, a most devoted spouse."

In the end they had no time for more than the most cursory inspection of the scene of the bloody Battle of Germantown, and Mercy was glad of it. It seemed to her extraordinary that a party of pleasure should even be considered to such a place when everyone was waiting in increasing suspense for news of the British attack on Charleston. "I shall never understand the Philadelphians," she said to Brisson and Ruth as they left the straggling two-mile-long village of Germantown. "How can they live such a frivolous life when they know what is going on in the rest of the country?"

"Ah," said Brisson, "but do you think it is really a country, madame? Is it not rather a collection of states only held together by their hostility to Great Britain? How much did you really care down in Georgia for what was going on in New England?"

"Well." She thought about it. "A good deal, in fact. But then"—she reached out to take Ruth's hand—"we had family there."

By pushing the horses, they managed to reach Mr. Benezet's inn in time for a late dinner, which they took on a verandah looking over the wide waters of the Delaware. Since the meal had been ordered in advance, it was long and elaborate. "A very different matter from our commons the last time we were on this road," said Brisson, toasting Mercy and Ruth.

"Yes, indeed. How well I remember those tough, raw beefsteaks. And how glad I was of them at the time." Mercy was finding it difficult to keep up her part in the light-

hearted conversation. Was this party really the prelude to a
dangerous voyage to France? It seemed impossible. The
way things were going, there would be no time, when they
had finished dinner, for anything but a return by the way
they had come.

But General Arnold had suddenly pushed back his chair
and walked over to the edge of the screened verandah. "The
day's wasting," he said. "Who's for a turn down the Trenton road before we start for home? We've not shown the
ladies nearly enough of the garden of America."

His wife seconded this proposal with enthusiasm, remembering a particularly beautiful view of the river a few
miles farther on, but Nancy Shippen looked grave and said
her mother had urged her not to be too late, and the other
members of the party also decided to start home at once
for fear of being benighted. In the end only the Arnolds
and Mercy's party set out to look for the beautiful view.

"I'm glad there is a moon," said Ruth, who had, Mercy
thought, looked unhappy while the question was being discussed. As well she might. It seemed an odd enough venture, with the heat already out of the afternoon and a
three- or four-hour drive still between them and Philadelphia.

Peggy Arnold had given Brisson careful instructions as
to how they would find the side road that led to her beautiful view, where, it was agreed, they would stop and drink
a glass of wine, provided, for a handsome consideration,
by Mr. Benezet. They all started out together, but the
Arnold carriage was drawn by four horses and soon pulled
ahead and, gradually, out of sight.

"Mercy," said Ruth.

"Yes, dear?" They were just entering a little wood, and
Mercy had a sudden memory of the wood where they had
first met Brisson.

"Do let us turn back. It's very late, and we are getting
nearer New York all the time. And I don't care what you
say, I cannot like Mrs. Arnold or her husband. I wish we
had gone home with Miss Shippen. I don't think Mother
would have liked us going on."

Mercy looked at Brisson. Suddenly this whole venture
seemed merest madness. What did she know about him?
What right had she to draw Ruth into such an escapade
without even consulting her? She was both ashamed of

herself and, most unusually for her, frightened. "Ruth, you must trust me." But why should she? "May I tell her?" She looked back to Brisson.

"Tell me what? Mercy, what's happening? What have you done?" And then, on a rising note: "Why are we stopping?"

"We change carriages here," said Charles Brisson.

# XIV )&⸺

Τ he mob was out again last night." Price had brought
Hart's breakfast to his room, as Mr. Purchis had ordered.
"Played hell in Moorfields, they say. An Irish Catholic district, but harmless enough, poor things. Mr. Malo, the silk
merchant, sent message after message to the Lord Mayor,
asking for troops, but that old bastard Kennet would do
nothing. In the end it was sheer luck the mob decided to
go home without doing much damage. Shall I pour your
tea, sir?"

"Thank you. What's happening today?"

"It's quiet, sir, so far. Well—Sunday. Please God it
remains so."

All morning Hart prowled about his room, racking his
brains, searching for some way, some faintly honourable
way out of his appalling dilemma. If he had really compromised Julia so fatally, he owed her marriage. He, a married man. And yet—it had been her suggestion that they
stay at the Bonds'. He could not understand it. She was
thoughtless, he knew, a madcap, of course, but surely she
would not knowingly have compromised herself. Unless . . .
He had sometimes thought she had a special look for him.
Could it really be a case of *All for Love, or The World
Well Lost* with her? Cockscomb to be thinking like this, but
what else could he think?

And nothing altered the fact that he was a married man.

166

For good or ill, nothing Busby or Purchas had said could shake his conviction of this. Bougainville and his officers, who had witnessed the ceremony, might be scattered to the winds, but that did not affect his position or Mercy's. Even if, horribly, the story about her and the French Minister in Philadelphia should prove true, he was still her husband. Her cuckolded husband? He would not believe it.

But why was she in Philadelphia? And why, most important of all, had she not written to him? He longed to talk to someone, but there was nobody. His feelings about Julia were not something he could discuss with Dick. Did Dick feel that? Was that why he was keeping away from him? Or had his father told him to keep away? He had looked hagridden, desperate, the day before, when he came to the Bonds' house. Not the Bonds. It remained incredible that they were not married and that knowing this (she must have known), Julia had taken him to that unlucky party of theirs. More and more he realised that he understood nothing about these English, about the way they lived their lives. He was not even sure that he wanted to.

And yet, when Price brought him his dinner tray and he saw the little folded note on it, his heart leapt up. Someone wanted to get in touch with him. Someone cared.

It was from Julia:

*Hart, I have just learned what my father is trying to do to you—to do to us. Dear Hart, I am so sorry. We must talk, you and I. I will not let this happen to you. Say nothing, do nothing, agree nothing, but meet me at Vauxhall tomorrow night. I will be* alone [*heavily underscored*]. *I can think of nowhere else safe for us to talk. Price will help you get away from the house.*
    *Ever your* cousin, *Julia*

Vauxhall. He did not like it. But then he did not like any of it. What was there to like? The very fact that Julia was behaving so well simply made his position with regard to her more unbearable. What in the world could he do? And the answer, of course, was that he owed it to Julia to do anything he could that she should ask him.

Mr. Purchas sent for him early next morning. "I trust you have reconsidered your position," was his uncompromising greeting.

"I am more sorry than I can say . . ." Hart began.

"Then don't say it. Don't waste my time with your idiocies. Don't make me angrier than I am already. I have news for you, young man, news that makes me wish Dick had never met you. If it were not for Julia, I'd turn you out of doors this minute, to take your chance of the Tower."

"The Tower? I do not understand you, sir."

"A fine fool's paradise you've been living in! Well, let me make a few things clear to you. To begin with, the mob was out again last night. Burned down Mr. Malo's house in Moorfields and every Catholic chapel in the district. And it's spreading; I'm told there was looting and burning in other parts of the city too . . . Fires all over . . . And the soldiers just standing by, waiting for the Riot Act to be read . . . And no magistrates to read it. God knows what will happen tonight. It begins to seem that it is all an immense conspiracy, aimed at overthrowing not just Lord North's government but Parliament itself, everything we Whigs believe in, setting up God knows what kind of revolutionary state. *Now* do you understand?"

"I hope not."

"Hope! Bah! I'd start fearing if I were you. Who has the greatest stake in a revolution here in England? Who but you damned American revolutionaries! Even the French, though they are our old enemies, have some sort of decent government, some respect for authority. For law and order. What can one expect from a pack of rascally radicals like you but this kind of underhand conduct? Fomenting violence, hoping for revolution, plotting it! There is something very strange about these riots. Why does the mob suddenly appear in one district or another unless someone is giving them orders? And why are the magistrates so slow to take action unless someone is bribing them? Answer me that, Hart Purchis."

"I only wish I could. But there is something both terrifying and unpredictable about a mob. It is as if it had a life of its own."

"Setting up for an expert now, are you? Well, I warn you, the word in town is that it is you Americans have plotted this whole business, and you will pay dearly for it when it is over, as, pray God, it will be soon. In the meanwhile, you need all the friends you can find. Were it not for Julia, I'd have you in the street already. As it is, you shall have until tomorrow morning to consider your position. I'd think hard, if I were you. You can kiss your exchange good-bye, to start off with. So—you are still bound by the terms of your parole. To Dick's custody! There's a good joke if ever there was one. Talk about the blind leading the blind!"

"What do you mean, sir?"

"That Dick's in black disgrace. You did not ask, I take it, why he was sent for to the Admiralty the other day?"

"No?" Hart was ashamed to remember that he had not done so and remembered Dick's haggard look. "What's happened?" he asked. "I hoped it was a ship at last."

"A ship! I should rather think not! Dick's had his last command. He's been at the Admiralty all weekend, being questioned about that crazy story you and he invented between you."

"That what?"

"The Canterbury Tale about you and the madman. How you saved Dick's ship! It always sounded havey-cavey to me, and it seems some of the crew told a very different story—one of attempted mutiny. Yes, I see you blench, and well you may. However you may come out of it, it will likely mean a court-martial for Dick. Lucky if he is just dismissed from the service! Were it not for the First Lord's friendship for our family, it might well have happened already."

Hart looked at him with blank horror. "Oh, poor Dick! And you still wish me to marry Julia?"

"What has Dick to do with anything? Of course, I do not *want* you to marry her. Think I want you for a son-in-law now? I would as soon have the devil himself. But it's not the devil that has compromised her; it's you. That will do!" He rose heavily to his feet, and Hart thought with a new qualm of conscience that the events of the last few days had aged him. "Go to your room, sir, and let me have a more rational answer in the morning. Once you and Julia are married, we can close ranks in the family. I am not entirely without influence. We Whigs hang together . . . I don't say I will be able to bring either you or Dick off scot-free, but there are ways and means. . . ."

"But, sir, whatever else you may think, you must know

in your heart that Dick would never have done anything that was not for the best interests of his country."

"He's not got a good record." Purchas looked at him sombrely. "Too lenient by a half. The punishment book shows it. Weeks without a single flogging! And not enough casualties either. It will be better for Dick if it never comes to a court-martial. He's at the Admiralty again this morning. More questions. God knows what will come of it. And all your doing. Now back to your room, sir, and think a little what you owe this family."

If he had been wretched before, Hart was desperate now. He could not even blame Mr. Purchas for wishing he and Dick had never met. He wished it himself. He seemed to have brought nothing but trouble on the relatives who had been so good to him, and welcomed him so kindly. Disgrace for Julia, court-martial for Dick—where would it end? Bitterly he felt that the Tower was probably the best place for him. And yet, thinking this, he found reason come to his rescue. He himself had always been a little anxious about the story Dick had made up to cover Grant's attempt to fire the *Sparrow*, but Dick had laughed off his doubts, secure in his inviolate position as ship's captain. And indeed, at the time it all had seemed sensible enough. As Dick had said, if he had admitted that the attempt was part of a planned mutiny, he would have had to name the other suspects. As it was, he had been able to keep them as members of his crew, carefully watched, and there had been no more trouble.

Until now. It was probably some of these very men, whom Dick had saved from the mutineer's horrible death, who had launched the accusation against him. Very likely Americans, turned members of the *Georgia*'s crew. And that brought him to the part of Purchas's tirade that he could not believe. Could not? Or would not? He thought it over. He could not. Inevitably he had met several Americans in London and had even visited the New England Coffee House, where the Loyalists met, in the hopes of getting news of Abigail's love, his old friend Giles Habersham. And the significant thing about that was that it had been possible. The passions that raged so high back in America seemed to cool in the temperate British climate. The Loyalists he met were mostly concerned with their vain attempts to get anything like adequate compensation for their losses out of the dilatory British government. And the Patriots? Well, they did not seem like Patriots. He thought of John Trumbull, son of the only Colonial Governor to take the Patriot side at the outbreak of the Revolution. Young Trumbull was in England now, studying art under Benjamin West, despite the fact that he had served with distinction in the revolutionary army. Hart had met him at Lady Garrard's house, and they had talked not about war or even home, but about the exhibition of paintings at Somerset House and Benjamin West's latest historical picture.

No, he absolutely refused to believe that the Americans in London had anything to do with the riots. And another thing, if there had been an American plot of the kind Purchas had suggested, he himself would most certainly have been approached about it. But that was small comfort considering his other problems. He was glad that he had tacitly consented to meet Julia at Vauxhall. He was ashamed now of that absurd suspicion of her. Vainglorious fool that he was, why should he imagine that she cared a rush for him? Surrounded by more eligible cavaliers, she very likely had a special glance for each of them. And as for staying at the Bonds', she was not a strong woman like Mercy; she had very likely been panicked by the violence she had seen and had not thought beyond the immediate danger. But now that she understood their position, she would advise him; she would know what he should do. In so much misery, it was a small miracle that he had her for ally and friend. Mr. Purchas was right, he thought. She was wiser than either of her brothers.

Price brought him his dinner early. "The master's gone out, sir. Dines at his club, and Mr. Dick's never come home. The mistress has one of her heads and Miss Julia dines out too. I'm to see you out by our entrance after you've dined. You won't mind it, sir?"

"Mind? Good God, no!" Hart had seen the folded note on his tray and was impatient to be alone. It was short:

*Hart. Vauxhall's too dangerous, with the mob still in the streets. Meet me at Cornelys's Rooms at nine. Wear the domino and mask Price will give you, and ask the man at the door for Mr. Fraser's party. I long to talk to you. J.*

He put the note in his pocket and sipped thoughtfully at the wine Price had poured for him. Cornelys's Rooms. He had gone there with Julia the first time they had gone out together and had not much liked the place. For all its elegance, there had been something faintly raffish about both the rooms and the company. But Mrs. Cornelys's establishment did have the advantage of being in Soho Square, an easy walk from Charles Street. And Price had told him that apart from Parliament and one visit to Lord George Gordon's house in Welbeck Street, the mob seemed to be keeping away from the fashionable West End of town.

He absentmindedly poured more wine and ate a little of the dry cold beef that had been sent up for him, thinking wryly that the kitchen must be fully aware that he was in disgrace. But Price, arriving half an hour later with domino and mask, was friendly enough. "You've eaten nothing." He looked at the tray. "I'm afraid we are all to pieces belowstairs with the mistress so poorly." He refilled Hart's glass. "Would you wish me to call you a chair, sir?"

"No, thanks, I'll walk. What's the word of the mob tonight?" Extraordinary that he had actually forgotten about the rioters for a while.

"Bad, sir. I reckon you'd be safer walking. Not that you're likely to meet them at this end of town, but it's been a strange day, and no mistake. With Parliament not sitting because of the Birthday celebrations there's been no line taken, no statement made; it seems as if the mob is to have everything its way. I don't like it." He leant closer to Hart. "It's almost as if it was planned."

"Planned?"

"For a time when Parliament wasn't sitting. The long Birthday weekend with nothing done and the mob getting more and more out of hand. There's a lot of talk in the streets."

"What kind of talk?"

"About people spiriting up the mob, giving it orders. Oh, not Lord George Gordon; everyone knows about him, only six in the shilling there. But other people, secret people . . ."

"Americans?"

Price looked uncomfortable and filled up Hart's glass. "Well, sir, it would be a lie to say I hadn't heard that. But

I don't believe it, nor do any of the rest of us belowstairs. Nor yet I don't think it's the frogs, neither. Frankly I don't think neither the one nor t'other of you has the power to stir up so much trouble, not here in London. But our local bad'uns, that's something else again. Just out for loot, as you might say, and anything else that might chance to come their way."

"Just for loot? But that's horrible!"

"So's the way most of London lives. Gin, and mud, and rags. And more gin, to make you forget the mud. Do you know how I came to be Mr. Dick's man, sir?"

"No?"

"I was a slum child, but happy. Our mother loved us; she worked like a dog, laundering to keep us all. When I was a boy, maybe ten, something like that—we didn't have birthdays, not in our family—I swept a crossing here in the West End. One day an old gentleman dropped his pocket handkerchief as he crossed the road. I picked it up and gave it back to him. "Keep it," said he. "It stinks of mud." Well, that was riches for me. I couldn't wait to tell my mum. Only—I never did. A little later there was a great crowd on the crossing, and a cry of 'Stop thief.' Someone stopped me —well, a crossing sweeper, of course. They found the handkerchief. Nothing I could say. Nothing my mum could do. When they gave me the choice of the navy or transportation for life, I took the navy. And a good day for me. I met Mr. Dick. He made me his servant; made a man of me. And—got me out of the navy, God bless him."

"And your mother?"

"When I got back, after seven years, she was gone—just gone. That's what happens to the poor. That's why you can't expect us to behave like other people."

"I wish you would drink a glass of wine with me," said Hart.

"Oh, no, sir, I couldn't. But thank you just the same for asking. Will you be wearing the domino?"

"No, I think I'll carry it."

"That's just what I was going to suggest. Nothing to make you look out of the way, just in case you should meet the mob, which I pray God you don't."

The conversation had made Hart a little later in starting than he had meant to be, though he knew Julia well enough, by now, to know that when she said nine, what she meant was nine-thirty or even ten. But that did not excuse him from punctuality, and he was angry with himself when he looked at his watch, by the flickering light of a tallow dip in the sinister basement hallway used by the servants, and saw that it was already just on nine o'clock. The mask was in his pocket; the domino over his arm. "No time to waste," he said to Price. "I'm late."

"Never you mind, sir." Price pushed back the heavy bolt on the area door. "Miss Julia will be later. Lord, look at that." He had opened the door on the flash of steel and the gleam of lanterns. "Soldiers, at last."

"But why? Why here?"

"Mr. Burke's house," he explained. "Down the street. I did hear talk. Mr. Hart, if you are going . . ." He was eager to close the door.

"Yes, of course. So long as it's not here."

"Oh, no, sir," said Price. "There's nothing for the mob here."

Emerging into the Haymarket, Hart found it full of an idle, drifting crowd. Not the usual fashionable loungers, though here and there a sedan chair or a carriage was making a rather cautious way among the loose knots of shabbily dressed people. "Ten o'clock," said a voice at his elbow, and he turned round sharply, but saw that the speaker had his back to him. "Burke's house." The man had not noticed Hart. "Crowbars." He spoke like a gentleman. "Time we put a scare into this end of town. Pass it on."

Hart moved away, thinking furiously. He ought to report what he had heard, which seemed clear evidence of planning behind the riots. But to whom could he report it, and more important still, what chance had he of being believed? Besides, he was late already for his meeting with Julia. She would know what to do. He hurried up the Haymarket, consoling himself with the knowledge that the soldiers had already been alerted and were waiting for the mob at Mr. Burke's house. He and Julia would have to stay longer than he quite liked at Mrs. Cornelys's Rooms. It would be madness to return to Charles Street until well after the inevitable confrontation between the mob and the soldiers.

He reached Soho Square, rather breathless, as a church clock struck the quarter, and paused under a tree to put on his domino and mask. It was quiet here, he was glad to see, except for a carriage drawn up to let a couple of young men go swaggering into the rooms. Quiet here, but listening, he could hear a low roar from the direction of Seven Dials. The mob congregating in the Haymarket was not the only one out tonight. Were there quiet men, quiet gentlemen, all over the city, directing operations? It was a thought to make the blood run cold.

"Mr. Fraser's party?" said the doorman. "Yes, sir. Bill" —he snapped a finger at a plush-clad page boy—"take the gentleman to number five."

The rooms were crowded tonight, the tone even more strident than Hart remembered it, and he was relieved when the boy led him upstairs, past the entrance to the main saloon, and through the curtained doorway that led to a further flight of stairs. Perhaps things were conducted more decorously in the upper rooms.

It was certainly quieter up there. The stairway gave onto a long corridor, discreetly lighted, with numbered doors to left and right. Pausing as the boy knocked on the door marked "Five," Hart heard a scuffle and a giggle from across the hall. This was no place to be meeting Julia. He was appalled that she even knew of its existence.

"Not here yet." The boy flung open the door and lit the candles in a chandelier beside it to reveal a luxurious living room. Heavy red velvet curtains; a supper table laid for two, with a three-branched candlestick. "Shall we serve when the lady comes?" He poured a glass of claret from a ready opened bottle.

"Yes. Yes, thank you." Horribly sure of the kind of assignation for which this room must normally be used, Hart was relieved that the only furnishings were the table, two chairs facing each other across it, and two others set back beside the curtained window. He was jumping to absurd conclusions again. He knew so little about England, about English customs. "Thank you," he said again, and nervously overtipped the boy.

Left alone, he sat down, sipped claret, and argued with himself. With her reputation already at risk, Julia would never have arranged to meet him here if there had been anything dubious about the place. He must quite simply be imagining things. Disgusting to do so. What kind of mind had he? Now he remembered, hot with shame, how he had jumped to conclusions about the club Mercy had run in his house in Savannah. If only I had had a father, he thought, or an elder brother. Instead, there had been Francis, always so worldly-wise, mocking, hinting, suggesting . . . Francis, whom he had killed. He shook his head as if to clear it, then got up, took off his domino and mask and laid them on a chair. Strange to be thinking of Francis now.

The claret was good. He poured more and looked hungrily at the table. He had known Julia would be late but found himself increasingly impatient for her arrival. Where had she been dining? he wondered. Suppose she should encounter the mob. He must tell her about that sinister man in the Haymarket. Maddening that all English gentlemen's voices sounded much the same to him. Otherwise, he would really have thought he had heard that one somewhere before. Absurd, of course. His mind was running away with him tonight, out of control. What am I going to do, he asked himself; what in God's name am I going to do?

It was almost a quarter to ten. Would the mob be assembled now in Charles Street? Ten o'clock, the man had said. Suppose Julia had decided to go back home before she came here? Buy why should she have? If he had known where she was dining, he could have called for her. How little I know about her, he thought; how little I know about any of them.

A knock on the door. "Come in." The same boy, ushering in Julia, almost unrecognisable in domino and mask.

"We'll ring when we want you." She dismissed the boy and turned to Hart. "I'm late, dear Hart, forgive me." She dropped mask and domino, revealing a low-cut gown of a material that changed under the light from darkest green to flickering blue. Her dark hair was unpowdered, and he remembered telling her how much he preferred it that way. "I am setting a new style." She smiled at him. "Do you like it?"

"More than I can say." As he seated her, her hand brushed against his and a flame shot through him. "But, Julia . . ." It was difficult not to look at what the dress revealed.

"I know." She smiled up at him and pushed luxurious dark ringlets from her face. "We are met here on serious business, and will come to it directly, but first, pour me a glass of wine, Cousin, and tell me that whatever my family try to do to you, you and I will remain friends."

"Dear Julia!" Drinking to her, he wished it was his first glass of the evening. Could his head really be swimming a little? Absurd.

"Dear Hart." She put her elbows on the table and leant her chin in her hands. "You are not to be looking at me like that, or you will distract me from the sober things I must say to you. You must not let yourself be entangled in my family's disaster."

"Disaster?"

"I begin to fear so. As if George's debts were not bad enough, now there is this terrible business about Dick. I suppose my father has told you?"

"I cannot believe it."

"I am afraid you must. But do not, I beg of you, be blaming yourself. Dick's always been a fool—oh"—she amended it—"the kindest, best creature in the world, but no more sense . . . My friends had warned me often enough that no good would come of those wild ideas of his. Lord George Gordon was the same. He wanted to reform the navy. Look what's happened to him! If it had not been you, Hart, it would have been something else with poor Dick. The Lords of the Admiralty know it all; they know he's never had enough casualties. He should have gone into the church."

"You mean—" Her father had said very much the same thing. "A man's success in your navy is based on the number of his own men he gets killed?"

"Well." She smiled her ravishing smile. "If no one gets killed, there must be something odd, must there not? But that's not what we are here to talk of. It's your position I care about. I think you should ask to have the terms of your parole changed."

"Changed?"

"Away from Dick. To Piers Blanding maybe. I asked him tonight. He said he would do it—for me."

"No!" He refilled their glasses. "That's not what we are here to talk about. What happens to me does not matter; it is you we are concerned with. Or—are you telling me?" He paused for a moment, digesting an extraordinary mixture of flaming jealousy and fierce relief. "Are you and Blanding—?"

"To be married! Oh, Hart, what a child you are, what a dear child. One can't help loving you for it. No one is going to marry me now; I'm to lead apes in hell. Don't look like that." She put out a finger to stroke away his frown. "We are met to face facts, you and I, and the fact of my position is that my dowry's gone with George's gambling, and my good name with Dick's disgrace. George's being caught with the Mohawks was bad enough—and now this! If I found a Croesus who would marry me without a penny, he would still balk at the connection. Bad enough to be a Whig, but to be a discredited one! Had you not noticed that I have not been able to take you to Devonshire House? That Mr. Walpole never did send that invitation to see his Strawberry Hill? I'm sure you have, but been too courteous to speak of it. English society's a small, tight circle, Hart, and heaven help the outcasts."

"An outcast? You?" But it made horrible sense.

"You're seeing it now, aren't you? The Bonds . . . Having to meet you here . . . My mother's ill; really ill this time; it's all been too much for her. When she is better, she and I are going down to the country. Once there, I shall put away my finery." A loving hand stroked the shimmering silk. "I shall learn backgammon and cribbage, take soup to the village sick, and, if I am very lucky, go into a decline and die young, of mere boredom."

"Julia! I won't believe it. It can't be true. You, so beautiful, so full of life. With all your admirers. There must be something—"

"Open another bottle, Hart. It's sad work, this. There must be something, you say. Well—I could beg you to buy me a passage to India. I'd be bound to snap up one of John Company's clerks there before I died of the heat. Or—do you see me as a governess, Cousin?" She smiled at his expression. "No need to try. If Dick's court-martialled, no respectable family would have me."

"I think I hate England. Julia, you must come back to America with me." The words filled him with terror as he spoke them.

"Dear Hart, as what?"

"As my cousin and dear friend. Our society's not mean-minded like yours—"

"You'd find me a husband?" Her eyes were huge with tears. She brushed them away patiently. "We're here to talk sense, Hart, not build dream castles. You're a prisoner, in danger of the Tower. It's you we should be thinking about.

As for me, I'm past praying for. I'm a proud woman, Hart; there's only one way I'd come to America with you."

"Julia!" How could he help taking her hand? "If only—" He was ashamed as he said it.

"Oh, ifs!" She rose gracefully from the table and moved over to tug at the bellpull by the door. "Let us eat and drink, for tomorrow we part."

"Tomorrow! You're really going?"

"I know now that I must. I've tried so hard to be strong for us both. I don't think I can keep it up much longer." She turned at a knock on the door. "At once, if you please," she told the page boy. Then, back to Hart: "So now, Cousin, let us make merry together on my last evening of London. I'm glad I am to spend it with you."

"Dearest Julia." He had thought he was hungry, but now the food choked him, and he was grateful for the champagne the boy had opened. "A strange thing happened to me on my way here." At all costs, he felt, he must get the conversation back to a more normal level.

"Yes?" She helped herself to lobster patties, her tone as neutral as his, and he blessed her for her understanding.

"I passed through the makings of a mob in the Haymarket." He paused to tell her about the soldiers and Mr. Burke's house, then went on. "I heard a voice in the crowd —a gentleman's voice. I almost thought I knew it. He was telling someone that they would attack Mr. Burke's house at ten o'clock. 'Crowbars,' he said. I'm sure I know the voice." For a moment he had almost had it. "But what shall I do, Julia? I must tell someone, but circumstanced as I am, who would believe me?"

"No one," she told him. "Dear Hart, even I, who love you, find it difficult. Are you quite sure you did not imagine it or, not so much imagine as misconstrue? A chance scrap of conversation, heard in a crowd? Whatever you do, I beg you will tell no one else. It could do us all infinite harm."

"Harm? I don't understand you."

"Don't you see? No, of course you do not. You are so open yourself, so unsuspecting, that you do not see how it might look to other people. That story Dick told, about the firing of his ship, was not entirely true, was it? No, no"— she put a restraining hand on his—"no need to protest. I understand it all and love you both for it. But look now,

here is Dick, threatened with disgrace, and you with him.
Suppose you come forward with another story, also uncor-
roborated. Do you not see how it might be interpreted?"

"Oh, my God! You mean I must do nothing because no
one will believe me? And let the plotters plot on, who
knows what horror and destruction?"

"What else can you do? But don't look so desperate. *I*
will do something. I will see Piers Blanding in the morning.
He is a good friend. If I drop a word in his ear, he will see
that it gets to the right place. Without involving you. I
wish you would let me ask him to take charge of you."

"Dearest Julia, you must see that I cannot seem to be
abandoning Dick."

"You would be well advised to abandon us all."

"Never! Julia!" Somehow he was on his feet; somehow
she was in his arms.

"Hart! Do you understand at last?" She raised her lips
to his, confidingly, like a child.

"I understand nothing!" Only that he was kissing her,
crushing her to him, helpless with a long hunger.

Afterwards his memories were blurred. It must have been
she who pulled back the curtain, revealed the door into the
next room. But he had picked her up and carried her in and
thrown her on the bed.

# XV 🙦

I'll never forgive myself." Cold sober, Hart looked down at Julia as she lay there, naked, luxurious, satisfied.

"Oh, dear Hart." She put up a hand to touch the lips that had fed on her so hungrily. "It had to happen. It was too strong for us, that is all. We must forgive ourselves, forgive each other. I love you, Hart." She raised pouting lips.

"No! Julia, it's no use." It was almost a groan. "I'm a married man." Quite horribly, just as she yielded to him, just as they moaned together he had remembered Mercy's body, the feel of it, the difference. . . .

"Married! Oh, my dear Hart! To the woman who's the toast of Philadelphia! Who does not even trouble to write to you!" She raised herself a little in his arms, and a hard nipple brushed his chest. "Hart!"

"No!" he said again, and began gently but firmly to disengage himself. "I'm sorry, Julia, more sorry and ashamed than I can say. I must take you home." He picked up his shirt and breeches. "I'll leave you to dress."

In the other room the candles had been snuffed, the table cleared, and a new bottle and glasses set ready. He looked at them with disgust as he put on his clothes. All part of the expected service. How many other men had Julia met here, for the same purpose, and had she really thought he

181

would not know? What an innocent she must have thought him. He felt sick with shame. A drunken fool; a sot . . .

She joined him as he was tying his cravat, exquisite as always. Even this disgusted him now. Did English ladies have special clothes that took off easily? And was that why she had worn her hair unpowdered? All planned, all carefully planned . . .

Like the riots. What in the world had put that idea into his head? "We must be going," he said. "It's late. Put on your domino and mask."

"Why should I? Dear Hart, I am proud to be seen with you. You must not blame me because I love you so much. I cannot help myself. You are my fate. I knew it the first time I saw you. Here, let me—" She reached up to the cravat with which he was still fumbling. "You're making a terrible botch of that."

"Julia, I tell you, no!" He finished tying the cravat. "If you wish me to take you home, you will put on your domino and mask this instant and come with me now." He put on his coat as he spoke, wrapped himself in his own domino, and picked up hers.

"Oh, so masterful." She smiled up at him over her shoulder. "You will make me fall in love with you all over again." But he had turned from her to pull the bellrope and demand the reckoning.

"And call a chair," he said as he paid the bill, which was even higher than he had expected.

The chairmen did not want to take Julia to Charles Street. "Mob's out down there, sir."

"Still?" He had hoped that the streets would be quiet by now.

"Making a night of it, by all accounts."

"What shall we do?" Julia was clinging to his arm. "I'm frightened, Hart! I can't stand anything more. Take me to the Bonds." Her voice rose. "I can't face the mob. Or my mother. Take me to Susan!"

"But we met the mob there last time."

"It never strikes twice. Like lightning. Then you can leave me there, Hart Purchis, and be quit of me." She was close to hysteria.

"Best get the lady home," said one of the chairmen. "Where to, sir?"

"Is the mob out between here and Lincoln's Inn Fields, do you know?"

"Not that I've heard of. They did their business there the other night, by what I hear."

"Very well. We'll go there. I'll walk beside the chair."

It was not so late as he had thought. But at least here the streets seemed quiet enough, though he could hear the horrible, too familiar roar of the mob from somewhere south of them, nearer the river, and saw the sky red in that direction. A sporadic outburst of shooting suggested that the soldiers must be out and actually going into action. In Charles Street perhaps? Should he have taken Julia back there? He knew, suddenly, that he could not face it. She would tell her father and mother what had happened. The pressure to a mad, bigamous marriage would become intolerable. He was a coward—he knew himself for one—but he was not going back there. He would find himself a lodging for the night. Things would look better in the morning. They could hardly look worse.

They were approaching Great Queen Street where he heard shouting ahead. The chairmen stopped and put down the chair. "Sorry, sir. They're ahead of us after all. You and the lady will be better on foot."

"On foot!" Julia leant out of the chair. "I never heard such impudence. Tell them to go on, Hart. The mob won't hurt us; why should they?"

"Sorry, ma'am." The spokesman opened the chair door. "You can risk your life if you fancy to; we're not risking the chair. It's our bread and butter, see? Take you back, if you like." He turned to Hart. "Charles Street, did you say? Might be clear by now. Ten o'clock was the word there."

"The word? What do you mean?"

"Nothing, I'm sure. You take a man up so short. Not Charles Street then." He reached up an ungentle hand and pulled Julia out of the chair.

"Bumpkin!" she exclaimed. "Hart—" She swayed towards him, and he had to support her, but his whole attention was for the chairmen.

"Who told you the mob would be in Charles Street at ten?" he asked.

"Why, no one, sir, how should they?"

And while Hart was still helplessly encumbered with

Julia, they picked up the chair, turned smartly to the right-about, and vanished back down the dark street without even waiting to be paid. If it had not been for Julia, he would have gone after them, tried to hold them as evidence that the mobs were being directed, but she was sobbing now, clinging to him. "I'm frightened! Take me to Susan."

"Very well." No hope of catching the men now. "Keep quiet if we have to pass through the mob. There is no reason why they should molest us."

"Or why they should not." She clung to him, trembling, and he could feel nothing but impatience with her. "I wish we had blue cockades," she went on. "Why did I not think of it? But you will cry, 'No Popery,' if they ask you to?"

"No." He pulled her forward toward the sound of the mob. Emerging warily into Great Queen Street, he saw it entirely filled with the now familiar torch-bearing, chanting crowd. "Nothing for it but to pass through them," he told her in a low voice. "Hold tight to my arm." Was it mad to venture? Well, if it was, he was mad. He wanted more than anything in the world to be rid of her, to escape. . . . He began, very carefully, very quietly to try to gentle their way through the shouting, chanting groups of people. Some had torches; some had crowbars; some were carrying an extraordinary variety of loot, fitfully illuminated by the tossing flares. An old, bent man hugged an armful of clothes; a boy carried a pair of fire tongs as if they had been a rifle; a young girl clutched a huge pie and bit at it as she walked. And everywhere was the smell of people and of spirits.

"Faugh!" said Julia.

"Hush." He tightened his grip on her arm, sensing a change in the movement of the crowd. When they had joined it, it had been making a fairly purposeful way up towards Kingsway. Now, from somewhere ahead, eddies of uncertainty seemed to be building up.

"Soldiers," said a voice, and, "Back," said another. "High Holborn's blocked." And then, buzzing through the crowd, came the words "Leicester Fields" and "Sir George Savile." And gradually, strangely, the crowd began to move again in the other direction.

Hart had an uncomfortable feeling that Julia's exclamation of disgust had been noticed and resented by the people immediately around them and thought it wise to go with the

tide of humanity for a little while, hoping to be able to
edge their way gradually into one of the side streets by
which they could get through to Lincoln's Inn Fields. But
Julia had her handkerchief to her face. "Faugh," she said
again. "The stink! Get me out of this, Hart, or I will faint."

"Gentry," said a voice beside them. "A gentry mort as
don't like the honest stink o' man. Faint, she will. Shall us
give her something to faint about, brothers?"

At the words the crowd solidified into a threatening circle
round them. A torch, thrust dangerously close, singed
Hart's cheek, and illuminated them for their tormentors. A
scarecrow of a woman reached out to pluck off Julia's
mask. "Look at the doxy then. And the swell cove, too!
Catholics, are you?" The crowd around them gave a growl.
"Bloody foreigners? Looking for that chapel of yours? She
has a foreign look, the doxy, don't she?"

"Not at all." Hart flung back the hood of his domino and
faced the woman. "We're as Protestant as you are. The
lady is English. Speak to them, Julia. Let them hear your
voice."

"Of course I'm English." Julia seemed to have forgotten
fear in rage. "And a better Englishwoman than any of you
scum. Now let me pass, please."

For a moment Hart actually thought it would work, that
the crowd were so trained to give way to the imperious
accents of the upper class that they would do so now. But
the woman who had first spoken barred the way, arms
akimbo. "Scum, is it? We'll show you scum. And you too,
pretty boy, who ain't English whatever you try to pretend.
Your talk gives you away, dirty foreigner."

The surrounding circle moved a step closer. "I'm an
American." Hart raised his voice in a last effort to hold
them. "A fighter for liberty. I won't cry, 'No Popery,'
friends, but I'll cry, 'God save George Washington,' and I
hope you'll join me!"

To his surprise and slight dismay, the crowd instantly
burst into a very free rendering of his words, to the tune
of "God Save the King." And at the same time an impatient ripple came down from the direction of Kingsway.
"Time's a-wasting," said a voice.

"On to Leicester Fields," said another.

And, "No violence, he says no violence," said someone

quite close to Hart, apparently to the woman who had questioned him.

"Oh, get along with you"—she gave Hart a push—"and take your woman with you, though it's more than she deserves. Scum indeed!" As she spoke, she was swept away in the southwards movement of the crowd, and Hart seized the change to guide Julia across the road and into Kingsway.

They found the Bonds' house brilliantly illuminated, as the mob demanded, but it took some time before they could make anyone open the door. At last, Bond himself leant out of an upstairs window in nightcap and dressing gown, identified Julia with a squeak of dismay, and came down to open the door. "Can't take any chances," he said apologetically as Julia subsided into his arms. And then to Hart: "You're not coming in?"

"No," said Hart. "You and Mrs. Bond will take care of her, I know. Good-bye, Julia. Forgive me." And before she could retrieve herself from her pretended swoon, he turned and got himself safe back into the dark entrance of Duke Street. Where now? Most certainly not back to the Purchas house. He paused in the shadows, away from the street's one inadequate light, and listened to the roar of the mob, still surging down Great Queen Street. Someone had been controlling them. Everything pointed to that. The change of direction had not happened spontaneously; word had been passed down from what had been the head of the unruly procession. So—whoever was in fact in command must be quite near now. He wrapped his domino more closely round him and insinuated himself quietly back into the milling, chanting crowd. The group who had tormented him and Julia should be well away by this time, and he had noticed other men in evening dress here and there among the rioters. It was only Julia's folly that had drawn the mob's attention to them. By himself, he should be safe enough.

Mad to be doing this. But he was mad tonight. And he could not shake off the strange feeling that he had known the man whose voice he had heard in the crowd earlier that evening. If he could only hear it again . . . A chance in a million, but one he felt he must take. In some curious way he felt it to be connected with Julia and all that disaster. Or was he merely clutching at straws, trying to make himself forget his own shameful behaviour? Either way he found himself moving down Great Queen Street, an un-noticed member of the mob. When they passed houses that had been looted in the previous day's rioting, the crowd stopped to give them three ironical cheers, but each time a new ripple flowed forwards through the crowd, and the words "Leicester Fields" and "Sir George Savile" passed from mouth to mouth. He thought that whoever was mas-terminding the riot must be behind him still and tried to slow his pace, but found it too dangerous. The only way to escape notice was to move with the tide.

When they reached Drury Lane, he could see a glow ahead, over the heads of the mob, and as they poured down Long Acre and spread into Leicester Fields, they were more and more clearly illuminated by the light of the huge bon-fire that burnt in front of Sir George Savile's house. "Too late," said a disgusted voice behind him.

And, "Look," said another, "the troops!"

The house itself still stood, with all its windows broken and its front door hanging ajar on broken hinges, but now Hart could see the glint of steel, the gleam of epaulettes in the savage firelight, as the Guards took over.

Now a new catchword was echoing through the crowd: "Rainforth." And, "Clare Street." He pushed his way back towards Long Acre, trying to see who had started it going but again found it difficult and dangerous to move against the crowd and made slow work of it. He ought to be carrying something; everyone else had a bit of booty or a weapon. He picked up a piece of wood from the road and, as he did so, noticed something. People with booty were detaching themselves from the mob and moving southwards towards the dark shape of St. Martin's-in-the-Fields.

He followed them quietly, clutching the bit of wood as if it had value. It was darker as he moved away from the great bonfire, and he was able to watch unobserved as one after another the men paused by a big old-fashioned car-riage that was standing in a dark corner by the church. They leant in at the carriage window, said something, and came away empty-handed. Or—not entirely so? One of them was muttering as he came back past Hart, "Six-pence!" angrily to himself. "Risk my life for sixpence! I'll see you damned first."

"Is that all you got?" Hart took his own purse out of his pocket. "Maybe I'll keep this myself, if so."

"I would," said the other man. "A paltry sixpence for a bit of plate I'd have hung for. Word was, pay was good! Good!" He spit loudly. "I'll prig for myself from this on."

"And so will I," said Hart. "Unless I can find the man himself and make better terms. Where is he, do you know?"

"Black George? As well ask me where the devil is! You don't know much if you don't know that." He gave Hart a sharp sideways look. "Why may you be, asking questions? And in a damned odd voice, too!" He reached out to grab Hart.

"An American!" Hart managed to evade him. "Who doesn't want to be hanged either." He threw it back as he turned and hurried back toward Long Acre. Clearly the carriage was merely a collecting place for loot; there was no chance that the man who was organising the riots would risk himself by being seen near it.

The crowd was thinning now. The bonfire still burnt high, illuminating faces to a dangerous extent, and the Guards were fully in command of Sir George Savile's house. Hart suddenly felt too exhausted almost to move. He must find himself somewhere to spend the night. He began to work his way in the direction of Fladong's Hotel, which Dick had told him was much used by country gentlemen. Perhaps a night's sleep would help him identify that mysterious, surely familiar voice he had heard earlier that evening. Black George's voice, presumably, or that of one of his accomplices. Horrible to think that this whole unspeakable outbreak of mob violence might have been planned simply as a means to loot. Planned . . . The word caught in his mind. Something else had been planned that night; Julia had planned to entrap him and had succeeded. And thinking of her, hating himself all over again, he had it. Black George. Not George Gordon. George Purchas. His voice. Part of him had known it all the time. Known it and not wanted to admit it? Very likely. It was a horrible bit of knowledge and one he did not know how to use. He had harmed the Purchas family enough already without branding George Purchas as the worst kind of criminal. Besides, he had not a shadow of proof. Thinking it miserably over as he prepared for bed at Fladong's, he decided that the only thing he could do was confront George himself with his knowledge and hope to frighten him out of further criminal activity. A forlorn hope, but in the end it helped him to a restless, nightmare-haunted sleep.

His first problem next morning was that of funds. The staff at Fladong's had welcomed him kindly enough the night before as a fugitive from the mob, which had explained his lack of luggage for the time being, but that would do for only one night. Either he had to go back to the house in Charles Street, collect his effects, and face Mr. Purchas, or he must go to Drummond's, draw some more money, and reequip himself. Feeling himself a craven, he chose the latter course. It would be time enough to face Mr. Purchas about Julia when he had seen George and done his duty there. He was pretty sure to find George at the Cocoa Tree later in the day, but he had no idea where he actually lived.

When he set out to walk to Drummond's, the smell of smoke hung heavy in the air. Many shops had not opened, although he had slept late, and it was now towards noon. Those that had opened sported bits of blue ribbon or scrawled slogans: "No Popery" or "This is a Protestant House." People went about their business nervously, hurriedly, heads turning this way and that, comparing whispered notes about their adventures of the night before. He remembered Mercy's description of Savannah after the British took it and thought that London today felt very much like a captured city. It made him angry with himself. His knowledge about George Purchas was too vital not to be used.

Was the clerk at Drummond's less cordial than before? Probably he was imagining things, but as he pocketed the money that had been—reluctantly?—handed over, he made up his mind. The one person he could and should consult was Busby, the Purchas family's man of business. He, surely better than anyone, would be able to advise him and could be trusted to do nothing to harm the family he served.

His office was in the Strand, only ten minutes' walk from Drummond's, and Hart went there at once. Clothes and a portmanteau were of infinitely less importance. Sending in his name, he was angry and ashamed to know that he was actually afraid he would find Mr. Purchas there before him. Cowardly and absurd: Mr. Purchas did not visit his man of business; he sent for him.

Busby greeted him, after a short wait, with his usual smiling effusiveness. "Mr. Purchis! What an unusual honour. You should have sent for me. I am always most happy to wait on the family in Charles Street. It is about the settlements, may I happily assume?"

"No, you may not," said Hart. He should have expected this but was glad of the chance to make his position clear. "Mr. Busby, you know as well as I do that I am a married man."

"I know nothing of the kind," said Busby. "I have taken the liberty of talking to my friends about your—ahem— unusual situation, and they are all of the same mind. Divines and lawyers, they all agree that it is but to take a firm stand, now, at once, over that lunatic travesty of a marriage, and you will find yourself a free man. You will let me act for you? It will be a most interesting exercise."

"I most certainly will not unless you are prepared to help me prove the validity of my marriage." This was not what he had come to discuss, and he wished to be done with it as soon as possible.

It did not look as if he would succeed. "Mr. Purchis"— the man of business put his white hands together and looked at Hart reproachfully over the fingertips—"I am deeply sorry to have to say this to you, but there is more to it now than a mere matter of the validity of your marriage to that young woman who is causing such a stir in Philadelphia. There have been hopes raised, Mr. Purchis, there has been courting done, and very publicly too, and a night passed, maybe not in the wisest possible manner, at the house of a gentleman of the name of Bond and his mistress. Mr. Purchis, I put it to you that you owe your cousin something."

"You are well informed, Mr. Busby." But not, thank God, entirely up-to-date, though no doubt he would be soon enough.

"I am the family's man of business," said Busby. "Its interests are mine. Now, Mr. Purchis, be reasonable, do. We do not wish things to come to a breach of promise action, which benefits only the lawyers and makes all kinds of bad such an action, so widely publicised as it must be, would blood . . . and which could have only one outcome. No English court is going to give a damn for your French-contracted marriage. And just stop to think of the harm do to poor Mr. Dick Purchas, circumstanced as he is. Have you not done enough harm, sir?"

"If it were only that!" Hart had wondered, in the course of the last speech, whether he had been right to come to Busby with the problem of George, but this final appeal decided him. Whatever other doubts he might have about Busby, there seemed no question of the man's devotion to the Purchas family and their interests. "Mr. Busby"—he plunged into it—"it is not about Miss Julia that I am come to see you, but on something even more serious, I am sorry to say, even more closely connected with the honour and well-being of the family. Of my family, if I may call them so?" And then, as Busby nodded approval, he plunged into the story of his encounter with George and belated recognition of him. "What am I to do?" he asked when he had finished. "What in the world am I to do?"

"Nothing." Busby had heard him out in cold silence. "Unless you wish to find yourself in Bedlam. I never heard such a tale of a cock and bull. Mr. George involved with the rioters! Really, Mr. Purchis, if you wish to invent a tale that will draw attention away from your own affairs, you will need to do better than that. A voice heard by chance in a crowd, and you leap to all these conclusions. If it were not such a case with Miss Julia, I would advise her to think again."

"Pray do," said Hart. When had he stopped deluding himself that Julia loved him and started wondering why she wanted to marry him? "I'm not good enough for her, Mr. Busby," he said now. "And with Charleston under such a serious threat, I may find myself penniless any day. I wish you would put that to Miss Purchas for me. It shows me in a shabby enough light, but the sooner she recognises how I am placed, the better for us all. I thought the clerk at Drummond's looked at me doubtfully when I was there this morning. It would be a real kindness to Miss Purchas if you would explain to her the true facts of my case."

"She loves you, poor fool," said Busby. "At least for her sake, if not for your own, I trust you will refrain from repeating these slanderous lies about her brother. Yes?" A clerk had put his head round the door.

"A message from Mr. Purchas, sir. He wishes to see you most urgently."

"Thank you." He rose to his feet. "I hope you will give

me the pleasure of being the one to tell Mr. Purchas that you recognise, at last, the great honour his daughter is doing you. And if that is too much good sense to expect from you, I trust that at least you will hold your tongue. I do not propose to add to Mr. Purchas's distress by telling him this wild tale of yours, but I warn you, if I learn that you have repeated it to anyone, I will take steps, at once, to apply for a commission in lunacy. I wish you a very good day, sir."

In the street once more, Hart stood for a few moments, wretched, irresolute. He had never felt so alone in his life. Even on the prison ship in New York Harbour there had been the companionship of misfortune, a kind of society in despair. Now, burdened with guilt towards Julia and dangerous knowledge about George, he did not know where to turn. Who would believe him? Busby was right about that. A voice heard in the crowd. His word alone against George Purchas and all his friends. If he went to Sir John Fielding, the famous magistrate, he would be laughed at for his pains. He thought, in his desperation, of trying to see Lord Stormont, the Home Secretary, or even Lord George Germain, the Secretary for the Colonies, but why should they believe him more than anyone else? He bitterly regretted now that he had stayed so close to the Purchas family, that he had made no friends of his own, and yet it had been natural enough, granted the terms of his parole.

"Hart! By all that's wonderful!" Dick's voice roused him from the squirrels' cage of thought. "Are you on your way to old Busby? He's not in the office."

"No, I've seen him." Hart gripped Dick's hand hard. "He's gone to your father."

"Yes. They told me. Where I do not propose to follow him. God, Hart, but I'm glad to see you."

"Handsome of you. I seem to have been your ruin, Dick. I can't tell you how sorry I am." They had fallen into step and were walking down towards the river.

"Not your fault," said Dick. "I remember how doubtful you were about that story of mine at the time. But I was so sure. . . . Being captain, I suppose I felt like God Almighty."

"I know. One does." Hart remembered his own disaster. "What are you going to do now, Dick?"

"What I'm told. I'm off to Plymouth on the night mail

to await my court-martial. God knows how long it will be before they can assemble enough captains. Maybe that's all for the best, though I don't much fancy the waiting. But father has high hopes of his friend the First Lord and his good friends the Whigs." For once it was not a joke. "Oh, don't look so sick, man. Bit of luck I'll just be dismissed from the service. I never did like it above half."

"But what will you do if you are?"

"Turn to my first love, the land. There's a young man called Coke doing great things up in Norfolk. If he'd take me on, as steward, bailiff, anything, I think I could earn my keep."

"You won't go back to Denton?"

"After the things my father has said to me? No. I wish you would marry Julia, Hart, and look after things there."

"Dick, believe me, I can't. I'm a married man." He turned away to gaze down into the turbid river, afraid that Dick would read the guilt in his face.

"You still feel that? After the news from Philadelphia?"

"Your father told you about that?"

"Oh, yes. He's mad for the match. I confess I do not entirely see why."

"No." Hart laughed grimly. "I'm not exactly a hopeful *parti*, am I? Dick, you've been such a good friend to me. I beg you to believe me when I say it is not possible."

"Oh, I believe you," said Dick. "I lived too closely with you all those weeks on the *Sparrow* not to know that for you the sun rises and sets in your Mercy. I told Julia so, back at Denton Hall, but she doesn't listen to me much. George was always the one with her."

"George! Dick, I've got to talk to you about George. It's horrible. You might believe me. Busby would not."

"What about George?" Dick turned to face him, and Hart was shocked to see how much he had aged during the last few days.

"I heard his voice last night. In the mob. Giving orders. Dick, I think he's their leader or one of them."

"Oh, dear God," said Dick. "Impossible!" And then: "No, I can believe it. I asked a few questions, after you mentioned the Mohawks the other day. He's been on the edge of bad trouble while I've been away. Not just the Mohawks . . . the Hell Fire Club . . . talk of a highway robbery. Father managed to get it hushed up. Father really has good friends. Poor Father, what this will do to him if it's true! But, Hart, why? George is no revolutionary."

"No." This was almost the worst of all. "I'm afraid it's just for gain." He described the sinister carriage where loot was being bought at cut price and got a savage laugh from Dick.

"How like George," he said. "He never paid a fair price for anything in his life. But he must pay for this. Hart, what are we going to do? Busby did not believe you?"

"No. And I don't blame him. A man in my position."

Again Dick laughed that savage laugh, so unlike his former cheerful self. "And one in mine! Not much use our going to the authorities, Hart. They'll say it's just another made-up story. I think we will have to take care of George ourselves, don't you? It's my duty. He's my brother. He should be at the Cocoa Tree at this time of day. Shall we pay him a visit, you and I?"

"He must have accomplices," Hart warned.

"Yes, of course. But there is no way he can know that you suspect him, is there? So if you and I pay a call at the Cocoa Tree and ask him to come out to us, there is no reason for him to be suspicious. He knows I wouldn't go into that den of Tory thieves for anything."

"Tory?"

"Did you not know? He joined it to vex my father. And succeeded. He's a coward, you know, my brother George. He'll contrive against you with all his might behind your back and smile like a very Judas when he meets you."

"What are we going to do to him?"

"Frighten him out of town. With a little violence if it is necessary, but I don't think it will be." They started off through the eerily silent streets. Most of the shops were closed and the few people who were about scurried along, looking anxiously over their shoulders, on the alert for a new appearance of the mob. But the Cocoa Tree Club was open, and Dick sent in a message to his brother asking him to meet them at a neighbouring coffeehouse.

"He's not in the house, sir." The page who had taken the message returned almost at once. "Mr. Mordaunt said to tell you he and some friends have gone to look at the damage the mob did last night. They were to meet at the

Brown Bear in Bow Street, he thinks. You might find him
there if it's urgent, sir."

"Thank you." Dick tipped the boy and turned to Hart.
"Shall we look for him there? It's a tavern just across the
street from Sir John Fielding's house, which might be con-
venient if we can persuade him to turn king's evidence."

"Do you really think he might?"

"I have high hopes of it. He's always been easily led,
George; that's how he gets into trouble. If we can just
catch him before he starts drinking . . ."

"Starts?" asked Hart doubtfully, but Dick had already
turned away, and Hart followed him more out of sympathy than conviction.

He was not sure whether he was relieved or disappointed
when they reached the Brown Bear and found no George,
but Dick had the bit between his teeth by now. "We'll wait
for him," he said. "If he is meeting friends here, he is
bound to turn up sooner or later. In the meanwhile, I'm
starving. We might as well eat here as anywhere else." And
before Hart could protest, he had called a potboy and ordered lamb chops and a pint of home-brewed for them
both.

Hart, too, was hungry, but he was also extremely
anxious. How could he make Dick understand that his
brother was no longer the persuadable creature he remembered? His voice, giving orders the night before, had been
the voice of authority. This was not someone who could
be persuaded to turn king's evidence.

Eating and drinking as fast as possible, he tried to put
this to Dick, but without success. "I hope I know my own
brother," said Dick. "Of course, he's wild—he always was
—but there's no real vice in him. He's just impulsive, like
Julia. And easily bored, like her. With the right friends,
they could both go so far . . . much farther than I ever
shall. But then"—he smiled ruefully across the table at
Hart—"I don't want to. To be a country gentleman, a
happy family man, is the most of my ambition. And much
chance I seem to have of achieving it." He pulled out his
watch and consulted it anxiously. "Whatever happens, I
must not miss the night mail for Plymouth."

"No." Hart, too, was aware of time ticking away towards
a decision he must make. He had still not confessed to

Dick what had happened between him and Julia. How could he? How could he not? He had to decide what he was going to do. If he asked Dick, could he release him from the terms of his parole? And suppose Dick could do so, might he not then contrive just to disappear? Perhaps Dick would let him go with him to Plymouth, even be able to help him find a smuggler there, who would set him over to France and so start him on his way home. But had he the right to ask this of Dick, who was in so much disgrace on his account already?

"Listen!" Dick looked up at the sound of shouting outside. "It's starting again. Hart, we must find George! Before he gets into any more trouble." He looked round the now crowded room. "There's a friend of his. I'll ask him." He jumped up before Hart could protest and returned a minute later. "We missed him. I've paid the reckoning. Let's go."

"But, Dick, where?"

"He's gone down to Newgate. There's a rumour that the mob is going there to try to release the prisoners taken on Friday. George knows Akerman, the keeper of Newgate. He would never have anything to do with harm to him. If he is there, he will be trying to hold back the mob and may need help."

"But, Dick . . ." Hart protested in vain. There was no persuading Dick that George was not the man he had known before he went to sea all those years ago. Still arguing, they emerged into Bow Street, which was now ominously thronged with people, chanting and screaming as they had the night before. Already they could hear the thud of axes, the crackle of flames, and, as they approached Newgate itself, a horrible screaming.

"It's the prisoners!" exclaimed Dick. "They've fired the building. They may be burnt alive!" And then: "Dear God, there's George."

George was standing on the sill of a burnt out window, clearly illuminated against the flames behind, urging the mob on with cries of "The prisoners! We must save the prisoners!"

"You see." Dick turned to Hart almost with triumph. "He's trying to save them." And before Hart could stop him, he had plunged into the screaming, seething crowd to try to make his way to his brother.

"Dick, wait!" Hart turned at the sound of rattling chains and saw a group of escaped prisoners with streaming eyes and smoke-blackened faces. As he did so, he heard a cry from behind him. "A Papist! A Papist spy!" A savage blow struck the back of his head, and he fell to the ground unconscious among the trampling feet.

# XVI ❧

I'm frightened." Ruth had received Mercy's explanation in stunned silence, now clutched her hand in the darkness as the carriage rattled on through the night.

"Ruth, dear, so am I. If this goes wrong, I'll never forgive myself." They were alone; Brisson was riding ahead on horseback. "But when Brisson made the offer, it seemed the only thing to do. Will you forgive me?"

"I wouldn't have if you had left me behind. It's not that —never that. But . . . do you trust Charles Brisson? Well, that's stupid. Of course you must, or we would not be here. But are you right to trust him? Sometimes . . . Mercy, sometimes he looks at you in such a way . . ."

"At me? Nonsense! It's you!"

"And thinking that, you brought me? Oh, Mercy . . . But you're wrong, you know, quite wrong. It's you. It's always been you. And now we are in his power."

"He is helping me get to Hart." Was she trying to convince Ruth or herself?

"You must love Hart very much," said Ruth.

"I do. I think I always have." Tears rose in her throat as she remembered the long disaster of the *Georgia's* cruise. Would they ever have another chance?

Sensing the tears, Ruth pressed her hand and was silent. They sat there together through the slow hours of the night as the carriage swayed onwards in the dark. At last, Mercy thought, Ruth slept a little, leaning against her shoulder, breathing quietly, like a child.

"It's getting light." Ruth's voice waked her. "We'll know soon."

When the carriage halted at last, the light was growing rapidly. "We must hurry." Charles Brisson opened the door and let down the steps. "We're late for the rendezvous. Will you ladies oblige me by doing just what I tell you and saying nothing? There will be time for questions when we are safe on board ship. This way." He said something quick and unintelligible to the driver and picked up their portmanteau. "It's not far to the cove." He led the way down a sandy path.

They followed in silence through scrubby woods, horribly aware that they must be deep into British-held territory. "Ah." Mercy breathed a sigh of pure relief as they emerged from the trees and saw the misty sweep of the sea and, half-revealed, far out, a ship, apparently motionless. A muffled shout from the shore greeted their appearance. A boat was waiting there, oars shipped, ready.

The sailors spoke a language Mercy did not understand, but there was no mistaking their urgent haste as they helped the little party on board. "Hush," said Brisson.

The mist was lifting fast as they were rowed swiftly out towards the ship. It was going to be a beautiful day. They could not be very far south of New York. At any moment a British frigate might appear. Well, Mercy thought, after all, she wanted to get to England. But she wanted to get there free, a volunteer witness for Hart, not a captive. She could see the ship more clearly now, a merchantman, lightly armed, for defence only. She strained her eyes: *Amsterdam*. Dutch. Of course. The neutral Dutch. So, it dawned on her, once they were aboard, they would be safe. Or as safe as one ever was at sea.

Ruth had seen too. Her hand found Mercy's and pressed it.

"Nobody speaks English." Brisson had carried their portmanteau to the tiny cabin. "Or very little. Captain van Loon asks that you keep to your cabin except when he or I summon you up on deck. It will be dull for you, I fear."

"Dull!" said Mercy. "Monsieur Brisson, I don't know how to thank you."

"Wait until we are safely there," he said.

"Tell me." She detained him for a moment. "What will they think in Philadelphia?"

He shrugged. "That we have been captured presumably. At first, no one will know whether by the British or by one of the marauding bands that operate in the debatable ground. You know as well as I do that it could be either Cowboys or Skinners."

"Yes, indeed. The French will be anxious about you. . . ." And then: "No, absurd. Of course, they must know. And no one will care much about Ruth and me. So—a nine days' wonder."

"Something like that. Will you mind if your meals are brought to you here in your cabin? Captain van Loon does not care much for women."

"Then it is very good of him to have us, and we will do nothing we can help to inconvenience him."

"I knew you would see it like that. Send for me if there is anything you need. And now—forgive me?"

Left alone, they looked at each other. "Well!" said Mercy.

"Dear Mercy." Ruth smiled bravely. "What an adventure!"

She did not think so when they met their first high winds a few days later. Although she had grown up so near the sea, she had never been on it before and became horribly sick as soon as the ship began to feel the weather. Mercy, a hardened sailor, ministered to her as best she might but grew anxious as the days passed, the storm raged on, and Ruth still lay sick and sweating in her cot. She sent for Brisson at last, by the simple expedient of repeating his name to the grinning seaman who brought their cold, unappetising food.

"Is there a doctor on board?" she asked Brisson when he came.

"I'm afraid not." He looked past her to the cot where Ruth lay so alarmingly still. "I'll speak to the captain."

Captain van Loon recommended liberal doses of schnapps, and Mercy, increasingly anxious, agreed to let Brisson help her try to get Ruth to take some. The storm was beginning to slacken at last. Things actually stayed in their places in the tiny cabin that had become almost a battleground. It was easier to get Ruth to take the curious mixture of schnapps and cold soup that Captain van Loon recommended, and to Mercy's deep relief, the unorthodox treatment, combined with the easing of the ship's movement, seemed to make a slow but unmistakable improvement in Ruth's condition. Watching anxiously, she saw Ruth's sleep become deeper, easier. "I really think she'll do now," she told Brisson when he next tapped on the cabin door to enquire.

"Her colour is better," he agreed. "Thank God for that. But you look exhausted. When were you last on deck?"

"I don't remember." She put a tired hand to her brow. "Before the storm."

"As long as that? No wonder you look so wretched, confined here all that time. Wait here, I'll find you a boat cloak, someone to sit with Ruth. . . . It's a little quieter on deck; the air will do you good."

"Oh, yes! But—Captain van Loon?"

"Fast asleep in his cabin. He's been on deck, almost all the time, since the storm hit us. It's a sign of how much better things are that he's gone below at last to get the rest he needs."

He returned five minutes later with a heavy cloak and one of the ship's boys to sit with Ruth. "He'll call us at once if she wakes."

It was good to get away from the noise and odour of belowdecks and take great breaths of salt Atlantic air. The wind had almost fallen, but the ship was still wallowing through mountainous seas, and the deck was a scene of ordered chaos as the crew worked frantically to repair the damage wreaked by the storm. "It's too rough to walk," Brisson told her, "and we must not get in the way. We'll stand here for a while and take the air. Hold on tight!" he warned as the ship rose to a huge wave. "I can see you are an experienced sailor," he went on with approval.

"Yes, it's not my first storm." The *Amsterdam* seemed huge after the little *Georgia*. "I love the salt air." She pulled the cloak more closely round her against a scattering of spray. "Monsieur Brisson, what day of the month is it? I have clean lost track of time."

"And no wonder, down there with the deadlights on. It's the fourth of June, though it doesn't feel like it. In England they will be celebrating the King's Birthday."

"Good gracious, the Birthday! Imagine your thinking of

that. Lord, I remember the first one I celebrated in America. 1774. And the mob already on the prowl."

"Mob?" He took her up on it.

"Well—yes. Oh, Sons of Liberty, of course, but some of the things that were done in the name of liberty . . . They killed my father. The mob." She had been in deep mourning for him, that fourth of June, but Hart had made her attend the celebrations just the same. Strange to look back and remember how Francis had squired her that evening. She had thought herself in love with him. Extraordinary. "It's a long time ago," she said.

"I'm sorry. I did not mean to remind you of the sad past. It is the future we should be thinking of. I have been wanting a word with you alone."

"Yes?" She braced herself against a great swoop of the deck and against what might be coming now.

"Mrs. Purchis—Mercy!" He had never used her first name before. "I want you to promise to trust me whatever happens. To go on trusting me. It must have been hard enough already, and I admire your spirit more than I can say."

"And Ruth's," she said.

"Indeed, yes. But she has you to rely on. If you are content, if you keep calm, she will do likewise."

"That's true. It's a great responsibility. Well"—she took a firmer grip on the rigging and smiled up at him—"having trusted you so far, Monsieur Brisson, there is not much alternative now, is there?"

"You're a woman in a million! Mercy, I must say it, for my own sake. Let me tell you, just this once and never again, how deeply, how passionately I admire and love you. I think you did my business that first day when you saved my life. And then—your courage on that terrible journey, through your illness, and the transformation in Philadelphia! Dearest Mercy, there is no one in the world like you. No, don't draw away from me. There is no need. I know you too well not to know that you are body and soul devoted to that lucky husband of yours. Why else are you here today? It is selfish of me to tell you how I feel. I know it. But I am allowing myself to do so because knowing I love you, you will know how completely you can trust me. I love you better than my life, Mercy Purchis. Whatever happens, remember that."

"Oh, dear Charles." She touched his cold hand with hers. "I do thank you." Spray or tears in her eyes? "I'll always remember, be proud to have been loved by a brave man. And yes, of course, I trust you. It's true, Ruth and I were afraid, that night in the carriage. But now you have brought us so far, what is there to doubt of now?"

"I beg you will remember that. And remember, too, the promise of secrecy you made me when we first spoke of this venture. Will you reswear it now? And promise me that you will get Ruth to do the same?"

"It was a strong oath."

"It needed to be."

"I cannot speak for Ruth."

"You can promise to do your best to persuade her."

"Yes, that I will do. And now I think I should go back to her. It's getting dark."

"Mercy." He had grasped her hand and now pulled her gently towards him. "Will you kiss me, just once? As . . . as a seal? Something for me to remember all my life?"

She looked up at him for a moment, puzzling to read his face in the gathering dusk. Behind them someone had lit a lantern, and its light made his face look pale as a ghost . . . as a corpse? "Yes." His lips were salt on hers. What were they saying to her, trying to say? She drew away at last, shaken. For an instant, as his lips held hers, she had forgotten Hart, forgotten everything, felt her whole body answer his. Shameful. Frightening. "I must go back to Ruth." She made her voice matter-of-fact. "But I do thank you."

"You believe that I love you? That you can trust me?"

"I believe it. Dear Charles, I shall remember you always."

She could not get to sleep that night, haunted by memory of that disturbing kiss, hoping that Brisson had not been aware of how it had stirred her. And when she slept at last, it was to dream shameful dreams, in which Brisson took Hart's place in her arms, and to wake, as she had so often on the *Georgia,* tense, frustrated, her whole body crying out for comfort it could not have.

When she finally woke, heavy-eyed and angry with herself, it was to the welcome sound of the deadlights being taken off the cabin window. The sky was blue, the ship was surging forwards on a following wind, and Ruth was sitting up in her cot and asking for food. The galley fire had been relit, and there was hot coffee for breakfast. Helping Ruth drink it, Mercy pushed last night's haunting firmly to the back of her mind. "It's a following wind," she said. "Not long now."

"Dear Mercy." Ruth smiled at her. "Do you feel it taking you to Hart?"

"That's it." And away from yesterday's dangerous encounter. When she saw Hart, everything would be right again. "It's June, Ruth," she said. "Brisson told me. It was the fourth yesterday, the King's Birthday. Wasn't it odd that he should think of that, a Frenchman?" She must not talk about Brisson. Not think about him. "England in June. You'll love it, Ruth. So green, and the little flowers in the hedges, and the smell of the country gardens . . ."

"My brother Mark always wanted to go to England," said Ruth. "He and Hart used to talk about it. They had a book, a book about fishing that they loved to read. They read it aloud to us children sometimes when we were eating our supper. About milkmaids, and cuckoos and ladies' smock, whatever that is, and sitting in the sun."

"Izaak Walton," said Mercy. "My father loved it too. Do you know, Ruth, I had no idea I had been so homesick for England."

"How are we going to get there, do you think?" asked Ruth, practical all of a sudden.

"Monsieur Brisson said there were always smugglers who would set one over for a fee," said Mercy. "I'm sure he will help us find one. And that reminds me. I've given him my solemn promise that whatever happens, I will say nothing about him, about the help he has given us. He asks that you should do so, too."

"It will be hard to explain how we got there—if we do," said Ruth, and Mercy was delighted all over again at how much better she sounded.

"I know, dear, but I think we have to promise—and cross that bridge when we come to it. It will be easier if we are deeply sworn and can say so." But she had a sudden, disconcerting vision of trying to explain to Hart.

"Captain van Loon says you have brought him luck." Brisson had taken them up on deck to see the dim shapes of the Scilly Islands far ahead. "He's never made so swift a voyage. It's not what he expected at all."

"Thought us a couple of Jonahs, did he?" Mercy had a swift, painful memory of the crew of the *Georgia,* who had thought her just that.

"He took a bit of persuading. But now he is full of your praises. Says he never had an easier pair of passengers."

"Well, I should think so," said Mercy. "He's hardly seen us. How long now till we reach Rotterdam?"

"Just a day or so, if this wind holds and we have no trouble."

"Trouble?" asked Ruth. "But this is a neutral ship."

"It was when it left the West Indies," he told her. "But think! That's over six weeks old. Anything could have happened in the meantime. There's been trouble enough between England and the Netherlands this last winter about the British and their search of neutral ships."

"You mean, this one may be stopped by the British?" This was a new and unpleasant idea to Mercy.

"It's possible. And if it should be, I strongly advise that you tell the whole truth and ask to be taken on board the British ship if it is heading for home. Do you see, it would be very much your easiest way of getting there?"

"But you? What would happen to you?"

"Captain van Loon and I have our story ready. I count on you two to keep your word and say nothing about me."

"Then how can we tell the truth? No one would ever believe that we arranged our escape from Philadelphia single-handed."

"Say that the Palmers helped you," he told her. "It has the advantage of being quite true. Did you never stop to wonder how they had come to get so rich so fast in the course of this war?"

"I never could like them," Ruth said.

"They'd sell their grandmother for a dollar's worth of feathers."

"And you trusted them to arrange this passage for us?"

"Oh, they are known to stick to their bond. Well, if they did not, they'd not last long in the business."

"I suppose not." Mercy shivered. "It's getting cold. Let's go below, Ruth. The light's going fast."

He took her cold hand in his warm one. "Sleep well.

And I beg you, do not plague yourself with imagined fears."

"Imagined! I don't know what's imaginary about them!" His touch had sent a flash of fire through her, and she feigned anger to explain her uncontrollable blush.

"I don't know why Brisson talks of imaginary fears," she said to Ruth, back in the refuge of their cabin. "Oh, Ruth, I wish we were safe in England. What a fool's paradise I've been in all this time, imagining us in no danger because we were on a neutral ship."

"Oh, well." Ruth was surprisingly calm. "Monsieur Brisson's quite right, you know. It would save us a lot of trouble if the British navy were to snap us up and take us in. We'd be safe with them, you know we would, two women. And I don't know about you, but I have not exactly been looking forward to crossing the Channel with a parcel of smugglers."

"Oh, Ruth, you are a comfort to me!" Mercy gave her a quick hug. "I don't know what I'd do without you." It was true. The long, quiet days of the voyage, even her sickness seemed to have completed Ruth's cure. The girl she had accepted as a burden back in the winter was now her invaluable friend and support.

"What's that?" Bleak light of very early morning.

"A gun?" It had waked them both. Now they could hear a volley of orders up on deck, the rush of bare feet, a change in the motion of the ship.

"We're lying to?" Ruth asked. Maddeningly the cabin window showed nothing but an expanse of calm, grey sea and sky.

"We'd best get some clothes on." Pausing to listen as she drew on her stockings, Mercy heard something bump against the ship's side and a new burst of orders. "I think we're being boarded."

"Suppose it's a privateer." Ruth had gone very white.

"The *Amsterdam* would have fought it off. Captain van Loon would never yield so tamely." Mercy tried to sound more confident than she felt. But how could she help thinking of the horrible deaths of Mrs. Purchis and Mrs. Mayfield and remembering that some privateers were little better than pirates? It would be a judgement on her if she should come to the same dreadful end as they had. But

Ruth was looking at her anxiously, sensing her fear. "Which would you rather," she asked lightly, "English or French?"

"Oh, I hope it's the British." Ruth had finished dressing and was swiftly braiding her hair.

"So do I. Except for poor Monsieur Brisson. I wish I knew what he meant to do." She must stop talking of Brisson, stop thinking of him.

"I expect that's him now," said Ruth, at a quick tapping on the door.

"Come in." Mercy fastened her last button as the door opened. It was the Dutch sailor who usually brought their meals, looking frightened, gesturing them to follow him.

"Lucky we dressed." Mercy ran a comb through her growing curls. "Are you ready, Ruth?"

They found Captain van Loon at his big desk, angrily biting his nails. Across the cabin from him a very young man was lounging against the wall. English uniform. A lieutenant, Mercy saw, with a swift breath half of relief, half of fright. No sign of Brisson.

"Ladies." The officer straightened up and made them a courteous bow. "The captain here tells me a strange tale about you. You are Mrs. Purchis and Miss Paston?"

"Yes." Mercy and Ruth bobbed token curtsies as he spoke their names. "But by what right do you ask it?" Mercy went on.

"Ah—rights. Must I remind you ladies as I have the captain here that we British are fighting a war. You ladies are Americans, he tells me. Enemies. So—when he took you on board, did Captain van Loon take American cargo too?"

"Indeed he did not," said Mercy. "And if he had, I do not see what affair it would be of yours. This is a neutral ship—is it not?" she asked, struck by a sudden qualm.

"Yes, ma'am." He smiled at her. "We are not at war with the Netherlands—yet. But neutral is as neutral does. If Captain van Loon will go out of his way to pick up an American party from the Jerseys, what other contraband may he not have on board?"

"None that I know of," said Mercy. "Miss Paston and I came on board in a rowboat, with one portmanteau between us. Not room for much contraband there."

"And you know nothing of the rest of the cargo?"

"Of course not. Except that it came from the West Indies. And that it is no concern of yours."

"Rum and sugar," he said meditatively. "A tempting haul, ma'am. As to its being my concern, you speak as an authority?"

"Of course not. I merely meant . . ."

"That this is a neutral ship. Quite so. You know a good deal about the sea, Mrs. Purchis. And you spell your name with an *i?*"

"Yes." Her hands clasped together. "Do you mean—can you mean that you know something about my husband? Captain Purchis of the *Georgia?*"

"Oh, yes," he said. "Everyone in England knows about him."

"About—what can you mean?" She clutched Ruth's hand.

"I'm sorry to give you bad news, ma'am, but when I left England your husband was in the Tower, suspected of complicity in the Gordon riots."

"The Tower? The Gordon riots? I don't understand—"

"And I have no time to explain. You are hoping to make your way to England, Captain van Loon says. I will take you if you wish it. I'm on my way to Portsmouth. I can give you ten minutes to get ready." He turned back to Captain van Loon.

"The Tower of London." Back in their cabin, Mercy sank down on her cot. "That's where they put traitors, Ruth!" It was a terror that had lurked at the back of her mind ever since she had first heard of Hart's capture. In the first years of the long war American privateersmen and even sailors in the regular American navy had been treated as rebel subjects by the British. Where captured soldiers had been eligible for exchange, sailors had been left to rot in the notorious British gaols. It was only after John Paul Jones had captured the entire crew of the *Drake* and held them for exchange that Parliament had passed an act allowing the exchange of naval prisoners. She had learned of this almost at the same time as she heard of Hart's capture, and it had helped soften the worst of the blow. But now. "The Gordon riots?" she said to Ruth. "What in the world?"

"We must hope to find out when we reach the British ship." Ruth was busy packing their portmanteau. "Dear Mercy, you've been so brave! Don't lose hope now." And then, as Mercy still sat gazing listlessly down at her own hands: "Just think how grateful you should be to Charles Brisson. We will be in England in a day or two. You will be able to speak for Hart at his trial if it should come to that."

"We may be too late," said Mercy dully. While she had been dreaming those uncontrollable dreams of Charles Brisson, Hart had been in the Tower of London, in danger of his life. It would serve her richly right if she never saw him again.

It was Ruth who took the lead as they were dangerously transferred by bosun's chair and small boat to the British frigate *Endymion*. The British sailors seemed friendly enough, and something about Mercy's white silence subdued the worst of the ribaldry that might have greeted the unexpected appearance of two captive young ladies. Alone at last in the small cabin assigned to them on the *Endymion,* with a marine on duty outside, Mercy spoke at last. "The Gordon riots," she said. "The Tower. My poor Hart. If only I knew. What can they have been, Ruth? And why should he have been involved?"

"I only wish we knew," said Ruth patiently. "But no doubt Captain Kemp will tell us when we see him."

"If we ever do. We're prisoners, do you realise?"

"I'm just as happy to be guarded," said Ruth. "The sailors were kind enough, but did you see how they looked at us?"

"Dear Ruth!" Mercy took her hand. "I'm ashamed. You are being so brave, and I can think of nothing but myself."

"Nothing but Hart," said Ruth. "That's a different matter. But, Mercy"—she had been casting round for comfort —"surely being in the Tower almost guarantees Hart's safety for the time being. It makes him a state prisoner, does it not? And that must mean a state trial, which I am sure would take a long time. What a blessing that we came. You will be there in time to speak for him."

"What shall I say?" Mercy had never been so close to despair.

Twenty-four hours of close confinement dragged by, and Mercy subsided into a silent trance of anxiety. At last, early next afternoon, a message summoned them to dine with Captain Kemp.

They found him alone in his surprisingly luxurious cab-

in. "Mrs. Purchis, Miss Paston." He greeted them kindly
enough, an elderly, sharp-featured man in immaculate uniform. "I am sorry to have left you in suspense for so long."
He turned to Mercy. "I understand that Lieutenant Fellows
told you about your husband."

"That he's in the Tower. Yes?" She had taken the seat
he offered her and leant forward eagerly. "Captain Kemp,
I do beg you will explain. What were the Gordon riots?"

"A terrible business," he told her gravely. "Half of London burnt and terrorised by the mob, from what I have
heard. Started by Lord George Gordon, a madman, if ever
there was one. I served with him when he was in the navy.
Crazy as they come! All kinds of mad ideas about equal
rights for the men. He didn't last long in the service, I can
tell you. Went into Parliament while he was serving. Got a
bee in his bonnet about the Catholics. Thought they were
going to take over the country: new Popish plot, something
like that. Crazy business." He gestured to his man to pour
wine. "The mob got out of hand, of course. He never could
control men. Terrorised Parliament, burnt all the Catholic
chapels in town, destroyed God knows how much property.
Lord Mansfield's house, Sir George Savile's, Mr. Malo's
distillery, the prisons—I don't know what else. Dreadful
business. Makes one grateful to be a sailor. Discipline.
Order . . . More wine?"

"No, thank you. But my husband. Where does he come
into it?"

"Baffling business." He held out his glass to be refilled.
"Somebody organised that mob. Must have. No one knows
who. Came pretty close to a bloody revolution. Six days of
it. Damned close-run thing. I beg your pardon. So—who
behind it? One obvious answer is you Americans. Everything to gain by a British revolution. And your husband
was in the thick of things, ma'am. Sorry to have to tell you.
Oh—made out a hero at first. Rescued a young lady, cousin
or something . . . Death or worse, that kind of thing. Ah,
let's dine." His servant had appeared with a steaming
tureen.

"A hero, you say?" Mercy prompted him when they were
seated at the highly polished table and the soup had been
served.

"That was the story. Saved this cousin of his from the
mob. That was on the Monday. Tuesday things grew

worse; the mob attacked the prisons: the King's Bench,
Newgate . . . I'm sorry to have to tell you, ma'am, but your
husband was in the crowd that attacked Newgate."

"I don't believe it."

"No? I suppose not. No wife would. Quite right, too."
He gave her a look of slightly bleary approval. "But he was
there, no doubt in the world about that, got a knock on the
head, picked up by the constables when the worst was over.
Of course, he *says* he was only trying to help the prisoners
escape because they were in danger of burning to death.
He's full of heroic stories, that husband of yours."

"What do you mean?" She tried to keep the anger out of
her voice.

"You'll need to know. There was an odd business about
his capture. Another tale of heroism. Got taken by a
cousin. Did you know?"

"Yes. I had heard."

"Well, he saved the ship. Caught a prisoner trying to set
it on fire. That was the story he and his cousin gave out.
There's another funny one: Dick Purchas. The cousin. We
were mids together. Midshipmen—" He amplified it.
"Never thought he'd get to be captain. Used to be sick over
a flogging. Wanted to wrap the men in cotton wool. Bad as
Gordon, if you ask me." He had rapidly consumed two
huge bowlfuls of soup as he talked, now summoned his man
to bring the next course.

"How do you mean, 'gave out'?" Mercy had been angrily
waiting for a chance to put the question.

"Too good to be true. The whole story. To people like
me. Oh, they swallowed it at first, in London, the First
Lords, the public prints. Hero's welcome, paroled to his
cousin's charge; all that. Then wiser councils, people began
to ask questions, people like me who had served with Dick
Purchas. Knew what he was like. And the men began to
talk. Bound to."

"The men?"

"Prisoners from your husband's ship. What was she
called? Privateer?"

"The *Georgia*."

"That's right. Most of them had turned their coats by
then, but the few who had refused were marched off to
Mill Prison when they landed. It burnt them up to see their
captain go off to his freedom. They talked, and so did the

others, sooner or later, when they got split up and found themselves serving on other ships. Away from young Purchas. A very odd story indeed. Attempted mutiny, arson . . . And all hushed up by Purchas, no doubt for good reasons of his own. He was awaiting his court-martial when I was last on shore. He was with your husband at Newgate, by the way. Swears blind they only meant to help. Well, naturally, he would. No use to your husband, of course. Nobody believes a word he says. Well, why should they? Just one lie after another. Too many stories of heroism by half. And of course, your husband's carryings-on in London didn't exactly help him."

"Carryings-on? My husband?"

"Nothing to it, I expect, really, but there was a bit of talk." He looked unhappy and gestured to his man to refill their glasses. "Understandable enough," he went on. "London for the first time, lionised a bit, hero of the hour, you know the kind of thing. By what I heard, he was lucky to get safe to the Tower, or he would most certainly have had to take refuge in the rules of court. You're safe there from debt, you know. He'd been spending money like water, like a drunken sailor . . . clothes . . . parties of pleasure." He had been carried away by his own eloquence, now stopped short, surprised at how far he had gone.

"You said he rescued someone." Mercy forced boiled beef down her throat. "A cousin, did you say?"

"Dick Purchas's sister. Julia Purchas. A goer by all reports. Quite a goer. Whig family, you know. Wild blood. The older brother's said to be a member of the Hell Fire Club. That kind of thing. Time you got there, ma'am." He helped himself to more beef and changed the subject. "Now I have to question you ladies. Decide what to do with you. Beauty in distress." He drank to them, one after the other, and Mercy did not like the leering admiration of his glance. "Gallant young ladies," he went on, "I'd like to make things as easy as possible for you. The British navy don't make war on females. Better uses for them." His speaking glance travelled from Mercy to Ruth, then back again. "Tell me how I can serve you?"

# XVII

"N o," said Hart. "I will not marry her. Not if it means I have to spend the rest of my life here."

"Which may be short." Mr. Purchas picked up his hat and gloves and looked round the bare stone-walled cell. "We have done our best for you so far. Not all the apartments here in the Tower are so comparatively luxurious as this one. When the turnkeys learn that you are penniless and we have washed our hands of you, you will find your treatment quite other. Commons here have to be paid for, you know. Though I doubt that will be a problem to you for long if we do not intercede for you. Did you know that they hanged some of the convicted rioters yesterday? A pity you are not allowed newspapers. You might have found the descriptions interesting. They were taken to the scenes of their crimes and turned off there. Made good ends, most of them. Merely hanged, of course. The delights of drawing and quartering are reserved for state criminals like yourself. I saw it done once. The man lived a surprisingly long time. I wonder where they will choose to execute you. Leicester Fields? Lincoln's Inn Fields? Or Newgate, of course. I hope for my poor Julia's sake that they do not turn you off in St. James's Square." He rapped on the cell door for the gaoler to come and let him out. "I will be at the house in Charles

Street another week. Consider my offer of help as open
until then."

"Consider it refused," said Hart.

Left alone, he moved over to stare sightlessly out of the
slit window that showed him only a strip of sky. The Tower
of London. All Hope Abandon, You Who Enter Here. Was
he mad to have refused Mr. Purchas's offer? But how could
he accept it? He had married Mercy for better for worse
. . . till death them did part. . . . Nothing she did could
alter that. And yet it was strange almost beyond belief that
he still had not heard from her. If she was really at Philadelphia, she must have heard of the deaths of his mother
and aunt. Impossible, surely, that she would not have written to him then. He had talked to enough Americans in
London to know that letters reached them by all kinds of
strange channels. So why not Mercy's?

"Till death us do part." Bougainville had not used the
words in that strange, hasty shipboard marriage. It had
not seemed like a marriage. He had never felt happy about
it, had intended to marry Mercy again as soon as they
reached Boston. That had been part of the whole disaster
of their "honeymoon" on the crowded *Georgia*. In his
mind, if not his heart, he could not help believing Purchas's
and Busby's assurances that his marriage was invalid. But
that was no argument for marrying Julia. Not now. Not
knowing what he did. Rather die?

Yes. He would not let himself think about that scene with
Julia. About how she had planned it, duped him, led him
on . . . Horrible . . . obscene . . . And going on from there,
in the long hours of wretched thought, he had found himself going back to other scenes, wondering about them. . . .
That visit to the Bonds'. Could she have planned that, too?
Hoped that the mob would come? That they would be
compromised? But why? He always stuck there but came
back to his one point of decision. Better to die than to
marry Julia. Besides—he moved back to gaze at the hopeful strip of blue sky—he would not believe in the threat of
death. This was England. This was the land of Parliament,
of Magna Carta and habeas corpus. The evidence that had
seemed so formidable at the committal proceedings would
never stand up in full court. On the Monday night he had
been among the crowd; he had proclaimed himself an

American, started them singing "God save George Washington," and so managed to get Julia safe away from them. Julia would support his story. And the next night he and Dick had been trying to rescue prisoners in danger of being burnt to death. If he could help it, now it was all over, he did not want to mention George, and this had told against him at his preliminary examination. So, of course, had Dick's absence, but it was understandable enough that when they were separated by the crowd, Dick had remembered the Plymouth coach he must catch and gone off to face his court-martial.

Dick would come back for the trial and speak up for him. If necessary, he would explain about George. He ought to have told Mr. Purchas that. But—drawn and quartered. Faced with that unspeakable threat, it was difficult to think clearly.

It could not happen. Not here in England. It was merely the long spell of solitary confinement that had opened his imagination to the unspeakable possibility. He had received no mail, seen no newspapers; Mr. Purchas had been his only visitor. After a month of this, if it was a month, he was beginning to wonder whether he really existed.

The surly gaoler, bringing his adequate, unappetising dinner, also brought paper, pen, and inkstand. "The gentleman said a line would bring him, any time of the day or night."

"And you would take it for me?"

"Of course."

"If I wrote to someone else?"

The man spit, neatly, between Hart's feet. "You'd waste your paper, and I've no instructions to give you more." He withdrew, slamming and locking the cell door behind him.

Left alone, Hart gazed from greasy mutton to the tempting pen and paper. Now, at last, he knew he was afraid. He had read of prisoners in France, confined to the Bastille by the infamous *lettres de cachet*. Could it possibly be that the same kind of thing happened here in England? He would not believe it. He must not believe it. And yet it was strange beyond belief that Dick had not come to him. He was cold to the very marrow of his bones.

Four days passed. Stale bread; lukewarm coffee; rancid beef. And the pen and paper always there on the table

beside the horrible food. The gaoler had grown careless
about emptying the sordid bucket in the corner of the cell,
and it stank. If Mr. Purchas had asked for a verbal message, he almost thought he might have sent it, but he could
not bring himself to write and sign an agreement to marry
Julia. . . .

She must know what was happening to him. Must she? If
she did and was letting it continue, death would be infinitely
better than marriage to her.

He was beginning to be afraid of losing his reason. Sleeping badly, he woke in a cold sweat, imagining himself back
in the hulks in New York Harbour. Mercy had reached
out her hand then, all the way from Savannah, and rescued
him from that living hell. On the fifth morning he woke
saying her name.

He thought it was the fifth morning. Best start counting;
it would help him stay sane, and here was a use for the
horribly tempting pen and paper. If the gaoler noticed, he
gave no sign. Was it not sinister that it was always the same
gaoler? It struck him, suddenly, on the fifth morning that
he might not be in the Tower at all. It had been dark
when the committal proceedings had finished. He had been
brought through crowded streets in a hackney cab. The hot
weather had broken at last. It had been raining. . . . He
remembered the sharp exchange of question and command,
the sound of a gate opening. . . . There had been flaring
torches; a flight of steps . . . a corridor . . . more steps . . .
and at last, this cell, darkness, and nothing to eat until the
morning. And since then the one taciturn gaoler and the
visits from Mr. Purchas.

"Where am I?" he asked when the gaoler brought the
slops that passed as his breakfast.

"The Tower." The man put down the plate and mug and
looked about him. "Stinks in here. Eat your victuals and
be ready to move. You've a visitor coming. If I bring you
a razor, will you promise not to cut your throat?"

A visitor? Julia? Horrible. But when the man came back
with hot water, a razor, and a clean shirt, he did his best
with his appearance. One felt better clean.

"Good." The gaoler returned. "You look almost human.
This way." Down the long corridor he remembered. Another cell, very like the one from which he had come, but
clean. A view, this time, from the slit window across a

grassy quadrangle to Tudor-style red-brick buildings. A big bird on the grass. A raven. "It is the Tower!" he exclaimed.

"Whoever said it wasn't? I'll bring your visitor."

Not Julia, mercifully, but Dick. Dick looking appalled. "Hart. What's happened to you?"

"Prison," said Hart. "I've never liked it. Lord, Dick, but it's good to see you."

"You won't think so when you hear what I have come to say." Dick was looking older, Hart thought. The strain of his disgrace must be beginning to tell on him. "Hart," he went on, "I wish you had told me."

"Told you?"

"About you and Julia. She told me it all. Asked me to come and speak to you for her. Hart, she thinks she is carrying your child."

"Dear God!" It stunned him for a moment. "Dick, what can I say?"

"Nothing. Save that you will marry her if we can just get you out of here in time."

"But I am married."

"You should have remembered that sooner. Think, Hart. My father has it on the highest authority that you have nothing to fear in treating that lunatic shipboard marriage as a nullity and marrying Julia. Circumstanced as she is, what else can you do?"

They were still standing, facing each other across the narrow cell. Hart turned away to stare out of the slit window so that Dick should not see his face. Memory of his seduction by Julia burnt in his brain. Now, at last, he thought he understood it. Another man's child. "I won't do it," he said.

Dick looked more wretched than ever. "Then I have no alternative but to call you out and kill you if I can."

"Fight you?" It made horrible sense. He looked about him. "It's not likely to come to that. By what your father says, the executioner looks like doing the business for you. Now the small fry have been executed, I imagine it will not be long before Lord George Gordon and I are brought to trial. I'll be glad when it is over. Dick, my friend, believe me, I am sorrier for this than I can say. And for what I have done to you. I have brought nothing but disaster to your family, after all your kindness to me. I wish I could hope that you would forgive me before I hang."

"You seriously expect to?"

"Why, yes." Hart was surprised at Dick's tone. "You will think me a coward, Dick, but I do pray that I will be spared the final horror, the drawing and quartering. I am an American citizen, not a traitor. And I . . . I am afraid I might disgrace myself . . . disgrace my country. . . ." He had lain awake at night, thinking of it, praying for strength to endure.

"Who told you of drawing and quartering?"

"Your father, of course. He has been my only visitor. He has warned me what to expect."

"Nonsense," said Dick. "You've not been seeing the papers?"

"No. And the gaoler won't talk. Says he has his orders. Dick! Don't make me hope; I don't think I am strong enough for that."

"Let me be sure of this," said Dick. "My father has been telling you—has convinced you—that it is a choice between marriage with Julia and the full barbarous sentence of the law?"

"Yes."

"And you believed him? You cannot think very highly of British justice."

"No," said Hart sharply. "I've seen enough of what is called influence since I have been here. I have only asked myself whether your family was really powerful enough to secure my release, granted that they have not been able to save you from disgrace because of what you did for me."

"But I am safe," said Dick. "You mean, you do not even know that?"

"Safe? Oh, thank God!" Hart turned and held out his hand. "That makes up for everything."

"You've not heard then of George's death?"

"Your brother?"

"Yes. His body was found, just the other day, in a gutted cellar in Moorfields. Nobody knows how many died there, from drink, from fire, from untended wounds. And no way to tell how poor George met his end, but I'm afraid you must have been right in your suspicions of him, and more grateful than I can say that you did not speak of them during the committal proceedings. He's dead now, poor George; it's over. We are hoping, my father and I, that we can keep his part in the riots a secret, for the family's sake. My poor mother has been ill ever since, and Julia is taking it hard. She loved him, you know. Hart—"

"Please! I must think. George is dead. Dick, I think I must tell you this. No one else. Ever. I believe your sister knew of his involvement with the rioters. I told her I thought I had heard George's voice. No one else, just her. She laughed it off. But I think she must have told George. Do you see? He knew why we were looking for him that night. I think he led us on, hoping for just what happened. It has to be her who told him." He found he could not use Julia's name. "Dick, you must see I can't. Not marry her. Oh, of course, I'll fight you if you insist and if I do get out of here. I've faced death for so long now I begin to think it would be a relief. My guilt about Julia . . . no word from Mercy . . . your disgrace. But you say you are clear of that?"

Dick laughed ruefully. "You've forgotten something. I am now the heir to the Purchas estate. It has made a great difference to my position. The Lords of Admiralty have been glad to close a painful episode by letting me send in my papers. My father sent for me from Plymouth as soon as poor George's body was found. I got here yesterday and found things well in train already. I am going to get my wish and settle down to run the estate and put into effect all those good ideas we had. Hart, if only . . . I would so like to have you for a brother."

"I am a married man," said Hart. "Nothing will alter that."

"Ah, poor Julia," said Dick. "She loves you, Hart. I think she truly loves you. It would be the making of her. It was George led her astray. With you, it would be quite different. If you had seen her this morning. In tears, Hart. Julia who never cries. She looks ill. Ill with unhappiness. If you saw her, I think you must relent."

"Dick, I'm married." There was so much he must not say. As Dick was pleading her case, he had had a sudden, horrible vision of Julia, the consummate actress, playing off her wiles on her gullible brother. Mercy was an actress, too, but how different. She had acted a part for her country.

With him, she had always been the soul of honour. Too honest, perhaps? What a strange thought. And why did talk of Julia now bring Mercy so vividly, so tantalisingly into his mind?

"You're hard," said Dick. "I'd not thought it of you."

"I'm honest, or try to be."

"And I must tell her not to hope?"

"Yes." There was no way of wrapping it up in clean linen.

"Then the first day you are safe out of here, which I trust will be soon, my friends will wait upon yours to arrange a meeting."

"Very well." He would not tell Dick that he had no other real friend in England. He held out his hand. "Good-bye. Believe me when I tell you how sorry I am."

Left alone, he could hardly cope with the flood of new ideas. Dick seriously seemed to believe that he was not in danger of death. If only he had asked him more questions, but how could he, with the shadow of Julia between them? He was beginning to hate both Julia and her father and was glad of it. But Dick he could not hate. The idea of fighting him was horrible. Was he in honour bound to fire in the air and let Dick kill him? Time enough to think of that when he was out of the Tower. He found he was actually beginning to believe in the possibility of freedom. George Purchas's body must have been found in incriminating circumstances, so he would be believed if he explained that his own actions during the riots had been caused by suspicion of him. So . . . if Mr. Purchas wanted to save his family's name, he would be wise to do everything to avoid a trial.

The gaoler confirmed the remarkable change in his position by appearing with a pint of porter. "The young gentleman said you was to have anything you liked, sir," he explained. "I'm glad of it. I do like to see my gentlemen comfortable. You won't take anything I've done amiss, will you now, not a gentleman like you?"

"Not if you will fetch me a newspaper . . . all the papers you can."

"I ain't got none, sir, and that's God's truth. I read them at the coffeehouse when I can. But I can tell you right out, sir, things look a whole lot better for you and even for

Lord George than they did. Things is quiet again, see, and
folks have turned to the right-about. What's fretting them
now is all the soldiers here in town. Amherst—the Commander in Chief—gave orders, see that no one was to carry
arms. First thing the soldiers did was disarm the citizens
who'd joined together for their own protection. Well, of
course, they didn't like that above half. So now the cry is
all to get the military out of town. And Parliament refusing
to sit while they are here. It's all quite different sir; you'll
find it so when you get out. Well, look at the executions
last week. All quiet as bedamned; just a nice day out for
the public, you could say." He laughed. "No need to look
so sick, sir. Government's had enough. The less said about
it all now, the better. Bygones be bygones; all that." He
looked a little anxiously round the bleak cell. "Anything
you need, sir, short of papers? My bet is you'll be out of
here before many days is passed, and I wouldn't want you
complaining of your treatment."

"No?" Hart could hardly help laughing. "Then fetch me
another pint of this excellent porter if my credit will stretch
so far."

"No need to be fretting about that, sir. The young gentleman said he'd stand the nonsense. A right down open-
handed good-hearted gentleman that one. Porter, sir, right
away."

I shall have to let Dick kill me, thought Hart. It would
be a solution, after all. His mother was dead. Mercy had
obviously washed her hands of him. And free now from
the immediate terror of execution, he remembered that if
he did emerge unscathed from the Tower, it would only be
to be recommitted to prison for debt. It was tragicomic to
think that in order to be able to fight him, Dick would
have to pay his debts. He looked back now on those first
mad, extravagant weeks in London with a kind of horror.
Fool . . . idiot. The fact that Busby and Drummond had
made it so easy for him to borrow was no excuse. He,
better than anyone, had known how his affairs really stood,
and yet he had let Julia lead him on from extravagance to
extravagance.

Disgusting to be blaming her like this. It was all his own
fault, his own foolishness, and if by some miracle he ever
got home to America, he would pay for it, in the sweat of

his brow, all his life. How happy he would be to do so. Suddenly, almost unbearably, he remembered the feel of working in the rice fields at Winchelsea, the soft, warm earth as one opened the sluices, the delight of seeing the first green shoots. Oh, God, just to get back there, to get home . . .

# XVIII ﷽⸺

"Mercy, try to rest." Ruth had unpacked their port-manteau while Mercy eagerly read through the back issues of the London papers that the landlord of the Portsmouth inn had found for her.

"How can I? With Hart in the Tower! For a whole month now, and no sign of a trial. And no clue in these papers to where I will find his family."

"The landlord says they'll most likely be at their country place, Denton Hall, since Parliament has been dissolved. He's been very kind."

"Everyone has." Mercy sounded surprised. It had been almost disconcerting to find that first Captain Kemp and now the landlord of the inn treated her not as an enemy, an object of suspicion, but simply as an unlucky woman whose husband was in prison, in danger of his life. The Mercy who had been the Rebel Pamphleteer seemed no longer to exist; instead, she had to live with this new crea-ture, Hart's wife.

"It can't be long until we hear," Ruth said once again. "Captain Kemp promised your letters would go off on the night mail. A pity there is no cross mail to Sussex so that the one to Denton Hall will take longer, but surely some member of the family will be in London since Hart is in prison there. And I am sure the captain was right to say we should stay here until we have heard from them."

"I wish I was." Mercy had only yielded after much persuasion. "Suppose they have washed their hands of him! It's so hard to make out from the papers what really happened in those terrible riots. First, Hart's a hero who saved his Cousin Julia Purchas from the mob, and then all of a sudden the story is that he led it, that the riots were an American attempt to dislodge Lord North's government."

"But nobody seems to believe that anymore," said Ruth. "So we should be grateful, Mercy dear, that there is no sign of Hart's being brought to trial, when so many others have already been tried and condemned. Time has to be on his side. And just think how much we have to be thankful for. We are not prisoners as we expected; we are in funds, thanks to Charles Brisson; and, best of all, we are here, in England, and treated as friends, not enemies."

"It's extraordinary," said Mercy. "But, Ruth dear, so far as I am concerned, the best thing of all is you. How would I ever have managed without you?"

"Or I without you." She smiled rather tremulously. "Sometimes I feel wicked because I do not think more about Mother and the others."

"They would not want you to. I feel the same about poor Mrs. Purchis and her sister. But it's the living one must think of."

"I do wish we knew what had happened to Charles Brisson." Ruth had found his letter, saying good-bye and containing a draft on Coutts Bank, in their portmanteau when she unpacked it, and they were almost sure that it had not been there when they left the *Amsterdam* for the *Endymion*. "Maybe he bribed a British sailor to put his letter in the portmanteau," Ruth went on. "And stayed hidden on the *Amsterdam*. I hope he is safe in France by now."

Mercy was not listening. She had returned to her anxious perusal of the shabby old papers, their tattered condition indicative of the frantic eagerness with which they had been read as they arrived with each day's batch of bad news from London. "It must have been appalling business," she said. "Half London in flames; the mob in command . . . And none of the ringleaders caught, by the reports of the trials so far. I'm so afraid, Ruth . . . that they are saving Hart and Lord George Gordon to make some terrible example of them."

"Don't think like that; try to be patient. Just think, by

now Hart may have had your letter. Imagine how happy it will make him."

"I wish I understood about this cousin whose life he saved," said Mercy.

The next morning's paper carried a description of the executions of a group of rioters convicted of taking part in the outbreak. An insignificant enough crew, by the report, they had been hanged as near as possible to the scenes of their particular crimes, and there had been no sign of sympathy from the crowd, nor was there any suggestion of a guiding hand behind them. Lord George Gordon was briefly mentioned as being still closely confined to the Tower, with all his letters read and his family allowed to visit him only for an hour at a time.

"So you see," said Ruth when Mercy read this out to her, "Hart will have been allowed your letter."

"They say nothing about him," said Mercy.

"Perhaps he has been released. He most certainly has not been tried. That would have been reported."

"Yes. Yes, of course. Thank you, Ruth!"

"I wish you would come out and walk by the sea. You've not been out of doors since we landed; it cannot be good for you."

"How can I," said Mercy, "when any moment there may be news of Hart?" She moved over to the window. "There's a private carriage driving into the yard now. It's a woman. I wonder . . ."

"My stars, how elegant." Ruth joined her at the window. "I never saw such deep mourning."

A few minutes later a chambermaid scratched at the door and announced, "Miss Purchas."

"I felt it!" Mercy advanced, trembling, to greet the black-garbed young woman, who had thrown back her mourning veil to show two huge dark eyes in an ivory-pale face.

"Mercy." She held out her arms. "I shall call you Mercy. And this must be Hart's cousin Ruth, of whom he has told me so much." She kissed them both warmly. "I came the moment I had read your letter," she told Mercy, seating herself in the room's one comfortable chair. "I knew it was what Hart would have wished."

"Would have?" Mercy had been afraid she knew what the deep mourning meant. "You mean, Hart—" She swayed where she stood, and caught hold of the window ledge.

"Oh, no, forgive me! I never thought . . . Dear Hart's as safe as a man can be when confined in the Tower for high treason. There's no move to try him yet, and Lord George Gordon himself is not to be tried until next month. No, alas, my blacks are for my beloved brother." She paused for a moment, using a delicate scrap of a handkerchief.

"The one who saved Hart? Oh, I am so sorry!"

"No, no. Not Dick. He survives to plague us. No, my beloved elder brother, George. Killed in the riots! The only man of rank to be so. And we did not even know until a few days ago! We thought he was in the country, on a repairing lease. And then"—now she really needed the handkerchief—"his body was found. In the cellar of a burnt building. Horrible! They only knew him by . . . by his clothes, a ring. . . . What he was doing there . . . we will never know. Please? Have you smelling salts?"

"I'm sorry. Ruth—"

"I'll find some."

"Thank you." Julia put out a shaking hand to clutch Mercy's. "Mercy, I have to talk to you. Alone. When she brings the salts, send her away!"

"I have no secrets from Ruth."

"But I have. And Hart . . . Please, for his sake, for ours . . ."

"Ours? What do you mean?" Still trembling, she let Julia pull her down into a chair beside her and received a warm, sweet waft of the perfume she was wearing. She was very beautiful, Hart's cousin Julia. "Ruth, dear." Ruth had reappeared with the landlady's sal volatile. "Would you mind leaving us for a little while? Miss Purchas has something she wants to say to me alone."

"Alone?" Ruth gave them both a straight, considering look. "Very well. I will be in one of the public rooms. But if I were you, I would decide nothing, promise nothing, on the spot."

"A very positive young lady." Julia sniffed at the sal volatile. "Surprising. Now." She put the bottle down and leant forward with another waft of heavy scent. "Dear Mercy." She sensed her instinctive withdrawal. "You won't mind my calling you that? Hart has told me so much about you . . . I feel we are friends already. Feel that I can trust you, thank God."

"Trust me?" Extraordinary how much she disliked the idea of Hart's talking about her to this exquisite young woman. And yet what more natural? She was his cousin. . . . Was that all she was? There was a cold feeling about her heart.

"Yes, trust you." Julia raised great tear-laden eyes to hers. "Mercy, I know you for the gallant, the splendid woman you are . . . The things you have done . . . The dangers you have braved . . . Compared with you, I am nothing, negligible. In myself, that is. But there is more to it than self. Mercy, dear Mercy, you are brave. I have to tell you this. Hart and I—it was too strong for us—we love each other."

"You—?"

"Love each other. We tried so hard to deceive ourselves, to pretend. . . . He talked a great deal about you, Mercy. I suppose he was trying to protect himself—to remind himself of you. That is why—forgive me—why I know something about your marriage. Don't—don't draw away from me. He could not help it, Mercy. We could not help it. It was the riots, don't you see, the danger. We had fought it off till then. He saved me . . . oh, from terrible things. You know the mob; you know what it's like. And in the relief, in the safety . . . Mercy, tell me you understand, you forgive us?"

"Forgive?" said Mercy. "Understand? Miss Purchas, I hope I do not."

"Oh, Mercy, so hard? Hart said you might be . . ."

"You have talked to Hart about this? About what you are trying to say to me?"

"But of course. Poor Hart, alone there in the Tower, afraid for his life . . . Abandoned, he thought . . . He is not even allowed letters now, but before . . . Why did you not write him? If you had cared . . ."

"Of course I wrote to him! He must have known I would, have understood that the letters could have been lost."

"After the way you parted?"

"What do you know about how we parted?"

"What Hart told me. Mercy don't make it harder for me than it is already. Must I go on my knees to you?"

"No! But I wish you would explain yourself, stop hinting about the bush and tell me directly what it is you are trying to say. After all, I am Hart's wife."

"But that's just it." Julia pounced on it. "Are you? The lawyers Hart has consulted are very far from sure of it."

"Hart has consulted lawyers?"

"Do you understand nothing? Will you not at least try to do so? Hart is in prison, in danger of his life. Naturally, he has consulted lawyers, and of course, he has told them everything."

"Everything?"

"Yes." Sudden colour flushed the pale face. "Everything. About us." And then, defiantly; "About his child, which I am carrying."

"His—?" She reached out for the smelling salts.

"Child. Our child. The Purchis heir, if you will let it be. Now, Mercy, do you understand what I am asking?"

"I think I begin to. You want me to help break my marriage to Hart? And he—he wants me to?"

"He begs it. I have a paper, drawn up by our man of business, which he says will do the trick. Mercy, I am asking you to sign it—and go."

"And go?"

"Back!" Julia ground it out. "Back where you came from. Back to your good friends in Philadelphia. Or to be treated? *la reine* in France if you prefer it. It's all here in the paper: an income for life from the Purchas estates, to be paid to you wherever you may be."

"How do you spell Purchas?"

"I beg your pardon?"

"This income you promise me. Is it to be paid me from the Purchas family estates in America or yours in England?"

"Now you begin to talk like a woman of sense! From the English ones, of course. Had you not heard that Charleston has fallen to the British? The news was the last straw for my poor Hart. He had been—I am sorry to have to say it —he had been living high on drafts on the South Carolina estate. My fault. I helped him spend it; we were so happy; we lived as if the world would never end. Then—the news of Charleston; Drummond's stopped payment. It would have been the debtors' prison if it had not been the Tower. So, you see, it is hardly an eligible *parti* you are to surrender."

"Hardly a *parti*," said Mercy. "A husband."

"A bankrupt one. My father is not best pleased with me. Were it not for the child . . . But as it is . . . he promises to do everything in his power."

"Oh, poor Hart," said Mercy. "Everything gone. His mother . . . his property . . ."

"He has me," said Julia, "if you will but make it possible. And think a little, Mercy, do you not owe it him? For the part you played in the deaths of his mother and his aunt. I am afraid, even if it had not been for the *coup de foudre* that struck Hart and me, it would have been hard for him to forget that if it had not been for your activities in Savannah, his mother and aunt would not have started on that disastrous journey of theirs. I had to break the news of their deaths to him. I saw how it hit him. It was when I tried to comfort him, to say what I could, that it all began between us. At our first meeting. Love at first sight. Do you know what that is like?"

"No," said Mercy. "I do not believe that I do." And thought at once of Brisson, that storm-tossed day on board ship, telling her that he had fallen in love with her at their first meeting. And then that kiss that had shaken her so. She dreamt of him still and woke in the morning, ashamed. But Hart was her husband, the man she loved. Charles Brisson's kiss might have stirred strange depths in her, but it was Hart's that she wanted. She looked at the seductive woman who was watching her so eagerly. "You are seriously suggesting that I leave England without even seeing Hart?"

"You must see that it is the only way. And there is another thing, though I had hoped not to have to point it out to you. Your appearance, now, could do Hart untold harm. You—the Rebel Pamphleteer, the American spy who duped the British in Savannah. You come forward and claim to be his wife, and it will immensely strengthen the argument that he was fomenting the riots for political reasons."

"You cannot believe that he was really doing so!"

"Of course I do not, but what is that to the purpose? I have it on the best authority that Government has still not decided how to handle his case. We have some influence, my family and I; some friends. If I come forward, claim him as my affianced husband, even if the worst comes to the worst, plead my condition . . ."

"You would do that?"

"I would do anything to save Hart. Can you say the same?"

"Oh, dear God." Mercy moved blindly to the window. Anything to get away from the strong perfume, the pleading voice. "I must have time," she said. "I must think . . ."

"Just remember that every hour you stay here in England you increase Hart's danger. You are passing here as Mrs. Purchis? Have perhaps spoken of Hart? Suppose it comes to the ears of some government agent that you are here. Think what it would mean to them to be able to prove that the terrible riots London has suffered were the doing of you Americans. Even the news of the capture of Charleston has not stirred up any public enthusiasm for this unpopular war. News of such treachery would do it. Don't think the government would not use it. North and his people are so committed to this absurd war that they would do anything to gain popular support."

"You mean they would use me to frame charges against Hart?"

"That's what I am trying to tell you. Here." She handed Mercy a legal-looking document. "Read this and see how generously we are prepared to treat you if you will just give Hart his freedom."

"No!" She let the paper fall to the ground. "Don't try to bribe me, Miss Purchas. If I go, I go of my own free will, for Hart's sake. I cannot believe that he agreed to your making me such an insulting offer."

"He did not much like it," said Julia. "But we could not let you starve. Nor do we wish to drive you back into the arms of your French friends."

"My French friends? What do you intend by that?"

"Well, they supported you in Philadelphia, did they not? An income . . . a house. Did you really think news of that would not have reached England? A very gallant band, it seems, the French in Philadelphia."

"This is the kind of thing you have been saying to Hart?" Mercy moved past her and opened the room door. "I must ask you to leave me, Miss Purchas. I will think about what you have said and give you my answer in the morning. I imagine you will not choose to stay in this inn, where your name might draw attention to mine. Send me your direction, and I will write to you. I do not think any purpose will be served by our meeting again."

"Very well. I shall be at the George." No pretence of sympathy now. "Just don't forget, ma'am, that every moment you delay may be a drop of Hart's lifeblood."

"Melodrama," said Mercy. "I wish you good day, Miss Purchas." But alone at last, she fell across the bed in a passion of tears.

"Mercy . . . Mercy! I saw her go." Ruth put a gentle arm around her and pulled her upright against the pillows. "She looked . . . I didn't like the way she looked. What did she want, Mercy? What did she say to you that you look so dreadfully?"

"She wants me to give up Hart."

"Give him up? But you are married to him."

"They do not think so. They think I endanger his life just by being here." And seeing Ruth's look of amazed horror, she plunged into an incoherent explanation.

"Yes. Yes, I see," said Ruth at last. "But who is this 'they,' Mercy?"

"All the family, I suppose. Ruth, I think I have to do it."

"Without seeing him? Without being sure it is what he wants?"

"If I see him, I endanger him horribly, tie him fatally to the American cause."

"Yes," said Ruth slowly. "I do see that. But . . . did you notice a curious thing she said, Mercy, right at the beginning, when you spoke of her brother's death? She said it wasn't Hart's friend Dick. 'He survives to plague us,' she said. Why do you think she said that, Mercy?"

"God knows." Mercy was not much interested.

"I wish we did." She picked up the paper from the floor. "This is their document?" She turned it over. "Signed by Richard Purchas, M.P. That's the father, of course. No word from Dick, who must be his heir, if the older brother was killed in the riots. Surely, if he had agreed to this monstrous proposal, he would have signed, too?"

"I do not see that it makes any difference," said Mercy wearily. "If I endanger Hart's life by insisting on our marriage, what choice have I? Yes?" She turned at the knock on the door.

"Thank you." Ruth had jumped up from the bed and accepted the letter that was handed in. "For you!" She

looked angry as she handed it over, and Mercy understood
why when she read the superscription: "To Miss Phillips by
hand."

"What now?" She opened it, and read rapidly. "She has
heard of a smuggler who will take us across to France tomorrow night," she said dully. "But, Ruth, there is no
reason why you should come."

"You really mean to go?"

"I think I must. I was wrong, madly, selfishly wrong to
come. But at the time it seemed the right decision. I love
him so, Ruth."

"Yes." Ruth took her hand. "I'm glad you said that.
Sometimes I have wondered. . . . Seeing you with poor
Charles Brisson. But, Mercy, think. When you decided to
come, you knew nothing of these terrible riots, of this
accusation. . . ."

"No, that's true. Perhaps I was right then. Now, just because I love him, I must go. But that's not to say I will
agree with any of Miss Purchas's other proposals. Not until
I have heard direct from Hart himself."

"That's good," said Ruth. "It does seem more than
strange that he has had none of your letters."

"I shall write him again, now, and enclose it to Miss
Purchas. No. That's no use. He's not allowed letters."

"And if he was, she would not give it to him. Mercy, do
you realise that you have only her word for all of this?"

"We know Hart's in the Tower."

"That, yes. But for the rest of it . . . It doesn't sound like
Hart to me."

Mercy managed almost a smile. "Dear Ruth, I keep forgetting that you know him too. But"—she flushed crimson
—"You don't understand. Our marriage . . . I refused him
at first. . . . My reputation was quite gone, you know. I
thought he only proposed out of pity, a sense of duty. . . .
Ruth, I think I should not have let him change my mind. I
loved him so much, but if he was only sorry for me. . . ."
It would explain everything. "Ruth, he told her things,
Julia. About our marriage. Things he could only have told
to someone he loved." It had been the hardest thing of all
to bear. "I think," she decided, "if he has really fallen
fathoms deep in love with Julia Purchas, I think I owe him
his freedom."

"In love with her?" Ruth's tone was scornful. "If he has, he's not the man I remember."

Mercy brushed away tears. "But none of this is to the purpose, Ruth. Everything the papers say confirms the danger Hart is in. My appearance in London might be fatal to him. I shall write Miss Purchas at once, accepting her offer of passage on the smuggler. I'll wait in France. Please God, when Hart is freed, it will be time enough to talk of an annulment, if he really wants it."

"I don't think you should go to France," said Ruth. "Certainly not on a boat of Julia Purchas's choosing. Why not go to Denton Hall? Perhaps Dick Purchas is there. He must know Hart better than anyone. He could advise you."

"Ruth, I dare not. I have killed Hart's mother and aunt. If I should kill him too . . . No." She sat down at the room's one table. "I shall accept Miss Purchas's offer. But, Ruth, will you not stay in England? Perhaps you could see Hart when . . . if he is released? Explain to him for me?"

"No," said Ruth. "Nothing would induce me to let you go off alone on a smuggling vessel recommended by that Miss Purchas. I tell you, I don't like it above half."

"But what else can I do?"

The note written and despatched, there was nothing to do but get through the long evening and longer night as best they could. Mercy refused to leave the inn for fear of some disastrous recognition by one of the English officers she had duped in Savannah. "I'm so far out of luck already," she told Ruth, "that that's just the kind of thing that would happen. And think what it might mean for Hart."

They had just finished pretending to eat breakfast when a maidservant tapped at the door to announce there was a gentleman to see them. "He asks if he may call on you in your room." The girl sounded dubious. "He said to give you this."

It was a scrap of paper with one word: "Charles."

"Ask him to come up," said Mercy. "It's Brisson," she explained to Ruth when the girl had gone.

"Oh, thank God! But how in the world?"

"We'll know soon enough." She turned to greet Charles Brisson warmly. "We were afraid we would never have a chance to thank you."

"I was afraid I would never see you again."

He looked exhausted, Mercy thought, as he kissed first her hand and then Ruth's. It must be hideously dangerous for him to be here. No wonder he had asked to see them in their room.

"Is it true that you intend to sail for France tonight?" he asked. "Forgive me for being so blunt, but I have no time. . . ."

"No, of course . . . After all your kindness, you have the right to ask anything. Yes, we do mean to go tonight, but how in the world did you find out?"

"Because I was offered passage on the same ship." He laughed ruefully. "You could call her the regular smuggler for illicit trips to France. An extraordinary war, this. When he offered me my passage, the agent here in Portsmouth asked me to bring two ladies to the rendezvous with me. I thought it must be you. But I refused the passage, and so should you. She is no place for two ladies. I do not like to think what might have happened to you. Besides, I don't understand Mrs. Purchis . . . Mercy . . . why?" He was still standing, looking from her to Ruth, every line of his body showing in exhaustion, eyes huge in his tired face.

Ruth picked up her bonnet. "There is something I must do," she said. "Will you excuse me? I'll tell them to bring wine," she told Mercy. "Monsieur Brisson looks worn out."

"Dear Ruth." He took her hand. "Thank you. But—no wine. There's so little time. . . ."

"God bless you," she said, and left them.

He turned to Mercy. "A girl in a million. Now quick, tell me why this sudden change of plan. You know your husband is in the Tower and yet plan to leave for France without even seeing him?"

"I think I have to. How much do you know about the riots in London?"

"A great deal. Like you"—he pointed to the pile of newspapers—"I have been reading about them."

"Then you know that there is talk that they were instigated by the Americans."

"Or the French. And no truth in either story."

"If only I could be sure of that. Don't you see, my husband is accused of being one of the ringleaders, of being, in fact, an American spy or agent provocateur? And then I arrive, a known spy. . . . Oh, it's no fault of yours. Do not for a moment imagine that I am blaming you. I am sure your advice to come was good. How were you to know what I would find when I got here? As it is, I see nothing for it but to get over to France and await events there."

"Your husband asks this?"

"I've not heard from him direct. His cousin came to see me yesterday. Miss Julia Purchas. With messages. With the warning of the harm I might do him by my presence." Telling him this, she found it more extraordinary than ever that there had been not one scrap of a word direct from Hart.

"Madame." He took her hand. "Mercy. Will you forgive me? I must ask you. What do you know of this Miss Purchas?"

"That I do not like her. But that is nothing to the purpose." She had no right to tell even this good friend more.

"You have heard the talk then? I'm sorry, I do not like to be the one to tell you."

"About her and my husband? She told me."

"Ah! And asked you to go?"

"Yes."

"And you are going. And on a ship of her choosing? So —you believed her."

"Yes, I believed her. How could I help it? And—you had heard of it? It is being gossiped about."

"I am afraid so. Paragraphs in the papers. You would not have recognised them. They have been together constantly, madame, since he reached England. At the playhouse, at . . . at other places of public amusement."

"She is his cousin." But what was the use of saying that? She knew the gossip about Hart and Julia was all too horribly founded in fact. "But it's not because of the gossip that I am going," she went on. "It's because I endanger Hart's life by staying." She owed it to this good friend to tell him the whole truth. "When I accepted the offer of passage tonight, I told Miss Purchas that I would agree to nothing else until I had heard from Hart himself. I am his wife," she concluded proudly, fighting tears.

"Dear madame," he said. "Dear Mercy. You love him still?"

"Yes. I think I did not quite know how much until this."

"Then do not go!"

"No? But—"

"Listen to me, Mercy, who love you and have fought the temptation of the devil to tell you this. You must believe me because it costs me so much. I have found another ship bound for France. A safe one. The captain's a friend. I could get you passage on her. Take you with me. Comfort you . . . Hope that one day you would turn to me for consolation. But no, when you learned the truth, you would never forgive me."

"What truth?"

"Miss Purchas is deceiving you. Oh, no, I'm sorry! Not about what has happened between her and your husband. That is indeed public knowledge. He was seen everywhere with her, at places of not the most savoury reputation. What you decide to do about that is your own affair, only, as you think of it, I beg you will remember that there is one heart that will love you always."

"I'm sorry . . ."

"You do not care! You are mad to hear what it is I am trying to tell you about your husband. Very well. You know me for what I am. A spy. Well, at least I am a well-informed one. There is no truth in this tale Miss Purchas has told you of danger to your husband. There may have been for a while perhaps. In the first reaction from the chaos in London there were all kinds of wild stories going about. I am not sure that the Tower was not the safest place for him. But now . . . the small fry have been examined, tried, executed. . . . There has been not a shadow of evidence to implicate either French or Americans. The government may have been tempted at first to mount a state trial and try and whip up some anti-American feeling, but they learned their lesson over Wilkes; they'll not risk having such a trial blow up in their faces for lack of evidence. They are merely waiting until feelings have calmed to release your husband."

"You are sure of this?"

"Would I tell you if I was not?"

"No." She reached out to take his hand. "I do thank you, Monsieur Brisson."

He raised her hand to his lips. "Love is a strange thing. I think I understand yours by my own. You will forgive your husband. I will never stop loving you. There we are. But you see, instead of taking this dangerous passage to France that Miss Purchas has arranged for you, you should be asking yourself why she has lied to you. I think, if I were you, I would go to Dick Purchas at Denton Hall." He turned over her hand and kissed the palm. "I must leave you, Mercy. I have stayed too long already. I am on my way back to America. If things go well with you here, and I pray that they do, you will remember me as a friend who loved you. If they go ill, come back to America, Mercy. Give me my chance to comfort you."

"Dear Charles, what can I say?"

"Nothing. Kiss me, Mercy, as you did before. God bless you. And good-bye."

# XIX

Hope, Hart found, was almost as restless company as fear. A mixed batch of papers, brought him by the gaoler the morning after Dick's visit, confirmed what he had said of the change in public tone. The riots were a thing of the past. English life was back to normal. The city fathers, meeting at the Guildhall, had been far from unanimous in passing a motion thanking the King for his care and attention to the citizens of London during the late riots. More significantly still, the Aldermen, meeting on July 18, had decided it was time to stop the allowance to the troops who had saved the City. At a hundred pounds a day, the expense of this had already amounted to four thousand. Quite enough in their view. The allowance would stop as from Saturday, July 22. After all, the executions were over, and the city quiet.

For Hart, the days dragged horribly. No visitors. No letters. Mr. Purchas's deadline had come and gone long since. Thanks to Dick, the gaoler continued obliging enough but turned a deaf ear to Hart's pressing requests for a lawyer. "No orders," he would say, and that, so far as he was concerned, was that. Hope sickened. Hart began to fear madness as much as, before, he had feared death. He made himself count things. Days. Nights. Ravens on the grass. The gaoler's visits. He was at the cell window, counting ravens, when he heard voices in the corridor. The gaoler's, fawning, pleading, and another, a gentleman's . . . Familiar? He was doubtless imagining things.

Rattle of keys. The cell door opening. Piers Blanding, falsely bonhomous, coming forward, hand outstretched. "My dear Purchis, deepest apologies for being so slow in getting you out of this hellhole. Never thought it could take so long to obey a command of Miss Purchas's but you've not been popular, dear boy, not popular at all. Took all my talent for special pleading to convince my revered principal that you'd be less of an embarrassment out than in." He looked round the cell with distaste. "Is this the best you could do for him, Miggs?"

"Orders," said the gaoler, with a pleading glance for Hart.

If he had not disliked Blanding quite as much as he did the gaoler, Hart might have mentioned the original, sordid stinking cell from which he had been removed before Dick's visit. Why bother? If he was really getting out, nothing else mattered. "You mean to tell me I am free?" he asked instead.

"Free as the air, dear boy. That will do, Miggs; I'll call when I need you." He moved closer to Hart as the gaoler left them. "To tell truth," he said, "we now find ourselves a trifle embarrassed by your plight. Had a bad time, by the look of you. Sorry about that! No intention of ours. Failure of communication. You know how it is. Less said, the better? Painful for the family. Things bad enough with them as it is. Rumours all over town about George Purchas. Sad business, but now a dead horse, don't you think? Hard on the family to have the whole thing opened up again. And not what Government wants either."

"Oh?" Where was this leading?

"You're a man of the world. Been reading the papers, I see. Well—things have settled down. No use stirring them up again, what? Trouble for Government; trouble for the family; very likely trouble for you."

"I've trouble enough of my own."

"Just what I'm saying. I'm authorised to make you an offer. Out of here, out of England, and no more said."

"Just like that?"

"Just like that. There's a closed carriage outside, will take you to Portsmouth. Enquire at the George for Mr.

Smith, and he will arrange your passage to France. Oh"
—he reached into a pocket and brought out a bulging
wallet—"you're somewhat embarrassed financially, I understand. This should take care of things for you until you
reach France and can make your own arrangements."

"And the terms of my release?"

"A gentlemen's agreement. Purely verbal. You trust us;
we trust you. And—you're out of here."

"Thank you." He wished he had not always disliked Piers
Blanding so much. "Very well then." He picked up the
portmanteau he had brought from Denton Hall. "I'm
ready."

"Your word that you'll say nothing about George
Purchas?"

"Given."

"Right." He pushed open the cell door, and Hart, following him down the corridor, thought that his own dislike
was richly returned.

The sun shone. The River Thames sparkled under the
bridge. The hired post chaise was comfortable, if not luxurious; the driver seemed civil. There had been a moment
when Hart had thought Blanding meant to accompany him
on the first stage of the journey. Instead, "You'll lose no
time?" he had said.

"Trust me for that." Hart remembered the exchange as
the chaise rattled through Southwark, where burnt and
blackened buildings still spoke of the savagery of the late
riots, and so, gradually, out into the country. It was good to
see green fields again. There had been a time when he
thought he never would. And now? Time to face it. What
was he going to do? He had promised Blanding that he
would not speak of George Purchas's involvement in the
riots. But he had not been asked to give any promise about
the offered passage to France. Presumably it had not oc-
curred to Blanding that one was necessary. After all, he
had every inducement to get clean out of England as fast
as he could.

It was early yet. With four horses, changed frequently,
he could be at Portsmouth by night, maybe in France
tomorrow. That was undoubtedly what Blanding expected.
The temptation was monstrous. France tomorrow. A fast
ship for America. Home . . . and Mercy. If she was still

alive. He would not believe her dead. He thought he would have known if she was dead. The bond between them, strained in those difficult frustrated days on the *Georgia,* felt strong as steel now. Night after night, in that grim cell in the Tower, he had dreamt of her in his arms and waked himself calling her name.

Portsmouth tonight. France tomorrow. Away from Julia; away from Purchas; away from debt. And away from Dick. Only Dick would know him for a coward. And Dick, he was sure, would say nothing. Might even be relieved? He did not want to kill Dick; still less, in the new delight of liberty, did he want to be killed by him. And yet . . . and yet . . . He had been brought up to the strict code of honour. He knew he would never respect himself again if he did not give Dick the chance of fighting him.

Denton Hall was not too far from the Portsmouth road. He could spend the night there, send a message to Dick, who was probably still in London, offering a meeting within twenty-four hours. Then, if he survived, he would surely still be in time to find Mr. Smith at Portsmouth. If by any unhappy chance he had killed Dick, he would be even more in need of Smith's good offices.

It was horrible. And he had to do it. Or rather, he had to try to do it. There had been no way of telling, from the brief exchange that had taken place outside the Tower, to what extent the driver of the post chaise was in Blanding's confidence. He might refuse to consider the proposed change of plan, and then, Hart felt, honour really would be satisfied.

But the driver did nothing of the kind. Approached with a casual suggestion of a detour and a night at Denton Hall, he agreed readily enough, "so long as the dibs are in tune."

Bribing him with some of the money made available by Piers Blanding, Hart was glad he disliked that young man so much. Was it government money, he wondered, or had it been made available by the Purchas family? He wished now that he had asked more questions but knew well enough that he would have received no answers.

It was late afternoon when he saw the long line of the downs and the clump of trees Dick had told him was called Chanctonbury Ring. Dick . . . Was he really going to Denton Hall, where he had been so kindly welcomed, made a member of the family, to try to kill Dick? Had he not done them enough harm? The point of honour? The point of dishonour? Madness. He reached out for the checkstring, then hesitated. He had come this far. He would go through with it, but fire into the air. Would Dick do the same? Well, he would find out.

Dick might even be at Denton Hall. It was some time since he had visited him in the Tower. Very likely he owed him his freedom, though Blanding had spoken rather of Government than the Purchases as concerned in it. The carriage swung through the little village of Denton and in at the lodge gates. He had walked along this drive with Julia, already her slave. It had been the first day, the day he learnt of his mother's death. They had gone to see old Granny Penfold, Dick's foster mother, and Julia had told one of her habitual minor lies. It was only now, remembering, that he even recognised it, but she had implied that Dick did not bother to visit his foster mother. When it became obvious that Dick had already been there, she had hurried rather crossly away. Captivated, he had not even noticed at the time but, looking back, thought it a characteristic, significant scene. Extraordinary, now that his eyes were opened and her glamour had lost its magic for him, how much he found he disliked her.

The carriage swung round the last bend of the drive, and he saw the hall as he had that first time, warm in afternoon sunshine. The front door stood hospitably open. Someone must be at home. Who? He was not ready for a confrontation yet. Once again his hand went out automatically to the checkstring. Too late now. Absurdly, ridiculously too late, and thinking this, he saw the woman's figure on the sunlit terrace below the house.

Julia? Horrible. This he could not face. Julia in black? Of course, George's death. But—this was not fashionable black. The skirts were not wide enough; the dress was too plain, cut too high; the bonnet was almost Quakerish in its concealing simplicity. A young woman. As the carriage drew nearer, she bent gracefully to smell a rose. Something about the way she moved . . . A wild, fantastic idea was growing in his mind. Absurd, impossible; it was only because he had been thinking so constantly of Mercy that this stranger reminded him of her.

Stranger? Now, violently, he pulled the checkstring. He was out of the carriage before it had stopped, over the ditch that divided the driveway from the terraced rose garden. "Mercy!"

She turned, saw him. "Hart!"

"Well, I'll be jiggered," said the driver to the postillion as they watched the long embrace that followed. "It almost looks like they was old friends, wouldn't you say?"

"It almost does," agreed the postillion, enjoying the spectacle. "Just the same," he went on a few minutes later, "maybe we should leave them to it and find the horses something to eat. He's just out of the Tower, didn't you say? Lord knows what'll happen next."

"Let's wait and see," said the driver, but the postillion was responsible for the horses, and prevailed.

"Hart," said Mercy at last. "Oh, my darling Hart, you have me backed against a rosebush. I believe I shall be marked for life."

"Our life," he said. "Mercy, it's a miracle. But how did it happen?"

"You may well ask. I can't believe it. Not yet. Hart!" He was kissing her again. "We're in full sight of the house. Your driver! The postillion!"

"They have very sensibly gone away," he told her. "There's a summer house." He had flirted in it with Julia; it did not matter a tinker's curse. He put his arm round Mercy to lead her towards it. "I nearly turned tail and fled," he told her, "when I saw you. I was afraid you were Julia." Absurd. What could she know of Julia?

Apparently a good deal. She turned in his arm to look up at him. "Did you so?" she said, the mischievous smile he remembered so well lighting up her face. "Lord, we've a lot to talk about, you and I."

"And a lifetime to do it." Was he taking too much for granted? "Mercy." He paused in the doorway of the summer house, his hand under her chin, gazing down at the beloved, well-remembered face. "You are going to forgive me?"

"Is there so much to forgive?" She met his eyes directly, as she always used to do.

"Julia." It came out as a groan. "I have to tell you . . ."

"Dear Hart. She has told me already. And"—she smiled

up at him and touched his lips with her finger—"I think
you told me all I need to know, back there on the terrace
when you said you nearly ran for it when you thought I
was her. Dear Hart, I have things I must tell you too. Let
us not spoil this blessed moment with apologies, with explanations. We are here, together, you and I." She drew
him gently into the summer house, which some Purchas
lady had furnished as an ornamental cottage. "It's our
miracle," she said.

"I lost our marriage lines." His fingers were busy with
the buttons of her dress.

"I don't see what difference that makes." She pulled off
his cravat. "You never believed they meant much anyway."

"We'll be married again." The threadbare fabric of her
dress gave under his impatient fingers, and he pulled it
away from her shoulders and buried his head on her
breast. "Mercy, I'm filthy. I'm just out of prison. I'm disgusting."

"I love you." Her small breasts were firm under his
mouth. She reached up to pull off his shirt and press herself
against him, breast to breast. "I love you so much."

When she cried out, he tried to go slow, to be gentle with
her. How could he? "Oh, my little love, forgive me."

"No need," she whispered. "Oh, my dear heart, no need."

Later she stirred gently, luxuriously in his arms. "I've
lain on some damp beds in my time"—she breathed it
comfortably into his ear—"between Boston and Philadelphia, and crossing the Atlantic, too, but I'm not sure this
isn't the worst. Darling Hart, you'll catch a gaol fever or
worse, if you haven't already. What miracle got you out of
the Tower?"

"I don't quite know." Reluctantly he followed her example and began to pull on his clothes. "Something . . .
someone made the government decide I was an embarrassment to it. Do you know, the more I think about it, the
more I wonder if the Purchases, for all their talk, really
have the power . . . Oh, my God!"

"What is it?"

"I'd clean forgot. Finding you like that. Mercy, I have
to fight Dick Purchas."

"Fight Purchas! But, Hart, why?" And then; "Stupid
of me. Julia."

"Yes. He challenged me, in the Tower, when I refused to marry her. That's why I am here." He explained quickly about Piers Blanding and the terms of his release. "Dick's not here?" he asked.

"No, but I sent for him when we got here yesterday. I hoped he might help me to see you. We thought, from the things Julia did not say, that he must be your friend."

"He was," said Hart. "Mercy, I have to tell you this. I shall delope."

"Fire in the air! Hart, you can't. He's a naval man; it would be death."

"Unless he does so too. And I cannot hope for that. Julia's his sister. Oh, Mercy . . ."

"Just the same," she said, "I'm glad you refused to marry her. Hart, we must go in, Ruth will be worried to death."

"Ruth?" He had been wondering who her "we" implied.

"Did you have none of my letters?" She pulled away from him in amazement.

"Not one," he said.

"Oh, my dear, what you must have thought of me! Your poor mother and Aunt Mayfield. All because of my playing God down there in Savannah. The great Rebel Pamphleteer! Making a display of myself at the expense of the family who had been so good to me. And all to send information to a state government so divided in itself that I doubt it used any of it. Oh, Hart, I wish this war was over. Do you find that nothing seems the same now you are here in England?"

"Yes, but we have to win just the same," he told her. "Mercy, you must look on my poor mother and aunt as casualties of war. I only thank God Abigail was not with them. Have you heard from her?"

"Oh, yes, everything that is kind. She is holding the Savannah house for you, Hart."

"For us." He remembered Dick. "If I survive."

"I don't think I can bear it."

"We have to, my darling. When did you send for Dick?"

"Yesterday."

"So he will very likely get here tonight. Mercy!" A new thought struck him. "What have I done? I cannot go out with Dick until you and I have been truly married. Suppose —just suppose . . . If I were to be killed and you should find you were carrying a child . . ."

"It would be my only comfort," she told him. "But, Hart, even by special licence, it takes a little time to get married, here in England." She let no hint of hope into her tone.

"How strange. I had quite forgotten that you were English. That you know more about life here than I do. Well, Dick will just have to wait, that's all. . . ."

"And Mr. Smith at Portsmouth?" Ever since Hart had told her about Blanding's arrangement, Mercy had been wondering if his Mr. Smith could be the same man as Julia's smuggler. Fantastic to think that if she and Hart had both taken the coward's path, there was still a chance that they might have met. And Brisson? She must tell Hart about him, but not yet. There would be a time for that, or so she must hope.

His thoughts had been following another line. "Mercy, who is Ruth?" he asked for the second time.

"I keep forgetting that you have had none of my letters. She is Ruth Paston—oh, Hart, that's another terrible story." She took his hand. "I'll tell you as we walk back to the house." She looked round the little summer house. "I'll never forget this place."

"Nor I." He pulled her to him again. "Oh, Mercy, oh my dear life."

Ruth came out of the house as they approached it through the rose garden. "Hart! Oh, Hart!" She was in his arms, laughing, crying. "After all these years! But I'd have known you anywhere. Hart, your hair's going white!" She looked from him to Mercy. "I'm so happy for you both."

"Ruth, it's so good to see you." He held her away from him to study her. "I never thought you'd turn out a beauty." And then, remembering; "Ruth, I am so sorry. Mercy told me about your family."

"Thank you. Both for being sorry and for sending me Mercy. If she hadn't come when she did, I would be dead, too."

"Oh?" He turned to Mercy. "You didn't tell me?"

"He's had none of my letters," Mercy explained to Ruth.

"Not even the one to the Tower?"

"You wrote me there?"

"Of course. Before we landed. The frigate captain promised it would catch the night mail. But Julia said you weren't allowed letters."

Ruth broke in with an odd question. "Hart, forgive me for asking you this, but did you talk to Julia Purchas much about your marriage to Mercy?"

"Much!" He did not try to hide his angry surprise. "Never! What do you take me for?"

"I thought so." She turned to Mercy. "That's when I began to distrust her. When you told me she said Hart had told her those things, those private things, about your marriage. Don't you see? She must have stopped your letters. Maybe his to you too. Read them. Used them."

"Oh, my God!" said Mercy. "Hart, forgive me. I should not have believed her."

"Ah, my dear love," he said. "When it comes to forgiving, I think we must just wipe the slate clean and begin to forget."

"But not until we have understood," said Ruth. "That's what baffles me. Why did the Purchases go to such lengths to keep you two separate? Dear Hart, you've always been one of my favorite men. Lord, how Naomi and I used to quarrel over you when we were young! But—you're not a British aristocrat; you're not rich. Forgive me, but I don't for a moment think Julia is in love with you. So what is it about you?"

Hart could not help laughing. "I always wanted a sister to keep me in my place," he said. "And it seems that at last I have got one. And of course, you are entirely right, Ruth. Should I be calling you Miss Paston?"

"You most certainly should not. But there is the dressing bell." She smiled mischievously at Mercy. "When the coachman told me who our mysterious guest was, I gave orders for a special dinner. And"—to Hart—"the housekeeper said she would have your old room made ready directly. You seem to be quite one of the family here."

"Yes." For a moment, in his new happiness, he had let himself imagine shooting in self-defence when he and Dick fought, but he knew he could not do it. "They've been wonderfully good to me. But I am not sleeping in my old room. Am I, Mercy?"

"Oh!" Ruth blushed crimson. "I never thought—"

"That we're an old married couple! Well, no wonder,

after the things that have been said. But just because of them, I do feel it is the least we can do to behave like one." He turned to Mercy. "If you will bear with a husband who smells of the gaol?"

"I will do my best." She flashed him a look of pure mischief.

Dick's clothes again. How could he wear Dick's clothes and imagine fighting him? No time now to be thinking of that. Mercy was putting on what she laughingly described as her "other dress." She smiled at him over her shoulder. "We'll not tell Ruth tonight," she said, "about the duel. Let us have one happy evening."

"Unless Dick comes. I should have thought he would have been here by now. You'll like him so much, Mercy. He's the brother I wish I'd had. One thing, and it comforts me, is that I know whatever happens, he will take care of you."

"Don't," she said. "We are having our happy evening."

It had not struck Hart before how much the servants at Denton Hall liked him, but when they got downstairs, they found the house bathed in a festive glow. While they were changing, someone had filled the saloon with flowers, and when they moved through into the dining room, it was to find it gleaming with glass and silver that Hart had never seen before. The special dinner Ruth had asked for had, assumed the proportions of a Lucullan feast, and Soames, the butler, welcoming Hart as a prodigal son of the family, murmured that he had thought the ladies would like champagne. "We are celebrating in the servants' hall, too, if you don't mind my saying so, sir. It's another happy day for the family."

Another? Thinking it over, as he helped Ruth to succulent chicken pie, he was afraid that the previous cause of celebration must have been George Purchas's death and Dick's accession as heir. Both the staff at the hall and the tenants on the estate must feel a great deal safer as a result of George's death. A strange thought struck him. If Dick should die, who would be his heir?

Dick was not going to die. Mercy was raising her champagne glass. "We must drink a toast," she said. "To our hosts. To the Purchas family."

They sat late at the table, enjoying their miracle while it lasted, exchanging stories, interrupting each other with questions, with explanations. "Brisson?" asked Hart, when Ruth spoke of him. "Who's he?" And noticed that Ruth left it to Mercy to reply.

"A good friend," she said. "You remember, I told you of him earlier, the one we met on our way to Philadelphia."

"The one you saved from the outlaws? I did not catch his name before. Did you not pronounce it differently?"

"Very likely. He pronounces it French or English as suits him for the moment. And Charles or *Charles*."

"A dubious sort of gentleman." It was an effort to keep his tone light. "You called him Charles or *Charles*?"

"I'd have called him George Washington if he asked me to. He's been the best of friends." There was no time, now, to say more. One day, please God, she would be able to tell him all about Charles Brisson. "Hart, dear, it's getting late, and we should not be lingering here, keeping the servants from their beds. You are sure you do not wish to drink a peaceful glass of port?"

"By myself?" All the time he was aware, and thought she was, too, of the minutes ticking away towards the duel with Dick. "Good God, no."

Later, alone with her in the room she had shared with Ruth, he turned to Mercy, put his hands on her shoulders, looked down into her eyes. "This Brisson must have loved you very much."

She met his eyes fearlessly. "I think so. It makes me a little proud."

"And you—"

"Love you." She smiled up at him. "I hoped for a while that he was in love with Ruth. Hart! What in the world are you doing?"

He had found the truckle bed tucked away under the big one and was pulling it out. "Taking no more chances," he said. "If you are to find yourself a widow in a strange land . . ."

"I shall need a child—your child. But I'll not believe it. Hart," she was busy with the fastenings of her dress. "Do you want me to think you are jealous of Charles Brisson?"

"No!"

"Then come to bed, dear Hart. Tomorrow is another

day." One last twitch of a ribbon, and the dress sank to the ground, half-supported by its own weight, as she stepped out of it and towards him, bare arms outstretched.

Much later Hart waked himself, crying out as he had in the Tower, and felt Mercy bending over him. "You were calling for me," she said.

"Of course." They turned to each other and, presently, slept again.

## XX

Waked by the far-off familar sound of the church
bell, ringing for early service, Hart dressed quietly while
Mercy still slept and walked across the park to the little
church with its graveyard full of Purchases. Was George
here? he wondered, and was answered by sight of a raw,
recently turfed plot close to the church.

Mr. Pym, the vicar, was wearing buckskins under his
cassock, and Hart remembered that Julia had described
him as a hunting parson. He listened courteously enough to
Hart's story but looked blank when he asked how soon he
could arrange to marry them. "Most unusual," he said.
"Highly unorthodox. I should most certainly have to consult my Bishop. . . . Yes, the Bishop, of course. Married
already, and on a French ship, too! A Roman wedding, no
doubt? We would not want any taint of that kind of thing
here in Denton, and at this time of all others. Yes, I will
most certainly need a word with the Bishop about it."

"How soon can you see him?" Hart controlled impatience
with an effort.

"The Bishop? Oh, well, my dear Mr. Purchas"—he mis-
pronounced it—"that is something else again. The dear
Bishop; not at all a well man, you know, not at all well.
Let me see, is it Cheltenham spa this year, or Harrogate?
We do try to spare him just as much as we possibly can
when he is taking the cure. I could write to him, I suppose,

but on a subject so delicate, so complex, really I believe
word of mouth would be better. After all"—he paused,
deciding how to put it—"you have lived together for some
time as man and wife, have you not? There can be no
particular reason for haste, surely? Unless . . . unless the
lady . . ." He made it a question.

"I wish to take her home to America," said Hart. He
could hardly explain that the real reason for haste was his
impending duel with Dick.

"Oh, well, in that case." Mr. Pym pounced on it. "Very
much better to be married in your own country surely?
Quite a different church, I have always understood. No
Bishops, I believe. Extraordinary." Somewhere behind the
church a horse whinnied. "And now, if you will excuse me,
Mr. Purchas, urgent parish business, you know. Most
urgent business . . ."

"But this is urgent."

"Oh, my dear sir." He smiled indulgently. "You young
people! So impatient . . . so impetuous." He pulled a huge
bandanna handkerchief out of the sleeve of his cassock and
tied a knot in the corner. "There! I will write to the Bishop
tonight or tomorrow perhaps. I wish I could remember
whether it was Harrogate or Cheltenham, but my dear wife
will know the direction, I am sure. No need to look so
anxious. We should have an answer in the course of the
next few weeks."

"Don't trouble yourself," said Hart. "I will take my wife
to London and marry her there by special licence."

"An admirable idea," said the vicar, relieved, and carefully undid the knot.

Hart strode back across the park, fuming with rage. All
very well to tell that obstructive parson that they would
go to London for a special licence, but how could they
when by doing so, he broke his promise to Blanding and
risked being rearrested? He had just reached the drive
when he heard the sound of a horse ridden fast and turned
to look back towards the village. Dick. What was he going
to say to him?

"Hart." Dick jumped down from his tired horse. "When
were you freed? And how?"

"Yesterday. You did not know? You've not had my
message?" But it was almost impossible that he should
have.

"No. I came because of a message from . . ." He hesitated. "From your wife. She's here? You knew?"

"Not when I came here. It was sheer good fortune." Hart quickly explained what Blanding had done. "I ought to be in Portsmouth by now. I came here—I felt I must—to give you the chance of a meeting. I wrote you I would wait twenty-four hours. Only now . . ." How could he explain his predicament? "Dick, I have to remarry Mercy, make her my wife indeed, before I can fight you. I have just been to see Mr. Pym. He won't help me."

"Old dodderer," said Dick. "He's never helped anyone in his life. He'd not have had the living if I'd had any say in the matter. It will have to be by special licence then. I can help you there, I think. The Bishop of London is one of my Godfathers." He looked at Hart ruefully. "Ah, poor Julia. I can see that this changes everything."

"Everything. When you meet Mercy, you will understand. She has had a desperate time of it, both in America and on the way here. None of her letters reached me." He stopped. He could not tell Dick of their suspicion that Julia herself suppressed their letters. "She is my wife," he said. "I'm sorry, Dick. I am ready to meet you, of course, just as soon as we are married. So long as I am not rearrested first."

Dick looked as wretched as Hart felt. "Yes, we will have to think of a reason—a pretext for fighting. To keep Julia's name out of it. Time for that when we have got you married. I'll go to London, naturally, and get your licence. Safer that way. It would be absurd if you should be rearrested now. They are strange, the terms of your release. And stranger still that I knew nothing about it."

"Your English law, Dick!" They had reached the house. "Come and meet Mercy."

One of the servants must have seen them walking up the drive together. A boy was ready to take the horse, and the staff were drawn up in the hall to greet Dick with loving respect. Watching him enquire after the butler's gout and the cook's granddaughter, Hart knew all over again that there was no way in the world he could ever shoot at him. Well, he and Mercy would have the few days it would take him to get their special licence.

Mercy herself appeared at the head of the stairs. "Hart, where have you been?" She saw Dick. "Oh, you must be—"

"Dick Purchas, and most entirely at your service, ma'am. I only got your message last night, or I would have been here sooner, but I am glad to find you in better company than mine."

"Thank you." She looked from one of them to the other, suddenly hopeful.

"No." Hart read her thoughts. "It has to be, Mercy. But Dick, God bless him, is going back to London to get us our special licence, so we can be married before . . ."

"You have to?" Seeing them together, so obviously friends, it seemed incredible to her that they should still be intending to fight each other. I will never understand men, she thought, and their absurd point of honour. "Please"—she looked from one of them to the other—"say nothing about it in front of Ruth. I haven't told her. She has had enough to bear. She feels that Hart and I are all her family now. Well, we are . . ."

"Ruth?" asked Dick.

"Here she is." Mercy turned to look up at Ruth, who had appeared at the head of the staircase. "Ruth, dear, here is Mr. Purchas, ridden from London. Mr. Purchas, our cousin Ruth Paston."

"Mr. Purchas!" Ruth had put on her one white dress this morning in Hart's honour but had not troubled to put up her fair hair, which tumbled in curls round her face. She held out her hand and came drifting down the stairs towards them. "Oh, I am so happy to meet you. Your housekeeper has been telling me such things about you! It is no wonder this is such a happy house."

"Happy?" He took her small hand in both of his and gazed down at her for a long moment. "You feel it so?"

"Yes. Do not you? From the first moment we got here, Mercy and I. I have felt—oh, safe, I think. As if I had been here before." She smiled up at him. "You will think me ridiculous, Mr. Purchas."

"I shall do nothing of the kind." He wrenched his gaze away from her with an effort. "But why are we standing here in the hall? I am sure Mrs. Soames has something ready for us to eat by now. I did not stay for breakfast at Reigate." A smile for Mercy. "I did not know then that you were in such good company." He offered his arm to Ruth. "Let us see what Mrs. Soames has for us?"

She smiled at him. "Devilled kidneys, of course. Your

favourite breakfast. And coffee, not ale, because you are not a drinking man." And then, blushing crimson: "Forgive me! We have made such friends, Mrs. Soames and I!"

"I can see you have made a conquest of her." He took her arm to lead her into the breakfast room, and Mercy, following with Hart, felt rather than saw the electric current that ran sudden and strong between them.

"I like your friend Dick." She hung back a little to speak to Hart. And then: "Oh, Hart, must you two fight?"

"My darling, you know we must. So come to breakfast, love, and smile."

Finishing his last cup of coffee, Dick announced that he had business with Glubb, the bailiff. "There is much to be settled since poor George's death, but I hope to be able to finish today and start back to London tonight."

"So soon?" said Ruth, and blushed.

"The sooner I go, the sooner I will be back. Believe me, I'll not stay away a moment longer than I must." He turned to Hart. "I shall enjoy presenting old Pym with the special licence. In fact, I think I will call in on him on my way over to Glubb's house and warn him to be ready to perform the ceremony early next week."

"Thank you," said Hart, knowledge of the reason for this haste heavy between the three who shared it.

"A wedding!" exclaimed Ruth. "I've not been to one since"—her face clouded—"since Naomi's."

Alone with Hart in their room, Mercy went straight into his arms. "Did you see?" she asked. "Your friend Dick and my dear Ruth? Love at first sight if ever I saw it." She shivered and looked up at Hart. "Nothing must happen to Dick," she said. "Ruth's been through so much."

"I know." His kiss was a promise. "Nothing will."

"But you! Hart, I can't bear it."

"We must. But I don't think Dick will fire to kill. A wound would satisfy honour. Mercy, don't look like that."

"It seems too hard," she said. "To have found you at last, and now this!"

He kissed her again instead of trying to answer. "Now we must go down, my darling, and talk about wedding finery with Ruth, or she will begin to suspect something."

They found that Ruth had been in conference with her new friend Mrs. Soames and was purring with delight over the result, a great bolt of the finest white India silk, which

Mrs. Soames had had laid by for a daughter. "Something happened to the girl, I am afraid," said Ruth. "Something to do with George Purchas. Mrs. Soames wants you to have it, Mercy, and I am going to make you a dress of it. This time your wedding is going to be done handsomely if I have any say in the matter."

"Which I can see you intend to." Mercy tried to match her happy tone, wondering how in the world they would be able to keep their wretched secret for the days Dick Purchas was away.

Luckily Ruth was happily occupied all morning with a set of fashion plates belonging to Julia that Mrs. Soames had found for her, and Mercy had only to pay a surface attention to her eager discussion of what a bride would wear for a quiet village wedding which also happened to be her second one to the same man.

Mrs. Soames had just appeared to suggest a cold luncheon and add her quota of informed advice when Dick strode into the morning room through the windows that opened onto the terrace.

"What's the matter?" Ruth jumped up. "What's happened?"

"Nothing." But his face was very white and his jaw set. "Hart, come into the study, would you? Glubb has just told me something . . . something I have to tell you."

"Yes?" Hart rose and went with him. "What's the matter?"

"I'm so ashamed," said Dick. "I—I don't know how to tell you, Hart, but at least"—he managed a travesty of a smile—"I have the comfort of knowing you will believe me when I tell you this is the first I have known about it."

"About what?"

"My great-aunt Julia," said Dick. "A very rich old lady and a very obstinate one. I swear to you, Hart, that's all I knew about her until Glubb let the secret out today. He thought I knew, of course. Well, as the heir, since George's death, I should have. I never did like Busby. Well . . . I was right. Of all the dirty games! And Julia . . . Up to the neck in it. God, Hart, what an escape you have had. Julia! My sister. I was so glad to see her, as I thought, head over ears in love with you. Someone worthy of her at last. And all the time it was only the money!"

"Money?" asked Hart. "What money? Take me with you, Dick."

"Great-aunt Julia's estate. She was a Miss Purchis of Harting. Cousin both to your grandfather and to mine. Flirted with both of them and died an old maid back in '69. I think she must have really loved your grandfather, for it seems she left a most extraordinary will. All her money in trust for any member of the American branch of the family who should return to England and claim it. I cannot imagine how any lawyer came to write such a nonsensical will, but I believe she was quite a Tartar in her day. And of course, it did mean that the claimant must be on good terms with the family over here, or he'd not know about the will. No one was to be in the secret but the head of the English family and his heir."

"But Julia knew?"

"I'm afraid so. She and George were very thick, you know."

"You mean"—Hart was working it out—"she intended to marry me and then tell me about the will? Good God, no need to look so unhappy, man! Don't you see what a weight you have taken off my mind! I have felt so wretched about Julia and so puzzled. I *knew* in my bones that she did not love me. More shame to me, you might say. Now, at last, I understand. As to the estate, naturally I won't touch it. I have no shadow of a claim. I can hardly be said to have come here voluntarily!"

"The will says nothing about that. You can imagine how Busby looked into that when I brought you home. All you have to do is make your claim."

"What happens if I do not?"

"The estate remains in trust until twenty-five years from the date of Aunt Julia's death and then reverts to our family. But Glubb tells me that my father and Busby between them hoped to break the will, once they had got you safe out of the country. There seems to be some doubt as to what should happen if a member of the American branch came here and did not make a claim."

"Well, now we are going to find out."

"No," said Dick. "I won't have it. I remember how you looked that day when I visited you in the Tower. What they had done to you. My father had let you believe you would be hanged, drawn, and quartered. The gaoler said

something about the way you have been treated. Sorry for
it, he said he was, when he saw how angry it made me. I
think we have to face it, Hart, that was not Government's
doing, but Piers Blanding's, acting for my father, for Julia.
To wear you down, make you give in and marry her. You
can see now, can't you, why they wanted you out of the
country so fast when you finally refused." He gave a short,
angry bark of laughter. "Poor Julia! Do you think she has
opened your note to me by now and knows the game is up?
I wonder what she will do. As to you, Hart, I am glad to
tell you that you have no choice in the matter of the estate.
As heir I have already lodged your claim with Glubb and
told him to pass it on to Busby."

"High-handed."

"The least I could do."

"Then we'll share it." Hart saw his way clear at last.
"Better than leaving the estate mouldering in trust or eating
it away with a suit in chancery. Half and half, Dick?" He
held out his hand.

"Generous! But think it over, Hart. Glubb seems to
think it a vast sum, but I don't trust any of them. Well, not
now, not after the way Busby has behaved to me." He had
taken Hart's hand and pressed it hard. "And if you think
I am going to fight you over that worthless sister of mine,
you're fair and far off the mark! If I have said anything to
offend you, Hart, I apologise."

"And so do I. For all the harm I have done you and your
family. You must see how happy it will make me if I can
make some small amends like this."

"Small! You're a good friend, Hart. The best I've ever
had. I've lain awake for hours, sweating about that duel.
But how could I not fight you? I was going to fire to miss,
of course. Only—when I met Miss Paston yesterday, it
seemed a pity even to imagine dying."

Hart laughed. "I was going to delope. How disappointing
it would have been for our seconds."

"Yes," said Dick soberly. "That's what worried me. I
have been racking my brains to think of two men who
could be relied on not to try to stir up more trouble or
start fighting each other or any nonsense like that. Just the
same." A new thought struck him. "Do you realise that but
for that ridiculous duel you would very likely be in France

by now, having missed Mercy and lost the chance of great-aunt Julia's estate?"

"Dear me, so I should," said Hart. "Poor Julia, how very nearly she succeeded. Will your father be very angry, do you think?"

"Not if he gets half the estate," said Dick.

"He's not going to; you are. But come, I cannot wait another moment to tell Mercy the good news."

"And I must start for London before the day is much older. Do you still want that special licence, Hart?"

"I most certainly do."

"Right. Hart Purchis with an *i*. Any other names?"

"No. But Mercy is Mercy Juliet Phillips. Her father was a friend of Garrick's. I wish I could take her to London, just for a visit, but I don't dare. There is no knowing what risk I run by remaining in England."

"I'll look into that, too. And have a word with my sister."

"Don't, Dick. It's not worth it."

"*She's* not worth it," said Dick. "I'll take Miss Paston for a walk in the garden, Hart, to give you a chance to tell Mrs. Purchis. Explain to her, please; make her understand how ashamed I am."

Hart took his hand and held it for a moment. "It's all over. Best forgotten. And, Dick, there is no reason now why Miss Paston should ever know we meant to fight."

"It seems quite absurd," said Dick. "What she would think of me!"

But when he invited Ruth to come and take a turn in the shrubbery with him, he found her quiet and rather pale. She admired the hearty growth of the rare Chinese azaleas he had planted the last time he was at home, but almost absentmindedly, without really looking at them. They were out of sight of the house by now, and she turned to him suddenly, holding out both hands. "Mercy told me," she said. "I made her. I could see something was wrong. About the duel. Mr. Purchas, you *can't!* You and Hart! My poor Mercy . . . I thought I knew . . ." She paused, looking down, a flush mounting in her pale cheek. "I thought I knew something about love. I knew nothing! Mercy—she lives for Hart, I think. Ever since I first met her, she has thought of nothing but him, of getting back to him. There was a man in America—a man called Brisson—who thought the sun rose and set in her. She never noticed." A little laugh. "She even thought it was me! Dear Mercy . . . And now that they are together at last, and happy, to have this happen!" She looked up at him, her blue eyes slowly filling with tears. "Mr. Purchas, I don't know how to ask you, but please, there must be something you can do. Oh" —impatiently now—"I know I am asking the impossible. Don't for a moment think I do not. But don't you see, the moment we met, I felt you were family. Our family. Mercy's and Hart's and mine. So I am asking you, as if you were my brother." She paled again. "My dear brother Mark. To spare Hart? Please?"

She was holding out her small brown hands to him in an eloquent, basic gesture of pleading, and he gathered them up and pressed them to his lips. "Not a brother, Ruth. I do hope not a brother! And thank God, there is no need for you to ask. Hart and I are not going to fight after all. He is telling his wife now. I'd not have fired at him anyway." He laughed. "Nor would he at me. You'll think us a couple of fools."

"Oh, no!" she said. "I just thank God." She smiled up at him. "And you."

"No need for thanks." Too soon, absurdly too soon to say more. He took her arm and led her back through the shrubbery, making a good story of Great-aunt Julia's will. Anything to distract himself from the feel of her arm on his.

"So Hart and Mercy will be rich?" she said. "I am *glad*. I wonder if they will stay in England."

"I hope they do. And you. What will you do, Miss Paston?"

"I don't know," she said slowly. "Do you know, I have never imagined parting with Mercy. But now she has Hart, it's all different. She may not want me. They may not want me." Her voice shook a little as the truth of it struck home to her.

"How could they help but want you? If they decide to stay on at the estate Hart has inherited, you'll be a neighbour, almost. Would you like that, Miss Paston?"

"Oh, yes," she said. "I have taken such a fancy to Mrs. Soames."

In the house Hart and Mercy had reached the same point. She had cried a little, with sheer relief, when he told

her that there was no longer any question of a duel between him and Dick, and then gone straight to the heart
of the matter. "But this legacy, it will make no difference
will it? We are still going home? Back to Savannah?"

"It will pay my debts here," he told her. "Which will
make a great difference to me. But do you want to come
home, Mercy? To the chaos and misery of Georgia at war?
Savannah fallen; Charleston fallen. God knows where we
will live. There is an estate here, Dick tells me, part of the
legacy. In the west of the country. Waiting for us if we
want it."

"Give it to Dick," she said. "You said there was money
in the Consolidated Funds too? If we used that to pay your
debts . . . Dear Hart, don't look so wretched! Would there
be enough left to start us out, in a small way, perhaps in
western Georgia? The British have never really held sway
there. We could be free. Be ourselves at last."

"There would be quite enough, from what Dick tells me.
I think we are going to find ourselves rich, my love, and
for the rich, everything is easier. If Dick finds that the
terms of my release are absolute—and authentic—I think
we could probably go back to Savannah, live in a quiet way
in the house there with Abigail, begin to pull things together again. Because there is one thing of which I am
certain, now that I have lived here in England: Sooner or
later we Americans are going to win this war. The British
might have beaten us if they had really put their heart into
it, at the start, but you must see as well as I do that they
never have. And now we are a nation. There's no beating
us now. And when it's over, the most important thing will
be to heal the wounds of this family quarrel, and who
better to set about doing that than you and I, who have
found so much to like here in England?"

"So much to love?" she asked him, teasing.

"Witch!" He pulled her to him for a quick kiss. "That's
settled then. We'll stay to be married, and then, however
dangerously, it's home to Savannah."

"Home to Savannah! Oh, my darling, yes," she said.

Dick returned a few days later, grey-faced with fatigue.
"I've got your licence," he told Hart, who had hurried out
to greet him. "No problem there. Everything made as easy
as possible. Orders from the highest possible quarters. Well,
no wonder! Your release was drafted back in June, Hart."

"In June?" Hart thought of the horrible, dragging days in the Tower.

"Exactly. Piers Blanding managed to 'lose' it under a pile of papers on the Secretary's desk. I couldn't discover just how it came to be found and signed at last just the other day. I ran into a wall of silence there. Well, government servants all hang together. I suppose when the three of them decided there was no breaking you, Blanding 'found' it again and tried to get you out of the country as fast as possible."

"Three of them?"

"Four really. My father, Busby, Blanding, and Julia. I'm so ashamed. Everything you went through in the Tower was our doing, my family's. The gaoler they bribed has been sacked, of course, but that's not much comfort to you. And, Hart, I am instructed to ask you, to beg you to say nothing about what you have gone through. Your story, given to the opposition papers, might enflame public feelings to the point of a fresh outbreak of rioting. It's a great deal to ask. I said so."

"Nothing of the kind," said Hart. "It's not at all something I wish to talk about. And I'd keep quiet anyway for your sake, Dick. It's horrible for you."

"Yes. I left my mother in convulsions. I told my father I do not wish to see him again. Julia and Blanding have gone off together." He threw it in almost casually. "They went the night she opened your letter to me. That's when it all came out. Of course, Blanding's flight makes it easier for Government to hush the whole thing up."

"And more necessary," said Hart drily. "Julia and Blanding. I should have known." He thought of all the parties for which he had paid: Vauxhall, Ranelagh, Mrs. Cornelys's Rooms . . . Julia hanging on his arm, egging him on to further extravagance, and Blanding always somewhere in the background. Blanding. "The child," he said. "The child Julia's carrying. It's Blanding's?"

"Hart, there is no child. I talked to my mother, made her tell me. Poor Mother, it's made an old woman of her. Julia was lying about that too."

"Thank God," said Hart.

"Yes. She was desperate, Hart. I had no idea. My mother told me the whole story in the end, hoping to make me sorry for her. But how can I be after what she tried to do to you? She lost her reputation, years ago, when I was a midshipman on the Mediterranean station. A cousin of yours came over from America. I suppose you must know him. Francis Mayfield. She thought he was rich. He thought she was. And they hoped to pass him off as the American claimant."

"Absurd." Hart had gone very white at the mention of Francis Mayfield. "He's no Purchis! Was none, I should say."

"He's dead?"

"Yes. Last year." Hart was taking it in slowly. "Francis Mayfield and Julia?" It made a kind of horrible sense.

"I'm afraid so. A pity he's dead. What in the world are we going to do with the child?"

"Child?"

"Julia's by him. She's real enough, poor little creature. Kept secret all this time, at least from me. Fostered somewhere. God knows what she's turned out like. And my father says he'll not pay another penny for her now Julia's gone off with Blanding. I'd hoped to persuade you and Mercy to take her back to America, to her father, but if he is dead . . ."

"And his mother too," said Hart. "I'm sorry, Dick. I'd as lief not even ask Mercy about this, for fear she should say yes. Francis Mayfield was nearly her death. Extraordinary . . . horrible to find his shadow still cast over us here. How old is this child, Dick?"

"In her teens. I'll have to have her, my sister's child. God knows how I'll manage, but I've sent for her. Hoped you'd take her, to tell truth, but I don't blame you for refusing. How I'm to break it to Mrs. Soames!"

Hart smiled at him. "You'll need to speak to Ruth, too," he said.

"Miss Paston? You know? You've seen? You're all the family she has, you and Mercy. Have I your permission to speak to her? I know it's absurdly too soon, but what can I do?"

"Speak, of course," said Hart. "May all your problems solve themselves so easily. From everything Mercy tells me about her, Ruth will make an admirable stepmother."

"It's a wife I want," said Dick. "Do you think I have any hope?"

"Oh, as to that, it's women's business. But I'd not despair, if I were you. Only—speak soon, Dick. Because Mercy and I are going home. We have made up our minds about Julia Purchis's estate. We are going to share it equally, you and I, as we agreed, but if you will, you are to have the property at Harting. Mercy and I are going back to America. When this war is over, as, please God, it will be soon, we mean to rebuild at Winchelsea. I hope the terms of my release will make it possible for us to live in Savannah for the meantime."

"You're going back to Savannah? Selfishly I'm sorry as can be, but, do you know, Hart, I think that would have pleased Great-aunt Julia very much. I have been thinking that she must have hoped your grandfather would send for her, to Savannah. Poor lady . . . Hart, it's more than generous of you, I do thank you. The property at Harting will make me independent of my father. I've told him I won't take another penny from him and have wondered how I was to live. I had even thought of trying to get back into the navy, but my enquiries were met in anything but a friendly spirit. I shall never be able to thank you enough. But at least I can tell you that you will indeed be able to live in Savannah. The terms of your release have been amended to allow you to take possession of all your properties in and around Savannah and Charleston. On one condition." He paused.

"Yes?"

"That you undertake not to bear arms against His Majesty King George the Third. It's what all the property owners in Savannah have sworn to. And in Charleston. Tell me honestly, do you want to go on fighting us?"

"I want America to be free."

"It will be. I was talking to Fox at Brooks's the other night. He says the taking of Charleston is just the last flash in the pan. A year, he says, two years at the outside, and we shall have peace with honour, and a whole new relationship to build. Could we not begin now, you and I? I'll give up all thought of the navy and cultivate my farm here, and you do likewise in Savannah. Paired, one might say. Two men of peace. What do you say, Cousin?"

"Well," said Hart, after a moment's thought, "considering that we have neither of us exactly covered ourselves with glory in our naval careers, I really find myself thinking it an admirable notion. The trouble is, ever since you were all so kind to me on board the *Sparrow*, I've not had much stomach for fighting you. If you really think your Whig party will contrive to bring about a peace?"

"I'm sure of it," said Dick. "It's just that you and I are declaring peace a little early."

"Good." Hart held out his hand.

To his relief, Mercy endorsed their decision wholeheartedly. "We've done enough, you and I," she said. "Too much perhaps. It's time to cultivate our garden. Oh, Hart, it seems too good to be true. Shall we really be able to rebuild Winchelsea? Do you think the Judas will still be flowering there?"

"We'll see next spring," he told her. "For now you had better finish hemming that wedding dress of yours. Dick's talking to Mr. Pym now." He looked beyond her to the double bed they had now shared for a whole week. "Perhaps I should sleep somewhere else tonight?"

"I never heard such nonsense," said his wife.

## XXI

To Mr. Pym's amazement, and Hart's fury, because it delayed the ceremony, the Bishop himself came back from Harrogate to marry them in the tiny flower-filled church. The entire village was there, wearing its best and watching with hearty curiosity as Ruth and Dick played their parts as bridesmaid and groomsman.

"Won't be long till we have another wedding, I reckon," said Mrs. Soames, surprising Mercy with a hasty kiss in the vestry. "And a good thing, too. Miss Ruth's the only one can make that hellbrat mind her."

"I know." Mercy glanced anxiously across the crowded vestry to where Dick's newly adopted daughter stood talking to Ruth and surveying the scene with a speculative, challenging eye. "Poor child," she said.

"Poor us! She's been here only three days, and we're all to pieces already. Practical jokes, Mr. Dick calls them. Should have been burned for a witch, if you ask me."

"Don't say that!" Mercy had a sudden chill memory of a cold night outside Boston and the mob approaching stealthily across the snow. "She's just unhappy and unsure of herself," she said. "She'll settle down with kindness."

"Kindness!" Mrs. Soames sniffed. "A birch for her backside would be my prescription for that young madam, but Mr. Dick won't hear of it."

"I'm sure he knows best." Mercy turned away to receive

Mr. Glubb's congratulations. This was an entirely village occasion, and the warmth of it was heartening. "You won't mind if they take the horses out of the carriage and pull you home?" said Glubb now. "One of my clerks has talked, I'm afraid. Well, it was bound to happen sooner or later. The whole village knows what you and your husband have done for Mr. Dick, and love you for it. When the news came that Mr. Purchas had agreed to take the Harting estate and leave Mr. Dick here . . . Well, Mrs. Purchis, I can tell you, I thought for a moment there was something wrong with my eyes. Tears come strange to a man my age, ma'am, but tears it was. And all your doing, yours and your good man's."

"I'm so glad we could. This is a happy day." She smiled at him, misty-eyed herself, as she remembered that other wedding on the *Guerrier,* the French officers laughing and toasting them in champagne, and all the time eyeing her speculatively . . . wondering. She looked down at her demure white silk and remembered bronze satin, low-cut, and the officer's eyes making the most of it. Even Captain Bougainville, marrying them, had had a roving eye for her. "I am so very happy," she said again to Glubb.

Mrs. Soames and the other house servants had left by now, and when the carriage made its slow way across the park, pulled by a laughing, shouting team of estate workers, Mercy saw that they had been busy. Trestle tables had been set out on the lawn in front of the house, and the whole village was to dine there.

Hurrying indoors with Ruth to straighten her veil after the windy ride, she found Mrs. Soames in the hall, fulminating. "That Frances," she said. "The young devil! Pepper in all my syllabub, and a whole crock of cream spilled! If I just catch the young varmint!"

"Oh, the poor child!" said Ruth. "Be patient with her, dear Mrs. Soames, it's all so strange and new to her. I'll speak to her, just as soon as the party is over, I promise I will. In the meantime, I am sure there will be plenty for everyone, if I know anything about your management."

"Oh, as to that," said Mrs. Soames, mollified, "I've sent to Joan Glubb already. She'll help out. She's got children of her own. She understands these things. It's a wonder to me how you do, Miss Ruth."

"I had brothers and sisters," said Ruth, her eyes suddenly shining with tears.

"Ruth, you're tired." Mercy noticed for the first time that Ruth's face was thinner, her figure almost too elegant in the plain white silk.

"Just a little." Ruth was looking past Mercy, out of the wide open window, to where Dick and Hart stood together among a crowd of tenants. "Oh, Mercy, do you think, perhaps, today—" She stopped, colouring.

"He'll speak? I'm sure he has delayed only because he feels it is so soon. He's afraid to be too quick for you."

"How could he be?" asked Ruth. And then. "Mercy, do you sometimes think of Charles Brisson? It must have been like this with him, I think. That first day we met him. Poor Charles . . . Just think, but for him none of this would have happened. I hope you think about him, Mercy, in your happiness?"

"Indeed I do. Often. I hope, when we get back to America, there will be news of him. Perhaps he is there by now. But, Ruth dear, what are you going to do? Hart and I would dearly love to have you come with us. Only . . ."

"Only . . ." Ruth looked at her, somewhere between tears and a pale smile. "Mercy, why doesn't he speak? Have I imagined it all?" She flushed suddenly. "I might have. I did before. With George. Thought he loved me. And then it was Naomi. Mercy! Let me come with you and Hart? Please? I won't be a trouble to you, I promise. Maybe I could live with Cousin Abigail."

"Dear Ruth, of course, you shall come if you want to. And live with us always. There's nothing I'd like better. But . . ." What could she say? She and Hart had been as puzzled as Ruth was distressed by Dick's failure to propose and had even begun to fear that he had changed his mind for some unimaginable reason.

"No buts." Ruth was frankly crying now. "Thank you, Mercy. I'll come. If you're sure."

"Of course I'm sure. I love you, dear; you're all the sister I've got."

Dick and Hart, coming in to look for them, found them in each other's arms, both crying a little.

"Mercy." Hart held out his hand. "The Bishop is asking for you. Come, dear."

Mercy smiled up at him, brushing away a tear. "Dear Hart, what a husband you sound."

Left alone with her, Dick took Ruth's hand as she stood there, looking down, fighting back tears. "We'll miss them very much," he said.

"Yes." It was all she could manage. What did he mean by that "we"?

"Do you know"—he reached out to where Mercy had left her bouquet of late white roses lying on a table—"you and I have known each other for just four weeks and two days?"

"And a few hours," she said. "You arrived early in the morning, remember?"

"Of course I remember." His fingers had been working among the roses, and now he pulled out one perfect bud. "Ruth, I have to put it to the touch. I've waited as long as I could. As long as I dared. Well, I had to wait until my affairs were settled, until I knew I could support you. And what kind of stepdaughter I was to cumber you with. She likes you, I think. Minds you better than anyone else. Miss Paston—Ruth—can I dare to hope that you will take us on, my poor Frances and me?"

"Take you on?" This was not how she had imagined it.

"Marry me. Stay. Help me make a home for Frances. Ruth?" Something about her continuing silence had disturbed him. "Have I assumed too much? I thought—I let myself hope that you loved me. Fool that I am. Vain idiot. Why should you? A disgraced sea captain, a pauper almost, were it not for Hart's generosity. Of course you could do better. I imagined it all? There's been someone else, perhaps, all the time? That man you and Mercy talk of—Charles Brisson? I always thought there was something about him, about the way you spoke of him. I heard his name the other day, at the Secretary's office. Wondered what he was doing in England still. Now I think I begin to understand." The rosebud crushed in his hand. "Forgive me for my presumption, Miss Paston. Try to forget the fool I have made of myself. I thought because it happened to me, like that, first day, that it had to you too. Idiot." He looked down wryly at the crushed flower. "I must return to my guests."

"Not yet. Not for a moment." She had been pale when he first spoke; now her colour was high, her eyes shining with tears. "Mr. Purchas, please, what happened to you that first day?"

"What happened? I fell in love, of course. The moment I saw you, coming down the stairs, in your white dress, smiling. Dear Ruth, I am glad to have had the chance to tell you. I think I shall love you till I die."

"So it's not just a housekeeper you want. A mother for Frances?"

"Good God, no. What made you think that?"

She was smiling at him now. "Well, it was what you said after all. You asked me to make a home for Frances. To be your housekeeper, said you could support me, as if I cared about that! I was afraid"—she got it out with an effort—"I was afraid I had been imagining things."

"Ruth! You mean, it did happen to you too?"

"Of course it did. When I saw you there, looking up at me. It was like . . . like drowning. The whole of my life before my eyes. All the sorrow; all the joy. Just waiting for this. Waiting for you."

"And I for you, dear Ruth." Slowly, almost deliberately, they moved into each other's arms. Drawing away at last from the long, deep embrace, she looked up at him.

"Just imagine your thinking it was Charles Brisson," she said. "Poor Charles, I think it must have been like this with him. But Mercy, not me," she added, her eyes sparkling mischievously. "Poor Charles," she said again. "But, Dick"—it gave her great pleasure to use his name—"I don't understand one thing. How could you have heard his name at the Secretary's office? Are you sure you did?"

"Yes. And the strange thing is that I thought at the time it was somehow in connection with Hart's release. Ridiculous, of course, now I know more about him. Well, just one of those things we will never understand."

"I suppose not. Do you know, I believe I would rather you did not mention it to Hart and Mercy?"

"Oh?" He looked down at her, smiling. "You think Hart might be as great a fool as I was?"

"Impossible!" He pulled her into his arms again, but the embrace was interrupted by a peal of laughter. Frances had come in from the garden and was watching them with delight. Her arms were full of flowers purloined from the dinner tables outside, and she began systematically pulling them off and throwing them at Dick and Ruth.

"The Bishop's mad as fire," she told them. "He says I'm a limb of Satan, but you'll speak up for me, won't you, Aunt Ruth? Or I'll tell him he'd better marry you too, and the quicker the better!"

"What did you do to the Bishop?" asked Dick severely.

"That would be telling! And I never tell! Come on, Aunt Ruth, the dancing's beginning on the lawn, and they won't start without you two. I've never been at a party like this before. Will you keep me with you always? You'll need me as chaperone, you know, when Mercy goes away. I'd be a good chaperone! Please let me stay."

"If you behave yourself," said Ruth.

"Hurray, hurray, I'm here to stay." Frances danced ahead of them out into the garden, and Dick took Ruth's arm.

"Why are you looking so conscious?" She smiled up at him with a question in her eyes.

"Well, as a matter of fact," he said, "you will think me the most presumptuous fellow alive, but I had been thinking about what would happen when Mercy goes. I will not ask my mother here. She does not admit it, but of course she knew what was being done to Hart. You will think me very ill equipped, but I have no other female relatives. I could not for the life of me think what was best to be done."

"So?"

"Well." He put up a hand to his cravat, which seemed to be throttling him. "While I was getting the special licence for Hart and Mercy . . ."

"You got one for us too! And never told me!" Now she was laughing at him. "Oh, my darling! And then thought it should have been for me and Charles Brisson! No wonder you looked so sick. But what are we waiting for! Let us find the Bishop at once. Besides"—she twinkled up at him—"it will take his mind off whatever dreadful thing your Frances has done to him."

"Our Frances," he said.

The Bishop fortunately thought it a capital joke to go back to the little church when the party was over and marry a second couple there. Blandly full of champagne by now, he and Mr. Pym made a good many broad remarks about happy events and standing godfather if necessary before they finally took their leave and the two couples were alone to toast each other over a light supper and retire to the beds that Frances had filled with prickly wedding flowers.

"Do you think she did it to Ruth and Dick too?" asked Mercy, removing the last bit of Michaelmas daisy.

"Bound to have," said Hart cheerfully. "But I think we will not go and ask."

"I should rather think not." Mercy was in her nightgown now, brushing her hair. "Hart, I'm so happy. It was quite different, wasn't it, this wedding?"

He took her gently by the shoulders and pulled her towards the bed. "And this honeymoon is going to be quite different, too, my darling."

# XXII ⬥⚬—

H art and Mercy left Denton Hall a week later, having learnt that a fast merchantman was to sail almost immediately with supplies for beleaguered Savannah. It was too good a chance to miss, though it was sad to leave Dick and Ruth in the first glow of their happiness. "I think your Ruth is going to manage that hellbrat admirably," said Hart as the carriage drove through Denton village. "She has really made her sorry for what she did to the Bishop."

"Dear Ruth," said Mercy. "I hate to part with her, but it is wonderful to see her so happy. If you had known her when we first met, back in January, you would not believe the change in her."

"All your doing, I'm sure."

"No, not all. We've been . . . lucky, Ruth and I. So lucky." They were holding hands, and she waved with the other one to a smiling village woman who had come to their wedding. "They're so kind," she said. "But, Hart, I'm *glad* we are going home."

Privileged passengers, they had their own cabin on the fast Baltimore-built merchantman that had been captured by the British a year before. They dined at the captain's table, and his boast that his ship could easily outsail any French or American privateer proved entirely justified. The voyage was an easy one, and as peaceful day followed day, Mercy was glad to see the shadows gradually disappear from under Hart's eyes. By the time they raised Tybee Light at the mouth of the Savannah River, early in November, he had almost stopped dreaming of the Tower and hardly ever woke sweating and screaming in her arms.

Since no pilot was available, and the captain had not sailed up the Savannah River before, he asked Hart to join him on the bridge for the hazardous journey up the slow-winding river, so Mercy stood alone, gazing at the golden acres of marsh grass that had given it its name. Passing the inlet that would have taken them up to the burnt bones of Winchelsea, she remembered a January day, four long years before, when she and Abigail and Hart had gone down river to look for forage for their hungry animals and had seen the sails of British warships making for the river. The British had been the enemy then. What were they now?

They anchored by the bluff below Factor's Walk just as the setting sun set the whole bronze marsh aglow. The bells of Christ Church were ringing for evensong. "We're home, Hart." She turned to him as he came hurrying down to their cabin, released at last from duty on the bridge. And then, remembering his mother and aunt. "A strange homecoming, I am afraid."

It was stranger even than she expected. The news came on board with the first official, and soon the whole ship was aflame with it, seething like a disturbed hive. "What is it, Hart? What's the matter?" Busy packing, Mercy had only gradually become aware of the change in the usual tone of the ship.

"I'll go and see." He returned, white-faced, the shadows back under his eyes. "Treachery!" he told her. "Benedict Arnold tried to sell West Point to the British."

"Benedict Arnold! I don't believe it!" But instantly, horribly, remembering the man, and his wife, she did. "How did they catch him?"

"They didn't. He's clean away to the British. They caught his go-between, a Major André. Washington has hanged him, Mercy. He wasn't in uniform. The British are terribly angry about it. Captain Graves is not sure whether he should let us ashore tonight; he says things are so stirred up in town; the news only came the other day; he's sent to Sir James Wright for instructions. He's asked me . . . he asks us both—to be very careful what we say. He's a good friend, Mercy."

"Yes." It came out mechanically. "I knew Benedict Arnold in Philadelphia. I never could like him. Or his wife. Oh." Her hand went up to her mouth. "I remember. There was gossip about her and Major André. He was with the British during the occupation of Philadelphia. Before she married Arnold. Hart!" It was all flooding back. "They must have been planning it when I was there in Philadelphia."

"I am afraid so." His face was very grave. "There is something else I have to tell you, Mercy. André was not alone when he was taken. There was another man with him. Charles Brisson."

"Charles!" Had she seen it coming?

"Yes. He was hanged too, Mercy. God rest his soul."

She sat down on the narrow bed, tears flooding down her cheeks. "Ah, poor Charles." It all began to make horrible sense. "He was working for the British all the time! Of course he was. Hanged!"

"They asked to be shot. But—they were spies, Mercy."

"So were we."

"Never again," he said. "Whatever happens. I think I'm glad now that I had to give my parole to the British. What monsters war makes of men."

"Not Charles," she protested. "I wish you'd known him, Hart. He was—" She broke off, remembering, understanding. "Lord, what a fool he made of me! Using me as his cover in Philadelphia. Even on the way there. We were stopped by the militia, Hart. They thought he was one of our party. They were looking for a man by himself. I remember how they cross-examined the boy, Jed, because he was riding alone. But Brisson was in the sledge. They did not question him. He must have come straight from New York. With a message for Benedict Arnold." Her eyes filled with tears. "And Arnold's free. Safe with the British, while Charles and André . . . Dear Charles. When he helped me get to England, he did it out of pure kindness. There was no advantage in that for him. Only danger."

"Not just out of kindness," said Hart. "Give him his due. It must have been out of love, out of pure love."

"Yes." She was remembering the last time she had seen Brisson. "He told me so," she said. "At Portsmouth. And,

Hart, he told me you were out of danger. He need not have. He could have let me think you as good as dead. Have urged me to go with him. Instead, he told me to stay, to go to Denton Hall and look for Dick Purchas. We owe him everything, Hart."

"I think I owe him my freedom too. Dick said something the night before we left. Said he had heard Brisson's name mentioned in the Secretary's office when he was there. I always wondered who in England, granted it wasn't the Purchases, cared enough about me to arrange my release. Now we know. Naturally, Brisson knew I was safe when he saw you at Portsmouth. He had just come from arranging it."

"So the war didn't make a monster of him."

"No. He must have loved you very much, Mercy."

"I'll never forget him." She was in Hart's arms now, crying quietly. "I wonder. If I hadn't been so oceans-deep in love with you . . ."

"You'd be his widow now." He bent to kiss away her tears. "I'm glad you're not. Poor Brisson . . ."

They went ashore next day and found Savannah apparently more firmly in British hands than ever. Abigail, welcoming them home to the house in Oglethorpe Square with tears of joy, congratulated Hart warmly on his acceptance of the British terms. "All right-thinking men have taken the oath," she told him. "Since the British took Charleston and the rebel governor, Howley, had to flee from Augusta, no one even knows where the rebel Assembly is. It's just a question of time now. . . ."

"But time is not on the Tories' side, dear Abigail," said Hart. "I warn you, the British are tired of this war. A year, two years, you'll see; it will be over. Happily over, I pray, and all friends again."

"Friends! After what's been done to André and Brisson!" And then, seeing Mercy's face. "Forgive me. I did not mean to remind you."

"I shall never forget him," Mercy said. "I don't want to. He may have been a spy, but he was a good man."

"He was a Patriot," Abigail said austerely, "not a spy."

"Oh, Abigail—" Mercy began, but Hart interrupted her.

"Dear Abigail," he said, "we must face it that this war has made contradictions of us all. Patriot . . . spy. Turn the coin; it's the same thing. I pray to God it will be over soon."

"And Giles Habersham home at last," said Mercy, and was horrified to see the change in Abigail's face. Sharp lines she had not noticed in the first joy of the meeting now showed savagely etched in the thin cheeks.

"Giles is not coming home," Abigail said. "He wrote me —at last. He seems to agree with you, Hart; I cannot imagine why. He thinks the British have lost interest in this war. He sees no hope of ever coming home. He wrote to say good-bye. To free me, he said. He has joined their regular army." The sentences came out short and stiff. "Don't be sorry for me," she said. "Please . . ."

"Oh, dear Abigail." Mercy threw her arms round her for a quick, impulsive kiss. "I am so glad we are home. We'll not be parted again."

"No." Abigail had changed, Mercy thought, hardened a little, and no wonder. "I have a letter for you," she went on now. "From Charles Brisson. He sent it under cover to me, asked me to get it to you if I could. He wrote it the night before he was hanged. How could George Washington hang them, him and André!" She turned to Hart. "It will never be forgotten. Never!"

"Nor will many other things," said Hart. "But let us not quarrel, not this first day at home."

"No, indeed." Abigail's smile was forced, and she made an obvious effort to change the subject. "Hart, there is something I think I should tell you."

"Yes?"

"Perhaps alone?" With an apologetic glance at Mercy.

"No." Hart made it gentle. "Mercy and I are man and wife. What concerns me concerns her too."

"Oh, very well. It's about Francis. After . . ." She hesitated for a moment. "After your mother and Aunt Anne died, I had to tidy their papers. I found a batch of letters to Francis from someone in England. Someone called Julia. She wrote as if . . . as if they were old friends." And then, bravely. "More than that. There was a child, a girl. She wanted help. I don't think he gave it."

"I know he did not," said Hart. "Thank you, Abigail. I'm grateful to you for telling me. It explains a great deal.

Do you realise," he turned to Mercy. "Why did we never think of it? No wonder Julia knew so much about me, about us . . . It was not just our letters that she stopped and opened. She had been in touch with Francis all the time."

"All the time?" Mercy thought about it. "Oh, poor Julia. Still hoping, do you think?"

"I'm afraid so. It's an old, sad story." He turned to Abigail, trying to remember how much she knew about Francis's death. "Best forgotten."

"Oh, yes," she said bitterly. "By all means let us forget."

Hart and Mercy were glad to be alone at last in Hart's old bedroom. "Poor Abigail," said Mercy. "If only she had gone with Giles Habersham when he asked her to that time."

"Yes," said Hart. "But how was she to know? Read your letter, darling. Best face it at once."

It was a brief scrawl, written the night before Brisson was hanged:

> *Beloved Mercy.*
> *Let me call you that, this once, before I die. And forgive me for the times I deceived you . . . used you. I think I am glad to die. I know I am glad to have known you; loved you. Give my kind regards to your lucky husband. I am glad to think that I saved your lives. Your murders were planned on that smuggler. You were to meet on her—and be killed. I pray that you will live happy and sometimes remember me. Mercy, spying's a shabby business. Don't go back to it; don't let this war tarnish you, as it has me.*
> *Yours, till death and beyond—Charles*

When she had cried over it, she showed it to Hart. "Nobody asked me to swear not to fight the British," she said. "But, Hart, I do. It's all too complicated for me now."

"I know," he said. "I feel the same."

They rode out to Winchelsea the next day, glad to be free of the currents and crosscurrents of Savannah society. "We'll rebuild and come out here just as soon as we can," said Hart as they took the familiar turning down the long walk with its occasional ilex tree, survivor of the avenue his grandfather had planted.

"I wish we could move out at once," said Mercy. "Poor Abigail, it's no wonder she's bitter. To have waited all those years for Giles Habersham and then receive a turn down like that! It's enough to turn anyone sour. But I'd as lief not live with her. Oh, Hart, I do bless Julia Purchis for her money."

"And Charles Brisson for our lives," he reminded her soberly as they reined in their horses at sight of what had been the house. Burnt almost to the ground during the abortive French attack on Savannah the year before, it was coming to life again now as a tangle of wild jasmine and scarlet-and-bronze-leaved creepers. Growing out of and up the remaining bits of wall and chimney, these even gave it something of the shape of the old house.

"We'll rebuild on the old site," said Hart. "Just as soon as the war is over and it's safe."

"I wish we could now."

"Oh, my dear, so do I. But this house was in the thick of the fighting last time Savannah was attacked. It may well be again. However we may hope for a negotiated end to the war, it would be madness to count on it. And in the meantime, there is always the danger of an Indian attack. I would never have a quiet moment if we came to live here now. I'd be afraid, always, of the same horrible fate for you as befell my mother and Aunt Anne. And—we must face it—I may not be able to stay with you all the time. I have promised not to fight the British, but I gave no undertaking not to work for peace."

She smiled at him. "And I have promised nothing since nobody asked me. How strange it all is." By tacit consent, they turned their horses in the direction of the old grave-yard. Reaching it, they stopped, surprised. The house had gone back to jungle, but the graveyard had been lovingly cared for. They tied their horses to the makeshift gate and walked across to where Mercy's father was buried. The stump of the Judas tree beside it had sprouted. The grave was covered with creeping evergreens, and the gravestone recently cleaned: "James Phillips. The truth shall make you free."

They stood for a moment, silent, hand in hand. "Do you remember last time?" she said at last. "I said we'd be back."

"And here we are. I thought we would bring my mother and Aunt Anne out here. And a stone for Charles Brisson?"

"By my father's?" She smiled up at him, letting the tears flow. "What shall we put on it."

" 'Love conquers all things,' " he told her.

"Even war?"

"Even war."